The Worst Guy Ever

Holly June Smith

Copyright © 2023 by Holly June Smith

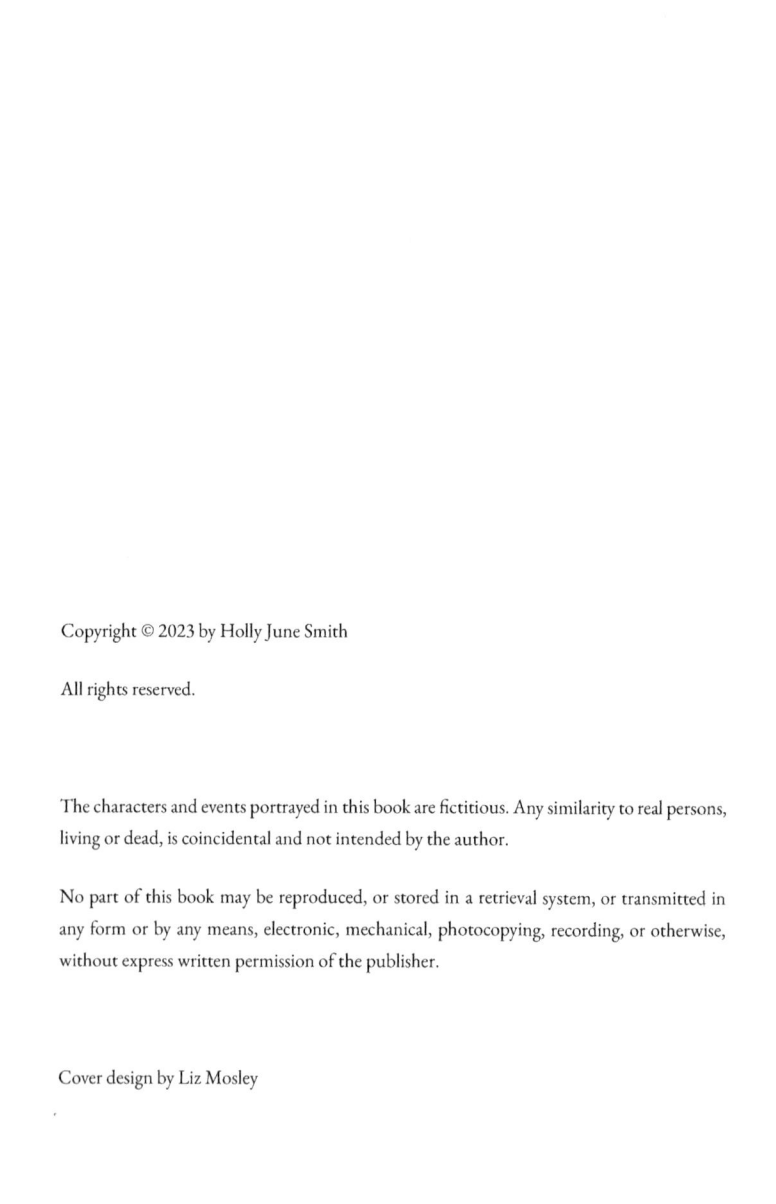

All rights reserved.

The characters and events portrayed in this book are fictitious. Any similarity to real persons, living or dead, is coincidental and not intended by the author.

No part of this book may be reproduced, or stored in a retrieval system, or transmitted in any form or by any means, electronic, mechanical, photocopying, recording, or otherwise, without express written permission of the publisher.

Cover design by Liz Mosley

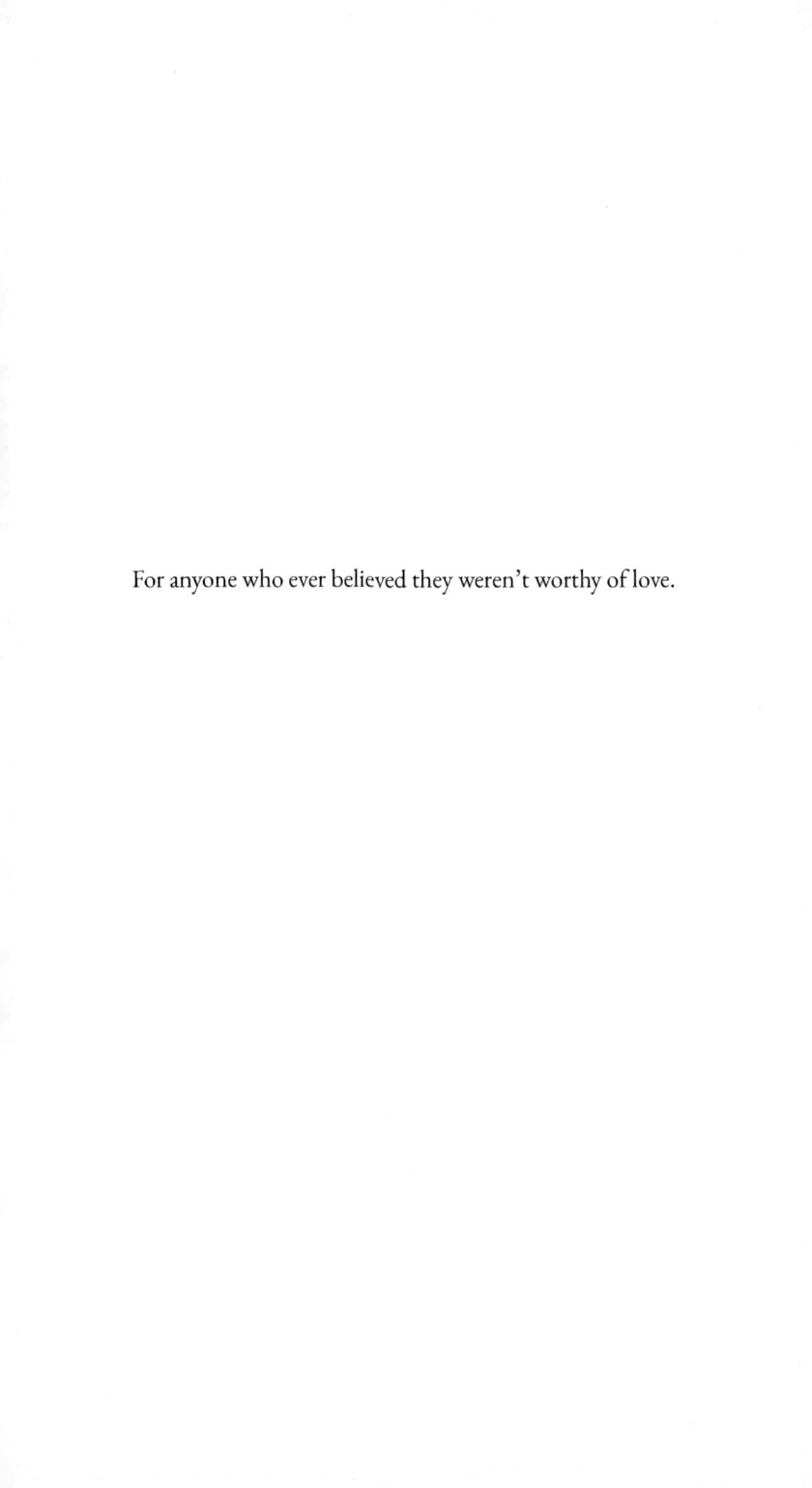

For anyone who ever believed they weren't worthy of love.

Contents

A Note From Holly		IX
Prologue		1
1.	Hattie	13
2.	Rob	21
3.	Hattie	30
4.	Hattie	41
5.	Rob	49
6.	Hattie	53
7.	Rob	62
8.	Rob	68
9.	Hattie	72
10.	Hattie	80
11.	Rob	88
12.	Hattie	98
13.	Rob	106
14.	Hattie	111
15.	Hattie	114
16.	Hattie	123

17.	Hattie	132
18.	Rob	138
19.	Hattie	147
20.	Rob	154
21.	Hattie	161
22.	Rob	165
23.	Hattie	172
24.	Hattie	180
25.	Rob	188
26.	Rob	196
27.	Rob	201
28.	Hattie	208
29.	Hattie	213
30.	Rob	221
31.	Rob	231
32.	Rob	241
33.	Hattie	249
34.	Hattie	257
35.	Rob	265
36.	Hattie	273
37.	Rob	275
38.	Hattie	288
39.	Hattie	294
40.	Hattie	298

41.	Rob	302
42.	Hattie	303
43.	Rob	311
44.	Hattie	313
45.	Rob	316
46.	Hattie	323
47.	Hattie	329
Epilogue		334
Acknowledgments		343
About The Author		345
Also By Holly June Smith		346

A Note From Holly

The Worst Guy Ever is the second book in the *Sunshine Book Club* Series. It can be read as a standalone but you may wish to read The Best Book Boyfriend first.

Please be advised that this book is an open-door romance featuring on-page sexual content for mature readers only.

While this is a light-hearted rom-com it also includes themes of childhood abandonment and grief (both off-page) on the way to Hattie and Rob's happy ending.

I hope you enjoy it as much I enjoyed writing it.

Prologue

It was only a matter of time before I crossed paths with Rob Morgan, a.k.a. the worst guy ever.

It all started when my best friend, Kara, fell in love with Rob's best friend, Luke. Soon our cherished girls' nights and their, whatever-it-is-boys-do, became mutual Sunday brunches. The sort of occasions that float on for hours and end with you collapsing into bed with a full tummy, a fuller heart, and a slightly spinny head. Luke's an excellent cook, Kara is a generous host, and these brunches would be perfect if not for the presence of one utter loser.

I knew of Rob's reputation, of course. When I first met Luke, I'd begged him to introduce me to his single mates. That's when he told me all about Rob, the serial dater who takes commitment as seriously as I do. Which is not at all. I know full well that men are good for one thing only, and that thing is their penises.

Luke had invited us all to get to know each other over a Sunday roast, and I'm not one to turn down a free lunch, especially where potatoes are involved. I'd actually been looking forward to it, until *he* turned up. It would be nice to say I look back on our first meeting with fondness, but the truth is that Rob has been a harbinger of hassle ever since that day.

In Luke's home, where Kara was spending more and more of her time, I arrived to find a beautiful table, laid with perfectly mismatched tableware, mood lighting, and crisp white linen napkins embroidered with *'please leave by nine x'*.

As an interior designer, this stuff comes effortlessly to Kara. My brain doesn't work that way. In the advertising world, *'effortlessly beautiful'* takes months of planning. We research and focus-group everything to within an inch of its life, until any semblance of creative spontaneity has been stripped away. Unfortunately, this means what other people fawn over, I see as overpriced and destined for a skip as soon as the creative execution is in the bag.

Kara and Luke sat on one side, unable to keep their hands and soppy eyes off each other. They were constantly touching each other in those early days, and still are. I find it hard to believe it doesn't get annoying. A hand on your thigh while reading, a kiss on the cheek when you've got a mouthful of food. All the squeezing and hugging. I swear I've caught them sniffing each other, the lovesick freaks.

My other best friend, Megan, filled water glasses around the table then took the seat next to me. The three of us have been friends since we were at school, and we're closer now than ever. After graduating from university, Megan and I got a place together back in our hometown and ten years later, she's the true love of my life.

That left the seat at the end of the table for Rob, who Luke had mentioned is often late. I was drooling at the table laden with buttery greens, crispy roast potatoes, and tender beef, so his tardiness had already landed him in my bad books.

I heard him before I saw him, but part of me sensed him even before then. There was a shift in the atmosphere, and I held my breath in a moment of silence before he filled it with his booming voice.

"Hello, lovebirds."

He stood behind Kara, leaning down to kiss her on the cheek with a familiarity that made me twitch. *Who on earth do you think you are? That's my friend.*

"These are for you, my darling. You look stunning as usual." He pulled a bright bouquet from behind his back. Proper flowers, already arranged for a vase, I noted. No last-minute wilting blooms from the petrol station from this guy.

I willed myself not to look at him, but I was powerless to stop my eyes from drifting his way. From my seated position he was unspeakably tall, with broad shoulders, big arms, golden skin. He took up all the space in my vision. My eyes coasted up and down, finding dark hair and dark eyes above the wall of his chest. Dressed in a grey sweatshirt and black jeans, he was everything that gets me fired up. Solid and fuckable, and I hated him for it.

"Thank you Rob," Kara beamed, "they're beautiful. We're just starting. Grab a seat and help yourself."

I had no reason to be nervous to meet him, so I concentrated on filling my plate while he hugged Luke from behind then pulled out the seat next to me. I kept my eyes down as he scooted in underneath and made himself comfortable. Legs spread wide, nudging against mine, he took up far more space than he was entitled to. It annoyed the hell out of me, but I also secretly hoped I'd get to feel if his thighs were as muscular as I thought they might be.

I was in the middle of pushing those thoughts out of my head when he bumped my shoulder with his. I looked up, and that's when he signed his death sentence.

"So you must be the single one?"

And then he had the nerve to *wink*.

"Excuse me?"

"The single friend. That's you, right?"

"I heard what you said. I just don't know why you think it's appropriate to make that sort of assumption about someone you've never met." I don't think I'd ever gone from breezy to bitchy so fast. Yes, I am happily single, by choice, but it's not like I'm wearing a badge to advertise the fact. You can't just say things like that to a stranger.

"Aren't you Hattie? The one who doesn't date? It can't possibly be this sweet angel next to you." He leaned across me, extending one hand, which Megan took politely. "You must be Megan. I'm Rob. I've heard so much about you."

"Nice to meet—"

"How dare you?" Why does she get a handshake and I get judgement? I slapped Megan's hand away and Luke froze, his fork halfway to his mouth. "Don't think I haven't heard about you."

"Oh yeah?" he smirked, resting one arm on the back of his chair. "What have you heard?"

"You're the man-whore who has a different woman in his bed every night."

"Hattie!" Kara gasped. "Don't be rude."

"Every night? Wow, if only," Rob leaned in closer. "You want to be next?"

My head snapped back. "I absolutely do not."

"Come on. Two sluts living it up, I'm sure we'd have fun."

"Did you just call me a *slut*?"

"You called me a whore first," he shrugged. "It takes one to know one."

"What are you, eight?" I shrieked.

"Yeah, eight inches," he laughed, reaching for the wine and changing the subject as if everyone apart from me found him charming. "This looks beautiful, Kara. Sorry for being late."

"I'll forgive you this once," she smiled sweetly, but he was not bloody forgiven as far as I was concerned.

I pushed my chair back and stood to take my water glass to the sink. Leaning against the counter, I refilled it while attempting to calm my breathing. *Who did this arsehole think he was?* It was supposed to be a nice day, two groups of friends coming together, and bonding over a shared love of food and each other. I would not cause a scene by blowing a fuse over something so stupid but how dare he insult me like that?

If a slut, by definition, is a woman with many partners, then yes, I guess you could call me that. I myself have proclaimed that I'm in my *slut era* on more than one occasion, and that's fine when I'm saying it about myself. It was absolutely not fine when said by *him*.

Back at the table, I leaned down and whispered in Megan's ear. "Swap places with me."

"Why?"

"I don't want to sit next to Rob. He's a prick and a manspreader," I said, not exactly quiet enough for him to miss. Megan did me a favour and shifted over, swapping our plates while I switched our glasses. Kara threw me a bemused look, and I reached for her knee under the table and gave it a squeeze. "Missed you, babe. This is lovely."

"So Rob, tell me about your work," Megan said, politely bringing him into the conversation. The traitor.

In my peripheral vision, I saw him nod and swallow his food. I perfected the art of stabbing my carrots with my fork.

"I'm a psychologist," he said.

"That explains it," I scoffed, a little louder than intended, and when I looked up from my food, all eyes were on me.

"What's that supposed to mean?" he asked, leaning in to look past Megan.

"That's how you get laid so much."

"I beg your pardon?" he laughed.

I took a long, slow sip of my wine, then dabbed the corner of my mouth with my napkin as I glared in his direction. "You're a psychologist. You use your professional knowledge to manipulate and exploit women for personal gain."

"I absolutely do not. I am fully able to switch between my work and personal life."

"Hmmm, it doesn't seem like the kind of career skill set that you just leave at the office each day."

He set his cutlery on his plate, his meal half eaten, and linked his fingers together, elbows on the table. "And what do you do, Hattie?"

My hands balled into fists, and I leaned back, keeping them still in my lap. "I'm an account director at a marketing agency."

"Oh, so you use your professional knowledge to manipulate and exploit the general public for profit," he mocked.

"Excuse me? That's not the same at all."

"How do you figure?"

"You know things. Techniques and whatnot. So you trick women. Use mind games. It's disrespectful."

"Oh trust me, there is nothing more respectful than the way I disrespect my sexual partners. I'm insulted that you think I need to trick them in the first place." He picked up his cutlery and loaded his fork with buttered greens. "And tell me, how would a man get you into his bed?"

"Men don't get me into bed, I get *them* into bed."

"Oh, so you're dominant?" he smirked. "I like that."

"You don't strike me as the submissive type." I instantly hated myself for letting him know I'd made any sort of observation about him.

"I'm not. But I like it when a woman thinks she's the one in charge." He lifted his wineglass to his mouth but held it there and licked his lower lip before taking a sip, never letting his gaze fall from mine. "I like it even better when I get to show her she's not."

"Are you two quite finished?" Kara interrupted. "Honestly, Hattie, give him a break. I've heard great things about your work Rob, it must be very rewarding."

"And Rob, stop being mean to her," Luke added. "We're supposed to be having a nice lunch and all getting to know each other."

"I think I've learned all I need to know," I said, leaning across Megan to scowl at him.

Rob let out that stupid idiot laugh again. "Au contraire, ma chérie."

"Why are you speaking French?"

"It's the language of love."

"It's revolting is what it is." I downed my wine and left the table.

Kara found me in the kitchen, struggling to get the corkscrew lined up with a new bottle of Montepulciano. "Are you OK?"

"Did you tell Rob I'm a slut?" I hissed at her.

"No," she gasped, laying her palm on my shoulder. "I would never say that about you, I can't believe you even needed to ask."

"Well then did Luke?"

"I doubt it. I tried to get him to call me a filthy little slut in bed once and he couldn't say it without apologising," she said with a grimace.

"Then what did you tell him about me?" Glancing over her shoulder, I could see him laughing away with Megan. I twisted the wine bottle in my hands, battling to wrench the bloody thing out.

"He asked if I had any single friends, and I said you don't do relationships and are happy with just hooking up and…" she trailed off as the reality of her words sank in. "Oh God, Hattie, I'm so sorry. I didn't mean it to sound like that."

I threw my head back and forced out an aggressive sigh.

"I'll make him apologise," she said. "But you'll have to say sorry for calling him a man-whore too."

"Forget it," I said, finally pulling the cork free. "I don't want him thinking I care."

"I'm kind of surprised you two haven't matched with each other on an app before now," Luke piped up over lemon cheesecake.

"Luke," I shook my head, "just when I was starting to like you, mate."

"I wonder why that is?" Megan mused.

"I think you're above my age range," the bastard said matter-of-factly, and I choked on my wine.

"Excuse me?"

"I cap out at twenty-eight."

"What the fuck. Why?"

"To avoid matching with women who want to settle down."

For once in my life, I was actually speechless. I pressed my lips into a tight, furious line, the way I have to hundreds of times a day around the idiot men I work with. "That is absolutely disgusting."

"It's disgusting to respect women enough not to lead them on thinking they'll get into a relationship when that's not something I'm capable of?" He cocked his head to one side and I felt my chest tighten.

"It's disgusting that you assume women hit twenty-nine and all they want is to find a husband and slowly die inside. No offence Kara," I said.

Her hand patted mine on the table. "None taken."

"How long will this go on for? Do you think you're Leo DiCaprio or something? You'll keep getting older and your conquests will stay in their teens?"

"Now hold on, I take offence to that. I never sleep with women in their teens. I'm not that fucked up."

"What's your age range, then?" I didn't even care. It was a stupid thing to ask.

"Twenty-two to twenty-eight."

"And you're thirty-three? Same as Luke?"

He nodded and rested his hand in the palm of his hand. "Are you telling me you've never slept with someone with an age gap?"

"Never."

"Bullshit," Kara coughed.

"Hey," I whipped my head and glared at her. "Whose side are you on?"

"Yours, obviously, but he has a point. You've had much older than an eleven year age gap."

"How much older?" His brow furrowed, and damn if he didn't wear a brooding scowl well.

"I don't have to explain myself to you."

"Try twenty," Megan chimed in from behind her wine glass.

"Woah. You've got a thing for older men."

"Oh no, she's gone way younger, too," Megan said, and she and Kara burst into tipsy laughter.

"*Megan!*"

"Oh, this is good," Rob said, rubbing his hands together. "How much younger are we talking?"

As if they had thrown me under the bus like that. How had a discussion about Rob's appalling, misogynistic attitudes towards women become an Everyone Take The Piss Out of Hattie festival?

"He lied about his age."

"Oh shit. Not a schoolboy?"

"No, fuck off. Nineteen." I focused on the view of the garden, desperate to avoid any more judgmental gazes.

"So basically a schoolboy. How old were you?"

"Twenty-eight."

Rob burst out laughing. "OK, so then I think we can all agree that there is nothing wrong with my age group settings."

"It's still sexist."

"Are you bitter because you don't make the cut? Is that what this is about? You wished you had matched with me."

"Absolutely not. I'd have blocked you on sight."

I tried to avoid him, I really did. As the meal moved from pudding at the table to mulled cider on Luke's patio, I was checking work emails ahead of a busy week when he settled himself down next to me on the garden sofa.

"You know, Hattie, I'm pretty sure we'll end up together at some point," he said, his voice low, for my ears only. *The utter pig.* What a revolting thought.

"You're not my type."

"I don't think you have a type," he said, leaning in closely.

"Yes, I do. *Not* arrogant. You don't fit the bill."

"I happen to think arrogance is a superpower in bed."

I could tell, even just from the warmth of him sitting next to me, the spicy cedar scent of his skin, that he would be good in bed. I wouldn't necessarily call it arrogance, but, in my experience, confidence is the one thing that elevates a hook-up from average to unforgettable. This guy had buckets of it, but so did I.

"If anyone's the arrogant one, it's me. I get in, get what I want, get out as fast as I can."

"How romantic."

"There is not a romantic bone in my body," I replied, deadpan, in an attempt to feign nonchalance and boredom despite the heat blooming in my belly.

He leaned in close, a hungry look in his eye that made me think I was about to get bitten right there in Luke's garden. "Would you like my romantic bone in your body?"

I screamed, and he sat back, snorting out a laugh as he stretched his arms along the sofa cushions. Before I ended up laughing at his stupid childish goading too, I thanked Luke and Kara, made my apologies, and told Megan to get an Uber home on my account.

It goes without saying that Rob Morgan did not make a good first impression. And would you believe it? He's only gotten worse.

Chapter 1

Hattie

"Well, if it isn't my favourite ice queen."

"Oh shit," I scowl, turning to Megan who is standing by my side on Luke's doorstep. "We've come to the wrong house, we must leave immediately."

"They're ten minutes away," Rob says. "Come in and let me look after you."

There are three things I hate about the man standing before me. One, he's an arrogant bastard. Two, he knows exactly how to push my buttons and takes great delight in doing it often. And three, he always smells incredible.

I've hated him since the day we met and you don't have to be some sodding psychologist to understand why. He's basically the male version of me: cocky, arrogant, and a serial bachelor. Of course, people would never describe me that way because I'm a woman. I'd be called feisty, hysterical, a drama queen, and a slut. If opposites attract, our similarities explain why I find him so repulsive.

Since our friends introduced us, I've had the misfortune of spending far more time in his company than I'd have liked: dinners, BBQs, and brunches that I scowl my way through. I try to get out of it when I can, but today is Luke's Granny Annie's birthday, and he and Kara are hosting a surprise lunch at their house to celebrate. That's not the sort of invite you turn down.

Kara officially moved in with Luke earlier this month, having sold the house she renovated for a tidy profit, and finally severing ties with her awful ex. I see she's already sprinkling her interiors magic with a new door knocker in the shape of an otter.

"Megan, you look stunning, as always," Rob says, as she crosses the threshold into enemy territory.

"Well, you look like shit," I say. "Whose bed did you crawl out of?"

"Hey, that hurts." He helps me out of my coat, stroking his thumbs down my arms in an unnecessary move that still sends a whisper of a shiver up my spine. "I got my full eight hours of beauty sleep and slept alone."

"Pathetic."

"You didn't?"

"On a Saturday night?" I laugh. "No, I absolutely did not sleep alone, thank you very much." Megan laughs, knowing full well we spent the night eating ice-cream and watching the latest action rom-com in the matching pyjamas we accidentally bought each other for Christmas. I glare at her and she takes the hint to keep that to ourselves.

"Who's the lucky guy?"

"That's none of your business."

"Ah, so you didn't know his name?"

"Oh, as if you can remember the name of every woman who's been through the conveyor belt you call a bed."

I push past him and make my way through the house to Luke's open plan kitchen-dining-living room. A happy birthday banner hangs on one wall, the table set for what looks like an afternoon tea.

"What can I get you ladies to drink?" Rob appears behind me and leans, both hands flat on the kitchen counter like he works here. His white shirt is rolled up at the sleeves, open at the collar, and in this position he might as well be saying *'here's your forearm porn'*.

If he served me in a bar, I'd most definitely be asking if he could get off work early. Unfortunately, any chance of that happening disappeared the moment he opened his mouth. Or perhaps I should consider it a lucky escape.

Rob is one of those guys who is disgustingly hot, but he knows it, and everyone else knows it too. I see other people lap it up, his charm, his schmoozing, but I've got him figured out and you won't catch me falling for any of it. I try to avoid him, but his favourite game is tormenting me, and apparently, that starts now.

"I'll get my own. Wouldn't want to get roofied at an eightieth birthday party."

"Hattie!" Megan scolds from across the room, and I spin to face her.

"What?"

"That's a terrible accusation."

"Whatever." I roll my eyes and walk behind him to add my wine to Luke's fridge. A small knot forms in the pit of my stomach. Why is it always me who ends up looking like the mean one when he's ten times worse?

At lunch, Rob takes the seat next to me, his thigh bumping up against mine. We both look down at the same time and then catch each other's eyes on the way back up. I scowl at him, sick of men taking up space that doesn't belong to them. I'm not moving, and I adjust my position, pushing back against him. He pushes harder, but he has underestimated how firm my quads are. Years of kickboxing will do that for you.

"Stop doing this pulling-my-hair-because-you-secretly-fancy-me shit. This isn't the playground and we're not five years old."

He leans in and whispers into my ear. "You would love it if I pulled your hair. And it's no secret that I think you're gorgeous."

"Are you negging me? That bullshit doesn't work, Rob. If I wanted to sleep with you, I'd have done it already."

Lunch is a feast of delicious sandwiches, perfectly fluffy scones with jam and clotted cream, and an array of miniature cakes including, apparently, Granny Annie's favourite treacle tarts.

"We used to serve this in our pub," she tells us. "Hot with double cream. Was famous for miles around. Do you remember that, Luke?"

"I remember coming home with syrup in my hair most nights," he laughs. If memory serves me correctly, he grew up in the pub his grandparents owned and later ran the kitchen there before they sold it.

Seriously, Kara got lucky landing herself an ex-chef, and as one of her best friends, I'm more than happy to reap the benefits. The treacle tart is borderline orgasmic.

After lunch, Kara takes Annie for a walk around the garden to talk about her plans for a vegetable plot, and everyone else tops up their drinks and follows. I live in a second story flat and can't keep a cactus alive, so I hang back and make a start on clearing the table.

With the plates and cutlery loaded into the dishwasher, I run a sink of hot water for the glasses. It's a welcome moment of peace and quiet, but of course, as soon as I think that I feel the heat of him behind me, hands bracketing me to the sink on either side.

"Sucked any good dicks lately?" he asks over my shoulder.

"Jesus, Rob," Luke interrupts, passing behind us on his way to the fridge. "Give it a rest, mate."

"Why, do you need some tips?" A swift elbow to the ribs has him bent double with a satisfying grunt. He moves to my side, leaning back against the countertop while rubbing the spot. I hope he bruises easily.

"No, just letting you know mine is always available if you're not getting your fill."

"I do just fine, thank you."

"Seriously, all you need to do is ask."

"Rob, you would beg for me before I'd *ever* beg for you. Like, centuries would pass before I got that desperate."

He leans closer. "You know that's my whole kink, right? I love getting women to beg."

The more he goads me, the angrier I feel, and the angrier I feel the more I want him. *What is wrong with me?* I feel lightheaded, heat pooling in my core, nipples hardening underneath my top. I have to get away from him before my body betrays me any further, though unfortunately, being elbow deep in soapy water means storming off is not an option.

"Leave me alone."

"Come on, we're having fun," he says, nudging his hip against mine.

"Gastroenteritis is more fun than this."

"I can tell you want me, Hattie. Look at you, shortness of breath, pupils dilated, goosebumps on your neck. I know what it looks like when a woman is aroused. I bet a hundred quid you're in my bed by the end of the month."

The *arrogance* of this man.

"A bet?"

"A bet. I like my odds with you. What do you say? Do we have a deal?"

"Get fucked, Rob."

He leans in again, hot breath ghosting the shell of my ear. If he touched me now, I'd probably come on the spot. "That's the plan, angel."

I dry my hands roughly on my jeans, and storm off to find Kara in the garden. "Ugh, I hate Rob so much," I whinge.

"Hattie, just sleep with him already. Get it out of your system."

"*Argh*," I scream, and when I see it draw his attention, I turn away. "For God's sake, why would you assume I want to fuck him?"

"I don't, it's just... you're hot, he's hot, you're both good in bed, apparently. I sense some chemistry."

"There is absolutely zero chemistry there," I huff out. "The man has more red flags than a jubilee party. He's the worst guy I've ever met."

"OK, so don't sleep with him, but please be nice. I really want my friends and Luke's friends to get along. You know how much you all matter to us both."

"But your man is so good. How is he friends with such a cave dweller?"

I was dubious when Luke came on the scene. Kara was heartbroken and completely sworn off men, but she's a true romantic at heart. Megan and I knew she didn't deserve to spend the rest of her life alone, so we agreed we'd wait a year before encouraging her to get back out there. Luke pipped us by a couple of months, and I'll admit I was worried she'd fall for the first guy to give her a little attention, but he soon won Megan and me over. He and Kara are perfect for each other. Even I, a non-believer in love, can see that.

"I think you're overreacting. He's a sweetheart. Look how close he is with Luke's granny."

I cast an eye back over my shoulder to where he's sitting with her leaning into his side. She's showing him something on her phone and they both cling onto each other, laughing uproariously at whatever it is. "He's dedicated to his work, he's a great friend to Luke. I don't see what you hate about him so much."

I can't explain it either. I just do.

As the evening rumbles on, I return from the bathroom to find Kara and Luke snuggled together on the sofa, his fingers stroking through the lengths of her hair while they talk to Rob. Kneeling by the coffee table, Megan deals cards, while Annie sits in the chair telling her a story from her childhood. It's a picture of friendship and domesticity, everyone in their place, at ease with each other. I'm not sure where to go or what to do. There's an aching feeling that I don't belong here, that I'm not needed, and it hurts. I want to go home.

"I'm gonna head off," I call from the doorway, and they all look up at the same time.

"Are you sure?" says Kara. "We're just about to play a game."

"Yeah, I need to squeeze in a workout this evening."

"Nice to see you again, Hattie." Rob leans back, his arms spread out across the top of the sofa cushions. "Hopefully, the next time I see you will be in my bed. Naked."

It's the kiss he blows in my direction that pushes me over the edge.

He's so bloody arrogant, so sure of himself. Utterly convinced that he has to do nothing more than simply exist and I'll be powerless to resist him. He's about to learn the hard way that underestimating me is the worst mistake a man can make. Guys like him are pathetic, and nothing makes me happier than taking them down and showing them up.

"You know what Rob," I stride across the room to where he sits on the sofa. "I *will* take that bet. You think you're so bloody irresistible, it's about time someone proved you wrong. Same terms. If I'm in your bed by the end of the month, the money is yours."

I shove my hand into his, shake it roughly, and throw it back into his lap like it burned me. I'm too angry to care about the spark the heat of his palm sends through mine.

"Megan, I'll see you at home," I say, retreating and leaning down to give Annie a kiss on the cheek. "Happy birthday. It was so nice to meet you, I'm sorry to leave early."

"I hope you know what you're letting yourself in for, lassie," she laughs, patting my hand with hers. "I wouldn't make a bet with him for a game of tiddlywinks. He's ruthless." *Oh shit. What's that supposed to mean?*

"Not as ruthless as me." I storm into the hallway, shouting back at him. "This will be the easiest money I'll ever make in my life."

Chapter 2

Rob

Kneeling before her, I wrap my hand around the base of her foot and rotate her ankle in small circles to the left. I repeat the movement in the opposite direction, then flex the joint up and down, paying close attention to how her body reacts to the pressure.

"How does that feel?" I ask.

"Much better."

"What about the knee? Show me what you've been doing."

"Oh, you're making such a fuss now." She sits herself up, pushing her foot against my chest and shoving me backwards against the coffee table. A stack of magazines and puzzle books slide to the floor. *OK, clearly no trouble with knee extension.* I scramble to my feet and put things back in order.

"Mum, I'm not making a fuss. You know you have to keep up with these exercises if you want to get your strength back."

Three months ago I noticed she was limping a little, and eventually got it out of her that she'd fallen in the garden. Scans revealed no serious damage, but I've had her on a physio plan ever since.

"When are you going to give me some grandchildren?" she says.

"Don't change the subject."

"Even a girlfriend would be nice. Surely you've met someone by now?"

I've met *plenty* of women in my time, but I'd never let it go far enough that I'd bring someone home to meet my mother.

"It's a shame. You're such a good-looking lad, I can't bear the thought of you being alone your whole life."

The curse of being my mother's only child is that I get this nonsense week in, week out. My answer never changes, and she needs to take the hint.

"I'm not alone. I've got you. I've got Sheila. I'm great."

"You know what I mean."

"And you know how *I* feel. I'm not interested in a relationship."

"Can you two shut up?" my Auntie Sheila scolds from her favourite armchair. "It's starting."

She turns up the volume, pulls a lap-tray from the side pocket of her chair, and that's my cue to head to the kitchen. *Tea Boy*, they used to call me, and still do when they want to remind me who's in charge.

I fill the kettle with fresh water and flick the switch. In the cupboard I find teabags and sugar, along with about fifty other mugs that Mum keeps but never uses. I find their favourite mugs upturned on the drying rack. They're pretty much in use or just washed and drying every waking minute of the day. There's no need for her to have so many others, but Mum can never get rid of anything.

The entire house is like this; drawers filled with ancient utensils, bookcases ready to topple under the weight of a million paperbacks she's never going to read again. She has a wardrobe full of clothes but wears the same three outfits on repeat, and everywhere you look there's some trinket or other gathering dust.

It's always been the three of us. Mum, Sheila, and me.

As the story goes, Mum was over the moon when she got pregnant, and excited to tell my dad she was expecting his child. He apparently felt quite the opposite, went to the pub and never came back.

She never speaks about him, but Sheila once told me she'd expected him to propose, that they'd get a big house somewhere, and I'd be the first of many happy children. He was her first boyfriend, the love of her life.

Instead, her outraged parents ignored her heartbreak and told Mum to find somewhere else to live. In solidarity, Sheila went with her. They moved to a small village, turned our little house into a home, and I never had a reason to think it wasn't enough. Sheila got a job in the pub that Luke's grandparents owned and looked after me while Mum found cleaning work during the day.

Growing up, Sunday was always bath night and Mum would get me to bed, read two stories, and sing three songs. Soon after she turned out the light, I'd hear this rousing music floating up the stairs, and it was the greatest mystery of my life. That and a chorus of *'oohs'* and *'ahhs'* and laughter from the women who raised me. What were they watching? I tried to listen from beneath the covers, but knew better than to leave my bed to find out.

As I got older, I pushed her to let me stay up late so I could be part of all the fun they were having. Sheila made a deal with me. I could stay up as long as I made the tea, and soon, that was my favourite part of the week. Sunday night, fresh and clean, snuggling on the sofa with my mum, weak tea and biscuits on a lap-tray, and Antiques Roadshow on the TV.

I know we've made a good life, but now, stirring sugar into their tea, it's pretty hard not to see Mum's situation as my fault. If it wasn't for me, maybe my dad wouldn't have left. Or maybe he still would have, but she'd have met someone better, someone who could have given her everything she dreamed of.

As far as I know, there's been nobody else after my dad, no support from my grandparents, who've both since died, either. She's done everything for me.

I'm not about to encourage my mum to get on a dating app, nor do I want to think about her having sex, but that life of solitude seems pretty depressing to me. It's no wonder she wants me to give her some grandkids.

Getting comfy on the sofa beside her, I distract myself with a text to Luke, asking for Hattie's number. That bet I made with her yesterday was such a dumb idea. I love flirting, but I've never been this cocky about it with anyone else.

I know I screwed up big time the day we met. The moment I laid eyes on her, sitting there at Luke's dining table, my manners and senses left my body. Soft pale pink hair, that beautiful body, those stunning blue eyes that refused to look my way. No wonder I lost my game entirely.

I felt terrible for calling her a slut, and still do. I guess I figured, *'hey, you like it, I like it'*, why not be upfront about it? Unsurprisingly, it didn't go down well, but since then there's been a level of banter between us, a chemistry that's borderline aggressive, and I can't get enough of it. I can't explain why I enjoy winding her up so much. Seeing her all stroppy and frustrated just does something to me.

She's changed her hair since then, the pink faded and was replaced with a bright blonde. Megan once told me Hattie's had all sorts of shades over the years. I'd have asked to see photos if I didn't think it would end up with her calling me a pervert or worse.

I'm screwed. She's not a woman you mess with. There's no game plan here. I don't even know when I'll see her again, and there's not much chance of getting her into bed when I don't know where she lives, where she works, or where she hangs out.

It's a safe bet she'll be at the Book Club Kara hosts at Sunshine Coffee, but romance novels aren't my thing, and it would be inappropriate to turn up somewhere else unexpectedly. I've never had to resort to stalking to get laid, and I'm not about to start.

Luke replies, and when I save her number to my contacts, it autocorrects to *Hottie*. The typo makes me smile so much I leave it that way.

Me: Hey this is Rob.

"Is this one sugar or two?" Mum asks.

"Two," I lie. It's fucking nuts how much sugar these two get through in a day with the amount of tea they drink.

"Bullshit," she says, shoving it back in my direction. "Can't get the staff these days. Sort it out Tea Boy. Give him yours too, Sheila."

Sheila shakes her head and holds it out, eyes glued to the TV. I stand up and take both mugs back to the kitchen and add half a spoon. There's a message waiting for me when I get back to my seat.

Hottie: Rob who?

Rude.

Me: Rob Morgan
Hottie: ???
Me: You know who I am. Luke's friend. The hot one. The object of all your desires. The man you'll soon be losing a bet to.

A photo appears in our chat, a screenshot of a Google search. *How to block dickheads from texting you.* That shit makes me smile so hard my face hurts.

Me: You're funny. I like you.
Hottie: Well I don't like you. What do you want Knob?
Me: Is that a typo or your brilliant wit?
Hottie: You'll never know.
Me: When can I see you?
Hottie: Never.
Me: Seems unlikely given our best friends are madly in love with each other.
Hottie: Then you can see me next month when you give me my money.

God, she's annoying. I can't get enough of it.

"What are you smiling at?" Mum asks.

"Nothing." I shove my phone in my pocket and lean forward for another custard cream.

"Is it a girlfriend?"

"No."

"Well, hurry up and get one. I'm not getting any younger, you know."

A few nights later, I'm heading to bed when my thoughts, as they often seem to these days, turn to her. I wonder where she is, what she's up to, what she's wearing. Is she smiling? She's got such a gorgeous smile. She smiles with her entire face; her mouth wide, cheeks full, eyes bright and sparkling. Though, of course, she rips it all away the second she sees me, so I have to catch it from afar when she's not looking.

I decide to give it another go.

Me: How do you rate yourself in bed?

She replies immediately.

Hottie: 11/10
Me: Interesting

And then nothing. She leaves me on read, and I lie there for what feels like hours checking to see if she's replied. It's pathetic how much I want her to. I'm too desperate to care about any rules against double-texting.

Me: I'm 11/10 too, by the way
Hottie: I didn't ask and I don't care

Liar.

Me: What are you doing right now?
Hottie: Working

Working? It's almost midnight. She shouldn't be working this late. She should be having fun, with me.

Me: Tell me about the best sex you've ever had
Hottie: Why?
Me: So I can make sure I claim the top spot
Hottie: I severely doubt you could top it
Me: Tell me
Hottie: No

I don't have time to come up with a reply before she messages again.

Hottie: What about you?
Me: Hang on, I just need to mark this on my calendar
Hottie: ?
Me: You know this is the first time you've asked me a question. Excuse me while I recover from shock.
Hottie: I take it back. I don't want to know shit about you

More lies. I can tell she wants me, but really, I don't know much about her at all. Kara and Luke aren't gossips, and though they've both told me Hattie doesn't date, I've heard enough to know she likes a good time. She strikes me as the adventurous type, and something tells me impressing her won't be easy.

Me: A weekend in a cabin in the woods where we fucked on every surface in every room
Hottie: Sounds unhygienic

Me: Maybe it was the car-wash

Hottie: Express service? Thanks for confirming my theory that you're a quick guy. Though I'm afraid your attempt to get me thinking sexy thoughts has failed. Car-washes will never be sexy for me because they make me think of something else.

Me: What?

Hottie: My dad. He used to take us to a car-wash for a treat. He'd let me lie on the parcel shelf.

Me: Used to. Is he dead?

Hottie: Deadbeat more like. Could be actually dead. No idea

Me: Sorry

Hottie: Me too. Fuck off now.

And with that one confession, Hattie becomes a bit less of a mystery.

Chapter 3
Hattie

For someone who claims to get laid so often, Rob certainly has a lot of free time to text me. It's happened every night this week, each of his conversations getting more and more suggestive.

Not content with asking me about the best sex I've ever had, truly a question rooted in male insecurity, he's covered favourite positions, unfulfilled fantasies, and even promised he can beat my personal record of four orgasms in one night.

I know what he's doing. He's trying to break me down so I'll cave and he'll win the bet. Unfortunately for me, it's working.

He clearly loves the chase, and I'm surprised to find that I don't exactly hate being the one he's chasing. Every stupid message has me craving him more, and by the middle of the month, I'm in the gym most days burning off excess energy and sexual frustration.

I'm about to round out my workout with twenty minutes on the stair climber when Rob appears, leaning against the equipment with that gorgeous cocky grin spread across his face.

"Hey, beautiful." He's his usual delicious self in a fresh t-shirt and shorts, exactly the right length to show off his toned thighs. He has a towel tucked under his arm, a full bottle of water in the other fist. "I didn't know you're a member here."

Bullshit, bullshit, bullshit. I've been coming here for years. It's my sanctuary.

I turn my head but keep my eyes on him.

"Jase," I call out to one of the PTs who works here, and my favourite sparring partner. "Have you ever seen this guy here before?"

"No, he just joined." He edges closer our way, no doubt sensing my frustration. This is a great gym, and the customers are decent, respectful people, but it doesn't mean we don't get the occasional creep in here pestering women who just want to work out in peace. "Do you need help with the equipment, Sir?"

"No, I'm good, bro. We know each other." Rob nods towards me in his *stand down, fellow good guy* tone.

Jase steps between us. "You all good, H?"

"I've got it, thanks." I stab at the buttons and Jase leaves me to program my workout speed. "Stalking is a pretty desperate way to get someone into bed, Rob."

"I'm just here for the gains." *Ew, cringe.* "But good to know you're thinking about getting into bed with me."

"Piss off." I fire up the machine and in the mirror I see him hop on the bike behind me. I start climbing and try to concentrate on my breathing, but it's not long before I see a text pop up on my smartwatch.

Knob: Your arse looks incredible

"I'll have you banned for harassment, Rob," I yell without turning, without looking in the mirror, my eyes glued to the monitor in front of me. Doesn't stop me sticking it out a little further, knowing he'll enjoy the view. I've worked hard for this peach.

Forty minutes later, my thighs are on fire and Rob is still going. This is longer than I usually do, but I'm not quitting before he does. Sweat rolls off me like I've just stepped out of the shower. I pull my t-shirt over my head and keep going in my leggings and sports bra, using the bunched up material to dry my face, my neck, and my chest. My watch buzzes again.

Knob: I could make you sweat more than that

The thought is heavenly, and I'm sure he could. Sex has always given me that same endorphin high that I get from exercise. I'm cursed with a busy brain and a loud voice in my head that never shuts up. Some people meditate to unwind, some people drink, some people get high. I fight and I fuck.

I learned long ago that the best way to keep my anger under control is to pound it out at the gym, or let someone else pound it out of me in bed.

At school I got into, not fights exactly, but a fair amount of arguments that had me sitting outside the Headteacher's office. It didn't matter who it was, I could always find something to argue about. With my classmates, with teachers who felt I didn't respect their classroom, which I didn't because lessons couldn't keep me entertained.

The first time I tried kickboxing, it was like everything went quiet. The first time I had sex, it was the same, and I've been chasing that inner peace ever since. If only my brain enjoyed both as solo activities as much as it does with a partner.

I keep my vision trained on the monitor, not giving him the satisfaction of meeting his gaze in the reflection. Doesn't stop me picturing him in my head though. Me and him at full throttle, wild and unleashed. The kind of sex that leaves you speechless, panting for breath, covered in each other's sweat.

My hands are clammy, my chest is tight. I don't even have the energy to respond, and as much as I hate letting him have the last word, I like that he sees me ignoring him. I reach for my water, but there's only a trickle left. I can't last much longer and he's on a bike. He probably has miles left in him. I've already done a full weights routine, this was meant to be a quick cool down.

I hate to admit defeat, but I've got no chance of winning this one. I slow my pace right down and step off, hoping he won't catch me wobbling. Stretching will have to wait. Knowing Rob, he'd take advantage of the opportunity and offer to help and get his grubby hands on me.

Knowing me, I'd probably break and let him.

I'm in agony the next day. Furious at myself for pushing it so far. I consider working from home, but I've got two important meetings with our creative team whose diaries are impossible, so I hobble into work in trainers and take the lift instead of the stairs. I never want to look at a staircase again. There goes Rob, ruining yet another thing in my life. When I finally sit down at my desk, my phone buzzes in my hand. I smile, knowing it's him before I even read it.

Knob: How are your thighs today?
Me: Perfect, as usual
Knob: You know, if you're aching, I'm really good at deep tissue massage
Knob: Great with my hands (and my tongue)
Knob: I could help you work out all that tension

Me: Or you could piss off
Knob: Nah, you'd miss me too much
Knob: Admit it, you love this game

I bite hard into my lip to stop myself smiling. I hate that he's right.

I must admit, but only to myself, and to my great horror, that Rob is bloody good fun to flirt with. Sometimes I meet men who are attractive on the surface, but underneath they're incapable of giving me more than one-word answers, grunts, and lip-licking that I'm convinced they've copied from an internet celebrity. Bieber. He seems like a lip licker.

If anything, our hate texts are more fun than real life flirting because this way I can imagine him stomping around, getting all hot and outraged, maybe even a little hard. OK, a *lot* hard. I like the idea of him being rock solid in frustration with me. I bet he hates it. Which of course makes me enjoy my power over him even more.

However, I will never admit it, and I will *not* lose this bet. Losing is not an option, because I know he'd never let me live it down, and it would be brought up at every dinner or party for the rest of my life. I'm not ending a two decade friendship over this fuckboy. No, I plan to win and taunt him for the rest of *his* life about it instead.

I have to be careful, though. I never show my hand, never text him first, but the second I get one from him, I'm smiling like a giddy schoolgirl while I fire off my replies. And he's fast, as fast as me, and cocky with it. I've never met someone like him. We're at war, and every round of flirting is a battle I'm determined to win.

I shove my phone in my drawer and log into my email before Rob can use up any more of my precious time. It's a big week at work, my key client's campaign strategy is shifting from research to planning stage and there are a lot of moving parts to oversee.

There are only two unread emails in my inbox since I keep on top of my workload throughout the weekend and always check first thing in the morning, too. Halfway through my breakfast protein bar, a third pings in.

From: HAWKINS, Andrew
Subject: See me ASAP

Oh shit. That can't be good. Immediately, my brain assumes I'm getting fired, but I manage to climb down fast. That won't be happening. I'm great at this job, the client is happy, and nothing has gone wrong over the weekend that I've caught wind of.

I peek up over my monitor towards Andrew's office just in time to see him welcoming another person in. It's not like him to call an impromptu meeting, but it's also not like him to use the term *ASAP* and mean anything other than *'you're already late'*.

I've never run for a man in my life, and I'm not about to start now, but I get up from my desk, brush oat crumbs off my lap and make my way along the bank of busy colleagues towards Andrew's door.

He's left it ajar, but I knock anyway and lean my head through the gap. "You wanted to see me?"

"Ah, come in, take a seat," Andrew says, gesturing to the unoccupied chair next to the one which is very much occupied by a guy I've never seen before. I perch on the edge, glancing back and forth between the two men, trying to get a sense of what's going on here.

Andrew's mouth pinches into a straight line, and the other man smiles widely, leaning back into his seat and spreading his thighs. He's young and fresh-faced, with floppy fair hair pushed back behind a thin elastic headband. He's kind of cute. I hope he's not a client, then maybe I can take him for a ride. Though dressed in dark jeans, clean trainers, and a red and white striped sweatshirt, I have an overwhelming urge to point and shout, "There's Wally!" The tension in the air tells me this isn't the time.

"Harriet, this is Lawrence Desmond." *Two first names. Idiot. Just like Rob Morgan.* "Lawrence, this is Harriet Buchanan, who you'll be working alongside." Shit. Not a client, a colleague. That's worse. I don't mess around with people I work with, and definitely not ones fresh out of uni.

"Call me, Loz," the graduate says, sticking one open palm out in my direction.

"Hattie," I reply, shaking his hand a little more firmly before shoving it back in his direction. Addressing Andrew, I lean forward and cock my head. "I didn't realise we were taking on new interns?"

"We're not. Lawrence is joining us here at the DFR Group. He's going to be providing support on the Spirited account." *What the hell?* I manage that account, I have done for years.

"Why?" I ask. The teenager laughs through his nose and makes an enemy of me.

"What do you mean why?" says Andrew.

"This is the first I'm hearing that the Spirited account, *my* account, requires any support. Is there something I need to know?" My fingertips grip tight to the edge of my chair. This is not normal business practice. Have I messed up somewhere and not realised?

"It was felt that the size of the account warranted an additional person to support the needs of the client." *Ah, what a heaping spoonful of bullshit.* I've been in this business long enough to know corporate spin when I hear it.

"So my role is a job-share now?"

"No Harriet, you're the account director, Lawrence is here to offer support."

"But I don't need any support?" This doesn't make any sense. "So I don't need him." I refuse to look at the child. I'm not having any of this.

"This isn't up for negotiation," Andrew says sternly. "Lawrence is on your account from today. I need you to bring him up to speed and identify the areas where he can add the most value for the client."

Andrew has been my boss for most of the time I've been at DFR, the company I joined fresh out of university. Although we've both worked our way up, he's always kept me under his line of management. We have a great working relationship, so I know something is afoot when he's talking to me as my superior and not as my friend. The fact that he's calling me Harriet is even worse. I'm in trouble and I've no idea why.

"Where were you before?" I ask, turning to face the infant beside me.

"Arden Murthly," he says, proudly.

"I've never heard of them," I say, then wince. They're one of the biggest advertising agencies in the country and a key competitor. "I'm kidding. Of course I've heard of them. What did you do there?"

"Account director, same as I'll be doing here."

"You seem a bit young to be—"

"Hattie," Andrew warns. We've all been through enough diversity and inclusion training to know that age shouldn't be a factor in the workplace. That always makes me laugh when I look up the chain of command in our company and see, yep, you've guessed it, a sea of old, white, male faces in every senior leadership role.

"I'm twenty-four," he smirks. "I was the youngest account director on staff there, but I graduated early. Starred first from Cambridge." *Ugh, prick.* Let's not discuss the fact that I didn't get into Cambridge back when I went to university a lifetime ago.

"What experience do you have with food and beverage accounts?" I zone out when he rattles off a list of some of the biggest brands in the UK. If I was recruiting for my team, I'd hire him off that list alone.

"This isn't an interview, Harriet," Andrew interrupts. He stands, and the baby and I follow suit. "Take Lawrence and set him up at the empty station next to yours. Lawrence, here are your login details and welcome pack from HR." Andrew hands him a manilla folder, opens his laptop and gets back to his own work.

I glare down at Andrew, but he refuses to meet my eye.

"Follow me," I grunt in Lawrence's general direction, fling open the door and strut back to my desk.

"This is my desk," I waft my hand over my stuff, both annoyed and embarrassed at the state I've left it in. A half-eaten protein bar, two empty coffee cups, and a well-thumbed copy of the latest pick for Sunshine Book Club lay amongst print-outs of the latest focus group feedback I was about to review before this idiot appeared to ruin my week. It's just my luck that this month's book has a topless model on the cover, and I scramble to hide it. Must thank Kara for that one.

The desk next to me has been free for months and I've gotten used to having the extra space to spread out. I sweep my paperwork back over the line where our two desks meet and nudge his chair out with my foot. "And this is yours. Get yourself logged in and I'll be right back."

I march back around our bank of desks and along the corridor to Andrew's office, throwing the door open without knocking.

"What the *fuck* is going on, Andrew?"

"Calm down, Hattie." *I will do no such thing.* "He's here now. Just let him get to know the account and use him where you can."

"What are you not telling me? Who decided this?"

He tips his head back and pinches the bridge of his nose. "I told you, it was felt that the size of the account warranted an additional person to support the needs of the client."

"Don't feed me bullshit. *Who* says that? Are Spirited not happy with my work? I'll call Brent right now and ask." Brent is my counterpart on the client side, the marketing director who commissions all our work.

"Brent's out. They're bringing in someone new."

"*What?*" I knew something was going on. That confirms it. What has he done? Has he been fired? Is this about to derail everything I'm working on?

"He's taking paternity leave, and apparently the baby arrived early."

"I didn't even know he was having a baby." *Jesus, you think you know someone.* I've been on weekly, sometimes daily, calls with Brent for a year and he never mentioned anything about it. Fair play to him though for trying to equal the playing field. You don't get many men in this industry stepping up to share the parental load.

"Look, it wasn't my decision, Hattie, but you're doing a great job here, and everyone knows you're still the big dog where Spirited is concerned."

"They'd fucking better. I don't like this one bit. You know I don't share my toys."

"Just give him the shit you don't want to do and keep your head down. I'm sure Brent's replacement will be in touch soon. Now skedaddle," he shoos me away, "I've got things to be getting on with."

Except there is nothing I don't want to do. I love my job and, despite the occasional self-doubt spiral, I know I'm fantastic at it. And I like the control it gives me. I have built a great team who deliver excellent work, and the relationship with the client is better than ever. Or at least it was. Now I've got not one, but two new dickheads to put in their place.

Chapter 4
Hattie

LAWRENCE HAS BEEN FOLLOWING me around like a bad smell since Monday. He tags along to my meetings and dials into my calls under the guise of *'getting up to speed on all things Spirited'*.

Meanwhile, I seethe my way through the days annoyed at everyone who welcomes him with big smiles and open arms. They lap his schtick up, fawning as he regales them with stories of his previous work like the golden boy arsehole that he is. Nobody is *that* good. I'd do some digging if he left me alone for two seconds. I bet he's got a rich dad in advertising who got him a foot in the door.

There's still no word from Brent's replacement, so all I can do is keep pushing things along and hope they don't decide they hate our proposed vision for the new summer campaign.

The worst thing about Lawrence, and I do appreciate that in any other employee this would be seen as a good thing, is that he works damn hard. He's in early, barely takes lunch, and stays late, which means I now need to work even harder to prove myself.

He's the very reason I'm late for book club, rushing into Sunshine Coffee halfway through Kara speaking, throwing my coat over a table, and awkwardly weaving my way to the seat Megan has saved me up front.

Luke opened this place last year, and it's my favourite place in town. Starting over after his wife sadly died, he moved here to open his own business, and it wasn't long until he met Kara. A self-proclaimed romance addict, he soon invited her to start Sunshine Book Club, and it's been a fixture in my social calendar ever since.

I love getting lost in a good book, though work is such a distraction that if it wasn't for book club spurring me on, I'd probably never finish one.

The other great thing about book club is that Rob doesn't come, so it's a good chance for Megan, Kara, and I to catch up without him sucking all the air out of the room. I don't dare admit I haven't finished the book, instead I just nod along and agree with everything Kara says. I normally cram a few pages here and there through the work day but with Lawrence talking *non-fucking-stop* I've not had the chance. Even when I'm at home, he's emailing me questions, requesting documentation and putting catch-up meetings in my diary. There's no need, he's practically attached at the hip, all I've done for three days is catch him up.

I should be grateful. Him monopolising my time has left none for fantasising about Rob, though that hasn't stopped his desperate games. Instead of taking the hint and fucking off forever, he's upped the ante by sending photos of himself. Unfortunately for me, every single one of them makes me want to ride him until the sun comes up.

I could say it's just great lighting and strong angles, but that would be a lie. I don't think you could take a bad photo of a man that attractive. It should be illegal to be that tall and broad, so chiselled and manly. It's an unfair advantage but I refuse to give him the satisfaction of knowing how much he gets to me.

I have a better strategy. For every photo he sends me, he gets one back with zero fucks about how I look, my middle finger raised.

On Friday night he sends a photo of himself all dressed up, clearly heading out for a date. If he thinks I'll be jealous, he's completely deluded. I part my lips and let the tip of my finger rest against my tongue. I send it off, knowing exactly what it will do to him.

When he doesn't reply, I send another, my lips wrapped tight around my finger.

Knob: Stop it dirty girl. I'm out
Me: You started it

He reads my message but doesn't reply and it drives me nuts. I want to know what he's doing? I've been too busy this week to arrange a date, and I'm bored with bouncing around between his messages and work emails.

"What shall we watch tonight?" Megan asks, plonking herself down on the sofa and pushing her hair back with a fluffy headband. On the coffee table, she sets out various lotions and potions ready for a night of skincare in front of the TV.

This is what Friday nights have come to now Kara's all loved up and living with her dream man. When her awful ex-boyfriend left her, she was in a pretty terrible place mentally, but the silver lining was Girls Night. Megan and I would head to Kara's after work every Friday, get into our PJs, eat takeout, watch rom-coms, drink wine and talk about anything and everything until we fell asleep on her sofa.

I think those nights were the happiest I've ever been. I was needed, I felt cared for, and I miss what the three of us had. Not that I begrudge my friend her Happy Ever After, of course. Megs and I still make a go of it, but the bubble has burst, and we both know it's not quite the same when it's just the two of us on the sofa we've shared for a decade.

"What do you think will happen to us?" I say, shoving my phone under my leg before I dare text Rob again.

"What do you mean?"

"When you move out. What will happen with this place?"

"I wasn't aware that I'm moving out?" she laughs, but it's not a funny one, it's nervous and defensive. "Is something going on?"

Megan and I have lived together since we both moved back to the area after uni. I lucked out when her dad bought this flat and she asked me to share it with her. He runs a construction company and I think he has a few places around town. I don't ask questions, but I'm not above living off a rich man's spoils. It's a two bedroom in a large complex above the supermarket. Central, convenient, and best of all, quiet once they close at 10pm.

We've got a good thing going, me and Megs. We split the bills and food, and I shove as much as I can of what's left of my salary into my pension and savings, well aware that there'll be no rich husband to look after me in my retirement. It will probably be best for everyone if I go quickly around sixty-five, dying as I lived, a cocktail in hand and a man's face between my legs. Wouldn't that be fun?

"What about when Max comes back? Don't you want to live with him?"

"I don't know," she sighs, her shoulders slumping. "We don't really talk about it."

They don't talk about it because he's a shithead. Max is ten years older than Megan, and he's been stringing her along for the best part of two years. He spends half the year in London, and half in Australia, where it's no secret that he has a wife and kids. Apparently he's waiting for them to start school before he leaves his wife to move here permanently, which is about a thousand red flags in one sentence, but of course you can't see the colour of flags when they're blowing in your direction.

"You might move to Australia," I say, poking the bear. She gives a little, almost imperceptible, shake of the head. There was a time where she thought he might ask her to go with him. She had a vision of what a new life down under might look like, fully under his rose-tinted spell. Something must have happened, because at some point, she stopped mentioning it.

"Hattie," she says, shifting sideways on the sofa to face me, "if I ever moved out, which I won't, you know you could still live here. You don't have to worry about that. This is your home, too."

"Your dad's hardly gonna let me stay here rent free."

"You're here rent-free now," she says. I know she doesn't mean for it to sound so harsh, but all I hear is that I'm a freeloading waste of space who isn't pulling their weight.

Maybe it's time I look for a place of my own. I'm in my thirties now, I need to grow up a bit. Two strong, capable, and frankly gorgeous women shouldn't be living together and acting like we're still students. I've probably got enough for a deposit for a little place, if house prices don't keep outrunning my meagre pay increases. The alternative is moving back in with my mum and whatever dickhead-of-the-month she's letting take advantage of her. I think I'd rather shit on a plate and tuck in.

My heart feels heavy, I don't want to live on my own, I don't even know why I've brought it up. I'd be lonely. Digging my phone out from between the sofa cushions, there's still no reply from Rob.

"I don't think I'm really in the mood for a movie," I say, getting to my feet.

"Are you OK?"

"Yeah, fine. Think I'll just get an early night." I've never in my life had an early night. Flopping onto my bed, I pull up Rob's messages again, desperate to know where he is and who he's with.

Me: Is she pretty?

Unread.

Fuck him.

If he's going out with someone else, I'm going to make sure he thinks about me the whole time.

Me: I bet I'm better in bed than her

An hour goes by with still no reply. I must type and delete a hundred messages before I catch myself. I'm acting like a jealous, needy teenager for God's sake. Why do I even care? He can go out with whoever he likes.

Me: Enjoy your mediocre shag

I'm fuming. At myself, mostly, because I don't do this shit. I never show my hand or let him into my head. I bet he *loves* knowing I'm thinking about him. His ego would float him into space if he knew just how often he's on my mind. How I imagine him naked, how I have pictured us alone together in that stupid fucking cabin that he probably made up. Honestly, who has sex in a cabin? It's like something we read at book club.

Doesn't stop me imagining it, though. Me and him, alone in the woods together. Me and him in a hot tub. Me and him on his desk chair. I imagine he turns up at my house, which is not my actual house but a fancy penthouse apartment where he finds me in a tight black dress and killer heels. He storms in and tells me I can win the bet, but he's the true winner because the real prize is me. He throws me a briefcase full of £100 notes and tells me there's one for every second he's about to spend making me scream his name.

I'm unhinged.

This is what this stupid, arrogant bastard has done to me. After a week concocting fantasies of him pulling me apart, I'm aching to be touched. I need someone to get me out of this funk and out of my head.

I pull up one of my dating apps and match with a guy a few towns over purely because his name is Rob and make it clear that I'm looking for a fun night. He replies straight away, so I shower quickly, pull my hair into a messy bun, then slip into a short green dress and wedge heels. I learned long ago that it's best to wear as little as possible. Makes it easier to find my clothes on someone else's floor as soon as it's time to leave.

"I'm going out, don't wait up," I call out to Megan, grabbing a G&T in a can from the fridge, and my leather jacket from the hook by the door. She must have whiplash from the shit she's getting from me tonight, but I'll make it up to her with bacon rolls tomorrow.

By the time I get there, it's nearly 10:30pm. The bar is crowded, but I find him hovering by a table in the back. Over two drinks, I nod and laugh, not caring that he only talks about himself. I just want to get out of here, and I try to push down the sick thrill that I'll get to moan *his* name tonight. This Rob's got a decent body, and a nice face, but by the time I'm in his bed, I realise he's lacking the skill, enthusiasm, and cocky attitude I'm after.

He's not *Rob* Rob. My Rob.

I fake my way through it in time to catch the last train home, unsatisfied and more than a little depressed about the whole thing. I hate that I'm thinking about him so much. That his stupid texts are getting under my skin. I wonder what he's doing now. He's probably got some twenty-two year old riding him like a bull. Lucky bitch.

I want to text him, flirt and argue with him a bit. Really, I want to see if he's still up, and if he fancies a visitor, but I don't dare ask. The state I'm in right now, I'd be losing our stupid bet in five minutes flat.

I tiptoe through the flat so I don't wake Megan. As I get undressed, I catch my reflection in the full-length mirror on the back of my door, and it occurs to me that I didn't even take my dress off tonight. My favourite mint-green bra, the one that makes my tits look fantastic, was entirely wasted on a guy who didn't know any better than to skip straight to the below the belt stuff. I feel irrationally annoyed, pissed off that nobody has seen how good I look. I want people to see me, to want me.

No, not people.

Him.

I hate that he's made me want him, hate that I've spent the whole night obsessing over him, and still can't get him out of my head.

Standing in front of my mirror, I take a photo and hit send.

Chapter 5
Rob

I reach for my phone with one eye half open and pull up the message Hattie sent me just before two in the morning. I'm wide awake in an instant, cursing past Rob who slept through perhaps the most important text I've ever received.

There on my phone is a photo of Hattie standing in front of the mirror in her bra, tits pushed out, hard, dark nipples visible through the thin fabric.

And in between them sits her raised middle finger. Her full face isn't in shot, but I can see that she's grinning, biting her tongue between her teeth. *The little shit.* I need her, all of her, and I need it now.

Me: Fuck you look good. Come over and show me for real.

She's probably still asleep. I lie there, picturing her walking into my room and crawling up the covers to straddle me. My fantasy has barely begun when my phone pings in my hand.

Hottie: Sorry that was for someone else

Fury bolts through me, and I sit upright, tossing a pillow to the floor. That had better be bullshit. I don't spare a second to think about why her sleeping with someone else doesn't bother me as much as the thought of there being some other fucker who gets to be on the receiving end of her flirt fighting.

If she wants to antagonise me, well, two can play that game. I'm rock hard, obviously. There's not a man on the planet who wouldn't get stiff at the sight of her in her underwear. Maybe they wouldn't all be fans of her attitude, but it definitely does something to me. It's been a few weeks since I got laid now, and I need to get this pent up energy out.

Last night was a work event, and I knew that a photo of me in a suit would get Hattie riled up, but I learned long ago not to get involved with colleagues. I was a good boy. Two drinks and in bed by 11pm. If I'd have known she was still up and looking that hot, I'd have rung her up and made her get on a video call with me.

I push my covers back and shove my boxers down my thighs. Angling my phone, I take a photo, making sure she'll get a good look at my abs, too.

Me: I want you so much my dick hurts
Hottie: I'm thrilled to know you're in pain
Hottie: And let the record note that I did not consent to dick pics

Fuck!

Me: Well I didn't consent to pictures of your tits either
Hottie: And yet with one photo you're begging me to get into your bed

Hottie: Told you you'd beg for me before I ever begged for you

Argh, she's impossible. I don't get it. I've never had to work this hard for it. She's hot. I'm hot. We'd have a good time, why won't she just give in?

As the end of the month approaches, I'm absolutely desperate, having built up a healthy bank of fantasies involving Hattie. Things I want to do with her, places I want to fuck her.

Last night I went for a few beers with the lads from football, and got chatting to a woman and her friends. She made it clear she wanted to go home with me, but I shocked myself by saying no. I'm sure we'd have had a good time, but all I wanted was Hattie on her knees. Even talking to another woman felt cruel.

Now I'm trying to watch some new crime documentary everyone's raving about, but I've spent the whole time checking my phone, re-reading her messages. Couldn't tell you a single thing this detective has said. Texting her clearly isn't working. I need to ramp things up, so I mute the TV and tap her number.

It rings and rings. My knee jiggles, eagerness tipping into a sticky feeling of desperation, and I'm about to hang up when the call connects.

"Yeah?" she pants, sending a jolt of electricity to my dick. What witchcraft does she possess that has this effect on me with just one word? "What do you want?"

"You're naked."

"What the fuck? How did you know that?"

"You're out of breath. So either you just got out of the shower or you just came, but either way, you rushed to answer my call."

"Maybe it was both." *Fuck.* The image is clear in my mind, Hattie all slick and soapy in my shower, peering back over her shoulder, eyes begging me to follow her in. "Why are you calling me?"

"Can I take you out for dinner tonight?"

"Gross, no," she scoffs.

"A walk then. With burritos on the way? I need to eat."

"I know what you're trying to do, Rob."

"What am I trying to do?"

"You're trying to make me lose the bet by convincing me to see you in the desperate, misguided hope that if I'm in the same room as you I won't be able to resist your advances, but there's a flaw in your plan."

"What flaw?"

"Do you really think I'm going to have sex with you on a walk?" she says, lowering her voice.

"What if the walk leads to my house?" She doesn't reply, her usual quick witted responses all gone. "Come on, you know you want to. I'll make it so good for you."

"Still begging? Pathetic," she laughs and hangs up.

Witch!

Something must be wired incorrectly in my brain because it doesn't respond the way a normal person would to her attitude. Instead of being understandably offended and turned off by her rudeness, my twisted grey matter actually likes this.

And my dick likes it even more.

Chapter 6
Hattie

SLAMMING MY FOREHEAD AGAINST my locker, I curse my stupid vagina. I'm so close to caving in.

I'm out of breath because he caught me changing after a gym class. Endorphins are screaming through my body and I can't think of a better way to keep this high going than a good screw. Fuck him for phoning me up, and frankly, fuck me for rushing to answer it.

Two days. That's all that's left of our bet. I just need to make it through two days and I'll have won. I don't trust myself, though. For the past few days, he's occupied all of my thoughts. He's in my head when I wake up and imagine him lying next to me, he's there all day long with his flirty texts. I love how bold he is about wanting me. He even sent me a dick pic that had me reaching for my vibrator and staring at it the whole time I got off. Who does that?

I could go and see him, I've got his address. I asked Luke for it in a moment of weakness. Could get in my car and be there in twenty minutes, tearing off his clothes and sliding down onto him. I press my eyes closed, forcing myself to take slow, deep breaths. Two days. I can last two days, I just need to keep my head elsewhere.

What I really need is to concentrate on work and make sure my project doesn't get derailed by Lawrence. I could barely sleep last night for worrying about it. Megan and I met Kara for dinner and drinks, but I skipped out early because they were in a gorgeous, silly mood, and I just felt like a black cloud dragging them down.

No, I can't go home or I'll flirt with him more. I tug my sweaty gym clothes back on, grab my gloves, and head upstairs. I can't get on my knees for him if I'm busy kicking the shit out of a punchbag and picturing his face.

An hour later, I exit through the turnstile, scrolling through five more emails from Lawrence who seems hell-bent on ruining my Saturday with yet more dumb questions. Before I can reach them, the doors ahead of me slide open to reveal the last person I want to see.

Rob Meathead Morgan is a vision in black sweatpants, a matching hoodie, and a fucking backwards cap. I don't think there is a woman on this earth who wouldn't want to climb him like a tree, tear those clothes off, and get to work. Though I'd let him keep the cap on.

He removes one earbud, a huge smile spreading across his face when he spots me. My face does the same before I can wrangle it back into a frown.

"Seriously Rob? Leave me alone."

He holds his hands up to his chest, palms towards me. "I didn't know you were here, I swear. I just came to work out."

"I don't believe you."

"Honestly. I work out when I'm tense."

"Why are you so tense?" I ask. He steps a little closer and lets his eyes fall down past my face.

"Why do you think?"

"Don't start," I say, hoisting my gym bag further up my shoulder. "I'm not in the mood for your shit."

"What's happened?" he asks, his tone turning sincere.

"Just work stuff," I shrug. When I duck left he does too, his bulky frame forcing me into a stand-off as he blocks my path to the door. I'm about to tear him a new one when he rests one hand on my shoulder and squeezes. One touch is all it takes. Warm, firm, the pressure soothing away tension he caused in the first place.

I roll my lips together, forcing my eyes down so he can't see how much he affects me. Hiding is futile. The next thing I feel is his hand on my jaw, tilting my face up to meet his.

I'm not short, but he is so tall. Looming over me, he takes up all the space in my vision. His eyes flit back and forth between mine, and when a little wrinkle appears between his eyebrows, he steals my breath too.

"Want to talk about it?"

I shake my head, but can't tear my eyes away. A month ago, I'd have punched him in the arm and barged my way past. Now I'm powerless to do anything but stand here taking in the dip in his top lip, the fullness of the lower one.

"Come on," he smiles, giving my cheeks a playful squeeze. "I can skip leg day, let's go get a bite to eat."

I open my mouth to object and he moves fast, his hot palm smothering it before I can get any words out. Part of me wants to kick and scream, but my eyes roll back because the traitorous bitch between my legs is apparently super into this. I think I'm about to lose our bet right here in the gym foyer.

"You do eat, right?" he laughs, and a deep rumble from my stomach gives me away. I am starving actually. I pull his hand away but he hooks his thumb over my fingers and doesn't let go.

"Did you say something about burritos?"

"That's my girl." He lifts my bag from my shoulder and throws it over his. "After you."

It's a short walk to our local Mexican diner, probably my favourite place to eat in a town with not that many choices.

"I need to reply to a couple of emails. Could you order for me?"

"Sure. What will you have?"

"Just order two of what you're having. I can handle heat."

He doesn't bother to conceal his smirk as he walks backwards away from me. I slide into a corner booth, open up my work emails, and groan out loud. Lawrence is relentless, sending me multiple access requests and questions about the project, but always copying in enough colleagues that it makes me look like I've fucked up somehow. I haven't, I know I haven't. He already has access to all the project files. Why is he even working on a Saturday?

It took me months to get this project and my team into a good place, one where we aren't having to work until 11pm and all hours of the weekend. I've pulled nearly twenty extra hours this week, all because of him. I'll need to have a word about company culture, make it clear that we don't pressure each other like this.

That's how it feels. Pressure. I know it's him not reading things properly, not listening when I've given him instructions. He looks a bit stupid to be honest, but I'll bet that come Monday there'll be comments from higher up about his dedication and enthusiasm. He'll make some smug comment about how he worked all weekend, but it didn't even feel like work because he's just *so excited* to be here. That's how it always is with men in advertising. Egomaniacs.

I reply to his most recent email and answer all his questions in one go hitting send just as Rob sits across from me, sliding a tray of food between us.

"Beef burrito, fully loaded. Jalapenos. Nachos with extra guac. Pineapple Jarrito. Sound OK?"

My exact order. I glare at him while I scroll through my memory bank, trying to recall how he would know this. Have we eaten Mexican food together before? Discussed it at a Friday night dinner? I can't remember. I can't remember most things we discuss when he's around, because I'm too busy hating his guts and trying not to get horny.

"That's perfect. Thank you."

"So, what's going on with work?"

"Ugh," I groan through a mouthful of burrito. "I don't really want to talk about it."

"You sure? I'm a great listener, you know," he says, scooping a crisp tortilla chip through fresh salsa.

"It's boring. There's a new guy who's been assigned to my project without my approval, and he's getting under my skin."

"You're hot for him?" Rob asks, his eyebrows shooting up.

"God no. He's twenty-four."

"Hasn't stopped you before," he teases.

"Please, stop," I lean back against the vinyl padding of the booth seats, sulkily. "I'm just feeling paranoid about why he's here at all. I'm the account director, I'm in charge, things are going well, we're on budget, the client is happy, the team are happy. Nobody will give me a straight answer, but in my world sneaky moves are made all the time without properly informing or consulting people. So it makes me feel like shit's about to go down."

"You think he's here to replace you?"

"I don't know. I've been asked to bring him up to speed on everything."

"Hey, maybe you're getting promoted?" he says. I know he's trying to help, but it's pointless, and I don't trust his motivations, anyway.

"It doesn't work like that. We have to jump through all sorts of hoops to move up. Nobody just *gets* promoted."

"Is that what you want to do? Move up?"

"Mm-hmm, absolutely," I say, finishing a mouthful of burrito. "Top job will be mine one day. What's new with you?"

"Oh look, the ice princess gives a shit." I roll my eyes and kick him underneath the table, but he grabs the back of my calf and holds it still.

"I'm OK, it's been a good week at work. A few of my patients have been making really good progress."

"Thanks to your mind control?"

"Hattie," he says softly, reaching out to cover my hand with his. "You know that's not what I do, right?"

"No," I shrug and pull it away.

"I work in neuropsychology. I'm part of a team who help patients recover from brain injuries. Stroke, head trauma, alcohol related brain damage, that sort of thing. I'm not off manipulating women day in, day out. I help people get their lives back."

Fuck's sake. Why didn't I know that? Now he's some sort of saint.

"How noble of you."

"It's incredibly rewarding."

"Any dates recently?" I ask without thinking, steering our conversation in the worst possible direction. This is why I hate small talk.

"Not this week, no. Been too busy thinking about you," he says without a hint of sarcasm. I don't have an appropriate reply to that, so I keep my filthy thoughts to myself while I finish my food. Thankfully he takes the hint and shuts up too, but after a while it's weird sitting here in silence across from him.

"What's wrong with you then?" I ask, cleaning off my hands with one of the lemon scented wipes they always give you here.

"What do you mean?"

"Why are you like this?" I sweep my open palm back and forth in front of him. "You're apparently drowning in women but never date, so you must be afraid of commitment. Why?"

"I'm not afraid of commitment," he baulks.

"Liar."

Rob shoves a nacho in his mouth and leans back, arms folded while he eats. "Dad shit, probably. He left before I was born, so it was always just me and my mum and my Auntie Sheila. I hate the thought that I could turn out like him, so I don't even take the chance that I could do that to someone."

Wow. He got deep real fast. "That's very self-aware."

"What's wrong with you?"

I walked into that one. "Nothing's wrong with me."

"Sorry, I'm not trying to be a dick. I'm just curious. I've never met a woman who's like me. You know, happy to keep emotions out of it. You don't want love, happiness, family, all that jazz?"

"My dad didn't want me either," I answer, stiffly. That's all he's getting. I don't tell him I've watched men hurt my mum my entire life. I don't tell him that the first time I liked someone enough to call him my boyfriend, I caught him cheating within days. I don't tell him my sister got out of it all unscathed while I'm a walking pile of trust issues with a hardened heart. I just tell him what I have.

"Kara and Megan are family to me. I love my life, I have a great job, I get laid plenty, and I love myself way more than anyone else ever could. Why would I need more than that?"

"Fucking hell. You're something else."

When Rob asks if he can walk me home, I relent. It's not too far and, against my better judgement, I am enjoying his company. We swap stories as we walk about where we like to drink, where we've had the most success meeting people. It makes me wonder how, just like Megan said, our paths haven't crossed before.

"Why aren't you trying to get me into bed?" I narrow my eyes and ask when we reach my door.

"Who says I'm not trying?" He steps closer, presses his hand against the wall above my shoulder, and just like that, Rob Cocky Bastard Morgan is back. Before I can push him away, his other hand catches my wrist, and the sensation of his thumb against the soft skin there disarms me. "You know, I could come in if you want. We could call in sick on Monday and spend the last couple of days really losing that bet in style."

It's a tempting offer. A two-day fuckfest would definitely lower my stress levels, but I never do sleepovers, I don't bring men to my house, and I'm certainly never doing *him*.

"Ah, but if we do that, you'd win. And I don't lose. Ever."

I move to step away, desperately needing some space between us, but he's got that maddening way of knowing what I'm going to do before I do it. He slides his hand around my waist, tugging me closer while pushing me back until I'm pressed right up between him and the wall.

He looks down at me, his eyes scanning my face, the tip of his finger reaching out to stroke a lock of hair out of my eyes. "Hattie. I promise you, we'd both win. Multiple times."

My eyes flutter closed as goosebumps prickle at the back of my neck. He tilts his hips forward, pressing into me just enough to feel the hard length of him behind his sweatpants. "I know you want this as much as I do."

I roll my eyes and try not to smile or push my hips back.

"Invite me in," he whispers, hot against the shell of my ear.

Resist, Hattie, resist!

"You need to go." I brace my forearm against his chest and fish my keys from the front pocket of my bag, squirming to turn away and unlock the door. Squeezing through the gap, I close it before he can follow, leaving him out on the street, and me gasping for air in the empty hallway of my building.

Jesus Christ. Two more days. I can manage two more days.

Chapter 7
Rob

She's won.

Today is the last day of our bet, and it's not as if I haven't given it my best shot. I've tried to seduce her with words, I've tried with photos, I've tried being a decent guy and actually getting to know her, which wasn't exactly a hardship. I thought I nearly had her when I took her out for dinner, though by the time I'd walked her home it wasn't even about sex. We were both different that night, and I just wanted to spend a little more time with her.

Joining her gym was a dumbass move that's going to run my losses closer to £1000 once the 12-month membership is over. I did it on a whim, but it seems especially stupid now I'm standing here in my garage, surrounded by the home gym equipment I set up just the way I like it. I have everything I need in here; weights, a treadmill, a bike, even a cable machine.

The only thing I get out of that gym membership is the chance to bump into her, and it's not like she lives there. I've been three times and not seen her at all. Maybe I'll get into boxing and let her kick the shit out of me. I'm sure she'd enjoy that, and I reckon I'd enjoy seeing her fully unleash her anger.

I set up my rack for push day and get myself into position for a heavy round of chest presses. This place saves my sanity after busy days at work, the ones that remind me how precious life is, and how quickly things can change. Halfway through my first set, my doorbell alarm rings on my phone. My house is on a quiet side street and I rarely get visitors, but a few of my older neighbours sometimes drop by for help with something.

Setting the bar back into the cradle, I reach for my phone and am pleasantly surprised to find a face that's not well known around these parts.

Rolling up the garage door, I step outside and lean against the wall of the house. There on my doorstep, she bounces gently from foot to foot, fiddling with her earlobe. It's not until I cough that she turns and sees me. I don't miss how wide her eyes go when her gaze falls down to my chest, bare except for a layer of sweat.

"What are you doing here, Hattie?"

She stalks over to me with a tight smirk on her face. I face her head on, my hands on my hips while her eyes roam over me. She drags one fingernail down between my pecs, over my abs, and hooks it into the waistband of my shorts. Pulling them away, she leans closer to take a peek inside, wetting her lips with her tongue before letting go. The elasticated fabric hits my skin with a sharp sting that makes my cock twitch despite the pain. My chin drops to my chest with a hiss, and she tilts her face up to mine, her nose grazing gently along my jawline before her mouth finds my ear.

"I think you know why I'm here."

Seriously? *Now* she's giving in? *Thank fuck for that.*

"Finally. Get in here." I grab her hand and pull her into the garage with me. Her laugh fills the space as she looks around.

"Why do you come to my gym when you've got all this here?" she asks.

"That should be obvious," I say, sliding my hands between her coat and her top, across her back then dipping lower.

"Mmm, I've been dying to get my hands on this ass," I whisper against her neck. She lets out a soft moan when I squeeze her tight, pulling her hips against mine.

"No, darling. Stop thinking with your dick for five seconds." She reaches her hand into her coat pocket and pulls out a folded slip of paper. She holds it up between us, but when I move to take it she yanks it away and pushes it deep into the pocket of my shorts, her fingertips a whisper away from my stiffening cock. "I just came to give you this."

Heat rises in my chest when I realise she's played me. Gripping her hips, I walk her backwards until she hits the wall and pin my elbows either side of her head, trapping her in.

"What is it?"

"My bank details so you can send me my winnings," she says, her laugh sounding a little more nervous now.

"You know you could have sent me those by text?"

She nods, then straightens up between my arms. "But then I'd miss the satisfaction of seeing your face when you realise you've lost our bet. And trust me, it's so satisfying."

She darts her tongue out to wet her lips and I lose it, pushing her harder, one knee wedged between her thighs, my chest against hers, forcing her to look up into my eyes. Her tits look amazing from this angle. "There are still three hours to go, angel. Come inside the house and lose. You know it will be worth it."

"I can't think of anything I want less." She pushes me away and squirms out of my grasp. Adjusting her skirt where I've nudged it up her thighs, she stumbles as she heads out the door. I don't know whether to laugh or to strip her naked and fuck her over the weights bench, neighbours be damned.

I know she wants me. If her flushed cheeks and shallow breathing didn't give her away, the speed at which she scurries off certainly would.

"Can you send it first thing?" she yells back. "I've got my eye on a new vibrator. Don't worry, I'll name it after you."

"Hattie," I call after her, and she turns around from the end of my path. "I will not forget this. One day, not too far from now, I'll have you in my bed and you'll love every single second of it."

She gulps and I slam the garage door down before she has a chance to even try to get the last word in.

Hattie drives me mad, but for some sick reason, it spurs me on. I power through the rest of my workout, easily motivated when my reward is playing out the alternative ending to her visit in the shower. The one where I hitch her skirt up and take her right there against the wall. Where I bend her over the weight bench and spank her for making me wait so long. Where I drag her into the house and don't make it past the kitchen before I get my mouth on her.

My poor dick has had zero action since our bet started, and I'm as disappointed as he is that it's ending just the two of us. I don't know where we go from here, but I don't want this game to be over. I text her as soon as I get out of the shower.

Me: How did you get my address?
Hottie: Same way you got my number dickhead

I punch her details into my banking app and lie in the dark, counting down the final minutes of the month. If I'm stuck obsessing over her, then I sure as shit want her lying in her bed thinking about me too. As soon as midnight hits, I transfer her winnings with the payment reference *'for your pleasure'*.

Two days later, I'm wolfing down a sandwich at my desk, catching up on typing patient notes when my phone buzzes in my pocket. I pull it out and see a photo notification from Hattie. My dick twitches instantly, desperately hoping she's sent me another picture of herself but when I open it up my excitement turns to confusion, then fury, then that hard ache that I never seem to be able to get rid of where she's involved.

There on her bed, nestled between crumpled sheets, lies a bright pink vibrator. A wide V shape, it's long with a thick bulb on one side and one of those clit sucker bits on the other.

Hottie: `Just arrived. Thanks for the best orgasm of my life.`

My brain turns to mush when I zoom in. It's shiny, glistening. Has it just been inside her? Is that what she's doing right now? Is she seriously in bed, getting herself off in the middle of the day and taunting me with the evidence.

The fucking tease.

I don't know what to say, don't know what to think. Instead, I lock my phone in my drawer and leave her on read. I don't want to give her the satisfaction of knowing how much she's wound me up.

I spend my day half hard, and head straight home into the shower, stroking myself off at the thought of her naked on her bed. No, even better, spread out on *my* bed. That toy buried inside her, writhing underneath me, grabbing fistfuls of sheets.

This woman is making me lose my mind, and the only thing I know for sure is that I'll die a very unhappy man if I don't get to make these fantasies come true.

Chapter 8
Rob

Hattie hasn't texted me all week. Now the bet is over, I'm struggling to come up with excuses to text her and it's ridiculous how much I miss our chats.

I torture myself by reading back through all the messages we've exchanged over the past few weeks. She's so fun and flirty, even when she's insulting me, I can't get enough of it. I've zoomed in on that photo of her in her bra so many times I might wear a hole in the screen. The vibrator one is even worse.

By Friday, I cave.

Me: Want to meet up tonight?
Hottie: Why?
Me: Bet's over, we can finally have our way with each other
Hottie: Rob, get this into your head. I took your bet because it was easy money. I don't want to hook up with you. Ever.
Me: Liar

She doesn't reply, and I don't believe her. I've seen the way her body reacts when I'm around, and I've been with enough women to know what it looks like when I'm turning them on. I'm an easy mark, I know we'd have a good time. Why doesn't she want this?

I didn't hook up with anyone while I focused on winning Hattie over and this month-long foreplay has me losing my mind. It's rare for me to go that long without sex, and my dick has spent more time with my hand than it has since my teenage years.

I can't take it anymore. A man has needs, and I don't owe her shit. If Hattie isn't interested, there are plenty of other women who are.

She's beautiful. This petite brunette standing in front of me, throwing her head back in laughter at god knows what. I've already forgotten what I said and I sure as hell couldn't tell you anything she's said tonight. This isn't like me, I'm never this much of a bastard.

I down my pint and set it on the bar. I'm about to make some excuse and apologise for wasting her time when she lays her small hand on my bicep and looks up at me through her long, dark eyelashes.

"What do you think about heading back to mine?"

It all happens fast, and I usually prefer to take my time. I kiss her in her hallway, grip her legs and lift her to wrap them around my waist like I know women love, but she's slippery in my arms, the fabric of her dress hard to keep hold of. I feel clumsy and out of control, so I pull it up over her head and the next thing I know, everything is off and we're naked on her bed.

I let her bounce on top of me for a while, but I can't enjoy the view. Instead, I close my eyes and wonder what Hattie would feel like on top of me. I bet she'd feel soft and firm all at once, and I'd be in heaven letting her take all her anger out on me.

The brunette moans and whips her hair around as she rolls her hips. She's hot, she knows she's hot, but she's trying too hard. Performing to make it good for me and I don't have the heart to tell her she'll never be what I need right now.

This isn't normal.

I'm a piece of shit. I should leave.

"Use me to get yourself off," I say, and it makes her squeal in delight. She reaches across to her bedside drawer for a vibrator. Normally, I'd slap it out of her hands before she had a chance to turn it on. Not that I have a problem with them, but I pride myself in giving it my best shot at making women come by myself before bringing toys into play. I can't summon the energy tonight though, so I let her take what she needs until she bucks and writhes and collapses onto the bed beside me.

Getting up, I grab my clothes from the floor and head into the bathroom to deal with the condom. When I get back, she's ready for round two, propped up on her forearms, wiggling her tits back and forth. They are great tits. They deserve so much better than me. Her face falls when she sees I'm already dressed.

"You should get some sleep," I say, setting a glass of water by her bedside and pulling her covers up over her body. It's the least I can do.

"But you didn't come," she pouts.

"I had a great time," I say from the doorway. "You look after yourself."

Never in my life have I slept with someone and not come. And never in my life have I walked out without making sure they're completely satisfied.

Hattie fucking Buchanan. This is ridiculous.

I can't have her. I can't escape her, but neither can I have her ruining my life. Am I supposed to never hook up with anyone again without her being stuck in my head?

This has to stop now. I'll be civil when we're with our friends, but no more gym stalking, no more flirting, no more texting.

And definitely no more jerking it over her photos, I tell myself as I climb into my own bed and open them up one last time.

Chapter 9
Hattie

I'VE MANAGED TO AVOID Rob since our bet ended by staying late at work or accidentally-on-purpose double booking myself. I skip Friday dinners, Sunday lunches, anything where I know he'll be there.

Kara's not happy about it and tells me she misses me every time we speak, but it's all different now. After her last relationship, she, Megan and I were our own little gang, and I don't understand why now everything has to be a big group activity with Luke and his idiot mate too.

Ah well, one more step towards that spinster life.

I haven't even heard from Rob since I told him I didn't want to hook up with him, but unfortunately my stupid brain doesn't seem to have gotten the memo because he's still in my head way more than I'd like. It's pathetic how often I think about messaging him, how often I pull up our chat and lust over all those selfies he sent when he was trying to seduce me. It pains me to admit, I kind of miss him and I'm annoyed that it was so easy for him to just give up our game.

I should be grateful, however, because this month has been hell at work and the last thing I need are more distractions.

Lawrence started doing exactly what I predicted he would, throwing ideas out into every team meeting with no consideration for how far into this project we already were. We'd already done our research, we had all the data, we'd taken preliminary ideas to focus groups, and the client loved their feedback. But no, Lawrence couldn't leave it alone and the next thing I knew, he was being sent off to pull together some new plans *'just in case'*.

Andrew must think I'm stupid, but I've been here long enough to know how these things play out. Lawrence can shove his new ideas up his arse as far as I'm concerned, and if I hear him say *'some food for thought'* one more time, I will start throwing things.

I really need to blow off some steam and the gym won't cut it tonight. Kara will be all loved up with Luke, rarely keen for impromptu plans since they moved in together. I'm all set to convince Megan that a night out is what we both need, but she refuses to drink during the week because she can't bear to teach with a hangover. Can't say I blame her.

I want to text Rob and ask if he has plans tonight, even though I know that would be the worst thing I could do right now. Desperate and needy is not a good look on me. The feeling is even worse.

I pull up an app and swipe through a few guys who are online now, pour myself a glass of wine and wait for someone to take the bait. It doesn't take long. My phone pings with that notification sound that makes my stomach twitch. Years of this shit and I still get an excited nervousness, not knowing what I'm about to read. Will it be a fun, flirty message that lets me know I'll be getting laid tonight? Will it be a boring bastard, or worse, an unsolicited dick pic? You never can tell.

Mark: Fancy a drink tonight?

Yes, Mark. You'll do.

My date is waiting for me when I arrive and after a friendly peck on the cheek, he holds the door open, following me inside. He's pretty cute, even if he's still sporting that shaggy 2000s indie boy haircut, and we talk about music while the barman pulls two pints. I nod along, agreeing with everything he says, dancing the dance even though we both know what we came here for.

This place is busier than usual for the middle of the week, so we grab a table up at the back, and while he tells me about his work, I admire his eyes. They're perfectly nice eyes, kind even. At least he's not looking at me like he hates me, hates his mum, hates all women, and can't wait to show me just how much. He's got nice teeth, and clean hands with neatly trimmed fingernails.

That's how I judge men. If he takes care of his teeth and his hands, I trust that he'll be a decent enough fuck. It's sad isn't it, how low my bar is? I wonder if he'll make the first move or if I'll have to. I don't mind if it's me, but it's nice to have a confident guy now and then. Rob would make the first move for sure.

Matt asks me about my work and I throw out a few of the big name brands I know always impress.

"That's so cool," he fawns. "Do you get lots of freebies?" They always ask.

"Sometimes, but never the stuff you'd really want," I say for the millionth time.

"So how long have you been on the apps, then?" They always ask this, too.

I pull my mouth into a tight smile and act all coy, the way I know they like. They don't want to think you've been on there for years. They don't like to imagine you're using it for hookups, even if that's exactly what they're doing. The hypocrites.

"Just a few months," I lie, not giving a shit whether or not he believes me. I'm halfway through my pint already and need to slow down. I take a small sip and feel that shift in the air that I've not felt often enough lately.

Rob Beautiful Bastard Morgan. Alone, and making his way to the bar.

I keep looking at Matt but tilt my head slightly so I can glance past him. The barman takes Rob's order right away, and they chat like old friends. He leans against the counter and takes a sip of his beer, while he scans the room. I snap my eyes back to Matt and scoot down in my seat.

So this is what he does. He just turns up and waits for the women to flock to him. I hate that it works, and I hate that a table of women between us are already melting into mush while they loudly whisper *'don't make it obvious'* while then making it incredibly obvious by all taking turns to look round at him.

Underneath the table, I slide my phone from my pocket and check my messages, but I'm disappointed. There's nothing from Rob. If he wanted to go out tonight, why didn't he text me?

Except, why would he? What would I have said? *Fuck off, Knob.* Even though I desperately wanted to text him myself, I know I would have told him to get lost. I'd never have given into him that easily.

I could text him now, but what would I say? It's a point of pride that I never contact him first, though I'd love to see the look on his face when he gets a message from me. I open my camera gallery and have a quick scroll through for a photo of me he hasn't seen before, but nothing fits the mood. I want him to lust over me, but all my recent photos were meant to take the piss out of him.

One of the women, a beautiful blonde in a red dress and skyscraper heels, has made her way over, and she's currently leaning into the bar, while he stands with his back to me. She flips her hair back over her shoulder and laughs loud enough for me to hear it all the way down here. God only knows what line he's fed her.

I watch, the room slowing as he lifts his hand, stroking down her back as he leans in to whisper in her ear. Cue more hysterical laughing and her slapping a hand against his chest as though she's scandalised. She's so obvious, and he's so pathetic that he falls for such moves.

I'm going to text him. I need to text him.

"I think I'm going to head off," Matt says, pulling my attention back to the table as he drains his pint. Shit.

"No, why?" *Yes, please go.*

"You seem great, Hattie, but I don't think your head's really in it. And you keep looking at your phone."

"You're right, I'm sorry. I am kind of distracted. It's a work thing." How many times have I lied to this man already, and why does this one feel worse than the others?

"It's cool," he says, standing to leave. "Hit me up another time if you like."

I nod. That will never happen. "Thanks Matt."

"It's Mark."

"Shit," I cringe, sinking lower into my chair. "Sorry."

And with that, he's gone.

Fucking Rob. Yet another night ruined by him getting in my head, and this time he's not even trying. I hate his stupid bastard face. I down the last of my drink, adjust my jewellery, wiggle my dress down to show more cleavage, and head over his way. With his back to me, he doesn't see me coming. He has no idea I'm here until I thread my hand through his. In his initial shock, he tries to pull away, but I grip it so tight it hurts. It probably hurts me more than it hurts him, but I'm not letting go.

If I'm not getting laid tonight, then neither is he.

"There you are darling," I say, looking up at him, my voice all prim and plummy. "Listen, I've just had a call from the babysitter and she says the twins have the most awful vomiting bug, diarrhoea everywhere."

"Twins?" the woman in the red dress asks, incredulous, looking back and forth between us. "You have twins?"

"Oh, he didn't tell you?" I say, tilting my head. "Little Margo and..." *Shit, think...* "And Robbie. Our angels. The poor darlings. And on our wedding anniversary too, what terrible luck." I turn back to Rob and pout. "And the worst part? It's all over your side of the bed. We'd really better go, honey."

"You're married?" Blondie shrieks and I have to bite my lip so I don't burst out laughing.

"Gosh, I hope it isn't norovirus again," I rub his bicep while smiling sweetly at her. "Last time we had it, this guy filled the toilet while puking in the sink at the same time. Honestly, it was the worst thing I've ever seen in my life. I wouldn't wish it on my enemy."

She does the understandable thing, stepping slowly away, a look of repulsion written all over her face. I am the very essence of smug, batting my eyelashes at Rob like a woman in love. His face is frozen in shock as he looks back and forth between the two of us and for a second I expect him to shout at me, but what he does is even worse.

He's not annoyed, he loves it. He wraps his arm around my waist and pulls me so tight to his side that I'm crushed against him. I feel the heat from his body scorching mine. His fingertips dig into my side and it would almost hurt if it didn't feel so good to be touched by him after weeks of silence.

"It was lovely to meet you Rachel. My wife and I best be off."

With one hand on my shoulder and the other around my wrist, his grip on me is relentless. Outside, he drags me along with him and down a side street behind the bar, my feet struggling to keep up with his long strides in these stupid heels.

"You sexy little minx. Now who's a stalker?"

"What the fuck are you playing at? Let go of me." He presses me roughly against the wall. It's his signature move and I've missed it like crazy. I punch my hands against his chest, but he catches them in his big fists, gasping when he looks down.

"What is this?" He barks, lifting my left hand between our faces. "Did you put a ring on your finger?"

"Yes. To be convincing." I try to pull it away, but his grip is firm. "Let. Go."

He reaches for my other hand, threading his fingers through mine, then he holds my arms above my head. His body presses so tight against me I can't look anywhere but up at him. The knot in my stomach tightens when the scent of him fills my soul.

"I don't think so. A good husband holds his wife's hand." His thumbs rub circles into my palms and he lowers his head, his mouth a whisper away from mine. My breath is shaky, and I have to pinch my eyes shut because he looks too damn good right now.

"A good husband takes care of his wife." He nudges one knee between my legs and the friction slides my dress further up my thighs, the exact way I've craved since he did the same in his garage. He presses his hips against me and - *oh my god* - there's no mistaking how turned on he is right now.

"A good husband makes his wife come *so fucking hard*." He says it right into my mouth with an upward thrust of his hips that drags the length of him against the underwear I know I've already soaked. If he touched me right now, I'd explode in seconds.

I just wanted to ruin his night. How did I end up here pressed against the brickwork, unable to think straight? I want him so much it hurts, and I hate myself for it. I want him to kiss me, I want to kiss him back, I want him everywhere, and I've never felt this kind of desperate longing for a man before.

It's not me.

It's not what I do.

And it's not OK.

I swallow thickly and open my eyes to find his dark and piercing. I don't recognise the look on his face. I don't know if it's anger or desire or a hint of something else, but it's so scary it makes me want to throw up.

"Well, thank fuck I'm not your wife." I knee him hard between the legs and run before he can recover.

Chapter 10
Hattie

Rob's not talking to me. I can't blame him after the way our last fight ended, but I've never had the silent treatment from him before and it's unsettling. Instead, he's preparing a salad in Luke's kitchen, Megan's mixing drinks, and I'm at the dining table, scowling at the back of his head and picking my way through a bowl of olives.

"Don't finish those before the others get here," he says without looking. I flip him my middle finger and eat two at once.

Kara and Luke are joining us late. They've been working all the hours they can spare at Moonshine, the new bar and music venue they're opening up in town. It's a really exciting project, and I wish I'd been able to lend more of a hand, but I can't take my eye off the ball for even five seconds at work right now.

It's been a while since we all hung out, so Rob offered to make pizzas for us all and he's been titting about in the kitchen since I got here.

Of course he cooks. Of course, he makes his own dough from scratch, and his own pizza sauce with his own special secret ingredient. Of course, he wears an apron and pushes his sleeves up and fucking *kneads* on the counter right in my eyeline. I bet he'd give my boobs the same treatment. Smooth, firm squeezes. I press my thighs together and try not to think about it.

He's at ease here in Luke's house - well, Luke and Kara's now - navigating the kitchen like it's his own. I've only seen the garage of his place that time I went to torment him about winning the bet, but I have been wondering what it's like inside. A sleek bachelor pad, or a grotty hovel, could go either way.

Who am I kidding? He dresses well, looks after his body, and his shoes are always clean. It will be minimalist and immaculate. I bet he has a cleaner, though. Maybe he hires one of those topless ones. I wouldn't put it past him, the creep.

Megan appears at my side with a fresh margarita. "Extra strong," she says, blowing me a kiss.

"You are my boozy godmother, thank you. How was your week?"

"Oh you know, same as usual, except my tutor group just finished their sex education module and now they keep pinging condoms across the room when I'm taking the register. One landed in my hair this morning."

"Ew, grim."

"What am I supposed to do, ban condoms? That's not the message I want to give them. And anyway, what does it say that it's the most action I've had in months?" she pouts dramatically, but I know there's a sadness underneath it. She hasn't mentioned Max for a while, but I'm loath to bring him up here where she won't want to get into the details. Instead, I wrap an arm around her shoulder.

"Olive?" I ask, nudging the bowl closer to her. "I'm not allowed to eat them all."

There's some commotion in the hallway, then Kara comes running into the kitchen, sliding to a stop next to the kitchen island, one hand held up in front of her face.

"I'm *engaged!*" she shouts at the top of her lungs.

Megan and I jump up, but before we can react there's an unholy scream from the other side of the kitchen and when I look up Rob is bouncing up and down, hands against his cheeks, mouth wide open.

"Oh, Kara," he runs over, lifting her and spinning around. "Oh my God, I'm so happy for you, sweetheart."

Luke appears in the kitchen doorway, smiling softly at the scene in front of him, and Rob drops Kara, pushing her aside to embrace his friend.

Megan gets to Kara first, so I hang back, unable to look away from the boys who've gone quiet in the doorway. Luke's face is pressed into Rob's shoulder, and Rob cups the back of Luke's head with one hand, the other rubbing up and down his back.

When they pull apart, Rob wipes tears from Luke's eyes with the pad of his thumb. His shoulders shake and he rubs his own face too, pulling Luke back in just as Megan drags me into a hug with her and Kara.

"Congratulations, babe." I squeeze her tight and lift her hand. I've seen the ring already because Luke asked me to help him find a designer, but here on her finger, it's even more breathtaking. "Do you like it?"

"I love it," she says, then drops her voice to a whisper as she leads her head against mine. "Thank you for helping. It means so much to me."

"I had no idea he was doing it today," Megan says. "Was it a big surprise?"

"The biggest. It was a complete shock."

She must have gotten over it quickly because she's definitely sporting sex hair right now. I fix where it's all wild at the back, and guide her to the dining table.

"Come and have a drink and tell us everything."

"So while we have you all here, we have some things we'd like to ask for your help with," Luke says over dessert.

"You're obviously both my bridesmaids," Kara continues, "Rob, you'll be best man. We want to have the wedding and the reception at Moonshine. We'll hire a local band and some street food trucks to come and cater. Megan, I'd love your help with some of the admin, and Hattie and Rob, we'd be so grateful if you could be in charge of a joint stag and hen do. Nothing big, just us five and our families."

Oh shit. It's a good job I love this woman because I can't think of anything worse than organising an event with Rob Billy Big Bollocks Morgan telling me what to do.

"Hang on a second," Megan interrupts, "you only got engaged five minutes ago. How have you decided all this?"

"We planned it all in the car on the way over," Kara says, as if that's a completely normal thing to do.

"But...weddings take a long time to plan."

"We're getting married in May."

"That's only two months," Megan shrieks. As a teacher, she's a hardcore planner and her brain must be working overtime.

"We don't want to wait any longer than we have to," Luke says, his eyes full of love as he tucks Kara's hair behind her ear. He pulls her closer to his side and plants a soft kiss at her temple. "I'd marry her tonight if I could."

Even my cold dead heart can't resist beating a little faster at that.

By the time we're onto after-dinner drinks, Rob still hasn't spoken to me, and it's gone from unsettling to infuriating. My need to butt heads with him is an act of self-harm at this point, but I'm powerless to resist it. I corner him in the hallway on his way back from the bathroom.

"For a man who doesn't believe in marriage, that was a pretty convincing performance earlier."

"Huh?" he says, adjusting the front of his shirt.

"All that shrieking was a bit much, though. Thanks for the tinnitus."

"Excuse me for being happy for my friend."

"Whatever." I push past him, but he grabs my shoulders, and he spins me to face him just the way I'd hoped. *Yes, there's the man I love to hate.*

"Hattie, Luke was dealt a shitty hand in life. He never knew his dad, his mum worked crazy hours, he and I were the ultimate latchkey kids, and then when he sorted his life out and fell in love, his wife got cancer and died." I try to push him away, but he pushes me back harder. "And it wasn't fast. It put them through hell, and me too. Heather was one of my best friends. After she died, I wasn't sure I'd ever see Luke smile again, let alone find another chance at happiness. So yeah, I'm over the fucking moon for him. And I know you're happy for Kara. Maybe if you quit your *'Hattie Buchanan, ice queen who doesn't give a shit about anything'* act you'd be able to truly experience their joy too."

My mouth opens, but no sound comes out. My breath catches in my throat. There are no words for how deeply he's cut me. Rob lets go, settling his hands on his hips as he takes a deep breath and stares up at the ceiling.

"I...I'm sorry," I eventually manage to croak out. I'm an awful person. Insensitive and cruel. I hadn't been thinking about any of that stuff. "I didn't mean—"

"And I never said I don't believe in marriage," Rob huffs as he walks away.

I avoid my reflection in the bathroom while I calm myself down. I consider leaving, but when I go to make my excuses, I find everyone on the patio. Kara has lit the firepit, and they've gathered on garden chairs to toast marshmallows. The only vacant seat is the one next to Rob's, so I take it begrudgingly. There's a chill in the air, so I'm grateful for the warmth of the flames, wiggling my toes as close as I can without scorching them.

"I can't believe it," Rob says to Kara as she presses plump marshmallows onto the end of our skewers. "You're gonna get married, and have kids, and I'm gonna be fun Uncle Rob. Do you think I'll be a good uncle?"

"I think you need to slow down," she laughs. "One step at a time." Still, she settles into Luke's lap and he pulls a blanket tight around them both. I give it six months before we're repeating this night with baby news. Christ, I'm miserable today. This is such a joyous occasion, and I'm just dragging myself down. I don't mean to be an ice queen, and I hate that it's how everyone sees me.

"Do you want kids?" Rob asks, shifting his chair closer to mine. I can only stare, partly shocked at the question, mostly that he's talking to me at all after scolding me so thoroughly inside the house.

"Do you know what happens to women in my industry when they have kids?"

"Ooft," he takes a big drink and turns his body sideways to face me. "I have a feeling I'm about to find out."

"They meet someone, they get all loved up, they shack up, get married and start a family. Then, they move away somewhere they can afford a bigger house to raise the kid in, and then they get a dog, and then they have another kid, and do they come back to work? No, they do not.

"And it's not because they don't want to, but because it's impossible for them to juggle family and career, in a decent house, even though they've been told their whole life that they can have it all. Except it's a scam because they don't get promoted, they don't get pay rises, and childcare in this country is a joke. The ones who do come back are almost always barely earning anything, and the workload makes them burn out fast." He sits back a little, out of reach of my jabby, furious hands. I don't give a shit though. I'm on a roll, my words unleashed as I twist my marshmallow over the flames.

"Meanwhile, what are the dads doing? They just keep climbing up and up in the world, taking everything they can. When I look up in my company, I see a bunch of boring old men at the top. You better believe I'm coming for them and nothing is getting in the way."

"So that's a no to kids?" he says, the corner of his mouth pulling up slightly.

"It's a hell no." I bite the crisped up marshmallow between my teeth and pull the stick away, throwing it into the fire. One is enough for me, and I'm going to need to go before my ranting ruins everyone's evening.

"Wow. I want a bunch of them. Though I think some of my swimmers might have gotten killed off this week," he says, nudging my shoulder with a gentle bump.

That lightens the mood, and I press my lips together to stifle a laugh. "Oh yeah? How's that?"

"Some psycho kneed me in the balls."

"I'm sure you deserved it." I move to head inside, then reconsider when his words truly sink in. "Tell me, Rob, how do you think you're going to become a father when you have a different woman in your bed every night?"

"Well, I don't want them yet. But someday."

What stupid, ignorant, patriarchal bullshit. Of course, he thinks he can have a lifetime of sticking his dick in anything that moves and then decide to have a baby whenever it suits him. "Well, please tell me when that day comes so I can channel some budget into an international ad campaign and warn the women of the world that Rob Serial Shagger Morgan is about to unleash his sperm on the world."

His brow furrows. "And what will you do with your child free life?"

"Whatever the fuck I want." I stand up and stare down at him. He spreads his knees wide to let me past and I hover between them. "I'll work, win awards, spend time with my family and friends, travel, have adventures."

Will I? It's not like I'm doing much of that now.

"And if I'm ever bored, I'll hop on a plane to Italy and spend my weekends eating pasta and screwing waiters." I shove past him and make my way inside the house for another drink. I guess I can stay for a little bit more of a spar with Rob.

"I'm a quarter Italian, you know," he calls after me.

"And three quarters dickhead," I yell back.

Chapter 11
Rob

LUKE IS ONE LUCKY guy. Not only was he blessed with the gift that was Heather, but now he's getting a second chance at marriage with another angel. In the wake of her death, I thought it was over for him. He didn't leave the house for weeks, I had to help him shave his beard at one point. To see him thriving is incredible, but bittersweet. We both know what it took for him to get here. I genuinely couldn't be happier for my friend, but I've woken up with an ache to match my hangover that I can't explain.

I'm not jealous, and I'm definitely not bitter, but I am feeling *something*. Their love is a beautiful thing to witness, but that life has never been for me. Commitment, love, all that jazz.

I've always seen sex and love as separate things. Sex is something you can have with pretty much anyone, consenting, of course, but I've never felt like I needed to be in love before I got into bed with someone. Love is a rare beast. You're lucky if you find it once in your life, and even luckier if they love you back.

Look at my mum. She had her great love, he didn't feel the same way, and she's spent the rest of her life suffering because of it. I can't imagine a greater punishment for putting your heart out there, holding it aloft, and giving it to someone who has the power to break it.

Fortunately, I've never been struck by a cupid's arrow, except maybe that time young Rob saw Britney Spears on TV in tiny shorts with a snake around her shoulders.

Maybe there's a small part of me that wants what Luke has. A beautiful home and someone to share it with. Someone to laugh with, someone to curl up in my lap and watch the flames dance in the firepit like the two of them last night.

And even though I've never been able to find that for myself, I don't think I was lying when I told Hattie I want kids. What I didn't expect was to have her point out the major flaw in my plan. How will I ever have a family when there's a different woman in my bed every night?

Well, not every night, but the point still stands.

She said something similar the day we first met. Something about me being like Leo DiCaprio, getting older while the women stay young. I guess I'd never really thought of myself that way. I'm in my thirties, it's perfectly reasonable to have fun. Nobody is getting hurt, but how will I ever bridge the gap between where I am now, and the life I've imagined for myself if I keep acting this way?

Truthfully, I haven't really felt like it much lately. I haven't been going out to bars. Matches and message requests go unread.

And as they do far too often, my thoughts turn to Hattie, who, despite my intentions, it will be impossible to avoid each other now there's a wedding on the horizon. Planning a stag do with her will probably be a nightmare, but part of me hopes it will help us get past this bickering and move us into a proper friendship, which means I need to make an effort.

Me: Want to grab breakfast tomorrow and start stag/hen planning.
Hottie: Maggie's at 10.

Sunday morning is mild, and I take a stroll to Maggie's cafe so we can plan the fastest stag and hen do known to man. I have a slight inkling we'd be accused of cheating on Sunshine Coffee if we were spotted here, but I'm not pushing my luck with Hattie when she's feeling amenable. Seeing me twice in one weekend will already have her acting twitchy and argumentative, as if it's my fault we've been thrown together for this mission.

Plus, Sunshine doesn't serve French toast sticks with maple butter, so who can really blame us for eating here?

Maggie's is a classic greasy spoon affair, red vinyl booths along one wall and the rest of the space filled with laminate covered tables and metal chairs. Framed certificates declaring it *'Hertfordshire's best cafe'* adorn the walls but every single one is at least a decade old. I'm pretty sure the black and white checked floors have been slightly sticky since 1995, but you don't come here for fine dining, you come for cheap, delicious food, cooked well and served fast. Besides, I've never seen the place empty, so whatever they're doing clearly works.

I nab a booth and sit facing the door, buying me time to clock Hattie's mood before she sits down. Usually I'm the one running late, but today I'm twiddling my thumbs, leafing through the Sunday paper, my head popping up like a meerkat every time the door opens. This had better not be a stitch up, or I'm going ahead with my plans and she can just put up with it.

10am was her suggestion, so where the hell is she?

Fifteen minutes later, she saunters in, her lower half wrapped in tight, black leggings, the rest of her hidden underneath an oversized, mint green hoodie. Her hair is pushed back, messy, like she's just rolled out of bed. And still she takes my breath away.

"You're late," I say, as she slides herself into the bench across from me without even a hint of an apology.

"Sorry, *Dad*. Had kind of a late one." My blood heats at her insolence, bile rising from my stomach at the thought of why she had a late night. *Don't ask, don't fucking ask.* "Then I slept in and missed the gym. All I want to do is kick the shit out of a heavy bag, and clock up enough miles on the treadmill that I pass out as soon as I get home."

"Sounds healthy."

"Don't start, dickhead," she says, slouching in her seat and hiding her face behind the menu. *Oh, I'll start, you rude little wench.*

"Morning folks." Our waitress greets us with a far cheerier disposition. Her name badge says 'Maggie' and I wonder if she's *the* Maggie, or if it's part of the uniform that they all play the role. "What can I get for you today?"

"Black coffee and the French toast sticks please," Hattie says, turning on the charm for our Maggie and handing over her menu. *So it's just me who's getting the attitude today, is it?*

"And for you, Sir?"

"I'll have the same, thank you."

"Coming right up," she says, leaving us to it.

"Are you doing that to wind me up?" Hattie leans back, her arms folded across her chest.

"Doing what?"

"Ordering the same as me."

"That's what I wanted," I shrug. "That's my order."

"Whatever." I almost repeat it back to her, but I catch myself in time. If she wants to act like a child, I'm not going to sail straight over the edge with her.

"So, joint stag and hen party. I have some thoughts." I pull up the browser on my phone to show her the research I did last night. The research I did while she was out with fuck-knows-who doing fuck-knows-what.

"Let me guess, you want to take us all to a strip club? Or some *Magic Mike* shit."

"I think that's more your vibe."

"Don't make assumptions about me," she says, nudging me under the table. "I find that whole thing really weird, actually. All those oily men slipping around on the floor, gyrating like a cat trying to throw up a furball."

Wow. What an image.

"I think we should do a tasting menu dinner, followed by drinks on a riverboat. It's classy and elegant."

"Oh, fuck you," she says, slouching backwards. "That's actually good."

"Here's the menu." I slide my phone across the table. "We can keep the meal part small. I know Kara said immediately family only, but I think some of the staff from Sunshine would love to celebrate, and maybe some folks from your book club too? That's why I think this..." I swipe to the next tab, "is the perfect way to spend the afternoon. And hopefully the weather will be nice."

While she scrolls through photos and reads the description of my proposed river tour, my hand comes to a rest on her wrist. I don't think either of us even realise until Maggie appears.

"Oh, look at you cuties," she says. "I almost don't want to interrupt such a gorgeous couple, but here are your coffees."

Hattie's eyes go wide and she snatches her hand away, rubbing her wrist as if my touch has left a mark. Her cheeks redden a little, and I've got the perfect view across the table. She's affected by me. I don't say anything, just lean back and keep my eyes on her while I sip my coffee.

"What are you smiling at?"

"She thinks we're a couple. A *'gorgeous'* couple. We've got *couple* vibes."

"She's deluded." Hattie tips three sugar sachets into her coffee, stirring so intently I wonder if she might be summoning a spell in her head. I want her attention back on me, craving the playful Hattie that jokes around with me, not the angry one that has my pulse racing and my cock thickening. Stretching my leg out underneath the table, I slide my foot in between hers until our ankles graze alongside each other.

She lifts one leg, kicking out at my knee, but I grip her calf in my palm before she can make contact, and lift it into my lap. I slip my thumb underneath the hem of her leggings, circling the soft skin there.

She leans in close and lowers her voice. "Let go of my leg before I scream this fucking place down."

I pull it towards me as she pulls it away, and somehow the back and forth ends up with a fast jab of her foot that hits me right in the balls.

I'm dead.

I've died.

Pain sears right through me, white light blurring my vision.

"*Fuuuuuck.*" I bend over the table, cupping myself and breathing through the searing agony. "Why are you so determined to destroy my nuts?"

"You're the one who grabbed my leg! Are you OK?"

"No I'm not fucking OK. Jesus, you're a monster. I can't believe I nearly fucked you."

"Oh, piss off. You were never even close." Her words sting, adding a pain in my chest to the one in my crotch.

"Bullshit. You wanted it. I saw it in your eyes. I felt your body heat up. You were so ready to give it up in my garage, you know I nearly won."

"That's all it was to you, wasn't it?" she says, a tinge of hurt in her voice. "A game."

Of course it was. A stupid bet between two hot people who would clearly benefit from a little time spent naked together. Except it wasn't just a bet in the end, and I know it's still not over for me. Regardless of what I've said, regardless of the fury in her words and the fire in her actions, every part of me still wants her. Even the parts she seems hellbent on smashing to pieces.

Hattie has no time for my epiphanies. "You're deluded too, Rob. You think I'll fuck anyone with a penis, but I do actually have some self-respect, you know? Why would I ever want to get with someone who treated me like a piece of meat from the moment he laid eyes on me?"

"Give me a break. You're not telling me you actually want people to get to know you first? That's bullshit too. And I'm not having that double standard either. You only want guys for one thing. I doubt you wine and dine them and ask for all their childhood stories before getting into bed."

"You're such an arrogant wanker."

"And you're an insufferable bitch."

"Wow," she rears back, her voice raised. "Don't hold back Rob, tell me what you really think."

"What I really think is that you're a scared little girl. You think you have to do everything yourself, nobody is ever good enough for you, and so you push everyone away before they'd even have a chance to get close to you."

Hattie's bottom lip wobbles. *What am I doing? Where is this coming from?*

"I hate you."

"Not as much as you hate yourself."

"Fuck this. I didn't come here for your psychoanalysis bollocks." I'm still rubbing my crotch when she stands up, throws cash from her purse onto the table, and leaves.

That was not how I meant for our conversation to go. I'm so ashamed of myself, of my words, that I think I'm going to be sick. I've been pacing the house for hours, I bailed on five-a-side, and told Mum and Auntie Sheila I can't make it tonight. I know I won't be able to concentrate on anything until I've apologised to Hattie. I need to fix this, fast.

I could get her flat number from Kara, but turning up inside her building might earn me a restraining order. The only thing I can think of is to stake out the gym and hope she summoned the energy to go.

Hours pass in the car, but time means nothing to me right now. I watch cars come and go, people complete whole workouts and still no sign of her. I'm willing to wait as long as it takes.

Finally, late in the afternoon, I spot her car pulling in and I wait until she's parked before getting out to approach her.

"Hattie?" I call after her and she stops, looking even more exhausted than this morning. Her hair is scraped back into a tight ponytail, and her eyes are red and puffy. That's my fault.

"What do you want?" She stares at the floor, scuffing her toes along the inside of her other shoe while I approach slowly.

"I'm sorry. I'm so sorry." My instinct is to hug her, but I fight it. If there's a way to make all of this even worse, I'm sure physical touch would be it. "What I said this morning was completely unacceptable. I don't expect you to forgive me, but I couldn't finish today without apologising to you."

"How long have you been waiting here?"

"A while. But I'd have stayed all night. I didn't want to say it over text. And I really mean it. You're not a bitch. You're not insufferable. And you're not wrong." She's still staring at the floor, so I inch forward, press two fingers underneath her chin and tilt her head to look at me. "I am pretty arrogant, and I do wank a lot."

That earns me a tiny smile, and I fold it up in my mind to keep with the other ones I've managed to get out of her.

"It's fine," she says, her hand circling my wrist as she pulls it away. "I am a bitch. At least I am to you."

"Hattie, I don't know why we always end up fighting, but I promise I'm going to stop this. You won't have any trouble from me again." She doesn't say anything, so I keep going. "I want to do a good job with this party, and I want to do that with you, without drama. I'll stop with the teasing, and I hope we can get along. Not just because of Luke and Kara, because you seem like you could use a friend."

"I've got friends," she says, shrugging dismissively.

"OK. So maybe I need a friend then." It slips out, a vulnerable admission. It's more vulnerable than I've been with her before and I feel as though she's peeled back my skin. "You should go enjoy your workout. I'm sure there's a punchbag in there with my name on it."

I turn to leave, but she calls after me. "Rob, wait. Are your balls OK?"

"I'll survive."

"I'm sorry too. And thank you. You won't have any trouble from me either."

It feels good to clear the air, but why do I feel like my trouble with Hattie is far from over?

Chapter 12
Hattie

Megan, Kara, and I have arranged to travel to London separately from the boys, and we're about to leave for our train when her doorbell rings.

"I'm here to collect the future Mrs Taylor and her bridesmaids."

Before me stands a gorgeous older man who is doing an incredible job of filling out his jet black suit. Behind him, a pristine, white limousine.

"I think there's been a mistake. We didn't order a car."

"No mistake, ma'am. Compliments of the best man." *That sneaky fucker.*

Spring rains have given way to a glorious summer's day. I'm determined to make the most of the warmer weather in a pale pink strapless dress that looks great with my freshly bleached and trimmed hair.

Megan and Kara have opted for floral and floaty and in the luxury of a limo, I think this is the fanciest we've ever felt in our lives. We open a bottle of champagne, and by the time we're weaving our way through London traffic, I've got a nice little buzz overriding my nervousness.

I haven't seen Rob in person since our bust-up over a month ago, and a low hum of anxiety has been rumbling away all week.

He got the worst of me, that morning at Maggie's. I already felt like shit after a night spent arguing with my sister on the phone about my apparent lack of effort with our mother. So what if I spent Christmas on my own and forgot to send a birthday card? It's not like she'd really want me there anyway, but George would never understand that because she's the perfect daughter who can do no wrong and I'm... well, I'm the opposite. I wish I'd never answered her call.

Despite the real reason for my shitty night and dishevelled appearance, Rob clearly assumed I'd been up with some guy, and that only fuelled my frustrations.

After making amends, we finished the rest of the planning over text and by 'we', I mean Rob did everything and sent me updates. The limo is a beautiful touch, and I'm starting to see there's a decent guy beneath the cocky exterior. Maybe if we can get through today, and the rest of the wedding celebrations, without bickering, we'll have a decent shot at friendship after all.

His casual carpark confession has stayed with me. I've always assumed that Rob has a perfectly content life, with plenty of friends, but those words hinted at a loneliness I've been unpacking ever since.

I know that, like Luke, Rob didn't know his dad, and they've been best friends since their school days. I know he's dedicated to his work, ambitious by all accounts, but he hasn't had the inclination to get into a relationship.

And I know from what he said the night of the engagement that he was pretty affected by Heather's death too.

Besides his loss, Rob's situation is a lot like mine, actually. I've always found that having a small group of tight-knit people keeps things simple and safe. There are a few friends from my university days who I occasionally check in with, but we haven't met up in years. I don't have the time or energy to have hundreds of acquaintances. There are plenty of people to schmooze with at work, but by the weekend I couldn't be less interested in seeing a lot of people.

My inner circle is small and safe, but is it enough? I love Kara and Megan to bits, but is there a part of me that feels a little lonely too? We've always been close, always there for each other, but I keep coming back to this feeling that everything will change now that Kara is getting married. Sure, we'll see each other, but I know it will be different. What's this life I lead going to feel like in my forties and fifties? Megan will settle down soon too, I'm sure of it. I just hope to God it isn't with Max. If he makes her move to Australia, I'm packing a case and going with her.

Outside the restaurant, Kara makes our driver take photos of us and I plaster on a big smile. Like always, I sense Rob before I see him, that deep, spicy, male scent filling the room and making my head spin. As we step inside the private dining room, he's there to greet us, and I rush in while he kisses Megan on both cheeks. I need to buy myself some time to take a deep breath and repeat what I've decided will be the mantra of the day. *Play nice, play nice, play nice.*

"You doing OK?" he says, appearing behind me. He gives my shoulders a squeeze, his hands coasting down to my elbows leaving a scattering of goosebumps behind them.

"Sure, I'm great," I say, turning to face him with a slightly manic nod. He looks too hot for his own good in cream trousers that fit him beautifully, a linen blazer over the casual navy shirt he's left open at the collar, pulling my gaze to his throat. The triangle of bare, tanned skin there looks thoroughly lickable.

Thank God we didn't have that second bottle of champagne in the limo or I might not be able to stop myself from doing just that. If he was an unknown guest at this party, I'd be luring him to a storage cupboard and dropping to my knees in a heartbeat.

"Did you enjoy your ride?"

"We did." I bite my lip, unable to ignore the innuendo. "You played a blinder there, thank you. Kara loved it."

"You're welcome. So, I know we cleared the air, but I just wanted to say sorry again. I've really been dwelling on it."

"Do you know, I think you're the first man who has ever apologised to me," I laugh, forcing myself to look up at his face. "You're already back in the good books, you don't need to keep saying it." *Jesus, Hattie, I said play nice, not massage his already over-inflated ego.*

I opt for a friendly pat on the arm and take my seat for lunch. We find ourselves seated at opposite ends of the long table and I'm grateful for the breathing space. Can't get in a fight with this distance between us. Can't flirt with him either.

The meal is exceptional and, thanks to the paired servings that come with each of the ten courses, my wine glass is never empty. Everything is dainty and beautiful, and despite my initial reservations that it wouldn't be enough food, I don't think I could manage another bite.

The restaurant is a short walk from the river cruise departure point, and Kara and Luke stroll down hand in hand, while I cling to Megan's side. Rob walks with Granny Annie and Luke's mum, and Kara's parents, her brother, and his girlfriend trail behind.

"Keep me away from Rob tonight," I whisper into Megan's ear.

"Why? What's he done now?"

"Nothing bad, but have you seen him? He looks hot, and he's being really nice to me. I might do something I regret, so I need you to vag-block me if I start acting horny."

"You're being ridiculous," she laughs. "If you wanted to sleep with him, you'd have done it by now."

The problem with that line of reasoning is the assumption that I'd want him less over time. Only me and my stupid vagina know the opposite is true.

At the riverside, we join up with the rest of our group. Luke's given the Sunshine team the day off to join us, and a few of Kara's clients have come along too. Luke and Kara introduce everyone who hasn't met before, then we make our way along the gangplank and board the boat we've chartered for the next few hours. After a short safety briefing from the crew, we're led up to the upper deck to continue our day of drinking.

I don't know whether it's the booze, or the sun, or the company, but I'm pretty high on life right now. The Hattie of my youth never got to go on a boat, never got to sit and drink champagne with a gentle breeze in her hair. I mean, childhood Hattie definitely shouldn't have been drinking champagne, but the point still stands. This is a good life I've built for myself.

Claude, one of Kara's clients, joins me on a bench towards the back of the boat. Rear? Stern? I don't know, I'm not driving the bloody thing.

"Your outfit is gorgeous," I say, admiring the beauty before me in a stunning, full-length kaftan and the biggest sunglasses I've ever seen. Kara has told me a lot about Claude. She's an icon and I immediately want to be her friend.

"Why thank you, darling. Now, you look like the girl to give me all the good gossip. Tell me everyone's secrets," she laughs.

We sit for a while and when the stories dwindle, we move on to ogling the cute waiter who circles the guests to top up our champagne.

He's far too young for me, and even younger for Claude, but that doesn't stop us flirting outrageously.

"Hattie, can I steal you away for a minute?" Rob asks, appearing in front of us.

"Is this your man?" Claude asks. I press my fingers to my lips and snort, trying not to spray my drink all over her beautiful dress.

"God no, I've never met anyone more mismatched. But he is single and afraid of commitment, so if you're looking for a good time he could be *your* man." I nudge her with my elbow and drain my glass while she looks him up and down.

Rob's smile falls right off his face, his shoulders slump, and he walks off, shaking his head. *Shit, shit, shit.* This is the opposite of playing nice.

"Please excuse my friend," I say, smiling sweetly at Claude. "He's such a moody bastard. I'll be right back."

"Oi!" I chase after him, but he takes the stairs two at a time, storming along the walkway and ducking back inside the area where we first entered the boat. It's empty and quiet, save for the churning of the water beneath us. "What's with your face?"

"Nothing." He rocks back and forth on his heels, his eyes glued to the floor. It's clearly not nothing.

"Bullshit. What were you thinking back there?"

"What was I thinking?" he scoffs, rubbing the back of his neck. "That's an awfully genuine question for a woman who claims to hate me."

"I don't..." I trail off with a sigh. I can't do this, can't get into another argument with him. I don't have the strength for it. "Fine, forget it. I don't care."

As I turn to leave he grabs my arm, pulling me back tight to his chest, and lowers his mouth to my ear.

"I was thinking the only woman I want here is you."

"What?" I wheeze out, pulling my head back to get a read on him.

"I was thinking about how much I want to see you on your knees."

My mouth falls open and heat pools in my abdomen. He traces a line around my lips with one fingertip.

"You'd like that, wouldn't you?" I really would, though I'd never tell him that. I don't tell him a thing, just stand there, speechless and lost in the espresso depths of his eyes. "I think you would love to be on your knees for me. Love the feel of my dick in your mouth. Would you gag on it, I wonder? I'm sure you're a goddamn pro, and I mean that in the nicest possible way before you start arguing with me."

He taps my bottom lip, pushing my mouth open wider.

"You're torturing me, Hattie." He slides two fingers into my open mouth until he reaches the back of my tongue and I grip his shoulders with both hands. My knees are about to give out. "I want to come here."

I can't help it. I try, but I can't stop myself from wrapping my lips tight around them and sucking hard. His mouth parts and his eyes darken.

"And here…" he withdraws and strokes them, hot and slick, down the column of my throat, over the notch of my collarbone and down until they nestle in my cleavage. Powerless under his touch, I'm frozen to the spot when he dips them inside the cup of my strapless bra, the backs of his fingers caressing as he watches. My nipples peak, exposed to the threat of him, and I can't even pretend to hate the way it feels when he cups my breast in his hand and squeezes hard.

"You'll look so good covered in my come." His voice is pained. He thinks I'm torturing him, but he's torturing us both right now. "I'll rub it all over you and send you off, knowing your skin tastes of me."

His hand caresses down over my stomach, showing exactly where he'd mark me.

"But best of all—" He reaches underneath the hem of my skirt and cups me hard. The nerve of it breaks me apart and my head falls against his chest with a heavy sob. He must feel the heat of me in his palm. Can he feel how turned I am on by the way he speaks to me? Who am I kidding? I've been soaked since the moment we walked into the restaurant. It's always like this with him.

"My God, this perfect pussy," he whispers into my hair, his other arm cupping the back of my head, keeping me pinned in place. "I want to fuck you until you can't bear to live without me. Until you wake up feeling empty and aching until I fuck you again."

Jesus, fuck. How does he do this to me? How does he make me feel like he is exactly what I'm missing?

"You're wasted," I whimper.

"Nope," he says, straightening up. He releases me from his hold and takes a step back. "These are non-alcoholic."

He's saying this shit sober?

His words hang in the air between us, and he waits. I don't know what his game is. If he touched me now, properly, I'd be helpless to stop him, but with inches between us it's my move to make. Part of me wants to turn around, lift my dress and let him fuck me into the wall right here, but I can't do this. Can't give him the satisfaction of knowing how much I want him, even though every wall I've built is crumbling so fast I feel like dust myself. I swallow hard, tug the top of my dress back up, and run.

I need to get off this fucking boat.

Chapter 13
Rob

HATTIE AND I HAVE done a stellar job of keeping things friendly this past month, our communication strictly limited to plans for today. I've missed her like crazy, though. Her sass, her smile, her sexy curves. They're still the first thing I think about when I wake up and the last thing on my mind when I fall asleep.

And I've tried so hard to be good today. I made sure we sat apart at lunch, and I vowed to stick to low alcohol drinks until we're all safely home, drama free. I've kept my distance and let her do her own thing, but when I saw her flirting with that waiter, all hell broke loose in my brain.

That and the pink dress that's been taunting me all day. The way the skirt tickles the backs of her thighs, the way the strapless top part just begs to be yanked down. It's criminal. I didn't mean to confess all the filthy ways I've thought about her, it just came out. Everything about her makes me act first, think later.

I don't want to fight anymore. I should follow her, apologise for overstepping, make all of this go away, but I don't know how. Nothing I say will make a difference. She's drunk, and angry, and probably hates me more than ever now. Despite what my brain says, my feet lead the way.

Pushing through the double doors, I climb back up to the deck and look amongst the guests, but there's no sign of her.

"Megs," I cup her elbow and gently pull her away from her conversation with Kara's parents. "Have you seen Hattie?"

She shakes her head and turns away. There's only so many places you can go on a boat this size. Where the hell is she? Leaning over the barrier, I spot her near the rear of the boat, arguing with one of the crewmembers.

"Please? Can't you steer a little closer and let me off?" *She's leaving?* We still have another hour to go. Well, of course she's not leaving. You don't just get off a boat when you decide you've had enough. I make for the stairs, ready to diffuse the situation, but she screams when she spots me heading towards them.

"Fine!" she shouts, slipping her heels off and hurling them over the railing. They sail through the air, landing on the grassy riverbank, and her clutch bag soon follows.

"Please, Miss, you can't do that," the young guy panics. He reaches for her elbow but she wrenches it away, climbs up the railings and leaps into the water.

All hell breaks loose as he shouts into his radio, staff come running, and my hands meet the edge of the railing just in time to see her head breach the surface.

"*Fucking Christ,*" she shrieks, shaking her head and gulping down air.

Seconds later, my feet hit the water too. I plunge into the murky depths, my ears filling with water, the world turning to treacle until I push up and swim to the surface.

"Are you OK?" voices call from behind me and I breathe hard, my chest tight from the shock drop in temperature. Turning circles in the water, I spot Hattie already halfway to the riverbank.

"We can't stop here," the crewman shouts at me through a loudspeaker. "Too busy. We'll pull in up ahead."

"We're fine, carry on without us," I yell back, then take a deep breath, duck my head and swim after her. We are so far from fine, it's not even funny.

"Are you crazy?" she shouts, her hands scrambling for purchase as she reaches the bank of the river and attempts to pull herself up.

"Are *you*?" I scream back. "What the hell are you thinking?"

"Get away from me."

We've drawn a crowd, not difficult when you've thrown yourself into the river after a madwoman on a stretch that borders a sunny pub garden. Two men rush down to the edge and scramble to pull her up.

Hattie finds her shoes and her bag, stumbling as she puts them on, her head swinging in all directions as she figures out her next move. I don't know where she thinks she's going to go.

All our friends are on the boat, we're pretty far out west, and we don't have a change of clothes. Clearly she doesn't think that's a problem, and storms off towards the car-park.

"Hattie, wait," I call out, finally managing to swing my leg up and heave myself out of the river. Water pours off me, and I pull away a clump of reeds from where they've wrapped themselves around my shoulders. Thank fuck I've barely had anything to drink, this is exactly the sort of drunken behaviour that lands people in my unit for neurological assessment. What if she'd hit her head?

"Are you alright, love?" one of the men asks, sticking close to Hattie and putting himself between the two of us. Behind him, I see two women doing a shit job of pretending they aren't filming this total fiasco on their phones. "Is this guy harassing you?"

"I'm not harassing her," I pant, bending over to shake the water out of my hair. "She's my friend."

"We're not friends!" she screams at me, shivering from head to toe in her now very see-through dress. I know I only saw them five minutes ago, but her nipples look even better underneath the wet fabric. I'm sure I'd be turned on if I wasn't boiling with rage.

"We are friends, we know each other," I say to the men, who are understandably confused. "She's just not my biggest fan."

I peel my jacket off, wring it out as best I can, and drape it round her shoulders. It's still soaking, but it's better than her losing even more of her dignity.

Her jaw is locked, mouth pressed into a tight pout, and she glares up at me, chest heaving. She looks like she could breathe fire, and I wonder why I'm getting the brunt of it since none of this is my fault.

I can't wonder for long though, as the sound of sirens snaps us out of our stand-off.

Half an hour later, we're wrapped in blankets on opposite sides of the beer garden being questioned by members of the police. I'm mortified, but apparently some busybody called them when they saw us go overboard, even though we couldn't have been in there for more than a few minutes.

Why did I jump in? What was she doing in the water? Who are we to each other? Their questions are ones I'd like to know the answers to myself.

"Technically, you've committed an offence here today, Sir. There's no swimming on this stretch of the river, as you can see." He points to a massive sign that says *No Swimming*, and I have to laugh. I definitely hadn't seen that. "However, on this occasion, since you were trying to come to the aid of the young lady, we won't take this any further and waste any more of your time or ours. Will you manage to get yourselves home?"

"Yes, of course. Sorry again for wasting your time."

I wait for the officers speaking with Hattie to leave and approach her the way you might approach an injured animal. Unsure whether she'll want my help or rip my arm off. She looks as miserable as I feel. How has it come to this?

"Can I sit down?" I ask. She looks up at me through her eyelashes, pulls her blankets tighter, and nods. I take a seat and we sit for a while, staring out at the river. A few people in kayaks pootle past, and I wonder where our friends got to.

"You hate me so much you'd risk your life to get away from me?"

"I'm sorry," she says, bursting into tears. I've never seen her like this, so lost and vulnerable. Shuffling closer, I reach my arm around her shoulders, and she folds into my chest. I wrap the other arm around her too, holding her close.

This is all my fault. I should never have said those things, should never have laid a finger on her. Flirting and teasing is one thing, but if my behaviour is going to make her put herself in danger, then this has to stop. After the wedding, I'll keep my distance. She can do all the friend things, and I'll see Luke some other time.

Against my chest, she begins to shiver and I don't know if it's the tears or the cold, but we need to get out of these wet clothes. I doubt there's anywhere to buy anything near here, but I dig my phone out of my pocket and, by some miracle, it still works.

"I'm calling us an Uber. Let's go home."

Chapter 14
Hattie

FRIDAYS ARE USUALLY QUIET in the office, with some of the team working remotely, and some taking advantage of our flexible working policy to have a long weekend. Today it's like a ghost town, and when I arrived, part of me wondered if I'd come in on the weekend by mistake.

I pull up my team's shared calendar to check everyone's status and my stomach roils when I read the words *Out of Office: Spirited Reset Away Day* in diary after diary. What the hell is this and how did I miss it? Am I sitting here like a mug when I'm supposed to be somewhere else?

I frantically search my emails, and my deleted ones, for mention of an away day, but there's nothing to be found. Which leads to only one conclusion.

Lawrence is running a coup.

Every part of me wants to kick Andrew's door off the hinges, but I've been told in the past that my communication style can seem a little aggressive at times, so I knock politely and wait to be called in.

"Morning, Hattie. What can I do for you?" he says, sucking down some green juice concoction I think his wife makes him drink.

"Good morning, Andrew," I say, sweetly. "Just a quick one, it will only take a second. Would you like to explain to me why my entire team is at a..." I pause to look at the shared calendar on my phone for effect, "A *'Spirited reset away day'*? And follow up question, what the fuck is going on?"

"I don't know a thing about it," he says dismissively.

My heart catches in my throat and my head rears back. I think this is the first time Andrew has ever lied to me. "You don't know *a thing* about it? Then why are you shown as declined on the invite list?"

"I am?" He scoots closer to his screen and pulls up his calendar. "Oh yeah, I am. Hattie, look, do you know how much bollocks I get invited to? I decline about 90% of my meetings requests, and my diary is still jam-packed. You're lucky you caught me, I'm due on a call with HR in two mins. I'm sure I would have assumed you were on the invite list too, I don't know why you aren't."

"It's called a Spirited reset away day? What is there to reset?"

"I have no idea. I'll ask Lawrence when they get back."

"Lawrence shouldn't be resetting anything. He shouldn't even be talking to the Spirited team without me present, so I don't know what the hell he's playing at organising an away day and leaving me out of it."

"I—"

"I'm not finished! This is so frustrating, Andrew. And utterly embarrassing. It makes me look like a fucking intern or something, not the account director, which I'd like to remind you I have been for two years. Why is my job being pulled out from underneath me and nobody has the decency to even admit it?"

He hangs his head and lets out a heavy sigh. "Listen, I don't know what's going on over at Spirited, but I will admit that we were asked for a bit of a freshen up, and they seem really happy with Lawrence's work."

I would laugh if I didn't feel like he's just stabbed me in the chest. A thousand questions rush through my brain all at once. Who said this, and when? Is this why Lawrence was brought on in the first place? How long has Andrew kept this a secret from me? What's going to happen now? And why can't anyone just be honest for five seconds?

"You've been on that account for bloody ages, anyway," Andrew continues, his voice unusually high in a chipper attempt to placate me. "You're ready for something more challenging." This isn't the olive branch I'm sure he intends it to be when I feel this cynical and insulted.

"What do you mean *'more challenging'*?"

"I don't know. I've got this call with HR shortly. Just be nice. Let me put some feelers out and see what's in the pipeline." *I'd like to shove my foot up your pipeline, mate.*

"What's your call with HR about?"

He answers with a steely glare, and I know I've pushed my luck. "Why are you here, anyway?" he says, changing the subject. "This says you're on leave today. That's probably why you weren't invited."

"I still should have been made aware. I would have rescheduled my plans."

"Isn't it your friend's wedding tomorrow?"

"Yes," I answer, sulkily.

"Then get the fuck out of here," Andrew booms, pointing at the door. "Take the day to switch off, spend time with your friends, and enjoy the weekend. This reset nonsense will just be a load of arse-licking, anyway. You hate that bullshit."

"I might hate it, but I don't want to be the only one not getting their arse licked." Andrew raises his eyebrows and I stifle a laugh. "That came out wrong."

Chapter 15
Hattie

I'm at Moonshine much earlier than expected having left Megan, Kara and the mums with the hairdresser, my own needing nothing more than a quick run through with the straighteners. Maybe I should have stayed, but the three of us were together all night, so I asked Kara for her keys and said I'd do a final check to make sure everything was in order.

Truthfully, I needed some air before being around so many people today. It's not even my wedding day and I'm nervous. The space looks absolutely stunning. String lights hang from the ceiling, bathing the normally dim room in a soft, warm glow. They've built a floral wall at the back of the stage, which, for today's purposes, serves as an altar of sorts. Kara hired tables and chairs that are better suited to a wedding than barstools, and we've placed gauze pouches of confetti on each, along with the Order of Service cards Megan designed and printed.

All there is for me to do is pace. I didn't sleep much last night, too busy replaying my conversation with Andrew and stressing about how to handle things on Monday. I stayed until 6pm, and nobody came back after the meeting, which means they all went to the pub and that pissed me off even more. The pub is where I get to work my true Hattie magic.

Clients love me because I'm a social butterfly. I network like a boss, ask fun and insightful questions, help put people at ease, and nobody's glass is ever empty. Seriously, I can work a fucking room, and I like to give them a chance to see the side of me that's not just work. I honestly don't know why they wouldn't want me there for the meeting.

I know it's ridiculous to be this jealous, but I can't get it out of my head. I pull up Instagram and search for Lawrence, who I do not follow but will absolutely stalk occasionally. Purely out of necessity, for potential ammunition and not any sort of desire to build a better connection with him, of course. I've locked my account so he'll never be able to do the same back, but he's a show-off, a feed full of photos of him out in bars and restaurants, posing in front of cars and private pools at who knows where.

He's at the top of my search history. *Shit.* I must have forgotten to delete his name the last time I checked. When I pull up his profile, there are no new posts, but there are a few stories. I tap them open and sure enough, there's the classic pints on the table photo. Predictable. So much for fresh new ideas, eh, Andrew?

There's nothing much to report. It's a typical Friday piss-up, and I'm about to close the app when something in the background of his last story catches my eye. Not something. *Someone.*

I press my thumb against the screen and hold it up to my face. I want to zoom in, but I can't remember if I can take a screenshot without him getting an alert. Things change so often on these bloody apps. I can't risk it.

Instead, I pull up LinkedIn, find Lawrence's profile and start scrolling through his contacts until I find who I'm looking for.

David Morrison.

It's so rare that I know their last names, but I wouldn't forget the man in the profile photo staring back at me. I can't remember when we met, or even how, but I can definitely remember that face staring down at me as I worked my magic on my knees. And now there it is in black and white, *Marketing Director at Spirited*. I jump over to Facebook and type in his name, clicking on the third profile, with a photo matching the one on LinkedIn.

This profile is far less professional, but filled – fucking, *filled* – with photos of him, a gorgeous brunette, and three children who all look to be under seven. Two boys and a girl. Pictures of them posing at what looks like someone else's wedding. Pictures of them at the beach, selfies with his wife, there's even one of David smashing through the ribbon at the finish line at a school sports day.

There's no getting around it. David Morrison is a family man. And my new client. And I've shagged him.

You have got to be shitting me. I have never done anything in my life to deserve this level of karma.

My cheeks burn, and I shove my phone in my bag, picking apart the past couple of months. David's employment dates line up with Brent leaving. Does he know who I am? Did he ask for me to be taken off the account? Has everyone been talking about me behind my back?

My heart pounds while I give the room another once over, adjusting all the candle jars a millimetre or so, as if that millimetre will help keep my life from falling apart. According to the wedding itinerary spreadsheet, it's much too early to light them, but I'm fidgety and need something to keep my hands busy. I've got no idea how to work anything at the bar, but I pull a Sauvignon Blanc from one of the low fridges and drink the final glass straight from the bottle. At one end of the bar, a box of crisps calls my name. I was much too stressed to eat breakfast, and I need food in my belly before I puke up nothing.

I grab a packet and tear them open, walking back around the bar to scan the room for other imaginary imperfections I can fix before the guests arrive. When I hear the door swing open, I don't need to turn to see who else is early.

Here we go.

Rob in a dark tweed suit, his hair styled away from his face, is truly a sight to behold. Christ, he has no business looking this good. Or smelling this good, a recent spritz of his favourite cologne filling my nostrils. It's the best smell on earth and a million times better than the last time I saw him, the two of us drenched in river scum. Turns out a man clambering out of a body of water looks a lot less like Anthony Bridgerton than you'd hope.

I still don't know what possessed me to jump into the river. Lately, I feel like I'm losing my mind, and being around Rob pushes me to my limits. I know it's the stress from work, all this Lawrence nonsense getting to me far more than it should. Yep, I'm categorically blaming Lawrence for this one.

Rob storms across the bar towards me, and for a second I feel genuinely intimidated, backing up against the bar.

"What's wrong?"

"What the hell are you eating?" he screeches.

"A snack."

"Are you out of your fucking mind? Cheese puffs! In your bridesmaid's dress?"

Kara chose floor length multi-way dresses for me and Megan in a beautiful sage green. After the fifth attempt to get the dress wrapped around me in the exact way we'd practised, I figured I'd just leave it on rather than change when I got here.

"Rob, I know you don't think much of me, but I am a grown woman who is perfectly capable of eating food without making a mess. I'm hungry. Just let me live my life." I pop another delicious puff between my lips and crunch right through it.

"This is not proper food, Hattie. What about your breath? You can't have disgusting cheese breath at your best friend's wedding."

"Oh, you must have not heard of this exciting new invention called mints." I grab a handful of crisps and shove them into my mouth.

"Give those to me right now," he reaches for the bag, but I snatch it away.

"Ha!"

"Give it to me."

"I will not. Get your own." Rob lunges out again, catching my wrist in one hand and the bag in the other. "How dare you? Let go of me."

We tussle a little and when I finally manage to wrestle out of his grasp, the packet rips open. The remaining cheese puffs, along with the layer of bright orange crumbs from the bottom of the bag, go flying through the air.

Everything happens in slow-motion. Rob's eyes widen and he tries to shove me out of the way, but it's too late. Cheese puffs rain down on the front of my dress, streaking it with bright orange lines before they land on the floor.

I stare down at the mess, clench my fists and force a deep breath before I lash out.

"You fucking idiot," I hiss through gritted teeth.

I run from the bar straight into the bathroom and quickly rinse my cheesy fingers before slipping out of my dress. I brush off what I can, but it's definitely going to leave a stain. *Fuck, fuck, fuck.* I wonder if I can get away with wearing it inside out.

The bathroom door opens behind me.

"Hattie, I'm sorry, are you... oh shit, sorry." He holds his hands up in front of his face. "What are you doing?"

"Cleaning my dress. What the fuck does it look like I'm doing?"

"Why are you naked?" he shouts.

"I can't wear underwear with this dress, you dickhead. It will show lines."

"You look…"

"Yes, I know, I look like a mess."

"No, you don't, Hattie," he says, peeking out from behind his fingers. "You look fucking incredible."

"Oh, piss off, you pervert. Guard the door so nobody else comes in." He turns away from me and thankfully lets me work in peace.

"Is it coming off?" he asks after a minute or two. I blot at a couple of sections with a damp paper towel and it does seem to be lifting, but there are a couple of marks that will be unavoidable. There's no time to fix this properly. Kara said she wasn't mad at me for jumping off the boat, but I can't handle another thing I've ruined this week.

I want to cry. This is supposed to be Kara's perfect day and now I'm going to look like I've been tangoed in the photographs. I can't cry. Not because of my makeup, because Rob is still in the room with me and, even if he is being a gentleman and facing the wall, I won't let him see me this weak.

I lift the dress over to the hand dryer and blast warm air on the damp spots, hoping it won't make it worse. I side-eye Rob who, to his credit, is standing with his hands in his pockets, eyes glued to the floor.

A twisted part of me is annoyed he's not looking at me anymore. In this moment, I realise that everything he does pisses me off. If he looks at me, I'm furious. If he doesn't look at me, I'm furious, but with the added unwelcome feeling of need and desperation. He can't win with me, and therefore I can't win either. Every minute in his company makes me feel like I'm going insane.

I kick the bin, and he jerks his head up.

"You're going to have to help me get back into this, but you are not allowed to be a sex pest about it. If you touch me, if you make even the smallest comment about my body, I will crush your balls. Again. I mean it, keep your mouth shut." He nods quietly, still looking at the floor.

I bunch the fabric together and pull it over my head, letting it settle around my waist when the skirt falls to the floor. The top part of the dress is made up of two long panels that can be stretched out or twisted and tied in different ways to suit different body shapes. I'm going to have to change my style and turn some sections around to hide the worst stains. After a bit of wrangling, I manage it, two wide straps rising from my waist, then criss-crossing above my boobs. I can spread the material out to keep my dignity, but the straps will have to twist around each other as they fall down my back.

"You need to help me with the knot," I say, and he steps up close behind me. "Are these two sections both the same width?"

"Yes," he says, coughing to clear his throat. I pass them around my waist at the front and gather them at the base of my spine.

"Can you please twist them into a rope, then tie them into a neat bow around my waist? You know how to do that, right?"

He pulls the ends of the fabric hard, yanking me closer towards him. I grip onto the edge of the sink and watch him in the mirror as he works, his hands looping the fabric together, his head dipping low now and then as he stands back and smooths out the sections, adjusting the length of the ends of the material.

"How does it look?"

"Perfect," he whispers. His hands are still holding onto fistfuls of my dress. I glance over my shoulder and shudder a little when he exhales, his breath catching my exposed neck. "I thought you might have a tattoo."

"Why did you think that?"

"You just seem like the type."

I turn to face him and slap my hands against his chest. "Well, there you go again, Rob, making more assumptions about me based on absolutely nothing. You really don't know me at all."

Silently, he lays his hands on top of mine and we stay like that for a moment. His heart gallops away beneath his shirt, as his eyes roam my face and settle on my mouth.

I wonder if he has any tattoos, but I don't dare ask. My fingertips shift a fraction, as if I might find the faint ridge of one across his firm chest. I picture him naked, tangled in white sheets, miles of skin for me to explore at my leisure. The thought makes me sway backwards and Rob's hands dart out, catching my hips and pulling me back to his body.

"What tattoos did you think I would have?" I ask, breaking the deafening silence.

His throat bobs and I hold my breath when he reaches around my waist and strokes his fingertips ever so gently across the exposed skin of my lower back. "Maybe a small thing here."

"You thought I'd have a tramp stamp?" I frown.

"Hattie," he laughs softly and shakes his head. "We don't tattoo shame."

I puff out air, awkward at being told off, but he doesn't stop there.

"A small thing here or—" he traces his fingers in circles and zigzags slowly up my bare spine, leaving a trail of goosebumps in his wake. "Maybe a bigger piece all the way up here. Flowers, a vine, maybe a nest of vipers snaking all the way up to your neck." He keeps going, his strokes dancing over my shoulder, sneaking beneath the material at the hollow of my throat.

He skims his fingers up my neck, spreading them out to take my jaw in his warm hand, tilting my face up to his. The pad of his thumb ghosts over my bottom lip and I'm certain I'm about to pass out. His eyes are full of longing, but his touch is so delicate it's almost painful. I feel it deep in my chest, an agonising need. I want him to touch me more. I want him to take me right here, dress be damned, the way he said he wanted me on the boat. It's been the only thing I've pictured in bed at night ever since.

This power he has over me has knocked something loose in my brain. No matter how hard I try to forget him, how desperate I am to ignore him, I always end up an aching mess in his presence. And he doesn't care about the effect he has on me. It's so easy for him to get on with his life, like his words don't imprint in my skin.

"Sounds like you've thought about my body quite a bit, Rob. You need to get a hobby, mate." I move to leave but his hand circles my wrist, thumb finding my pulse point and caressing there so tenderly it's impossible to pull away. He pulls me gently into his arms, the front of our bodies pressed together, one hand cupping the back of my head. The sound that escapes my throat is mortifying. He lowers his mouth to the shell of my ear and the warmth of his breath sends heat flowing through every part of me.

"You know I've thought about it," he whispers. "And now I know what it looks like, I don't think I'll ever get you out of my head."

Chapter 16
Hattie

"Congratulations, you may kiss!"

The celebrant steps aside, and the room explodes in applause. My hands follow their lead without thinking. Up on stage, I watch my best friend and her husband - *husband!* - wrap their arms around each other, lock lips and turn slightly, Kara's bouquet rising to her cheek to give them privacy just like we planned.

"This is amazing, so amazing," Megan sobs beside me, pulling a tissue from her clutch bag and patting her face. "I'm so happy for them."

"Me too," I say, fixing my mouth into a tight smile. "So happy."

Maybe if I keep saying it, it will feel real. It's not that I'm *not* happy for them. I've never met two people more deserving of each other's love. It's more that I don't really feel happiness the way I think other people feel it. Sometimes I wonder if I've ever been truly happy.

The afternoon passes in a blur of champagne, canapes, and camera flashes. I'm briefly introduced to Rob's mum and aunt, which seems fucking weird until I remember that it's not, given how close Luke and Rob were growing up.

Kara asked if I wanted to invite my mum, but I said no. Although Kara and I hung out plenty as kids, we mostly went to her house or Megan's, so they aren't as close with my mum as I am with their parents. I never wanted to take friends home because I never knew what state the house would be in, or which boyfriend of the month would be making himself at home on our sofa. If I'd invited Mum, knowing my luck, she'd have turned up with some dickhead in tow who'd try to act like he knows me based on the limited information mum seems to give them.

I don't want to be dwelling on this shit today, but seeing Luke and Kara combining their happy families really drives home what a mess mine is.

By the time the street food trucks are ready to serve I'm absolutely ravenous, and first in line for pizza. I grab a stack of napkins and carry my plate to a table, bagging a seat beside the second most amazing woman in the room.

"Hi, Granny Annie."

"Oh hiya doll, don't you look smashing," she says, her Scottish accent already soothing my soul. She rests one hand on my forearm. Her nails are painted a pearly pink, to match her lacy dress, her glossy ballet pumps, and her enormous hat. I don't give much of a fuck about weddings, but I respect that the older generation are still so into hats. It's a dying art, I think.

"Are you OK? Can I get you anything?"

"I'm all good, sweetheart, Luke's getting me some food. Come here, tell me how you are." *Christ, where to begin.*

"I'm doing well, thank you."

"That boy still giving you grief?" she waggles a finger in Rob's direction. Having been witness to a few of our spats, and the dreaded boat disaster, she knows exactly what the two of us are like.

"What was your husband like?" I ask, changing the subject. I know Luke's grandfather died long before he came into Kara's life, but I haven't heard much about him.

Her eyes light up and she angles her body towards me. "Oh my goodness, you're so sweet to ask. He was the best man you could ever meet."

"Tell me about him."

"Derek was my husband, but he was so much more than that. He was my best friend, and my business partner. Did you know we used to run a pub together?"

"Luke mentioned it, yes."

"Nearly fifty years we had it. Luke's mammy grew up there, then when Luke came along we moved to a house nearby, but we were there every day and we loved it. It was the heart of the village, and my Derek, well, he was the life and soul of the place. He always had time to stop and chat with everyone, no matter how busy it was. It was like he had more hours in the day than everyone else, you know?"

She smiles softly, a little hum at whatever memories she's conjuring.

"Sarah was useless in the bar, have you met my Sarah?" she points across to where Luke's mum is standing at the bar and I nod. We met at the engagement dinner, but I wasn't sat near her so we didn't get to speak much. "Always had her head in a book. That's why she's so good at what she does, she's a surgeon, you know. But my Derek didn't mind. He'd let her sit at one end of the bar and he'd quiz her while he pulled pints. Then the customers got in on it too, always quizzing her when she was doing her studies. They were all bawling their eyes out when she passed her exams."

"He died not long after Heather got her cancer diagnosis," she continues. "And I know it sounds awful, but sometimes I'm glad he went then, because I don't think he'd have survived seeing what she and Luke went through. He loved her to bits. She was like a granddaughter to us."

Luke's first wife isn't exactly a secret, she comes up in conversations often, and we went to visit her tree on her birthday. It had been Kara's idea, and Luke and Rob had spent a couple of hours regaling us with stories about her. This is the first time I've heard someone mention Heather today though, and it's sweet that Annie doesn't treat her like an elephant in the room.

"I wish I'd been able to meet her," I say, though the reality is if she'd survived, Luke would never have appeared in our lives. And if I hadn't met him, then I'd never have met Rob. And if I hadn't met Rob, then… My chest tightens at the thought. I don't know how I would feel about life without him. He's such a fixture now, whether I like it or not. I shove the thought down and knock back the rest of my wine.

"Derek would have just loved Kara. I tell him all about her." She points skyward, then holds my hand. We watch my sweet friend across the room, biting into a huge slice of pizza with a napkin tucked into the front of her dress. "And he would have loved you too, doll. He always liked lassies with a bit of fire in them."

I burst out laughing and wrap my arms around her. "That's probably the nicest thing anyone's ever said to me Annie, thank you."

And I mean it. My attitude is usually a problem for people. Bossy and unlikeable. Doesn't follow instructions. Too demanding. Not compliant enough. That's what they say.

The sound of metal clinking against a glass draws my attention. From the stage, Megan adjusts the microphone to her height.

"Good evening everyone," she begins. "It's almost time for speeches. If I can ask you all to please take your seats, the lovely team here at Moonshine will make their way around to top up your glasses. Afterwards you can gather around the dancefloor for the cake cutting and the first dance."

"I need to eat some more food, Annie," I say, rising from my seat.

"Come and find me later for a dance, doll."

"I will, I promise."

This is the bit I've been dreading most of all. I'm no stranger to public speaking, but the subject of love is definitely out of my comfort zone. Megan should be the one to do it, she's a believer in all that shit. Plus, as an English teacher, she manages to keep entire classes of teenagers engaged every day, but she handed Kara's request for a bridesmaid's speech off to me before I could object.

"Are you ready for your speech?" Rob asks, appearing out of nowhere as I finish a mouthful of a second slice of pizza.

"Yes. Are you?"

"Sure am. Think you're going to like it." He bumps my shoulder with his and when I look up at him, he gives me one of those smarmy winks that still somehow sends heat racing through me.

"Rob, please do not use this as an opportunity to wind me up. This is Kara and Luke's day."

He walks backwards away from me, that gorgeous grin taking all my oxygen with it. "What kind of monster do you take me for?"

I find my seat at a table up front with Megan on one side, Kara and Luke on the other.

While Kara's dad shares stories of her as a little girl, I force a smile and pick at the skin at the side of my thumb. I haven't been a guest at many weddings, but this bit is always my least favourite. These public declarations of love and belonging are too much to handle. It hurts to know nobody would ever stand up and do the same for me.

Fortunately, it's a short speech, and Luke takes the stage to tell the story of how he offended Kara when they first met. He thanks her for giving him a second chance, tells the room how much he loves her and before I know it, Rob is up behind the mic.

"For those of you who don't know me, I'm Rob. I'm Luke's best man and his oldest friend, and I couldn't be happier to stand up here with him on this beautiful day.

"Kara, you look absolutely stunning. Luke tells me every day how lucky he is, and I'm sure he tells you, too. To the bridesmaids, Megan and Hattie, you've done an amazing job of getting this place ready this week. Megan, you look beautiful, and Hattie..." His gaze locks on me and my stomach turns to cement. Of all the ways he could humiliate me, this would be it. On stage, mic in hand, knowing full well I won't cause a scene.

"I'm just... I, er—" he clears his throat. "There just aren't words to describe how incredible you are."

Kara and Megan both gasp and shoot their hands out to rest on my knees. I press my fist to my mouth and will myself not to smile, or cry, or do anything to make it obvious I'm hanging on by a thread right now.

"I'm not exactly the best candidate to make a speech about love since I've never been in it," he continues, finally tearing his eyes away from mine. The room is filled with an *'awww'* from the seated guests and I roll my eyes and angle my body back towards the table. As if he needs sympathy. It's probably one of his tactics to get laid.

The rest of his time on stage is a blur. I smooth out the skirts of my dress, drink my water, make the appropriate noises, giggling along on auto-pilot with everyone else, but my ears refuse to hear anything else except *'there just aren't words to describe how incredible you are.'*

'How incredible you are.'

'Incredible'.

'You'.

"To the love of today, and the love of tomorrow," the voices around me roar, raising their glasses to the sky. I fumble the words, sip my drink and take a deep breath. Knowing how nervous I am, Megan squeezes my hand and I stand, desperately wondering how on earth I'm going to follow whatever he just said.

It's stifling up here on stage. With the lights pointed towards me, I can't see anyone in the crowd, and I'd rather be anywhere else right now.

"Hi everyone, I'm Hattie, and I'm an even worse candidate to give a speech at a wedding because I've never been in love and personally can't think of anything worse." An awkward laugh rumbles out of me, but I'm met with silence.

"Um, but that doesn't matter, because today isn't about me." *Come on, Hattie, fake it 'til you make it, babe. Big smile.* "It's about these two amazing people, who have so much love for each other that it spills over and passes on to everyone they meet."

Nice save.

"I'm not great with words. Um, Kara..." I shield my eyes with my hand so I can see her, sitting in Luke's lap, her head resting on his shoulder. "I'd be doing a much better job if you wanted a wedding creative brief or a PowerPoint presentation."

Finally, a little laughter spreads across the room. "So, instead of trying to write something, I found some words that say everything I want to, but a million times better. And I want to read them for you today."

There's no reason for me to feel this nervous. I've stood up in front of rooms full of strangers more times than I can count. Presented client pitches with millions of pounds on the line. Here, surrounded by people who I know and love, this should be the safest room in the world, but I'm terrified. I cough to clear my throat, take a deep breath, and force myself to stand a little straighter.

I pick a spot near the back of the room and train my eyes on it. It's a terrible way to address a crowd. I'm supposed to look guests in the eye, take my time to glance around the audience, keep my body language open, and use hand gestures for impact. Instead, I freeze and look at nobody, as if somehow it will mean nobody looks at me.

"So, er, this is a poem called Married Love by Guan Daosheng, who was a Chinese painter born in 1262. At the time she was alive, it was not uncommon for men to take more than one wife, the bloody bastards," I wince. "Anyway, as the story goes, once her husband read this poem, he decided not to take a second wife and remained faithful to her. I've adapted it slightly, but since she wrote it 800 years ago, I hope Guan wouldn't mind."

Deep breath, Hattie.

"OK, here goes.

You and I
Have so much love,
That it
Burns like a fire,
In which we bake a lump of clay
Molded into a figure of you
And a figure of me.
Then we take both of them,
And break them into pieces,
And mix the pieces with water,
And mold again a figure of you,
And a figure of me.
You are in my clay.
I am in your clay."

If possible, the room is even quieter than before. I can hear my blood whooshing in my ears, my heartbeat threatening to explode from the cavity of my chest. Keeping my eyes on that spot in the crowd, I will myself to disappear. I need to get off this stage and out of this room.

"Um, to Kara and Luke," I manage to squeak out, raising my glass in the air.

"To Kara and Luke!" the guests repeat back, and it hits me like a wave. Thunderous applause, cheers and whistles, the sound of chairs scraping the floor as everyone gets to their feet. I feel unsteady on my feet as adrenaline rushes through me.

Blinking away tears, I step out from beneath the spotlight and into the shadows, forcing myself to breathe. Casting my eyes back to that comforting spot at the back of the room, the light has shifted, and the sea of faces cheering me on are now clear as day. There amongst them, in the place I've addressed this entire time, Rob cheers loudest of all.

Chapter 17

Hattie

My feet hurt in these shoes. I'm wondering if everyone's drunk enough for me to sneak away early when Rob appears in front of me, his arm outstretched, palm open.

"Hattie Buchanan, please may I have this dance?" I'd think he was a true gentleman if I didn't already know otherwise. His tie and suit jacket are long abandoned, his hair dishevelled. He looks happy, and I don't trust him.

"Why?"

"For God's sake, Hattie," he snaps. "Just let me dance with you."

I huff out a breath, but stand anyway. My hand settles in his palm and I let him lead me to the dance floor just in time for the DJ to switch to a slow song. Rob bites back a smile and I know he must have requested this, never one to miss an opportunity to rile me up.

"You're unbelievable," I say, shaking my head.

"Why thank you." He settles one hand on my hip and takes my hand in the other for a, I don't know, *waltz*? I don't know a thing about dancing unless it's jumping up and down to release my demons on a dancefloor or grinding up against someone in a corner. And I certainly won't be grinding up against Rob. My other hand hangs awkwardly by my side. I'm not sure what to do with it, grateful when he lifts it to his shoulder. Heat radiates through the cotton of his shirt. Or is it my hand that's hot?

Held to him like this, it's hard to know where I end and he begins. I let him guide me through the song but keep my head turned away, my eyes on the other couples on the dancefloor.

Kara and Luke are wrapped around each other, the picture of newlywed lovebirds who can't believe their luck. Her mum and dad spin their way past and they switch partners, Luke and his brand new mother-in-law, and Kara back in the arms of the man who loved her first.

I wonder where my dad is right now. Would he dance with me on my wedding day? Not that I'd ever have one.

I can't make out what they're saying as they move together, but it's beautiful to witness the love that passes between them, the joy in their smiles. It makes me smile too. You can't not smile when love is that pure. It's infectious. Of course, it doesn't last long because Rob opens his big dumb mouth to remind me whose arms I am in.

"Your poem was incredible."

"Not my poem," I say, batting his compliment away.

"You know, in some cultures, it's traditional for the best man and maid of honour to hook up," he teases.

"What cultures?"

"Sexy ones."

I hate myself for laughing. "You never quit, do you?"

"Nope," he spins me a little, tugging me closer. "Not where you're concerned."

"Great. A lifetime of torture. I must have really screwed up in a past life to deserve this."

"Do you believe in all that stuff? Karma?"

"I guess not. I don't think it's fair to suggest the shitty things that happened to me are payback for something I don't even know I've done. What could I possibly have done to deserve my dad leaving me? Or you with yours."

That shuts him up, though I feel his thumb rub the palm of my hand. It's a kindness, a reassurance that I didn't know I needed. His small intimacies always make me want to run, but I'm tired of running. I let my forehead fall against his chest and we stay like that for a while, rocks filling my throat, my jaw pressed tight shut.

"Hattie—" he whispers against my hair, and I lean back a little to see his face. There's that look again. Eyes ablaze, hypnotic, and full of need. I couldn't look away even if I wanted to. "How the hell am I supposed to concentrate on dancing when I know you're naked under here?"

I hadn't even noticed we've stopped moving. He skims his hand from my waist up to my ribcage, his thumb sneaking under the hem of the part of my dress that covers my boobs. I shiver under his touch, my nipples pulling into tight peaks.

I wish I could just get out of my head for a minute and enjoy this for what it is, a slow dance with a gorgeous man with an incredible body who isn't being subtle about his hand placement. I wish I could loosen up, lay my head on his shoulder, and sway to the music with him. It could be so easy. Instead of tensing and pulling away, I could just let my body melt against his, safe in the knowledge that he'd hold me up.

I could be obvious about inhaling the scent of him, maybe tell him how good he smells, and how much it makes me want him. I could let go of his hand and take it again, but this time thread my fingers through his in that intimate way other people do. I could kiss his neck, his jaw, his mouth. I could do it right now and I'm certain he'd let me. And then maybe, in some other timeline, on some other planet, in some other universe, I could do it again. And again tomorrow. And every day after that for the rest of my life.

But that's not possible, because what I'm wishing for is to be a different person entirely. I'm not Hattie Buchanan who slow dances and swoons, I'm Hattie Buchanan, good-time girl. Hattie Buchanan, who doesn't know any better than fucking and fighting. Hattie Buchanan, who men leave.

The thought coincides with the end of the song. Rob keeps me held in his grasp, but it's far too painful now.

"Stay," he pleads when I let go of his hand and twist out of his arms, but I mumble my excuses and escape to the loos, locking myself in the far cubicle. I take my time peeing, sitting in the cubicle trying to calm myself down until I hear the main door swing open.

"Hattie?" I hear the voice I'd know anywhere. My beautiful Kara. "You in here?"

"Yeah."

"You OK?"

"Yeah, just a sec." I finish up, meeting her out by the sinks. She tries to hug me while I wash my hands, but I don't want her to see my face. She always knows when something is up. "I know I've said it a few times, but you look absolutely gorgeous, darling. This dress is amazing. You must wear it every day forever."

"Can you imagine? I'll wear it to paint and do the garden," she says, laying her head on my shoulder and swaying with me the way I wanted to with Rob. She's more than a little tipsy, and we've all had enough to drink that no amount of artisan pizza is going to put a dent in it. "You're not yourself. What's going on?"

"It's just work stuff, babe." And Rob Beautiful Bastard Morgan getting under my skin. "You are absolutely not to worry about it on your wedding night. Do you want me to call a cab for you soon?"

"Actually," she pulls her head back and blinks a few times, her eyes widening to stay focused. "There's been a bit of a mix-up with that."

"What? What can I do?"

"Luke thought our flights were 7pm tomorrow, but we've just realised they're 7am, so we're going to skip the hotel and go straight to the airport and sleep there."

"Kara, you can't spend your wedding night in an airport. What about all the consummating?" I laugh.

"Trust you to think of that," she swats my arm, missing by a fair distance. "Anyway, there's no point in us staying at the hotel for only a few hours. We've had so much to drink we'd probably sleep in and miss our flight."

"That would be awful."

"I thought you might like to stay there." She fishes a keycard out of her bra and presses it into my palm. "My brother already picked up our bags, I don't want it to go to waste."

"Wouldn't your parents rather stay there or something?"

"No, you know they're just keen to get home to their own beds. You've been working your sexy butt off," she gives me a firm spank and it's so loud we both burst out laughing. "You need a break. There's a jacuzzi bath and everything, just go enjoy it. We booked a late checkout too."

My eyes feel spiky and tears well up as I swallow the lump in my throat. The weight of my exhaustion hits me, everything catching up all at once. I hug her tight and choke out a thank you.

"Honey, you deserve it."

"I love you so much. I know you're only going for a week, but I'm really going to miss you."

"I know, I can't believe it, me going on holiday? On a plane? Did you ever imagine!" My darling angel sacrificed so much of her twenties on her house and her business, she deserves this more than anyone I know.

"You'll love it."

"And you'll love the hotel," she says. I know I will. Especially sleeping in a massive bed and sitting in that tub until I'm wrinkly all over.

Chapter 18
Rob

Something is wrong with Hattie. She's not been herself all day, and I would know, I've been watching her every minute. She's barely said a word since the speeches, and when she has she's been quiet and soft, not the firecracker I'm used to sparring with.

I'm completely thrown, with no idea how to handle her when she's like this, all shut down and sad. It's not even my place to *want* to handle it. I thought a dance might cheer her up and help her relax, but like always, I've somehow made it worse and now she's run off again.

At the bar I find Luke and his Mum laughing away, both more drunk than I've seen them in a long time. I give Sarah a peck on the cheek and slide my arm around Luke's shoulders.

"Have you seen Hattie?"

"No, sorry mate," he slurs. "Hey, do you want to stay in the honeymoon suite tonight?"

Wow, he really is drunk. "Pretty sure you'll be needing it yourself, bud."

"I got the flights wrong," he hiccups, then thumps his chest, releasing a burp. "Excuse me, sorry. Going straight to the airport. Here, you take it. 401." He fishes the hotel keycard out of the inner pocket of his suit jacket and hands it over with a flourish.

"You're serious?"

"Yeah, it's all yours," he giggles like a teenage girl. "Go screw a bridesmaid or something."

If only.

I find Kara on the dancefloor with Megan, barefoot and ripping it up. I bend to yell in her ear. "Where's Hattie?"

"She left, darling. Everything OK?"

"Of course. I'm gonna head off too. Congratulations again, sweetheart. You have an amazing honeymoon."

"No, *you* have an amazing honeymoon!" she shouts, not realising her error.

I considered going home, but there's nothing like the luxury of a hotel bed and if there's one thing that will take the edge off today, it's having breakfast delivered in the morning. I've stayed in this hotel a few times, usually with women passing through town for a conference. It's a nice place, a grand old building but pretty modern and fancy inside. I bet Kara chose it.

I bypass the receptionist, a petite brunette with a long, sleek ponytail. If I was in a better frame of mind, maybe I'd suggest she come and see me if she gets a break, but to be honest I just want to shower and sleep. The whole day has been full on with stressing about making it perfect for Luke, too much socialising, and whatever the fuck this thing with Hattie is.

We had some intense moments today, moments where I felt that we were more than just our usual bickering. She must have felt it when I stroked her skin in the bathroom. To be honest, I think I deserve a fucking trophy for keeping my hands to myself while she stood there in nothing but heels and a scowl. Holy fuck, her back is incredible. Those strong, lean muscles under soft, supple skin. That ass, tight and high and just begging to be squeezed. She *must* have known.

If not then, I'm sure she felt it when we danced. At least until she mentioned her dad. She rarely mentions him. I guess it's not exactly a regular topic of conversation, but maybe that would explain the drop in her mood.

The lift doors close and I lean against the wall, rolling my neck from side to side. I'm tense and weary. Perhaps there's some sort of massage package I could have delivered to my room.

It's Hattie's fault. I've never felt this level of tension build up with anyone else. I know she thinks it's all a game to me, but I've been trying to get her into bed for so long that my dick and my brain can't keep up about who wants what. Every time I get a little closer to her, she pulls away, but there's something behind it I just can't seem to ignore.

I need to get over her, but I honestly feel like I won't be able to get her out of my head until we've fucked and burst this bubble. Other women don't hold the same appeal any more.

I don't know why she's so against the idea. I'd sit down and have a serious chat about it with her, make an actual proposition, but I think she'd rip me a new one for even suggesting it.

The keycard readers flashes, illuminating the dim corridor, but when I let myself in the lights are already on. The short corridor leads into an open lounge area with a kitchenette and through the double doors I spy the bedroom with the biggest bed I've ever seen.

Jackpot.

I kick off my shoes and head through, but pause in the doorway when I see the covers are already out of place. From the bathroom I hear the sound of running water and... *is that singing?* That doesn't make sense. I left Luke and Kara at Moonshine. Who would be here?

"Hello?" I call out from the entrance to the bedroom and the bathroom door flies open to reveal Hattie in a silky robe that she hasn't bothered to tie, a bottle of champagne swinging in her hand.

Oh shit. I am so fucked.

"Ugh. You," she sighs. "What do you want?"

"*Christ*, Hattie. How is it possible that I am seeing you naked for the second time today?"

She stalks towards me, swigging straight from the bottle. She wipes her mouth with the back of her hand and gives me a look I've never seen before. *How many versions of this woman are there?* She points her finger and stabs me in the chest. "Take your clothes off."

"Excuse me?"

"Strip," she says, one eyebrow raised. "Then we'll be even."

"This feels like a trap."

"Actually leave the tie on," she waves a finger at my neck and cackles. "All the better to choke you with."

"What are you doing here?" I fight my instincts and keep my gaze strictly at eye level.

"Kara gave me the room," she says, picking up her phone from the bedside table. "I'm swiping for a hookup. You should probably leave. Or stay and watch. You might learn a thing or two."

I round the bed fast and snatch the phone from her hand. "You hate me so much you'd let me watch another man fuck you?"

"I'm not opposed to a bit of exhibitionism," she shrugs, her face tilted up to mine, goading me. I can't tell if the tightness in my chest is because I would love it or hate it, but as much as I love fighting with her, she's clearly not in a good headspace right now.

"You should leave." I take two steps back, pointing to the door. "Luke gave *me* the room. I'm planning on starfishing in that bed and draining the mini bar on his account."

"Well, that is unfortunate, because I'm the one who'll be having the best sleep of my life tonight." She stands with her hands on her hips, which has the unfortunate yet incredible effect of pushing her robe wider. Somehow, her tits look even more delicious than they did this morning. I can't look away, and she doesn't ask me to.

"Can you at least put some clothes on while we have this conversation?"

"No. I don't think so. If it makes you awkward, then… what's that saying? If you can't beat them, join them?" She closes the gap between us, reaches for my belt and starts unbuckling it. I grip her shoulders and push her away.

"Stop it."

"Why?"

"It's not a good idea for me to be naked around you right now."

"Oh please," she scoffs. "You feeling shy?"

"No, because…"

"Because you'll never be able to resist all this?" She jiggles, *literally jiggles* her boobs at me and saunters away. My hands ball into fists at my sides.

Deep breath, Rob, deep breath. "Anyway, I've already come in that bed, so it's mine."

"*What the fuck?* You only left ten minutes before me."

"What can I say? I'm great in bed."

At the edge of the mattress, she flops back onto the covers, stretching her arms above her head. With the length of her body exposed, I want to lick that beautiful dip in her stomach. My head and my dick are at war now, but my mind has the edge.

"Fine. I'll go. This is ridiculous."

"Is it because I'm too slutty for you, Rob?" she calls after me. "I'm sure you wouldn't dream of sullying yourself with someone like me. Hattie the slut."

"You have no idea what I dream of," I say, turning back to face her.

"Is it this?" She parts her legs and my knees go weak. She looks so goddamn gorgeous, I want to worship her for hours. "I'm sick of playing your games. I need you out of my head. Just fuck me already."

That right there is the hottest thing she's ever said to me, and yet, I'm frozen to the spot.

"Well? Are you going to stand there all night?"

"I... I can't." I'm not lying. I genuinely can't seem to move. Can't breathe. Can't do anything except stare at her perfect body spread open for me. After everything she's done to tease me since we met, I can't believe this is actually happening. I must be hallucinating.

"Why not?"

"I'm—" *Earth to Rob*, engage brain, move your ass, fuck the woman already. "I... I think I'm nervous."

"*Nervous?*" she half shrieks.

"You're intimidating. I haven't had time to prepare myself mentally."

She props herself up on her elbows and glares at me. "Rob Dickhead Morgan. You're not getting this chance again. Get your head in the game and fuck me, you prick."

Why are her insults always the thing that tip me over the edge? I drop to my knees in front of her like a man possessed. Bewitched. Enchanted by the feast laid out before me. My mouth hangs open, I can't think straight. I look up at her, and she waves her hand back and forth, telling me to get on with it.

"How drunk are you?"

"Drunk enough to back down, unfortunately not drunk enough that I won't remember you in the morning."

"You'll never forget me angel." I trail my knuckles slowly up the inside of her leg. "You really want this?"

She laughs, that laugh that makes my cock twitch. "Yes Rob, fucking eat me."

With my eyes locked on hers, I move closer, wet my lips and let the warmth of my breath coast over her. There's a little tremble at the back of her thigh, and I drag my tongue lazily along the crease of her hip and down the other side before lapping at her clit. She throws her head back and moans so loudly I know she'll hate herself for it. It's the most glorious sound on earth. I wrap my arms around her thighs, yank her closer and keep going, watching her lose her mind from my slow, teasing strokes. Gripping the sheets, she is everything I've ever imagined and more.

From somewhere beneath her, music blares. Prince's unmistakable vocals singing about the most beautiful girl in the world.

"Fuuuuuck," she shouts, thumping the bed with her fist.

I pull away, confused. "Are you soundtracking me going down on you?"

"No, it's my phone. Get off me."

"Leave it." I bark, pushing her thighs further apart. I dive in again, firmer this time, ravenous for her, but she wrenches out of my grasp.

"It's Megs. I have to answer. Where is it?" She throws the covers back, not giving a shit that she's flung them over my head.

"How do you know?"

"That's her ringtone. A-ha!" I hear her answer. "You OK, babe?"

I wriggle out from under the sheets and sit on the floor by the foot of the bed, trying not to be obvious about listening in. I can't make out what she's saying, but Megan is clearly upset. Hattie climbs off of the bed and rifles through her bag on the chair by the window.

"Oh shit, yeah, I've got them. Don't worry babe, I'll be right there."

My heart sinks when she grabs her dress from the floor and steps into it, giving me a great view of her pert backside. "Are you warm enough? You want to go and knock on Mr Michaels' door and see if you can sit in with him for a bit? ... No fair point, he's probably asleep ... OK ... See you soon."

She throws her phone at me and it lands in my lap, hitting my aching dick square on. If she hadn't been looking in the opposite direction, I'd swear she'd done it on purpose.

"Book me an Uber while I sort this stupid fucking dress out."

"You're going?"

"I've got her keys, and she's locked out." She fiddles with the straps while I try not to crush her phone in my hand. I book the car and she struggles on, trying to cover her chest and her shoulders, but the fabric keeps slipping from her hurried fingers. Eventually she yanks the skirt part up over her boobs, crosses the straps around her waist and ties a big knot in the middle. I'm almost certain it's not one of the suggested styles, but she's still a knockout.

"Will you come back?" I ask, even though I know her answer will destroy me.

"No," she sniffs. "Saved by the bell. Fuck knows what I was thinking." Perching on the end of the bed, I watch her hobble through to the lounge and she winces putting her heels back. I don't want her to go, but I don't know what I could do to make her stay, either.

"Here, take my jacket." I grab it from the lounge chair and place it over her shoulders. She won't even look at me.

"My phone?" She reaches out and I set it in her hand, wishing I could leave mine there with it.

What a mess. I've never been so disappointed in my life. I dip my head to force her to look at me, but she's busy checking her booking, refusing to meet my gaze.

"Seven minutes. I'll wait downstairs," she makes for the door. "Bed's all yours. Enjoy!"

"Hattie, wait…" I say, even though there's no end to that sentence.

"Bye Knob."

The door swings shut behind her and I'm left to, what, sleep? I flop onto the bed and scream into a deep, downy pillow. It doesn't make me feel any better.

Chapter 19
Hattie

SOMEHOW I'VE MANAGED TO escape the aftermath of the wedding with just a medium sized hangover which I'm certain could be fixed with coffee and a bacon roll. Alas, the energy to make either escapes me. I'm also lonely as hell, so I get up and trudge through to Megan's bedroom. She's awake, but reading, and scoots over to make some space for me.

"How are you feeling?" she asks.

"Been better."

"Me too. I did *not* need that last gin and tonic."

I snuggle down on her pillows and try to find my voice. "I think I know why I'm being shafted at work."

She puts her book on her nightstand and turns to face me. "Why?"

"I didn't tell you, because I didn't want to stress you or Kara out right before the wedding, but on Friday I was excluded from a client meeting and Lawrence went instead."

"Ugh, Lawrence," she mock retches but it's a bad move. A real retch quickly follows, a disgusting one that sets me off too and we both start laughing, gulping air to stop ourselves from being sick.

"So I was furious, and I tried to get to the bottom of it, but Andrew wouldn't give me a proper explanation. He said he's going to find me something more challenging. And then he told me to, get this, '*be nice*'."

"Uh oh. Nobody tells Hattie Buchanan to be nice."

"Exactly. Anyway, they never came back from the meeting, which means they all went to the pub, and yesterday I watched Lawrence's stories and he'd posted a load from their night out like a twat. But in one of the group photos I think I recognised someone."

"Who?"

I bury my face in the pillow. "A guy I hooked up with last year."

"*Nooo.* Who?"

"His name is David, that's all I knew. But I did some internet stalking and found out he's the new marketing director at Spirited."

Saying all of this out loud makes me feel even worse. What a mess I've made for myself.

"Oh Hattie, darling. What are you going to do?"

"I don't know. I think if he knows who I am then maybe he asked for me to be taken off the project."

"Can he do that?"

"Men can do anything they want, Megan. They're awful. I don't even know for sure it's him but from the way I thought I was about to shit myself I think it might be. And there's no way I can go in on Monday and say *'oh by the way I think maybe I shagged the client's new director, has he happened to mention it?'* They'd have even less respect for me."

She strokes my hair, knowing full well there's nothing she can say to make this better.

"Also..." I pull the covers up over my head. I have to tell her, but I can't bear to look at her when I say it. "I very nearly almost slept with Rob last night."

"*What?*" she sits bolt upright. "How? When? And why didn't you lead with that?"

"When you rang me I was at the hotel in Kara's honeymoon suite. She told me I could stay the night since they went to the airport early."

She frowns. "Why didn't I get the offer of a night in a luxury hotel?"

"Shit, sorry. She said she wanted me to have a rest after all the work stuff."

"That's fair enough, you have been working so much."

"Anyway, turns out Luke had said the same thing to Rob. So just as I was getting comfy, he turned up."

"Oh my god," she lies back, kicking her legs in the air. "Only one bed! This is a romance book."

"I told him I'd already swiped for a hookup and he was furious."

"Had you?"

"No, I genuinely wanted a good night's sleep, but when he turned up I was naked, and that was the second time he'd seen me naked and—"

"*Excuse me?*" she interrupts.

"That's a story for another time. Anyway I'd had enough to drink that I told him to strip so we'd be equal." Megan takes her fist between her teeth and groans. "We argued about it for a bit but eventually he gave in and he'd just started going down on me when you rang about the keys."

"I'm sorry, what are you *actually* saying to me? I rang you mid-coitus?"

"Well, pre-coitus. I know, you saved me."

"Oh my God, Hattie. Nobody should ever stop receiving oral sex to answer the phone. You idiot," she whacks me through the duvet cover. "I'd have figured something out."

"No. No, I'm glad you rang. It was a bad idea, in a bad moment, after too much booze. I'd have regretted it if we went any further."

"Would you really though? From what I gather he must be pretty good in bed."

"Please, he's all mouth and no trousers Megan."

She snorts. "Well you'd know."

Megan grants my wish for a bacon roll, and after a shower and a second coffee I feel mostly human. We head over to Moonshine to pack up all the wedding decorations, as promised, before the afternoon staff arrive and open up properly.

Rob sidles up next to me at the bar where I'm wrapping church candles in tissue paper. He gets stuck in and wraps a few and I ignore him until we reach for the same one, my fingertips grazing the back of his hand.

"So, are we going to talk about last night?"

God please no. "The wedding? Yes, it was wonderful wasn't it? I think a good time was had by all," I singsong, meaning no, we definitely aren't talking about it.

"No," he leans in close. "About me fucking you with my tongue and then you running out on me."

"For fuck's sake Rob," I hiss. "Megan is right over there, keep your voice down."

"She knows," he laughs and I whip my head around to face him.

"What the fuck did you say to her?"

"Nothing, but I can tell you did from the way she looked at me when I arrived. I'm surprised," he says, his voice low. "I thought you'd want to keep me your dirty little secret."

"What? No! I mean, yes, I do. I don't want anyone else to find out about this. And anyway, nothing happened."

"I'm just going to take these jars out to the car," Megan calls over from the doorway. *Cheeky cow.* I know what she's up to, and I do not want to be left alone with him.

"I'll help," I say, desperate to get away from him, but Rob grabs my wrist and pulls me into his arms.

"If nothing happened, how come I can still taste you?" *Fuuuuck.*

"Please stop. I'm going to be sick. Just hurry up and tidy so we can get back to our respective homes and never see each other again."

His jaw drops, eyebrows knitting together. "Why won't you see me again?"

"The wedding is over. Our work here is done. There's no reason for us to be in each other's company."

"Except the fact that we're friends? Or that our best friends just got married? We're hardly likely to never see each other again."

"We are not friends, Rob."

I leave him to finish the candles while I dismantle the flower wall on the stage. A few minutes later, my phone pings, but it's not in my pocket. I've left it on the bar, right next to where he's standing.

"Who's George?" the nosy bastard asks, looking at my screen.

"None of your business."

"Well he says he wants to see you soon." I press my lips together and turn away, trying not to laugh. "Must be one very satisfied customer. He says it's been far too long."

Of course he would think the worst of me. I dump an armful of flowers on the end of the bar, and reach for my phone, shoving it into my back pocket.

"George, *Georgina*, is my sister, if you must know. She keeps harping on at me about not visiting enough."

"Oh." His shoulders slump, and he seems almost disappointed that he hasn't got a fight out of me.

"Get the bunting down."

He reaches for the scissors at the same time as I pick them up, but I think he's about to touch me and swerve out of reach, batting his arm away.

Suddenly he's screaming. His eyes are wide, hands covering his face and when he pulls them away, we both look at his hand, then each other, and then back to his hand, which is covered in blood.

"You've fucking cut me."

"Oh my God, oh my God," I look around, panic, and ball up a wad of tissue paper to hold up to his face. "I'm so sorry. Let me help."

"No, get off me," he pushes me away and I stumble backwards.

I run behind the bar to get clean napkins and he bends forward to avoid getting blood all over himself.

"Here," I hand the napkins to him, my other hand on his shoulder.

"Get off me, Hattie."

"Calm down, it's not that bad."

"Not that bad? It's my fucking face Hattie, how you do expect me to be calm? I'll have a scar."

Megan chooses this moment to reappear, with Rob doubled over and me crouching down trying to help.

"Well, this escalated."

"I need to go to hospital," Rob shouts at her.

"No, really?" I physically feel the colour draining from my face. "Come on, it's not that bad. It can't be that bad. Can it? *Fuck.*"

"Get me my coat and my keys," he screams, pointing over to the end of the bar and grabbing another wad of napkins.

"I'm really sorry, Rob. It was an accident. I'm so sorry." I want to cry but I think I'm in shock.

"My coat. Now!"

"No, you can't. I'll drive you."

Chapter 20
Rob

My fucking face.

I know Hattie is an angry, mouthy, sometimes volatile little firework, but never in my life did I think she'd go as far as slashing me across the face.

After a frankly unacceptable wait at reception, we're pointed towards the drab blue waiting room, full of patients in various states of distress. Hattie finds two seats together in a far corner, although right now I think I'd prefer she sat as far away from me as possible. I slump down on the hard plastic and she folds her coat over the back of the chair next to mine. "You sit here and I'll get us something to drink."

"I'm hardly likely to leave, am I?" I huff loudly.

She comes back five minutes later with two Styrofoam cups of warm brown slop and a digestive biscuit, which I eat in two bites. I'm starving. The hotel bed was as great as I hoped, and by the time I woke up I was pretty fuming to discover I'd slept through breakfast service. The only suitable thing I could find was a Snickers from the mini-bar, and I ate it in the shower.

A Snickers and a biscuit. Is this the effect hanging out with Hattie has on me? Shoot me in the head if you catch me eating cheese puffs and calling it lunch. I was hoping after we'd finished with the clear up she'd let me take her out for food somewhere. Megan too, anything if it meant I got to spend a bit of time with her.

Last night was... Well, I'm not sure what last night was, except I know in my gut that I walked in on her at a vulnerable moment and she raged right into it. I should have left immediately, but that's the thing about Hattie. Walking away is the hardest thing to do. Either it's because she's locked me in a battle for the last word, or because it's just so enjoyable to watch her get herself fired up into one of her rants. Or lately it's because a few of those arguments turned into moments of connection that I haven't felt with anyone before. Whatever it is, it's impossible for me to turn my back on her, no matter the mood.

"I wasn't sure if you took milk and sugar, so I added both. I'm sure the sugar will help with the shock," she says with her shit-eating grin plastered across her face. Just when I was starting to give her some grace.

"This is not funny, Hattie. I'm so angry with you."

"I really am sorry. I didn't do it on purpose." She angles herself sideways on the seat and leans in close to my face. "Is it still bleeding?"

"How am I supposed to know? I'm not removing this napkin until I see a professional."

"Let me take a look," she reaches out, but I swat her away.

"What are you going to do Hattie, *marketing campaign* my face better?"

"That doesn't even make sense," she sulks, sitting back in her chair. In the corner, an ancient TV plays old episodes of quiz shows, but of course the volume is down so low that watching is completely pointless. Still, we both stare.

"I'll probably need plastic surgery to make sure there's no scar, you know. This hospital better have a Jackson Avery on staff."

A perfect arc of tea sprays out of her mouth and rains down over her jeans. "You tit!" she says, fishing a tissue from her bag and dabbing at the thankfully tepid liquid. I won't give her the satisfaction of an apology. On the TV, another re-run of Wheel of Fortune begins.

"You watch Grey's Anatomy?" she asks quietly.

"Yes. Is that so surprising?"

"Yeah, it kind of is, actually."

"Well, there you go again, Hattie, making assumptions about me based on absolutely nothing." Her eyes flare as I repeat her words from yesterday. The words she said before I showed her where I thought her tattoos would be. The words that clearly bruised my ego.

She picks at her nail varnish for a while then crosses the waiting room to leaf through a pile of old magazines. She comes back a few minutes later with Practical Camping and I force myself not to comment as she loudly flicks through the pages.

"Do I have my own ringtone?" Her brow furrows, until she pieces it together with the memory of our interruption last night and laughs.

"Yes."

"What is it?"

"You'll never know."

I pull my phone from my pocket. "I'll ring you right now."

"You're not supposed to make phone calls in here," she pouts and wrinkles her nose, pointing at a big sign on the wall with an 80s mobile phone and a red cross in front of it

"Fine. You win. For now." Mere seconds later, her phone rings in her hand, and she quickly rejects the call. "You're the only person I know who has their phone off silent."

"My job is important. I can't risk missing a call or an email."

"Hattie, with all due respect, your job is sending emails and making people rich. You're entitled to your time off. It's the weekend. What could they possibly be ringing you about today?"

"It's not work. It was my sister," she huffs and something tells me now is not the time to get into why Hattie is rejecting her sister's calls.

Eventually, we're taken through to a small room and I oblige when the nurse tells me to hop up onto the bed, still holding my face. Hattie hovers by the door and steps to the side when the doctor appears with a trolley of medical supplies.

"So what happened here, then?" she asks, snapping on gloves. She places my hands in my lap and gently removes the napkins, which, now that I see them, aren't as bloody as I thought they would be.

"The monster over there slashed me with a pair of scissors."

"Jesus, Rob, it was an accident. I thought he was about to grab me." The doctor looks back and forth between us, assessing the situation. I know how it must look. She's probably seen all sorts in here. Broken legs, stabbings, assaults. Suddenly my face doesn't seem like such a big deal after all.

"Perhaps this would be quicker if you could wait in the waiting room?" she says to Hattie diplomatically.

"No, it's not like that. I know she didn't do it on purpose," I concede. "She can stay."

I don't want her to leave, anyway. She should have to see what she's put me through.

"Well, the good news is the bleeding has stopped," the doctor says, swabbing my cheek with an antiseptic wipe. "And you won't need stitches."

"I won't? Oh, thank God."

"No, it's just a small superficial cut." Hattie squeaks and when I whip my head around she's covering her mouth, her eyes closed and head tipped up to the ceiling.

"Hold still please," the doctor says, twisting me back into position. "The body is an amazing thing. Injuries to the head and face can often bleed what seems like an alarming amount, but it's not deep. In fact, it's already healing, but I'll give you a couple of butterfly stitches just for the next day or so."

She applies them in seconds, a seasoned pro, then sits back to assess her work. "Do I know you?"

I groan inwardly. It's a huge hospital, but there was always a chance this would happen. "We might have met. I'm Dr. Morgan, I work in the neuro team."

"Ah yes, you were my consult on those boys in the quadbike accident last month. I knew you looked familiar. How are they doing?"

"Taking each day as it comes," I say with a pinched, dismissive smile. I can't talk about this in front of Hattie, and the truth is those kids have got a long path of recovery ahead of them. They're lucky to be alive.

"Well I'm glad to see you under better circumstances."

"Will I have a scar?" I ask, desperate to change the subject.

"Perhaps a thin one but it should fade quickly. Once it's scabbed over, you can use something like bio oil to improve the elasticity, but you've got fantastic skin. I think you probably already have a solid regimen, yes?" That sets Hattie off again with the squeaking and she turns to face the wall.

"What are you laughing at?" I bark across the room.

"Nothing," she breathes deeply.

Hattie would probably take the piss out of my skincare routine, but I'm not ashamed of taking pride in my appearance.

"OK, you're all set," the doctor says, peeling off her gloves and throwing everything into a waste bin. She taps a few things into her computer. "I've discharged you from here so you can head straight out."

"Thank you." I'm starting to feel like a bit of a tit for walking in here thinking I'd need reconstructive surgery and walking out with two little plasters most commonly seen on children with bumped heads.

"Excuse me doctor, I was just wondering..." Hattie says as we're halfway out the door. "Could we have handled this at home?" *You little shit.*

"Probably," the doctor throws her a small smile that says *'yes, you idiots'*. "But it's always good to come in if you're worried about things." Hattie presses her lips tight and nods.

"Why have you asked that?" I say.

"No reason." Her shoulders shake.

"I'll let the two of you go enjoy the rest of your Sunday together."

That's the final straw. Hattie bursts out laughing. "Oh God, no. We're not together."

"Oh, my mistake. Apologies. See you around Dr. Morgan."

Storming down the corridor, I feel Hattie at my side, struggling to keep up. She's usually the one running out on me, but right now, I need to be as far away from her as possible.

"Slow down," she says, and I stop abruptly, her body slamming into the back of me.

"Why is the idea of us together so laughable to you, Hattie? It's not enough to scar me, you've got to piss yourself at a stranger's simple mistake?"

"I'm sorry Rob," she hangs her head. "It's not you. It's laughable that anyone would look at me and think I'm in a relationship."

I can't go there with her right now.

In the car I examine my cheek in the passenger sun visor mirror. It really isn't that bad and the longer we drive, the more guilty I feel. I've made a mountain out of a molehill here. Hattie's been decent enough to drive me, and mostly keep her mouth shut, despite my outbursts. By the time she pulls up outside my house, I know I owe her an apology, or at the very least to make sure she knows I've accepted her numerous ones.

"Do you need me to get anything for you?" she asks, scratching off the last bits of nail varnish on her thumb.

"Are you offering to nurse me back to health?"

"Am I fuck. Get out of my car." *Dammit. I knew that would be bold.*

When I get out I lean down before closing the door. "I'm sorry for shouting at you so much today. I just panicked, I really like my face."

"I suppose it's quite a good face," she says, repressing a smile. "I'm glad I haven't scarred you for life."

Quite a good face, huh? I'll take it.

Chapter 21

Hattie

Rob answers Kara and Luke's door wearing a bright yellow high-vis jacket, safety goggles, and a hard-hat.

"Hurrah! You're here," he says, rubbing his hands together and stepping aside to let me into the house.

"What the fuck are you wearing that for?"

"Ready for battle with my favourite girl."

"No," I hold my hand up to his face. "Can we call a truce? I've had a long, stressful day, I worked through lunch, I've not had enough water, and I'm in no fit shape to fight with you. Give me five minutes."

"Oh, shit guys," he shouts as he ushers me through to the kitchen. "Hattie's had a tough day. Quick, Luke, get the kettle on."

He pushes me past a very tanned looking Luke, who is standing at the counter arranging snacks in little bowls. Kara is equally bronzed, and watches the scene unfold from where she and Megan are sitting at the dining table. I barely have time to say hello before Rob rushes me towards the sofa. With both hands on my shoulders, he pushes me to sit.

"Here we go, my Queen. You put your feet up, and relax." He lifts my legs and spins them round, stretching me out while he fluffs a cushion and props it behind my back. From a wicker basket by the window, he pulls a blanket and makes a show of throwing it open wide and floating it gently down on top of me, tucking it in at my sides.

"OK, you precious thing, you just sit tight here for a minute and I'll be right back with a lovely cuppa and a snack for you."

"What is going on?" Kara calls out.

"I have no idea," I half-laugh, completely bemused.

He's such a dick, but I'm not exactly hating being made a fuss of. After a frustrating day with still no answers about what I'm supposed to be working on, I'm glad to be off my feet for a bit. I let myself fully rest my head on the cushions and enjoy the view of the garden, which is full of colour thanks to Kara's green fingers. Whatever Luke is cooking smells amazing, and I close my eyes listening to some folky song he's chosen. The man has great taste in music. I used to be really into music at university, but somewhere along the way I've had less time for it.

Rob appears at my side, crouched low with a cup of tea in one hand. When I take it, he gives my shoulder a squeeze before he leaves.

"Thank you," I whisper, hoping it reaches his ears only. I daren't let the rest of them witness anything that might resemble gratitude for this man.

He's ditched the personal protective equipment by the time he returns. On the coffee table, he sets a glass of water, a glass of red wine, and a bowl of olives. Lifting my feet, he takes a seat underneath me and settles them in his lap. I'm too tired to object.

"How was your day?"

"It was fine." I sip my tea and narrow my eyes. "Why are you being so nice? Did you poison this?"

"It's good manners to ask how someone's day was." He adjusts his body, one arm against the back of the sofa, his head propped up in his palm. "Aren't you going to ask how mine was?"

"No, I don't care."

"Indulge me."

"Fine. How was your day?"

"Just got better," he winks. *This idiot.* I bite the inside of my cheek to stop myself from smiling. "What happened today?"

"I'm being screwed over at work. I don't want to get into it."

"I'm sorry, sweetheart." Underneath my blanket, I feel him take one of my feet in both hands, tugging my sock off. I'm about to kick him in the face, but he pushes his thumb along the arch of my foot, pressing hard and soothing away the tension. It feels so good I almost forget to hate him.

After dinner, Luke hooks his laptop up to the TV, and we all squish up on the sofa while Kara talks us through their honeymoon photos. They spent a week at an all-inclusive resort in Greece and, judging by the photos, it was all sun, sea, and a frankly obscene amount of selfies. It's amazing to see my girl so happy though, and the resort looks truly incredible. Adults only, six pools, private cabanas on the beach.

"We get it," Rob whispers in my ear after the fifth or sixth photo of grilled prawns, "you like seafood."

I scratch my nose and smile behind my palm. "Don't be mean. This was a big deal for them. Although I'd have been fine with edited highlights."

"I'm just teasing. Do you fancy going somewhere like that sometime?"

"Sure," I shrug. "Looks nice."

"Really?" He looks shocked. I hadn't realised quite how close we've been sitting, or that his arm is stretched out behind me, or that with my feet underneath me I'm basically tucked into his side. "With me?"

"Oh," I pull away a little, and his face falls. "I thought you meant in general."

"Yeah, cool, yeah," he says, rubbing at the back of his neck. "Looks nice."

Later we find ourselves in Luke's hallway, leaving at the same time. My arm brushes against him when I push it into the sleeve of my coat, and I end up awkwardly half-in, half-out of it, turning in circles. Silently he stills me, pulls it off and helps me slip into it properly.

"What are you doing tomorrow night?" he asks over my shoulder, quietly. My heart has the nerve to flutter. Is he going to suggest something? He's been on excellent form all night, and I've felt calmer than I've been in weeks.

"I've got a date," I say. I catch his reflection in the hallway mirror, and the look on his face makes me wish I was lying.

Chapter 22
Rob

I TAKE A SEAT at the bar and order a beer, wondering what the hell I'm doing here in the first place. I don't want her to see me but I'm also curious about who she's out with, since she's so adamant she doesn't go for guys like me.

The long mirror behind the bar means I have my back to their table but I can still keep my eyes on her. I've got no reason to be sitting here, drinking alone, and the last thing I want is for her to spot me.

She's gorgeous in a tight vest top and jeans, her hair tied back, exposing her slender neck, but her body language is far from happy. She hasn't laughed once, and she definitely hasn't touched her earring either. Anyone can see this guy's not doing it for her. Surely she's not going to go home with him? The thought of this boring arsehole with all the charisma of a plain yoghurt getting to see her naked is unbearable.

I'm nearing the end of my beer when she excuses herself. Hopping off my stool, I dash past the end of the bar and down the dark corridor that leads to the toilets. I lean against the wall, ready to stop her, but I don't expect the force with which she slams into me when she turns the corner.

"Oh shit, sorry."

"Hey," I say when she looks up. Her eyes shift from the shock of our collision to something I think is delight before heading straight into fury. She takes a step back from me.

"What are you doing here?"

"Kara might have mentioned you'd be here. I was passing."

"Dammit, Kara," she says, kicking the wall. "She knows I only tell her where I'm going in case I get murdered or something."

"Well, I thought I'd best check you aren't about to be murdered."

"Since when do you care?" she jabs her finger into my sternum with all her might.

Only from the second I laid eyes on you. I rub the spot and wonder if she'll have left a bruise. "Who's the guy?"

"That's none of your business." She tries to side step around me, but I hold my arm against the wall, blocking her in.

"Let me guess. Theo, 36, finance for a startup, works hard but plays harder," I mock him in my best rich, boring twat accent. "Never had a serious girlfriend because he's just been so focused on making his first million. His mum is called Minty. Has he mentioned skiing in Chamonix yet?"

Her mouth pulls into a tight pout and I clock her hands balling into fists on her hips. God, she's fun to wind up. "Fuck's sake. How do you do that? Have you tapped my phone?"

"Come on Hattie. If you're desperate for a good time, all you have to do is ask."

"A night with you is so far from my idea of a good time." Those furious eyes bore into mine. She looks right on the edge of confessing how much she wants it.

When another customer comes out of the bathroom, I lean in to whisper in her ear. "Tell me what you need and I'll give it all to you."

"I'll manage fine on my own, thanks." She snaps up straight and punches her fists into my chest, pushing me away from her. "I need to pee. Be gone by the time I come back."

The urge to storm into the bathroom, throw her over my shoulder, and drag her out of here caveman style is intense, but I don't want to risk another physical assault when I've put her in a mood this sour. For once when it comes to Hattie, I do as I'm told.

Back home, I pull up her texts and scroll through our messages, right back until she told me about her dad and how he used to take her to the car-wash. I read through her messages, and even the mean ones make me want her. Then there's the photo of her vibrator. The vibrator I paid for.

I hate the thought of some loser sitting with a great view of her tits all night. I don't want her to go home with him. Or if she does, I at least want to be so stuck in her head that she thinks of me. I take a quick photo of my bed.

Me: Wish you were here.

I start a follow-up message, but I'm interrupted by a knock at the door, loud and impatient. There's only one person it could be. I rush downstairs and practically pull the door off the hinges. Hattie barrels into my hallway like she's been set on fire.

"I don't know what the *fuck* you're playing at, but don't you ever sabotage me like that again."

This is not good. I'm not sure I've ever seen her this angry. Not during our argument at Maggie's, not in the hotel the night of the wedding, not even after almost drowning because of me.

"Shit, I'm sorry, I just—" My words are cut off when her hands yank my t-shirt up. I have no idea what's going on here, and battle against her to pull it down again, but she's bloody strong. I try to spin around and wrestle myself free from her grip, but her hands are up underneath now, her nails digging into my chest. *Fuck, that feels good. Good and wrong.* "Stop it! What are you doing?"

"You owe me an orgasm," she shouts, one hand reaches for my waistband, tugging it away from my skin, her nails catching me again with a sharp scratch that makes me yelp like a little girl.

"Excuse me?"

"Get your clothes off." I don't know whether to be turned on or terrified, but mostly I am intimidated by how quickly she fights. This is *not* how I want this to go down. Wrenching her hands away from me, I pin them at her sides, holding her as far away from me as possible while still keeping her under control.

"I am so angry at you right now," she screams. "I really wanted to come tonight and then you had to show up and ruin everything."

Thank fuck that douche didn't get his hands on her. "Theo wasn't doing it for you?"

She pants, her breath short and fast as she regains her composure. "His name is Harry."

"That's not better," I smile. "What happened?"

"You got in my head. Plus, his mum actually is called Minty, and he facetimed her while I was in the bathroom then made me say hello."

I burst out laughing. I knew he was the sort. We stand there, staring each other down for a few moments until she glances towards the stairs.

"Have you got someone else up there?"

"Don't be ridiculous." She jerks herself free from my grasp and bolts, taking the stairs two at a time. "Hattie—"

"Shut your mouth and get up here." She's at the top by the time I can fully register what's happening. Her top and her bra lie abandoned in the hallway. I pick them up and carry them through to my room with my palm covering my eyes. This doesn't feel right.

"Hattie, put your clothes back on, *now*." I throw the discarded items back in her general direction and turn to face the wall. "I'm not going to fuck you like this."

"You've been trying to get me into bed for months, Rob. You'd do well not to tease me much longer or I'll start swiping for a hookup."

"What are you gonna do, call a guy round and make him wear a mask of my face?"

"Anyone could be you from behind."

"That's *enough*." I'm on her in a flash, rushing her back towards my bed. Spinning her round, I press her onto my covers and she lands with a gasp. In seconds, I'm straddling her perfect arse, pinning her down and growling in her ear. "That's what you want, is it? You want to be bent over, you want me to fuck you through the mattress?"

Her little whimper tells me all I need to know, and it's almost enough to tip me over the edge. She's so tempting, lifting her hips, grinding into me, I know she'll be able to tell that I'm already hard for her.

"You *will* fuck me. When I want something, I don't stop until I get it."

"Then you'll lose the bet."

"The bet was over months ago. *You* already lost, remember, and I don't give a shit anymore."

She might not give a shit, but I sure as hell do. Everything has changed between us. It's not about the challenge anymore. The woman before me isn't a bet, or a game, or an easy mark. Sure, she's a nightmare most of the time, but beneath all that fire Hattie is someone I've come to treasure. I couldn't just fuck her and send her away, no matter how much my dick wants to get inside her right now.

"Hurry up," she screams, grinding into me more. I squeeze my eyes shut and think of all the ways this could go down. If I send her away, she'll hate me. If I give her what she wants, she'll hate me anyway, and I'll hate myself for taking advantage of her when she's out of her mind. It takes everything in my power to stay in control, but I let go and climb off the bed, tucking my aching erection into the waistband of my jeans.

"We're not doing this tonight."

"*What?*"

"Listen to me." I press my fists into my eyes and take a deep breath. "You know, I've always said this is inevitable, but we're not doing this when you're in a shitty mood and taking it out on me. Plus, I was about to go to bed and read my book."

"Fuck your book!"

"Hattie, I'm serious," I say. "I don't want my only time with you to be a quick fuck when you're pissed off at me."

"Ha," she scoffs. "There will never be a day in this life or the next that I'm not pissed at you, you prick."

"You really know how to charm a man." She glares at me, her face twitching with frustration until she grabs her top, pulls it back over her head and shoves her bra in the pocket of her jeans. With the beast at bay, I step closer, cupping her elbows, my thumbs doing their own thing, stroking softly. "If you really want this, just say the word and I'll make plans."

Her lips press together and she rubs them back and forth over her teeth. Even though I'm offering exactly what she came here for, I know she'll never give in and say the words. I dip lower, my eyeline level with hers.

"Here's what I propose. You and me, one night, no strings attached. We get all this stupid shit out of our systems, and we never have to talk about it again. Would you like that, Hattie?" She makes the softest whimpering noise, her forehead falling against my chest. I feel the slight pressure there as she nods, and I push away the desire to jump up and down and punch the air.

I step away, putting some distance between us, and point at the door. "Go home, and calm down. I'll text you the details."

"You're pathetic." She storms out of my bedroom and I hover, waiting for the front door to slam and wondering if one night will ever be enough.

Chapter 23

Hattie

IT'S BEEN DAYS SINCE I stormed out of Rob's house, and I haven't heard from him once. I don't know what is going on in this stupid brain of mine, but I'm feeling wildly unsettled and sick about the whole thing.

Part of me is mortified that he turned me down. I assumed he'd jump at the chance and it stung like hell that he called me out on my anger. The rest of me is embarrassed he saw me acting so desperate and emotional. Yet the more I think about it, my feelings of shame are turning to fury. He hasn't even been in touch to check if I'm OK.

This is what happens when you start to get attached to someone. I'm getting needy. I can't stop thinking about him, wondering what he's thinking about me, checking my phone for messages from him. It's pathetic.

And this bullshit about him arranging a night for us to sleep together, was that just a ploy to get me out of his house? Am I supposed to sit around waiting? I sure as shit can't text him to chase it up.

Oh hi there, was just wondering when we might be getting together for all this sex we've been talking about? As if.

He wasn't wrong though. This tension has been building between us for months. It would be a shame to waste it on a quick hate-fuck. When I close my eyes all I can see is that image of him about to go down on me after Kara's wedding. If he's half as good as he claims to be then it would be better to have at least a few hours together.

Whatever he has planned, I need it to happen soon so I can get him out of my system, out of my head, and out of my goddamn fantasies.

I'm in a quarterly review meeting with Andrew, his boss, Bob, and a woman from HR who I've never met when the text arrives. My heart leaps into my throat at the sight of his name and the notification.

Knob: I'll pick you up on Friday at 8. Wear something hot.

Here we fucking gooo.

I cross my legs and instinctively squeeze my thighs together while I slide my phone towards me, silence it, and discreetly text him back. I'd much rather text him than listen to any more of Bob's wittering on about the direction the business is taking this year. I'm not sure why I'm even needed here.

Me: Bit presumptuous. What if I have a date that night?
Knob: Cancel it.

I roll my eyes. Arrogant shithead. I should hate this, him telling me what to do, but there's no ignoring the pang that I get in my belly when he gets all bossy. I'm still thinking of an appropriate reply when he texts again.

Knob: Shit, do you really?
Me: No, but it's fun to wind you up. Have a meeting in London until 6. Come straight to yours?
Knob: We're not going to mine.
Me: Where?
Knob: Top secret. Somewhere you can get out of your head.
Me: And into your pants?
Knob: Exactly x

I should not be this excited, but if I was alone right now I'd almost certainly be jumping around and squealing. Instead, I'm stuck with this bunch of bores wondering what I should wear.

"Are you with us, Hattie?" Andrew's voice interrupts my train of thought, pulling my attention back to the room.

"Yes, absolutely," I smile and nod.

"Is there an account that you're leaning towards, then?"

"Leaning towards for what?" I shrug.

Andrew sighs and pinches the bridge of his nose. I look around, confused, and Melissa - *or was it Melinda* - from HR scribbles something in her massive notebook.

"For your next project. These are the new clients we have in the pipeline and we'd love to utilise your skills on some of their accounts. You can take your pick."

Oh, crap, I definitely wasn't paying attention to that. "What about Spirited?"

"The Spirited account is moving in a different direction," Bob says, matter-of-factly.

"So Lawrence is taking it over?"

"For the time being, yes."

I turn to Andrew, and throw my hands up in the air. "This is how you're telling me?"

He can't even look at me, and now I see why Bob and HR Lady are here. He's too much of a coward to deliver this news himself, and because they think I'm going to kick off he's brought in back-up. To be fair, every fibre of my being wants to go apeshit right now, but I know how to play the game.

"For the record," I say, turning to Michelle - *yes, it's Michelle!* - "this meeting was scheduled in my diary as a quarterly review. I think I should have been given more of a heads up about its true purpose. You can write that down in your notebook."

If they're going to try to manage me out, I want a record of all of it so I can take them down with me.

"Can you also please note down that I have a two year record of excellent work with Spirited, and ten years prior to that on various other accounts here at DFR." Michelle just stares at me, eyes wide, clearly unsure what to do.

"You're not writing." I stare back until she picks up her pen and I clear my throat. "Lawrence Desmond was brought in to *'support'* my work, without request or consultation, and in the subsequent weeks all of my work has been re-allocated to him, again without request or consultation. You've now pulled me into a *'quarterly review'* which is actually a meeting to discuss my future at the company, and are offering me mid-tier accounts which sounds a lot like a demotion to me."

You can't bullshit me. I've seen it all here.

"So with all gratitude, Bob," I say, turning to face him, "you can take your mid-tier accounts and shove them. I have a great relationship with Spirited. Brent and I—"

"Brent is no longer with Spirited," Andrew interjects.

"I know that, and his replacement hasn't even had the decency to contact me for an introduction. It's like I don't exist to him. It's incredibly unprofessional, and frankly rude. If this relationship went the opposite way I'd be terminating our contract."

"Are you finished, Hattie?" Bob says, wearily, and I slide my pout from side to side while I think about it.

"Yes, I am."

"This is not a demotion. This is an opportunity. There'll be a promotion available later in the year and—"

I snap my head towards Andrew. "You're leaving?"

He shakes his head quickly, and Bob continues. "We'd like to see you spend some time with other clients to strengthen your experience. Two or three of these should be easy for someone of your caliber and talent."

Oh Bob, flattery will get you everywhere.

My brain is rattling and I bite back my smile. I thought I was about to have to throw a chair through a window and now it turns out they want to nurture me for a promotion. Why didn't Andrew tell me this months ago? Promotion opportunities get less and less frequent the higher you move up in this industry, and there hasn't been one for a long time.

"Fucking hell," I put my head in my hands and roll my chair away from the desk until my forehead is resting on it. "Why can't anyone in this company just speak candidly? It's all fucking mind games. Don't write that, Michelle."

I sit up, wipe my hands over my face and take a second to compose myself. Operation Promotion begins right now, in this room. I'll do whatever it takes.

"Thank you, Bob. I'm extremely keen to progress in the company, as Andrew knows, and I welcome the opportunity to expand my client base." God the ass-kissing rolls so elegantly off my tongue. I wasn't paying proper attention when Bob ran through his presentation on new clients, but I know the brands listed on his screen and any of them would suit me.

"Are there any clients you're particularly keen to see me lead on?" *Gold star, Hattie, throw it back on them.*

"You can take your pick. Why don't I send you a briefing on each, and you can take the rest of the week to immerse yourself before you make a decision."

"That would be great. Budgets and top line objectives too?"

"You've got it. We'll reconvene on Monday."

Rob's ringtone blares from the depths of my bag while I'm leaving the gym. My arms and legs are buzzing after unleashing my anger through kickboxing, and I dig it out, then throw the bag into the boot as I answer.

"What do you want?" I grunt, hiding the smile spread across my face.

"Hello, Hattie." Why does he have to have such a sexy voice. He can't even say hello without it sounding dirty. "I'm just calling to give you a heads up."

"About?"

"I'm not going to come between now and Friday."

"Excuse me?" I laugh. I squeeze in between the car and the wall, open the door and slide into my seat. "Why not?"

"I'm gonna save it up for you."

"That's... a weird thing to do."

"I don't think you should come either."

Jesus Christ. Even just talking about this with him makes me want to get off right this second. "Well luckily for me, you don't get to make decisions about my body, so you can piss off."

"Hattie," his voice drops to that growly, teasing tone I've come to love so much. I bite my lip, tilt my head back against the headrest and close my eyes. "I mean it. You don't touch yourself until Friday. The next time you come it's going to be in my hand."

Fuuuuck. Yeah fucking right, mate. One, you're not the boss of me, and two, as if you're gonna stop me. I slip my hand under the waistband of my leggings and into my underwear. I find myself hot and slick, the way I always am when talking to him. I moan gently as my fingertips sweep over my clit, and bite my lip to stifle it. Fuck it, I don't even care if he knows what I'm doing.

"Where are you Hattie?" he asks.

"Gym," I whisper, pressing harder.

"Get your hand out of your underwear." My eyes fly open and I pull my hand out.

"What the—"

"On your left." I look across the car. Over the phone I hear him laughing, and through the passenger window I can see him, sitting in his car parked next to mine. He gives me a smug little wave.

"I hate you so much." I hang up and drive.

Knob: Hattie Buchanan you filthy minx. It's pretty hot knowing you were going to get off thinking about me but hands off until Friday. I promise it will be worth the wait.

Me: Deal is off. I'm not coming.

Knob: Oh you're coming, sweetheart. 70 hours to go. I'm counting down every minute until I get my hands on you.

Chapter 24
Hattie

I can't concentrate at all on Friday. I'm too jittery to eat lunch, and spend the afternoon clearing out my inbox and clock-watching until the genuine quarterly review meeting with Andrew, Bob, and the other account directors that sit under his management. Only a total bastard would schedule it last thing on a Friday, but I'm determined to make a good impression, play nice and show willing.

Andrew corners me as I'm leaving to wish me a happy weekend, and I make my train home with seconds to spare. I'm desperate to shower off the commuter stink, but I pause when I find Megan in the living room surrounded by school books she's marking. We've been like passing ships this week.

"Hey," she says, clearing her work away to make space for me. "Kara's free tonight. You want to get a takeout, like old times?"

Shit, I really do want to do that. I loved those nights we spent, just the three of us, eating, drinking, and curling up on Kara's sofa. OK so I don't miss the ones where she was so distraught about being dumped she cried until she fell asleep, but when we were happy, we were really happy. We didn't need these stupid men.

"I'm so sorry, I've got plans."

"Oh, OK."

"I really want to do that soon though. I feel like with all the wedding stuff it's been ages since we had a girls night."

"Yeah," she says, her voice sounding sadder than usual.

"You OK?"

"I'm fine," she says, "Kara's coming anyway. Don't let me get in the way of your plans."

I get the feeling she's lying, but at least she won't be alone tonight. After months of build-up, I can't bear to cancel on Rob and drag this out any longer.

"Shall we do some nice things this weekend?" I suggest. "PJ day, facemasks, I'll cook a mountain of carbonara?"

"I'd love that," she says, picking up her red pen and returning to her marking.

I shower in record time, straighten my hair, and get myself into a panic over outfits. Rob said to wear something hot, but what type of hot? Men are so useless when it comes to this sort of thing. I look great in denim cut-offs and an old t-shirt, but am I supposed to trawl my wardrobe and find a gown of some sort? I swear to God, if he picks me up in a tux I will put a dent in his car.

In the end I opt for a black halterneck bodysuit underneath a dark green, floaty skirt that hits at mid calf. I throw my leather jacket over the top and dig chunky ankle boots from the bottom of my wardrobe. It'll have to do. If he tries to take me to a place where I get refused entry based on some stuffy dress code then that's on him.

"Have a nice night," Megan calls after me.

"You too babe, don't wait up."

I don't know where we're going, but I know I'm not normally feeling this excited about the prospect of getting laid. As much as I hate to admit it, I've been thinking about Rob constantly this week, so I hope the reality lives up to my high expectations.

He makes small talk with me as we drive to the outskirts of town and on to country roads. We pass through a couple of little villages and then take a turning that, as far as I'm aware, only leads to one place.

No. It can't be here.

Another half mile on, he takes the left turning and there's no mistaking the giant sign.

"Seriously? This is where we're going?"

"Yup," he says, a huge grin spread across his face.

He parks the car and dashes round to open my door, holding his hand aloft to help me out. With his bag in one hand, he takes mine in the other, interlacing our fingers as if we do this all the time. When we walk inside I marvel at the beautiful foyer, its grand domed ceiling and giant floral arrangements, all things I'd neglected to notice the last time I was here at Fettleworth Lodge.

There's no queue at reception, and I linger behind him, nibbling my fingertips while he checks us in. The reality of what we're about to do is finally hitting me. I'm no stranger to a hotel hookup, but I can't put my finger on why this feels so different, so terrifying.

"Welcome, Mr and Mrs Morgan." *Mr and Mrs?* Don't these people have training not to presume their guests names? "You'll find complimentary champagne in your suite and room service is available 24 hours a day. If you'd like to take advantage of our spa services just call us and we'll arrange whatever we can to meet your needs."

"Thank you, Cheryl," Rob says, tucking our room key into his jacket pocket. He takes my hand again and gives it a little squeeze as he leads me towards the lifts. He hits the button for the top floor and silently pulls me close to his side. The top floor. *Oh God, surely he hasn't?* I get my answer when the doors open and he leads me along to the end of the corridor, to the door where I left him just a few weeks ago. My head is spinning. This is really happening.

"Rob, please do not tell me you've booked the honeymoon suite."

With his arm around my shoulders, he grins down at me and wiggles his eyebrows. "They had a cancellation, and I thought we should come back and finish the job."

Dammit. He has no business being this romantic. "You are such an idiot. That must have cost a fortune."

"You're worth it," he says softly, tapping his keycard and opening the door for me. "After you, darling."

It's literally the same room, and a flood of excitement hits me when I see the bedroom through the open sliding doors. I'd forgotten how massive it is. He places his bag in the wardrobe as I wander around the suite, taking it all in. The heavy curtain fabric, the paintings on the walls, the vase of fresh flowers on the side table in the lounge area.

I'm stalling. I don't know what to do with myself. I can't even look at him. We both know why we're here but I have no idea what to say or how to get things started. This is too much, it's beginning to feel like a terrible idea.

Men pay for hotel rooms all the time but those are cheap, basic rooms and I can't think about the cost for long or I start feeling that I'm as cheap as they are. Nobody has ever spent money like this on me, or taken the time to do something so thoughtful. I don't belong here.

"Champagne for my wife?" Rob asks from behind me, and I find him standing with two glasses and a perfectly chilled bottle. I nod and take off my jacket, suddenly too hot.

"Is that the game you want to play?" I frown. "I'm your wife and you're my husband?"

"I don't hate the idea," he smirks, popping the cork. "It's a pretty hot fantasy, don't you think?"

I can't say I've ever thought about it. "If I had a husband, he'd probably be sleeping with someone else. Or I'd be shagging the pool boy."

Rob pours two glasses and stalks across the room to hand me mine. The room doesn't feel so big at all now, and when he holds my gaze and clinks our glasses, time stands still. I can't read him when he's like this. I much prefer him when he's being a dick to me. I snap out of my trance and take a big drink, the bubbles filling the back of my mouth so quickly it makes me splutter.

"So…" I whisper, staring at the floor when I've regained my composure. The silence between us is making my skin itch.

"So?"

"What do we do now?"

"What do you want to do?" He takes a seat in one of the armchairs, and leans back with his legs spread wide. I want to climb him. "This is your one night with my dick, Hattie. You'd better make the most of it."

Ah, there's the Rob I know.

"God, your ego really is through the roof, isn't it?" I shake my head and laugh, perching my bottom on the arm of the sofa opposite.

"Come and sit here," he says, patting his thigh. Half of me is screaming to run for it, to call a taxi, to never, ever give in to his demands.

The other half wins. I do as I'm told, but I'm awkward about it, sitting too close to his knee and throwing myself off balance when I cross one of my legs over the other. He grabs me around the waist and hoists me further up until I'm fully in his lap. I glance around the room, desperately hoping for something to focus on that isn't the heat rising from his body and threatening to scorching mine.

"Hattie," he says, reaching for my face and turning it towards him.

"Hmm?"

"You're so tense. What's going on?"

"Yeah, sorry." I swallow down the rest of my champagne. "I think I've just built it up in my head."

"Ah," he grins while his thumb caresses my jaw gently back and forth. "So you admit you've thought about this before?"

The smug prick. "Oh, fuck off."

"Hey, I'm flattered. Does it help to know I have too?"

"Of course you have. You're incapable of seeing women as anything other than sexual objects."

"Don't be rude, that's not true at all." His thumb inches upwards, to sweep over my bottom lip, pulling it out from where I've trapped it between my teeth.

"Why don't we start with a kiss?" he whispers, bringing his mouth closer. His breath mingles with mine and it scares the shit out of me. My shoulders tense and I pull away, though his arm around my waist still grips me tight.

"I don't kiss."

He cocks his head to one side, his eyebrows knitting together. "Why not?"

"It's just too personal. I don't like it."

For some reason he finds that hilarious and his laugh stings. "So you'll put a dick in your mouth but not a tongue?"

"Don't mock me." I uncross my legs and try to stand, but he pulls me back to his lap, where there is no mistaking how turned on he is, even if he's not getting what he wants from me.

The feel of his erection pressed into the back of my thigh has heat racing up my spine, heating the back of my neck. I set my glass on the table and scoop my hair up for some relief. I roll my earring between my fingers, a tic I have when I'm unsure what to do with my hands. I'm aching to touch him, but this is all a bit too slow. I'm used to guys who just want to get straight to the good stuff, why is he wasting so much time?

"Do you know you play with your earring when you're horny?"

"I do not," I protest, dropping my hands to my lap.

"You do so."

"I'm not horny, I'm nervous." *Well, I've fucked it now.* As if I've gone and confessed to Rob Lothario Morgan that I'm nervous to have sex with him.

"Honey, I've watched you do it for months. You do it when you're talking to Kara about her sexy books. You did it the entire time we watched that Chris Evans film Megan picked out on her birthday. You do it when you're arguing with me. So I don't believe you for one second if you try to say you're not turned on right now."

He must feel the way my core tightens at his words because he keeps going, his voice dancing millimetres from my ear. "I know you've thought about this. Us. Late at night with your hand in between your legs, all wet for me."

Jesus, this man and his dirty talk. I can't bear it. Just shut up and do something. Anything. I'm actually trembling with nerves, and he notices. One hand settles on top of mine and strokes the shakes away.

"Hattie," he says, sitting upright, his voice all serious. "Do you want me to take you home?"

"No, fuck no. Absolutely not." *Hattie is my name, mixed signals are my game.*

"OK," he laughs, relieved. "So tell me what you need."

I need to get out of my idiot brain. I need to just fuck all of this stress away, and I need for my hands to work, to take his clothes off and get this show on the road. And I need to be honest with him, which I hate most of all.

"I'm really sorry, Rob. For all my bravado, I actually just feel a bit awkward and stressed out, but there's no real reason why."

"OK, honey." He presses a kiss to my shoulder and lifts me up to my feet before standing himself. "Let me help you unwind."

Chapter 25
Rob

THIS IS A DISASTER. She's built it up as much as I have. We agreed to one night after months of tension where we dropped hints, teased each other, and set high expectations of what we'd get from a night in bed together. Now it's finally here, I want to take my time, but her nerves are sending mine through the roof.

To be honest, I was hoping we'd close the door behind us and she'd go into full horny Hattie mode and get my dick out before we'd even taken our shoes off. Now it turns out she won't even kiss me, and she's freaking out when I touch her. I don't know how to handle this, and the only thing I can think of is to get back to basics. She's having a stressful time at work, I've destroyed my brain anticipating this all week, we need a moment to pause and clear the day away.

With her hand in mine, I lead her through to the bathroom and turn on the shower. It's a huge open one behind a glass panel with two separate shower heads. A shower made for lovers. It is the honeymoon suite, after all. I get a flash vision of all the people who must have fucked in here, and it makes my dick twitch.

"What are you doing?" Hattie asks.

"Let's take a shower."

"Together?"

"Yep." I begin to unbutton my shirt and try not to smile too much at the look on her face as she watches me slowly reveal more skin.

"Come on then," she says, forcing herself to sound bored. "Let's see what all the fuss is about."

"You've seen my dick before," I let it fall to the floor and move onto my jeans, loosening my belt buckle and undoing my zipper. "Don't tell me you haven't studied that photo in great detail."

Her cheeks redden. "Yeah, but I haven't seen you in the flesh, so to speak."

My eyes never leave her face as I push my jeans and my boxers down together, and pull my socks off as I step out of everything. Standing with my hands on my hips, my cock hangs thick and heavy. I kept my promise when I told her I wouldn't come until tonight, and the evidence is right there, absolutely raring to go.

"Oh for fuck's sake," Hattie groans, tipping her head back to stare at the ceiling. "Well, that explains the ego."

She needs this. She needs me to be vulnerable first, and boy do I feel it standing here in front of her, ready for her appraisal. I wait for her to make a move, but she's rooted to the spot while her eyes roam all over me. The room fills with steam, and still she doesn't move.

Was this a bad idea? Is it too much pressure on us both? Something inside me rips apart and suddenly I can't bear it any more. She has all the power, and I half expect her to laugh, or leave, or give me hell about something. The thought that she might change her mind about all of this is terrifying. I need her naked, now, more than anything in my life.

"Can I undress you?" I ask, taking two cautious steps towards where she's backed herself up against the sink counter.

"Yes, please," she whispers and closes her eyes, standing straight, so close to me.

This high-necked top she's wearing is gorgeous, fitted tight to her curves, and I've wanted to get her out of it since the moment she got into my car. I slip my hands into the waistband of her skirt to tug it up but it's stuck on something. I pull harder and she smirks.

"Are you pranking me? Why isn't this coming off?"

"It's a bodysuit, you idiot."

"Get it off."

"I am!" she laughs, reaching down inside the front of her skirt to release the fastening. "Hold on."

When Hattie laughs, when she forgets to hold herself back and really goes for it, it's the purest sound on earth, but I can't think about it for long because soon she's dragging her top up and over her shoulders.

Finding her naked underneath has me grunting like a caveman. When I undo the zip at the back of her skirt and let it slip off her hips, I have even less control of myself. She steps out of it and kicks it to one side, leaving her in a scrap of lacy underwear with double straps I immediately wrap around my fingers.

"I love this," I snap the straps on one side against her skin and she gasps. "You and I are gonna have a lot of fun tonight."

Pushing my fingers through her hair, I tug her head back to pepper her face with soft kisses. She's putty in my hands when I cup her ribcage, my thumbs stroking up and down her sides, sweeping over the curve of her perfect tits. My mouth is so close to hers, and I dart my tongue out to taste the corner of her lips.

"I told you, don't kiss me," she says firmly, twisting her head away from me. I move my mouth to her neck and kiss her there instead, caressing her throat with my tongue.

"Please?" I push her hair back from her forehead and look her right in the eyes, desperately hoping she'll give in to me. How can she be standing here almost naked with me and not want to kiss? It's all I've thought about for months. I want to feel her tongue in my mouth so much it hurts. "Let me show you what you're missing."

"Rob, I mean it. You can kiss anywhere but my mouth. Don't push it." She covers her lips with her hand and I push my luck and plant a quick kiss on the back of it instead.

"You're the boss." I drop to my knees, dragging her underwear down with me. I don't need to be told twice, and frankly I'm amazed this wasn't the first thing I did when I got her alone tonight. "You know I haven't been able to stop thinking about kneeling in front of you since we were last here?"

My eyes on her face, I run my knuckles up the inside of her leg, teasing slowly towards her apex until she sways backwards. She catches herself on the edge of the counter, and her thighs part slightly, exposing her, all pink and slick beneath that dark strip of hair. It's the best fucking view. I'm starving for her, but I plan on taking my time. Every part of me wants to take her right here, but getting Hattie to beg for me has become my biggest fantasy. I'm not blowing this.

"Soon, wife." I know I'm playing a dangerous game, pushing her buttons like this. I press a kiss just below her belly button and rise, leading her into the water.

Underneath the spray, she turns away from me, and I swear she trembles slightly. She closes her eyes, letting the water rain down over her face, and in this moment she looks so vulnerable, so unlike any of the versions of herself she's shown me so far.

Although I'm hard as hell, I realise that even if we left here without doing a single sexual thing that would be enough for me. I thought I'd bring her back to this room to finish what we started, and spend the night getting her off, but right now all I want to do is hold her.

So that's what I do.

Stepping into the space behind her, I wrap my arms around where she has hers held in front of her chest, and pull her back against my body. My chin falls to her shoulder and her head tilts to rest softly against mine. Water rains down from above, the high pressure easing some tension I hadn't noticed I've been carrying in my shoulders. My arms rise and fall with the cycle of her breath. I watch the water cascading over her tits, but apart from that, I don't move. Being this close to her, this still, is a peace I haven't felt in a long time, maybe ever.

"This is so nice," I moan, angling my neck to get the pressure on a sore spot. "Just this. I swear, we don't have to do anything."

"I'm OK." Hattie inhales sharply, spins in my arms, and reaches down to grip my shaft in her warm, wet hand. "I'm ready."

Having her hand wrapped around me, after months of dreaming about it, gets me even harder. As does the way she's staring at it, biting down on her lip while her slim fingers tease me with slow strokes.

Much to my dick's dismay, I slide her hand away and settle it on my chest, along with her other one. "You're not in charge tonight. Your job is to relax, and let me take care of you."

I reach behind her for the shower gel, dripping something woody and exotic into my hand then lathering it between my palms. The best thing about fancy hotels is their abundance of luxury toiletries, and I plan to use plenty to help her unwind.

Hattie drops her forehead to my chest. I hook her hair out of the way with my thumb, sending a shiver down her spine when it sweeps along the nape of her neck.

I take my time lathering her up, and with every minute that passes she softens more. She doesn't speak, barely looks at me, but that's OK. I want her to get lost in the feeling of my worship. I close my eyes and get lost in her too, letting my hands roam, but never too close to where I'm most desperate for her. My touches vary between firm and featherlight, teasing their way over the toned muscles of her back, down over her hip bones and back up to squeeze that perfect ass.

Soon she's reaching for me again but I turn her away and press her face first against the wall. I pin her wrists at the base of her spine and Hattie tilts her hips, pushing back, rubbing harder against me. I nearly come right then from the friction between us, this needy woman searching for release. I drive my hips forward, pressing even more of her body into the tile.

"Does that feel good? The cold against your nipples?" I take her earlobe between my teeth.

"Yes," she hisses and I fist her hair, pulling her head to arch her back.

"Rub them against the wall."

She whimpers at the sensation, rolling her slick body between me and the tile, and I groan, pocketing this memory for later.

"Please, Rob," she chokes out.

"Please what, angel?"

"Please fuck me."

Those three little words, I've been dying to hear them, but I never thought they'd make my head spin quite like they do. It takes every ounce of strength to pull away but I have to. I'm not fucking her here. I need her in that bed, laid out for me to explore, to feast on, but I'm only a man, and if she says it again I won't be able to resist a second time.

I leave her there, gasping, shaking, holding onto the wall, and grab the detachable showerhead so I can rinse us off.

"Turn around."

Hattie is always beautiful, but right now, head tipped back, chest heaving as rivulets trickle all over her, she's a fucking bombshell. Rinsing off her legs, I'm tempted to angle the showerhead and make her come right here in front of me, but that's not in the plan. I need to be inside her the first time I make her come. The orgasm I owe her belongs to my dick.

I turn off the water and step out to grab towels, quickly wrapping one around my waist then the other around her shoulders.

"I can dry myself," she says, shoving me away, but I grip both sides and yank her in close. Fighting with Hattie gets my blood pumping like nothing else, but I need to rein it in unless I want another one of her specialty kicks in the dick.

"Let me." I pull her out of the shower and kiss her neck softly, rubbing the towel over her back and up and down her arms. I stand behind her to dry her hair, then spin her and drop to my knees again. Lifting one leg, I rest her foot on my thigh, and only when I'm satisfied that she's thoroughly dry do I lead her through to the bedroom.

"Lie down. On your front."

She does as she's told, scooping her hair to one side and settling into position with her head resting on her palms. On the bedside table is a bottle of oil in the same scent as the shower gel, and I warm it in my palms before spreading it over her back and her shoulders, sweeping down over the slope of her gorgeous backside, on and on until I reach her ankles.

I could spend hours running my hands up and down her shapely calves, the firm muscles of her thighs. Could get high on the way her body reacts when my fingers graze the softer skin on the inside of them, the quiet moans she makes when my touch grows firmer. Climbing onto the bed, I straddle her and force myself to focus my attention on her back, and not the incredible view of my erection resting between her cheeks.

Her shoulders are tight, full of knots and I take my time to warm her up with more oil, rolling them out with the pad of my thumb. It shouldn't come as a surprise that Hattie is full of knots. I don't think

I've seen her relaxed in the entire time I've known her, and I know she doesn't take proper care of herself. Answering emails at all hours, not eating properly, running her angry little mouth at me every chance she gets. They're hardly the actions of a woman at peace, and that's not the life I want for her.

I'll do whatever I can to help her unwind tonight, and make it my mission to ensure she never gets this wound up again.

Sifting my fingers through the hair at the nape of her neck, I roll her head gently from side to side, but a small squeak makes me pause.

"Are you crying?"

"No," she sniffs, then sniffs again. The little shudder of her shoulders says otherwise.

"Liar. You want me to stop?"

"No."

"OK, well, I'm going to." I lay down next to her, brush her hair away from her face, and rub her shoulder. "What's up, sweetheart?"

"I don't know. Honestly, I don't know. This is really nice, I'm not upset, you're just making feelings come out of my face."

"Have you never had a massage before?"

"Of course I have, but not from a gorgeous guy while his dick is pressing against me."

"So you think I'm gorgeous," I tap the end of her nose with one finger. I want to kiss her, but I know she won't let me. "I knew it."

"You are insufferable." She rolls her eyes and lifts a little, wiping her face with the back of her hand. "Can we please have sex now? I'm honestly fine."

"You feel ready?"

"Yes, I promise."

"Roll onto your back."

Chapter 26
Rob

My restraint is hanging on by a thread when she rolls over, exposing more of her beautiful body to me. The months since I met Hattie have been the longest foreplay of my life, but I can hang on a little longer.

Gripping her ankles, I tug her closer to the foot of the bed, positioning her the same way I had her last time. The way I've dreamed of every night since. I kiss my way up the inside of her thigh until my mouth hovers at the crease of her hip.

"If that phone rings, I'm throwing it out the window, do you understand me?" Her nose wrinkles, and she bites back a smile and nods. *So fucking cute.* "Good, you're all mine."

My first lick is long and slow, and I savour the taste of her arousal, the way her fingers rake through my hair. She moans softly, her back arching away from the bed, and I take my time exploring with my tongue, learning all the ways that I can make her feel good.

Hattie hitches a knee higher up the bed and lets it fall to the side, opening herself more to me. There's nothing hotter than when a woman is unashamed about her desires, her need for pleasure. Hooking her other leg over my shoulder, I splay one palm across her stomach and hold her steady while I work her clit with the flat of my tongue.

I'm in no rush, but I can tell she's already close, her breath shaky, eyes squeezed shut, the muscles of her stomach contracting and releasing under my hand. I slide a finger inside her, then another, crooking them upwards, strokes matching the rhythm of my tongue.

Her thighs clamp around my head then, hips riding against my face, her moans kicking up a gear. I tear my mouth away just before she crashes over the edge, denying her the orgasm I want to give her so much. Her moans of frustration make me harder than ever.

"What the fuck," she growls, throwing her head back against the bed. "I thought you were the kind of man who prides himself on making women come? Not giving up."

"Who said I'm giving up? We're just getting started." I suck her clit hard between my lips, my tongue striking firmly across that tender bundle of nerves that makes her arch up from the bed. *Fuck,* I love seeing her possessed like this, but I stop again.

"*Ahh!* So like a man to get a woman close and then switch things up."

"Oh honey, I can tell you're close. You're out of your mind if you think I'm going to let you come yet. I'm in no hurry, beautiful. I know once you come, you'll start freaking out. We're doing things my way, nice and slow." One arm still wrapped around her, I keep her pinned and bring my fingers up to tease her with lazy strokes that drag up and over her clit then back down again, soaking her more. "I want to hear you beg more. Want you aching for me."

"Please, Rob, just fuck me already." She's genuinely feral, squirming underneath my hold.

"I can't, baby."

"Why not?"

"You've got me so worked up, feel what you're doing to me." I stand up, angle my cock against her and push up hard, slipping easily against her wetness. "I won't last five seconds inside you."

She tries to squeeze her legs around me, jerking harder against my grip. "Please, I can't take this any more."

I don't know how much more I can take either. Bending over, I suck one perfect nipple into my mouth, biting a little just because I can. "Give me a second."

Our time together this evening has been achingly slow, but I still forgot to move condoms closer to the bed before coming in here. I hop up and grab one from my bag, tossing the wrapper and rolling it on as I stalk my way back to the bed where she's laid out for me in the middle of that huge mattress.

Hattie props herself up on her elbows, eyes wide as she checks me out. I tower over her, committing all of her to memory.

"Don't look at me like that," she says.

"Like what?"

"Like you've won."

"Of course I've won, you're a fucking prize. Look at you, so hot." I kneel between her thighs, nudging them apart. My fingers trace the soft crease where her leg meets her hip. "So beautiful."

She throws an arm over her face, unable to take the compliment. I pull it gently down, leaning over so she can't look away. "I don't think you've been told enough just how beautiful you are, Hattie."

I swipe my thumb between her legs, pausing to circle her clit, and she groans under the teasing pressure. With my other hand I cup her jaw, and make her watch me lick my thumb clean.

"So delicious. And all for me." I link my fingers through hers and press her hands above her head. "Are you ready?"

"Yes," she says on a shaky exhale. If I can't kiss her mouth, I'll settle for the inside of her wrist, the soft, pure skin where I can feel her pulse fluttering against my lip. My dick notches against her instinctively, and this is the point where I lose it. I can't hold on anymore, can't resist pushing deep into her in one swift thrust.

Hattie moans against my throat, tits pressing up against me. I give her a second to adjust to me before rolling my hips. She tugs one hand free, snakes it in between us, but I pull it away.

"Rob, please," she whimpers. "I need to come."

"Am I not doing what you like?"

"Oh poor baby egomaniac," she laughs on an exhale. "You're doing fine, but I can't come from only penetration, I need more."

"You said I owed you an orgasm, and I promised I'd deliver. What's your favourite way to get there?"

Her brow furrows while she thinks about it, and it makes me wonder if nobody has ever asked her, if nobody has ever put her first.

"This is good," she pants. "I want to come with you inside me, I just need more."

I reach for a pillow to tuck underneath her and sit up on my knees. With my hands on her hips I keep her pulled flush to me, and push her legs out wide. Seeing her like this, spread out with my cock buried inside her, I don't know how I haven't come already.

My brain needs a second to stop short-circuiting, but my hands take on a life of their own, stroking their way around her body, worshipping the way goddesses should be worshipped. It softens her, my touch, I see it happen right in front of me. Her anger dissipates, her body sinking into that heavenly state of bliss. Her eyes open slowly, we take a deep breath together and something passes between us, but like always with Hattie, these moments don't last long.

"Well, are you making me come or not?" she says, summoning her insolence and reminding me why we're here in the first place.

"Play with your nipples for me. I want to see."

I suck my fingers, wetting them with my tongue and reach down to play with her clit, stroking, rolling, pressing gently to test what she likes. Finding my rhythm, I move at a teasing pace and watch her writhe as she squeezes her tits, head rolled to one side as she bites that perfect pouty lip that has taunted me for months.

Hattie rolls her hips, sliding herself up and down my shaft while I rub harder, watching the pink flush that creeps up her neck. I let her fuck me like that, so strong, so needy, until I can't take it any more.

Throwing her left leg over my shoulder for leverage, I thrust hard, slow at first then pick up the pace until I'm giving her everything I've got, my hips pistoning against her.

White heat blooms from the base of my spine, my balls tighten, but I hold back and wait for her to get there with me. Hattie slams a hand over her mouth and I yank it away.

"Don't be quiet baby, let me hear you."

Her pussy is my entire world right now, clenching around me as I fuck harder, harder, harder.

"*Fuck*, Rob, yes. More," she moans.

The sound of my name on her lips as she comes is what pushes me over the edge. My vision turns to stars when I slam into her and topple forward, catching myself with my hands either side of her face. I thrust a little deeper, a groan surging from deep within me as I come, and come, and all I can see is the pleasure on her face as her orgasm races through her. A face I'll never be able to get out of my head.

Chapter 27
Rob

HATTIE'S HAIR IS STUCK to her face, a light sheen of sweat coats her skin, as I balance myself above her. I never want to move from this spot.

"You're..." she gasps, "the biggest... idiot... in the world."

"What have I done now?"

"We could have done this months ago."

"Ah, but doesn't the anticipation make it so much sweeter?" I lick her shoulder up to her neck, and her skin tastes incredible, hot and salty.

"Please, I have not been anticipating this," she laughs, her belly rumbling against mine.

"Always lying to me." I drop to one elbow and pinch her nipple playfully. "You've been a frothing, squirrelly mess waiting to have me inside you."

"You're thinking of someone else," she says, pushing me onto my back. I think she's about to straddle me, but she surprises me by climbing out of bed.

"Where are you going?"

"Home."

What the fuck? No.

"You're not serious." I jump up too, dashing to the bathroom to deal with the condom.

"You know my rules," she calls through. "I never sleep with the same guy twice. I'm not changing the habit of a lifetime just for you."

"Not even in the same night?"

"Nope."

We'll see about that.

I fill a glass of water, down it, and fill it again. "You've been depriving yourself of so much pleasure."

Walking back through, I find Hattie rummaging in my overnight bag. I lean against the doorframe, watching as she grabs a plain white t-shirt and pulls it over her head. I'm half-hard at the sight of it, fabric skimming the top of her thighs but knowing she's naked underneath. That right there is the filthiest thing a woman can do.

"I'm borrowing this," she says, sauntering over to take the glass. I circle her wrist and she tugs it away, but my grip is firm. She tries again then relents, draining the glass with my hand still wrapped around her, pulse fluttering away beneath my fingertips. Her slender throat bobs and it makes me want to see what it looks like with my dick in it. When she finishes I set the glass down on the bedside table, cup her elbow and tug her closer.

"I booked us a late checkout. We aren't done."

"Oh, but we are." The beautiful eyes staring up at me don't match the tone in her words. "The last thing I'm going to do is lie here all night and let you steal orgasms from me."

"*Steal?* Don't take the piss, you can't tell me you weren't one hundred percent into that." I nod back at the bed and when she smirks, I know I've got her. "I've barely started. There's no way I'm letting you leave our one night together early."

I walk us backwards until I hit the edge of the bed and sit down. With one fingertip, I lift the hem of her t-shirt, stopping just above her belly-button. Goosebumps follow my tracks, and when I kiss her there she leans into it. Nudging my knee between her legs, I pull her down sharply until she straddles my thigh. My hand keeps moving upwards, her t-shirt slowly lifting higher, bunching against my wrist until I push my hand through the collar and wrap my hand gently around her throat.

Hattie's head tips back, eyes fluttering closed, mouth parting on a moan.

This.

This is the vision I'll keep with me forever. The full curve of her tits peeking out from where I've lifted her top, pale flesh begging for my tongue. The line that dips down the centre of her stomach to where her hips are rolling against me, already desperately seeking relief. Her hands grip my shoulders and I guide her in close so I can whisper against her mouth.

"If I had my way, you'd be full of my dick this entire weekend." My other hand finds its home on her hip, gripping her there, moving with her as she rubs back and forth against me. "You've only come once. It's not nearly enough. I need more."

"I faked it."

"Such a pretty little liar," I say, licking her throat. "Keep grinding."

"I hate you," she moans and bucks faster.

"I hate you too, sweetheart."

After our second round it's late, I'm starving, and Hattie doesn't take much convincing when I suggest we order burgers from room service. I throw on a robe to collect them at the door and set everything up in the lounge.

"Dinner is served, my darling," I call through, and she appears a second later in a robe of her own. A robe I immediately want to get my hands inside.

Her hair is wild, the skin around her neck and her chest red from my kisses, and I add that image to my memory too. She picks up a plate and settles at one end of the sofa, but stretches her legs out until her feet are in my lap. Hattie so rarely makes the first move, but I don't draw attention to it in case she changes her mind.

"Do you want to watch something?" I ask.

"Sure."

"Anything in particular?"

"I don't mind. I mainly watch rom-coms with Megan and try not to point out how ridiculous they are." Hattie takes a big bite of her cheeseburger and I'd be offended by her satisfied moan if I hadn't already made her make that same noise with my tongue.

"I had you down as more of a true crime fan."

She points a fry in my direction. "You thought I'd enjoy watching shows about women getting chopped into pieces then glorifying the men who've murdered them?"

"Well, not when you put it like that," I laugh, slightly horrified at the reality check.

"What do you watch?"

"Not a lot. My mum is a big fan of Antiques Roadshow though, I sometimes watch it with her."

She doesn't reply, and I turn to find her staring at me, her head cocked slightly to one side. That cute little wrinkle appears between her eyebrows and I want to reach over and smooth it out with my thumb.

"You're a real mystery, you know that?" she says.

I shrug and leave the remote for now, happy to just be here with her like this.

"Where did you learn to give massages like that?" she asks, finishing her burger and wiping her hands on a napkin.

"I studied physiotherapy for a while. It helps a lot of our patients, so I wanted a better understanding of how I could help with more of their issues. Massage therapy was a part of the training. Speaking of which, you've got some serious knots in your shoulders."

"Mmm, I know," she says, swallowing. "I've been pushing it hard at the gym lately and not allowing enough time to recover."

I sense a hint of something there. "Any particular reason?"

"There's a lot going on at work. Boxing is a good way to deal with the stress of it all. That and orgasms," she says with a smile.

"Well, I'm glad to be of service on that front."

Truth is, I can't get enough of her. I'm not ready to go again, but after clearing away our plates and washing my hands, I'm very happy to return to the sofa and lift her into my lap. She doesn't resist, and I sit back and let her get comfy, straddling me, her warm, smooth skin on mine.

"Tell me about a time you were happy," she says, her tone so calm, peaceful. To my shock, she leans in and settles her head on my shoulder, one arm sneaking into my robe to wrap around my back. I close my eyes, settle my head back against the sofa cushions, and she wiggles in closer.

Her question brings to mind a day from my childhood. The summer Luke, Heather, and I were old enough to disappear for the day without raising alarm bells. Beyond Luke's granny's meadow was a hayfield, and our quest was clear. Stacked like giant Lego bricks, we knew we needed to build a house with the freshly baled harvest.

I stroke through her hair, down her back, and tell her everything. The details are fresh; the heat, the scent of summer, the scratches that covered my arms and legs the next day.

Our house had bedrooms, a kitchen, an enormous living room with, somehow, its very own window. We'd run home for blankets to use as a roof, and nabbed Granny Annie's best cushions to sit on. Heather had even drawn pictures to tuck into the twine, turning our bare walls into a gallery of sorts.

I tell her how the hay house had a second story, with a lookout tower, and underneath it a space for a bathroom, a real feat of engineering. Though we all agreed peeing in the house was strictly forbidden, we'd stick to the hedgerow instead.

In my memory, it was a palace. We'd grafted through lunch and dinner, existing on the boundless energy and determination of youth. By dusk, we were all set to camp out in our new home, but the farmer had other plans. Riding in on his quad bike, we were ordered to put it all back in piles of eight and clear the field.

We never played in that field again. At least, I never did. And though things didn't go our way that night, I'll never forget how good it felt to build something that was just ours.

Hattie's eyes are closed, the only sound is her gentle breathing and the sweep of my fingers through her hair. It's dark outside, and with only a side lamp on, I've lost all sense of time in our cosy cocoon. I'm content though, here with my hand underneath her robe, stroking lazy circles over her hip.

If she asked me the same question on my deathbed, about a time I was happy, I think this is the moment I'd come back to. I want to ask about her memories, but a small part of me is terrified she wouldn't hold this, *us*, in such high regard. Will she even remember it, the day she fell asleep in my arms?

"Mmm, you're so soft," I whisper. There is so much I want to say to her, but it never seems to be the right time.

"That doesn't sound like a compliment," she murmurs against my chest, and I try not to shake her while a laugh rumbles out of me.

"Oh, it is. I just thought you'd be firm everywhere."

"Well, I'm super relaxed right now. I'm firm when I tense up." I can't tell you what it does to my ego to know I'm the one who got her feeling this way. My well fucked, well fed girl.

"Tense up here," I open her robe, spread my palm across her stomach and when she does, I move to the smooth insides of her thigh. "Now here."

I need more of her. All of her. When my hand slips up between her legs, I find her soaked again. My fingers slide underneath her, gripping her ass, taking her with me as I stand to carry her back to bed.

"Now here."

Chapter 28
Hattie

He wasn't lying. Rob Incredible Penis Morgan is the complete opposite of a shit lay.

I have no idea what time it is when I wake up, heavy curtains shielding us from the outside world. All I know is I'm naked, he's still asleep, and we're far too close to each other in a bed this enormous. I look down to find his warm hand against the curve of my stomach, his arm fitting snugly around mine. I'm not a hugger, and there's no explanation for how good it feels, but damn if I didn't sleep long and well.

The empty champagne bottle on my nightstand triggers a memory of him pouring it down my spine, lapping up the bubbles before they could pop, and more visions come with it. Rob washing me in the shower, his big hands taking their time to massage every inch of me, the look on his face when he filled me up for the first time.

Behind me Rob stirs softly in his sleep, and I stay deathly still, not ready to wake him and face the reality of what we've done. This feels so warm and nice, but it's also something else. Claustrophobic.

"Stop thinking so loudly," he says, pulling me closer. His arm wraps around my chest, his hand finding a home on my shoulder.

I want to escape, but all I can do is soften into his hold. "See, you're already obsessed with me. This is why I don't do sleepovers."

"I'm obsessed with this," he cups me between the legs and my head tilts back against his shoulder instinctively. He nuzzles into my neck, the scruff of his stubble dragging back and forth sending sparks zipping through me.

Oh God no, please don't want this.

"Coffee?" he mumbles somewhere beneath my earlobe.

"Yes, please."

He climbs over me, pressing a kiss to my cheek as he goes, and walks through to the lounge naked and brazen. Fuck, he's gorgeous. Those wide shoulders, every muscle working exactly as it should do. I roll onto my back and cover my face with a pillow.

I want to scream into it, but I also don't want to appear any more insane than I'm sure I already do. Last night was not normal. I don't recognise the woman who cried when he touched her, who pleaded with him to make her come, who curled up in his arms afterwards.

Rob hums his way around the kitchenette so I sneak into the bathroom, grabbing my phone from my bag on the way.

```
Me: I fucked up
Kara: what's wrong?
Kara: where are you? I'm about to leave
yours, shall I come and get you?
Me: no need, I'm safe
Kara: what's happened?
Me: Rob happened
Kara: OH. MY. GOD.
Megan: OHMYGOD
Me: my words exactly
Megan: So that's where you were all night!
Me: I am ruined
```

Me: RUINED

Me: He'll drive me home. The bastard.

I freshen up, throw on the fluffy hotel robe I wore last night, and tie the belt tight, covering as much of myself as possible. I don't know what to do. If I shower, he'll join me. If I get back in that bed, he'll have me naked again before I can blink. The thought keeps me frozen. I can't stand the idea, and I've also never wanted anything so much in my life. I need to get out of here, fast.

In the lounge I attempt to get my things together, but I don't make it far before he's standing in front of me, that wall of fucking manliness.

"So, darling wife," he says, turning the mug he's holding so the handle faces towards me. "Did I live up to your expectations?"

"Get over yourself Rob. It was a one night stand, I'm not here to stroke your ego."

"I've got something you could stroke instead," he laughs, and because I am my own worst enemy I palm his half-hard cock and step closer. It swells beneath my fingertips and I run them up and down, my eyes on his as I lift my cup, take that perfect first sip and let out an obnoxious moan.

"I've ordered breakfast in bed for us both. I bet…" he trails off, loosening the belt of my robe and dropping to his knees. "I bet I can make you come before it arrives."

I close my eyes, take another sip, and let him win.

"You're welcome," Rob says on the drive home.

"For?"

"The orgasms."

"Whatever. Like I said, I faked it." I gaze out of the window and hide my smile in my palm.

"Oh honey, no." He reaches across the centre console and slides his hand between my thighs, gripping firmly. "You see, I've got a superdick with magical powers and it could feel it. Every flutter, every pull, every tight clench as you came around me. You might want to lie, but me and my dick know the truth." *Fuuuuuck.* I won't even make it home at this rate.

"Superdick, eh?" I yank his hand out, throw it back into his lap like hot garbage and angle my body away from his. "Maybe I'll chop it off and send it to a museum of curiosities."

I wonder what will happen to us now. Will things be awkward at Friday Night Dinners, or will we exchange knowing glances in the company of others? Will he still text me? I don't know why I even care, I've never had a problem with hooking up and drawing a line under it before.

"Hey, we're still friends, right?" Rob says, clearly plagued with similar thoughts.

"If we must," I sigh. "I don't normally see guys I fuck again. So keep it to yourself."

I neglect to mention I've told Kara and Megan. They'd better swear to keep it a secret, I don't need Luke finding out about this and judging me.

Rob drops me off outside my building and I find myself standing in the kitchen wondering what the hell I'm supposed to do now. Megan is nowhere to be seen, I have chores to do, groceries to shop for, work to catch up on, and all I want to do is go to bed and relive last night. And cry.

I never cry. The stupid prick has broken me.

In my room, I change out of last night's clothes and realise I'm still wearing Rob's t-shirt, tucked into my skirt. I shove everything into the washing basket, but then I lose my mind and do the stupidest thing I have ever done.

I pull his t-shirt back out, lift it to my face and inhale.

The scent of him, his skin, his hair, brings it all rushing back. Everything inside me tightens, an unbearable ache from the memory of last night, and what I hate to admit is the best sex I've ever had.

Chapter 29
Hattie

Desperate for sugar and carbs, I turn down the bakery aisle and spot someone I recognise.

Marcus, I think his name was. Michael? We met in a bar and went back to his hotel room not long afterwards. He was a lot of fun, and we left amicably, he didn't pester me for more or act like I'd broken his heart. Those are the best kind of hookups. I didn't think he was from around here, but maybe I was mistaken?

I walk towards where he's choosing a loaf of bread but I'm so busy checking him out I don't notice the woman standing on the other side of him. It's only when he steps back and turns to face me that I see her. The woman holding his hand. The woman with her other hand on a pram.

His eyes meet mine and I cover my mouth so I don't throw up right in front of the crumpets. It's too late to turn, he's seen me now, and his face goes as white as mine feels when he realises who I am. I need to keep walking but between them, the pram, and the trolley, they're taking up most of the aisle. I just have to stand here awkwardly and wait for them to move. My gaze drops to the loaf of bread in his hand and there it is. A shiny band on his finger.

You arsehole.

He has a wife and a baby. A little baby too. A baby definitely too little to have not yet been conceived around the time he was balls deep inside me. My heart starts racing as his beautiful wife apologises for getting in my way.

You utter shit.

"No problem. What a gorgeous baby," I say, peering into the pram where I see their little girl. There's no mistaking that since she's dressed head to toe in pink with one of those bow bands stretched around her soft, fair hair.

"Thank you so much," his wife says.

"How old is she?"

"Twenty weeks today," she beams, as if I'm supposed to know off the top of my head what that means. I do the maths.

"So what's that, about 4 months?"

"Yeah, she's growing so fast. It feels like she was just born yesterday."

Bastard.

I look up at him and his eyes plead with mine. A subtle shake of the head says *'please don't'*. He knows I could ruin his life, right here in the middle of Tesco on a Saturday afternoon.

That's not my style though, and why would I even bother? I'm not the winner, there's no upper hand here. She's the wronged woman, even if she has no idea. And I'm the woman who slept with her husband while she carried his child. Who benefits from a confession or confrontation?

No, the only winner is the man who gets to fuck around and get away with it. These men who have beautiful wives and perfect babies, and, still not satisfied, they make a whore out of me with their secrets and lies. I would never, *ever*, knowingly sleep with a married man, and if I knew they were expecting a baby I'd punch them so hard in the dick they'd never make another kid again. I hate him, and now I hate myself.

"Well congratulations, she's an angel."

"What a nice lady," I hear her say as I leave them. I'm going to be sick. I slept with a pregnant woman's husband and I had no idea. And he lives here, so I'll probably see them everywhere I go now. I drop my basket at the end of the aisle and walk out, blinking back tears.

The sofa is my saviour. When Megan gets home that night, Kara is with her, and they find me curled up under a blanket on my fifth episode of The Repair Shop. At least I can pretend I'm crying about some old man being reunited with his childhood train set and not the truth, which I can barely admit to myself, let alone anyone else. They drop their bags in the hallway and rush in to see me.

"Right, pause that and tell us everything," Megan says. I do as I'm told and she gets under the covers at the other end of the sofa, while Kara scoots in beside me. I want to explain, but when I open my mouth to speak, only a sob comes out.

"Oh honey, what's wrong?" Kara asks, putting her arm around me. "Did he hurt you? I swear if he hurt you I'll kill him."

I shake my head and sniff uncontrollably. Megan fetches a box of tissues.

"What happened? Why are you so sad?"

"Remember how we almost hooked up the night of your wedding?" I nod towards Kara.

"*What?*" she shrieks. Oops. I'd forgotten she was absent for that update. Megan presses her fingertips to her lips, she'd clearly forgotten too.

"Um, yeah, you know how you gave me your key to the honeymoon suite?"

"Yes?" she says, eyes wide, her fingers digging into my forearm.

"I don't think you realised, but Luke had given his key to Rob. So he turned up shortly after me, and I was in a shit mood and pretty drunk so I let him make a move, but thankfully Megan called because I had her house keys. I got a cab home and left him there."

"Oh boy. I have a confession to make," she says with a grimace. "We did that on purpose."

"You set us up?" I sit upright and pull my knees to my chest.

"I'm sorry, Luke and I figured it was inevitable and that you might both welcome a little nudge."

I cannot believe what I am hearing. "And you told me off for meddling in your love life?"

It wasn't so long ago Megan and I helped Luke come up with a plan to win Kara over by recreating a fake date from her favourite book, but it was so obvious to us all that she needed a little push, and look where's it's gotten them. Married, and happily so.

"I'm sorry, we were pretty drunk too. It seemed like a good idea. But it sounds like it didn't go anywhere? So what happened last night?"

Oh God, this is so pathetic to explain. I rip the band-aid off and get it out fast. "Last week he sabotaged a date I was on, and so I went to his house and told him he owed me an orgasm."

"*Excuse me?*" Megan gasps.

"Oh Jesus, that's hot," says Kara. "That's proper enemies-to-lovers stuff."

Of course she would view the mess that is my life through the lens of romance novel.

"Shush, you. I was just angry at him, I didn't think anything would happen. But then he agreed, and said he'd arrange a night away for us.

He picked me up last night and drove me back to the hotel so we could *'finish what we started'*. He booked the same room and everything."

"I'm sorry. Are you telling me Rob booked the honeymoon suite for your one night stand?"

I nod. "And it was awful, because I was nervous, but he was so patient and encouraging. He showered with me, and gave me a massage, then, you know." I can't even say it out loud. "And you know me, I don't do sleepovers, so I tried to leave but somehow he mind-tricked me and convinced me to stay. Then this morning he went down on me while I drank my coffee. So, now I think I'm addicted to his penis, but every time I think about it I want to cry."

"He went down on you while you drank your coffee?" Kara stares at me, mouth wide open.

"Yes," I half sob, half laugh.

"You lucky cow," Megan says.

"Not lucky. Cursed. I think he's ruined me for other men." Genuinely, how am I supposed to get by with some random Ben, Rich, or Matty, knowing that I've had a night like that? It is deeply depressing to know that I could sleep with a thousand more men and none would make me feel as good as he did.

"Do you think I'm a terrible person for sleeping around so much?" I ask, slumping back under my blanket.

"Absolutely not," Megan says. "I wish I had even an ounce of your confidence."

Kara agrees. "I think you're amazing Hattie. I've always loved the way you're so independent and do things your way."

"How long can I keep this up, though, really? You must be sick of my shit."

Kara pulls me into a hug and Megan rubs my back. They attempt to pacify me with words of kindness, but nothing can cut through the murk I've kicked up inside my head.

First David joins my favourite client, and I still haven't managed to figure out how he's casually destroyed the career I've worked so hard for. Now I've bumped into another married man, which takes the number of people's husbands I've been to bed with to two. And that's only the ones I know of. It's a horrible thought, but I know there are probably more, and all because I like a quick round of pass the orgasm?

It's not fair. I bet these men aren't sitting in on a Saturday night feeling shit about themselves, even though they've got way more at stake than I do. This behaviour might have been cute in my twenties, a series of scandalous stories to share in the pub, but I'm getting older. Forty will be here before I know it, and then what?

One day this will all end and I'll be a shrivelled up old shrew with nothing and nobody. That's not the life I want for myself. I want... well, I don't bloody know. How am I supposed to know? What does a good life look like when you're someone who has to do it all on their own?

The only thing that's certain in my life right now is that I want this promotion, and I'm going to work my arse off for it. It's a big step up. Professionally I'm ready, but personally, I think I need to whip things into shape. That means no more distractions, no more energy drains, and absolutely no more thinking about Rob's delicious dick, thoughts of which keep unhelpfully racing through my head. Memories of the weight of it in my hand, of me straddling him, the incredible sensation of feeling so fucking full.

Stop it, brain.

"Are you feeling better?" I ask Megan. "I should have stayed with you, I'm sorry."

"It's over with Max," she says, softly. "Properly over."

Oh, God, I didn't see that coming. I mean, I did, and of course it's over. It was over the moment he left to go back to his wife who he said he was separated from, but it's not Megan's fault she couldn't see through his philandering ways. She always wants to see the best in everyone.

"Babe, I'm so sorry." I wrap my arms around her. "Shall I book a flight to Australia and kick his arse? I'll do it right now. I've got a lot of anger to get rid of."

"Shall we do an angry clean?" she laughs, and it sounds like the perfect remedy to our blues.

Kara leaves, and Megs and I get to work cleaning and tidying with shouty punk rock turned up loud. I spend the rest of the evening overhauling my life. I tidy my bedroom, throw out a bunch of old makeup and skincare products, return all my books to the bookcase, dust, vacuum, and change my bedding.

I shower and slather every inch of my skin in moisturiser, trying not to think about the way Rob massaged me last night. That heady mix of delicate caresses and firm strokes. The way he slipped his fingers into my hair to soothe the tension at the base of my skull. Some kind of wizardry that lit up every nerve in my body.

Slipping in between fresh sheets I delete all my dating apps, which haven't gotten much use lately anyway. Instagram goes next. There will be no more stalking Lawrence, but then I remember I need it for work so I re-install it but set a limit so I can't use it after 10pm.

I hit play on a meditation, and pull an eye-mask on, all set for the best sleep of my life, but the second I lay back against freshly plumped pillows, my phone beeps.

Knob: I'm glad we got that out of our systems. You're a good friend, Hattie.

Is he fucking joking? This absolute bastard. He's wheedled himself so deep into all of my systems I feel like I'm wearing his skin and breathing his air.

Friends? Is he insane?

I can't be friends with him now. I don't even think I can be in the same room as him knowing how much I'm craving his touch.

I hate him. Hate him for being so hot, and so eager, and so good to me. I've never been with anyone with his confidence. Nobody has ever been so attentive and encouraging and committed to my pleasure. If sex was like that every time, I'd never leave the house, and the only way it could be like that every time is if...

No, no, no.

It's a bad idea.

I pull my eye-mask back on refuse to even finish the thought.

It would never work, and I would hate myself even if it did.

Chapter 30
Rob

This was not supposed to happen. When I first met her I figured we'd hook up and carry on with our lives.

But you don't forget a woman like Hattie Buchanan.

I'm not supposed to be sitting in work meetings daydreaming about the way she tastes. Or reading her old texts in bed and wishing I could ask what she's up to. Or reaching for her when I wake up. When I find the other side of my bed empty I have to push down a longing I've never felt before.

She hasn't replied to any of my messages this week, and I would know if she had because I've been checking constantly.

At work I've had a record number of patients referred for assessment this week, each with wildly differing needs. It's been a real test of my skills, and the rest of the team, as we work together to come up with the best plan for each patient. I've done my best to keep my head in the game but my brain is running on overdrive and all I want to do is eat a mountain of pasta, sleep through Saturday, thrash it out at five-a-side football on Sunday, then see Mum and Auntie Sheila. The last thing I need is someone ringing my doorbell at nine o'clock at night.

Correction, the last thing I need is *Hattie* ringing my doorbell at nine o'clock at night, but here she is, standing on my doorstep wearing a very un-Hattie like black trench-coat, heels, and a smile.

"Oh hi, friend," she says, her casual tone unfamiliar. I think this might be the first time she's ever greeted me with anything other than a scowl and an insult. I'm happy to see her, of course, but deeply suspicious. I cross my arms and lean against the doorframe.

"What are you doing here?"

"Can't a girl just drop in on a good friend and say hello these days?" she shrugs, her voice like warm honey. I can't do anything but stare, wondering what she's wearing beneath that coat. I have a sneaking suspicion it's nothing, but would she really be bold enough to turn up at my house naked? She'd better not have taken a cab. My chest tightens at the thought of her practically naked with some strange man making small talk about potholes and the weather. I glance over her shoulder, and relief washes over me when I see her car.

"Aren't you going to invite me in?"

What I want to do is throw her over my shoulder and march her up to my bedroom, but Hattie has never pulled a stunt like this before. After all her months of resisting me, a little payback seems only fair.

"Why do you want to come in?"

"I think you know why," she bites her bottom lip, but then half a second later she releases it, her smile replaced with a look of horror. "Oh shit, do you have company?"

"No, I'm alone."

"Then get out of my way." *There's my girl.*

She pushes past me and, despite myself, I close the door behind me. "Aren't you going to offer to take my coat?"

"What's under your coat, Hattie?"

"Take it off and find out."

Fuck my life. I knew it, and I'm desperate to know but this is a very, very, dangerously bad idea. This has to be karma kicking me in the nuts, right? Payback for everything I put her through when we first met. The bet, the taunting, all of it. My hands tingle as I reach for her belt, but I pull back and shove them deep into my pockets.

"You need to go home," I say, but she's not in the mood for listening. She struts down the hallway and into my kitchen like she owns the place. My heart rate kicks up a notch, my dick stiffening behind my zipper. This feels like a game, but I don't know the rules, how to play, or even if it's one I want to win or lose.

Hovering in the doorway, I find her sitting on the kitchen counter, her legs dangling apart, making just enough room for her hands to grip the edge between them. The front panels of her coat have slipped aside and ridden up, exposing the firm, smooth, bare inner thighs. The memory of kissing her there floods my brain and I want to get on my knees, crawl to her, and feast. In my pockets my fingernails prick the skin of my palms.

"Have you seriously got your bare arse on my kitchen counter?"

She nods seductively and wiggles her hips. "And the marble feels *so* good on my warm skin."

"That's not marble. It's laminate. You're nuts, get down."

"Come on, Rob," she whines. "What's the problem? We both have itches to scratch. We've already seen each other naked. Why can't we do it one more time?"

One more time wouldn't come even close to scratching the itch.

"You know why. We don't sleep with people more than once and you're kind of proving my point about why not. People get too attached, though I have to say you're the first who's gone this far."

She bursts out laughing. "Get over yourself, I'm the last person in the world who is going to get attached to you."

After so long trying to get Hattie into bed, I can't say I hate being on the opposite side of this battle. The idea that she would beg for me is too tempting to ignore. I must have left quite the impression. She tormented me for months before giving it up, I'm not letting her get what she wants so easily.

I move past her, grab a beer from the fridge, and take a seat at my small kitchen table. I open a magazine, sit back and flick through the pages, refusing to make eye contact with her.

In my peripheral vision she slides off the counter, loosens her belt and pulls her coat open. She settles her hands on her hips and waits for my reaction. Glancing sideways, my eyes drag up her gorgeous calves, and it's impossible not to keep going. Up, up, up to the top of her thighs, to the skimpy black underwear that leaves little to the imagination. Up to the soft dip of her hips, her toned stomach, and the swell of her tits in a bra with cups so tiny I'm amazed they're held in at all. She doesn't belong here, she belongs on a billboard causing multiple vehicle pile-ups. What did I do to deserve this punishment?

I prop my elbow on the table and press my hand across my forehead, the worst shield ever as Hattie stalks her way over to the fridge.

"Do you have any whipped cream in here?"

A low growl rumbles in my chest. "Stop it."

She opens the low freezer next, bending over to peer inside. I get the perfect view of her lace thong peeking out from underneath her coat. "What about ice? I'm so hot, I need something to cool me down."

She rummages around, and when she finds it she takes a cube between her fingers, kicks the door closed and turns to face me. My jaw hangs slack when she swipes her tongue across the frozen surface and wraps her lips around it. I can practically hear it sizzle. My eyes lock on a trickle that runs from her mouth, down her hand to her wrist. She dips her head to catch it, lapping it up ever so slowly, and I'm reminded of her running it along the length of my dick that night in the hotel.

She doesn't stop there, tipping her head back, hissing as she drags the ice along her jaw and down her neck. Her throat rolls and on it goes, tracing wet circles across the top of her breasts then down between them. She bites her lip and her moan imprints on my memory.

"You're making a mess."

"So come clean me up."

I turn back to my magazine but my brain misfires, the words on the page jumbling together while I attempt to ignore her.

"What do I need to do? I'm not above begging." She drops to her knees and crawls towards me. *Fuuuuck.* So much for resisting, this will be my undoing. "Oh please, Rob, please baby, I need you so bad. Nobody makes me come like you do. I can't breathe, I need you so much."

I don't dare look at her, though I can feel her gaze drop to my groin where the tent in my trousers will give her no doubts about the impact she's having on me.

"We're not doing this." *My dick hates me so much right now.*

"Fine," she says, springing to her feet and storming out of the room. "If you won't help me I'll do it myself."

When I hear footsteps on the stairs I jump up and dart after her. "Where are you going?"

"Your bedroom."

Not this again. "Get back down here."

I rush up behind her, reaching out to catch her ankle when she gets to the top. I tighten my grip, yanking her back down the stairs and she stumbles into my arms, taking me down with her.

"Ow!" she yelps, legs kicking out as she tries to climb back up.

"What the hell is going on with you?"

"You fucking prick," she grunts. I pin her with my weight as she struggles to get free, and she delivers a swift elbow to my ribs that knocks the wind out of me. "You couldn't just be crap in bed, could you? Why did you have to go and have a massive cock and the skills to back it up. Upstairs, now."

Now there's a sentence I never thought I'd hear.

"Wait, are you saying—" I wrestle her onto her back while leaning to keep my face clear of her frantic clawing. It takes me a second to realise she's not fighting me off. Instead her hands are scrambling with my belt buckle. She really wants this. "Are you saying I'm the best dick you've ever had?"

"Go to hell," she says through gritted teeth. I pull her arms free, pinning her wrists above her head with one of my hands. Nearly naked and stretched out beneath me, she's more beautiful than ever, and I wonder how on earth we've ended up here. I tried really fucking hard not to look in the kitchen, but it's impossible now. I fill my palm with one of her perfect tits, tugging the lace down so I can pinch her nipple then bend and take it between my teeth. When she moans I shift my knees, forcing her legs apart to rub my aching hard-on against the scrap of her underwear.

"Are you saying I've ruined all other men for you?"

"I hate you," she says through gritted teeth, but her body says otherwise, her legs hooking around my waist, lifting to press up into me.

"Are you saying you can't live another moment without having me inside you?"

Hattie screams and it turns me on far more than it should.

"Just fucking fuck me, you fuck!"

I pull back, reaching behind me to unhook her legs. Pushing her knees apart, I set one foot on the stair below her, and jam the other up high between the spindles of the bannister. She's fucking perfect, spread out for me like this and with two fingers, I tug her underwear aside, and drop my head to sweep my tongue straight through her. Her back arches on a moan, tits heaving, neck bared to me. I'm about to ruin her.

"Don't move," I point my finger in her face and turn away. I find my wallet in the kitchen, grateful for the condom I stashed in there, and hurry back, shoving my jeans and my boxers down over my hips, and rolling it on.

I find Hattie exactly as I left her, save for one hand stroking her clit in slow circles. She wets her lips when she sees me stroking myself too.

"Tell me how much you want this."

"Fuck you, I don't *want* to want this."

"I'm not asking you to beg, Hattie, I just need to know I'm not crossing a line. Is this what you came here for?"

"Yes," she nods, her breath shaky with anticipation. A whisper of vulnerability hangs between us, and for a moment I think I should stop this, wrap her up, make her a cup of tea and give her a cuddle. She'd murder me and not even bother to hide the body. The urge passes when she reaches out for me, her angry expression switched for one of desperation. "Please, Rob. Please."

"I'm not holding back this time. Hold your underwear to the side."

She obeys, and I line myself against the spot where she's slick and ready. I know she'll never let me kiss her, but with one hand on her jaw I hold her still, my mouth hovering, ready to feast on the cry she can't contain when I finally get inside her. My other hand holds her thigh to the stair and I slide straight home in one deep thrust.

"Oh God, Rob. *Fuck!*" She moans like she's needed this as much as I have and I breathe her in. It's only been a week since our night at the hotel and I've missed this, missed her, so damn much. Her legs wrap around me again and I thrust deeper, lifting her a step higher. I bury my face into her neck, shoving my hands into her hair while she claws at my t-shirt, balling it into her fists.

Hattie Buchanan. This temptress, this witch, making me break the rules because I can't get enough of her skin. She feels so damn good wrapped around me. I know I won't last long, and I don't care.

I let myself go, hips pistoning in and out of her, the stairwell filled with the sound of her skin on mine, heavy breathing, and guttural moans. She clenches around me, and I thrust deep and hold myself there, groaning open-mouthed against her cheek as I fill the condom between us. I know she's close but I can't hold on, I'll make it up to her in other ways.

I pull out and hoist her up another step, lifting her to my mouth and clamping around that slippery pearl, tongue sweeping in firm circles. My eyes stay on her face but when hers lock with mine she squeezes them shut. She looks incredible and unleashed, stomach tightening, hips rolling, right on the edge of her bliss, but it pisses me off that she can't even look at me. I suck hard, then harder again, refusing to let up until she cries out, hands tugging at my hair, thighs pressed tight around my head.

We ride her orgasm out together, her legs over my shoulders, my hands stroking them up and down until her moans turn to whimpers and she pulls away.

Pushing off the stairs, I leave her there while I deal with the condom and get my clothes back in order. I'm not proud of myself for being so fast and out of control, but that's the effect she has on me.

"You're the worst guy *ever*," she huffs out, her breath still coming in shallow pants as she follows me into the kitchen. "I hate you."

Great, back to this are we?

"Hate fucking isn't my style, Hattie. We're not doing this again."

"Oh, but we are," she shakes her head and laughs.

"What are you talking about?"

"Look, I'll be honest with you," she says, pulling her coat back around her and taking a seat at the table. I run a glass of water and set it down in front of her. "I want to make a deal with you. I'm up for a promotion at work, and it's a lot of pressure. A friends-with-benefits situation would save me a lot of time. It's such a waste of time swiping for hookups, and I had one that was a bit dodgy, but a girl has needs so whenever I need a fix, you're gonna help me."

This is a terrible idea. Dangerous. Potentially catastrophic. And I'm grinning like a Cheshire cat.

I don't know how many people Hattie's slept with. It's none of my business, but knowing that I'm the one she'd break her rules for too? That's a sense of pride I feel from my head to my toes. I can't deny I like the sound of it. She's a fireball in bed, and guaranteed sex without having to jump through hoops getting to know someone first would save a lot of time.

Standing over her, I lift her chin with two fingers and force her to look at me. "What I'm hearing is you saying we're friends."

"Gross," she says, jerking her face away from my touch. "We can call it enemies with benefits if you'd prefer." *Now that's a kind of hatefucking I could get on board with.*

"Wait, go back. What do you mean you had one that was dodgy?"

"Forget it."

"Who hurt you?" The thought of someone laying an unwelcome finger on her is a punch in the gut.

"It was nothing like that."

I crouch down in front of her, one hand gently resting on her knee. "You can tell me."

"I bumped into a guy I'd slept with and he was with his wife and brand new baby. Timing seems like he must have cheated on her with me."

Fucking men. We really are the worst. There's no shame in having multiple partners, but cheating is one thing I'd never do. I always ask if women are attached before things go too far.

"You know that's not your fault though, right?"

"I know." She knots her belt a little tighter. "It just fucked with my head a bit. I'm getting older, the pool of decent guys is only going to get smaller."

"And friends with benefits is your solution?"

"Don't try to talk me out of it. I've given it a lot of thought, we're doing this."

"I don't get a say in the matter?" I tease, though my head was on board with her plan five minutes ago, my dick long before that. "Sounds a bit morally grey. I thought you girls only liked that stuff in books."

Her shoulders slump forward and she sighs heavily. I can see now how hard this is for her, to come here and ask for what she wants, to be this vulnerable with me. "Please?"

"Fine, we can do this. I'm in." I pull her into a hug and squeeze tight, "but I'm only agreeing to this because one night wasn't enough time to do everything I wanted with you."

"Oh," she says, sitting back. I notice her picking at her thumbnail again. "Like what?"

"That's for me to know and you to find out, sweetheart."

"You have the worst lines," she laughs, standing up to leave. "I don't know how you ever get laid."

Chapter 31
Rob

"Who are you texting?" Auntie Sheila asks. "Is it that girl?"

"What girl?"

"The one who cut your face. The one you were making eyes at all night at Luke's wedding." *What the fuck?* Nothing gets past Sheila.

"She's a woman." A woman I'm desperate to see again. "Be quiet and watch your show."

Hottie: We need to agree to some ground rules

Me: Way to kill the mood

Hottie: I'm serious. I don't want this to be more complicated than it needs to be

Me: Want to come over Wednesday and state your terms?

Hottie: I have book club, but I can come after?

Me: Oh you'll come alright. Wednesday works. See you then, fuck buddy.

Hottie: Call me that again and you'll lose a testicle

"What the hell are you wearing?"

"A suit." Deep black, it fits me in all the right places. I've loosened my tie, and undone the top two buttons of my shirt. I knew exactly what I was doing when I opted not to change after work.

Hattie has made considerably less of an effort than the last time she turned up here, though she still looks gorgeous in grey sweatpants and a matching hoodie, her dark grey cap doing little to disguise her.

"I can see it's a suit. Why is it on you?"

"I had a management meeting." I lean closer and plant a kiss on her cheek. She baulks, then lets me. "Is something the matter?"

"I can't come in with you looking like that."

"Why not?"

"Fuck's sake, Rob! I'm wearing jogging bottoms, and I've got a rotisserie chicken in a carrier bag. You look like some billionaire book boyfriend who's off to a ball. I'll come before I've taken my shoes off."

I grab the front of her hoodie, and pull her over the threshold. "Get in here you nutter, I'll get changed."

"Oh you absolutely will not," she says, toeing off her trainers and making her way to the kitchen.

"No?"

"Leave it on. Just keep your mouth shut and let me enjoy the view. Management meeting, for God's sake. Where do you work, the mafia?"

She unpacks her shopping on my kitchen counter and I hang back, happy to watch her make herself at home.

"Where do you keep your plates?"

I press against her back to pull one from the cupboard above her head. "What's with the chicken?"

"I told Megan I was going to the gym after book club, but I haven't eaten all day." There's a spiky feeling in my throat knowing she's lied about where she is, and I swallow it down. I don't know what I expected, of course she wouldn't tell her friends about this dirty little secret of ours.

"This is just chicken and coleslaw."

"This is the best dinner on the planet."

"Your diet is atrocious, you know that?" I lift her cap off and sweep the hair from her neck to one side. I know we haven't discussed her rules or set any boundaries yet, so don't know if I can do this, but wild horses couldn't stop me from kissing the slope of her shoulder, that spot where it meets her neck and makes her moan.

"Christ, you do my head in," she says, but her body betrays her, perfect ass pressing back against my groin. "I don't know whether to punch your dick or suck it."

"Can I express a preference?" I grip her hips and pull her back, then slide my hands up underneath her clothes, desperately seeking bare skin. She makes a pathetic attempt to push me away, but when I suck her earlobe and roll her nipples into tight peaks her resistance falters.

"I need to eat," she moans.

Spinning her around, I lift her into my arms and head for the stairs. "So do I."

"Your place is not what I expected," she says after we've had our fill of each other. The bed is a wreck, sheets pinged off from two corners, a well fisted pillow mauled loose from the cover. Her body is settled between my legs, head resting on my chest, fingertips skating up and down my side.

"What were you expecting?"

"I don't know. Bachelor pad. Worn carpet, ancient sofa. Mug rings on the coffee table. New York skyline on the wall. Navy sheets and one thin, grotty pillow."

"This is telling me so much about the men you sleep with. You've been in here before, remember?"

"I know, but I wasn't in my right mind then. It's so sparse," she says, lifting her head to look around my bedroom. "You don't have a single candle in here."

"My mum is a bit of a hoarder."

"Oh." She drops her head back to my chest but everything else tenses and I wonder what's behind it. Having her this close is new. She so rarely lets her guard down, and I'm acutely aware that she could bolt at any second. Pushing her is the worst thing I could do, so I do the opposite and let her in further.

"Growing up with so much clutter made me want to keep things minimal. It's less stressful, saves a lot of time cleaning, better for my brain."

"I can relate to that."

"You can?" I brush her jaw with my thumb and she softens a little more.

"My mum had this one boyfriend who stepped on some Lego while we were at school. By the time we got home he'd binned it all. Mum acted like that was a normal thing to do. I think it rewired my brain, ever since then I haven't really cared about possessions."

"Except candles, apparently?"

"Candles are a vibe."

"You can buy me one," I say, and she groans in revolt and pulls away. Bonding time is over. I roll her onto her back and shift down the bed to scatter kisses along her collarbone. "You stay here. I'll get you some dinner."

I pull on fresh boxers and make my way downstairs to scope out Hattie's version of a food shop. Chicken and coleslaw for dinner, the absolute state of it. Between work and the gym, she's always on the go, she can't be living on coffee all day and eating like this. She needs a balanced meal, more nutrients.

I toss spices into a pan with a squeeze of tomato puree, and once the toasted aroma fills the air I add a can of mixed beans and stir it all together. While it heats, I shred chicken and add it to the pan, along with a handful of spinach and some fresh lime juice. I plate up two bowls, top with a dollop of sour cream, and carry them upstairs.

Hattie is sitting up in my bed, t-shirt on, covers back in order. Arms folded across her chest, that familiar scowl back on her face. I've fucked up, and I've no idea how.

"What's the matter?" I set her bowl down on the bedside table.

"Have you got a girlfriend?"

"No."

"Secret wife you've neglected to mention?"

"Also no."

"Housemate?"

This could go on all night. "What are you really asking?"

"Your bathroom cabinet is full of women's toiletries," she huffs then pouts her perfect lips. I try not to laugh.

"You've been snooping?"

"Yes. Don't avoid the question."

"Eat and I'll explain." I push her bowl into her hands and hold out a fork which she takes, begrudgingly. "I don't ever want anyone to feel uncomfortable here, so I keep a supply of stuff guests might need. It's no big deal. You can use anything you like."

"You bring women here?"

"Sometimes." I perch on the edge of the bed and eat too. "Depends on the vibe. I'll bring them here if I get the impression they'll want to leave soon after. If they're the type who'll want to cuddle for a bit afterwards I'll suggest we go to hers instead. I don't like doing the whole morning after thing here. Do you bring guys back to your place?"

She drags out her answer while she eats. "Never. I always go to their house. Or ideally a hotel."

"Why don't you bring them home?"

"I don't want them knowing where I live if they can't take the hint," she says, taking another mouthful and moaning around her fork. "God, this is good. Plus Megan is a sweet angel, I don't need her knowing what a filthbag I am."

"I have a feeling she probably already knows," I nudge her thigh and eat some more. "Wait, does that mean I can't come to yours?"

"Never, we have to meet here. Also because I really like these sheets. They're so soft."

"This is what it's like when you sleep with men, not teenagers."

"Piss off. The nineteen year old paid for a hotel I'll have you know."

"Aww, with his birthday money?" I tease.

"He was great actually. Very receptive to feedback."

"Yeah, because he was a beginner just learning the ropes. Now you have a man who knows what he's doing." I slide my hand, warm from the bowl, up the inside of her leg. "Who has spent his life mastering the art of pleasuring a woman."

"Give it up, you sound like a cult leader."

"Some women have described my penis as a religious experience."

"Stop it before I throw up this excellent food."

I take the compliment, and let her finish her dinner in peace. When we're both done, I take everything downstairs, load the dishwasher, wipe down the counters and head back upstairs with a glass of water. Nothing about this feels unusual. If anything, it's kind of nice knowing she's up there waiting for me. Even nicer knowing she's not running.

Back in my bed, I roll onto my side and face her, one hand propping up my head. "So tell me about these ground rules of yours. They sound pretty serious."

Hattie is the opposite of relaxed. She sits up straight, crosses her legs and stretches out her neck as if this is about to be a major effort for her. "I just think it's smart to be clear about expectations and capacity."

"You're not at work, Hattie, tell me what you really mean."

"OK, number one. This is just two people helping each other out if it's late at night and we have an itch to scratch. We don't need to meet up or go out or anything."

"What if it's an early morning itch?" I stroke my thumb over her knee while she takes me through the rules I know I'm about to have a great time breaking.

"Mornings are for sleeping."

"Damn that's a shame. I love morning sex."

"Number two, no sleepovers. Number three, you can't tell anyone. This is just between us."

"Better cancel the full page announcement I took out in the newspaper then." That earns me a playful kick in the stomach, but I grab hold of her foot and begin to massage it.

"Is this exclusive?" I ask, suddenly feeling nervous about her answer.

"Don't be ridiculous. We can see other people."

My chest tightens. I thought the whole point of this was to make things easier for us both while we're so busy. I'm happy to keep things casual, but the truth is, I haven't wanted to sleep with anyone else for a while, and I'm starting to hate the idea of anyone else getting even within an inch of her. How did we go from friends-with-benefits to me craving something exclusive in the space of a week?

"You wouldn't be jealous?" *I'm sick just thinking about it.*

"I don't get jealous," she laughs, dismissively. "You're free to do whatever, whoever, you want, but I also don't want to hear about it. Just be safe."

"Always."

"You should know I have an IUD and I get tested regularly. My last results were clear."

"Me too. I mean the testing, not the IUD, but condoms are non-negotiable for me."

"Fine."

"Fine."

She climbs out of my bed, and while I watch her pull her clothes back on I flick away the urge to ask her to stay. She was pretty adamant about the no sleepover thing. In my bedroom mirror she adjusts everything, pulling the strings of her hoodie so they're equal, then rakes her fingers through her hair. I want to tell her she can leave a hairbrush here, spare clothes, anything she wants. I'll clear a drawer. This is so unlike me to feel needy, but I know I won't be able to go long without having her here again.

"When shall we see each other?"

"Do we need a schedule?" she groans. "Surely that takes the fun out of it."

"I think maybe we do, just so we're clear what to expect of each other. I don't want you getting pissy if you turn up here looking for sex and I'm not home." I can't even begin to imagine how pissed *I* would be if I found out she'd come over and I'd missed her. "When works for you?"

"Hold on while I get my diary out," she mocks. Standing behind her, I reach up under her hoodie again, my new favourite game. I pinch the soft skin at her side and she squeals.

"Tuesdays and Sundays are out for me." I do need to be clear about that.

"Why?"

Shit. "Um, standing engagements."

"That's fine, I don't actually care and I box those nights, anyway." I bet she does care, I bet she's dying for answers, but I'm not ready to give them. "Fridays are out because of Friday dinners," she continues.

"Those are my best nights of the month."

"They are?"

"Yeah, I get to see my favourite people. It would be even better if I got to take you home afterwards." I kiss her neck, sneaking my tongue out for a taste.

She moans softly, then spins around and pushes me away. "Fine. Occasional Fridays, but I mean it. Nobody can know about this, so promise you'll keep your hands to yourself when we're around our friends."

I cross my fingers behind my back. "Promise. What about Monday?"

"Eww, nobody has sex on a Monday."

"I could have sex on a Monday."

"Monday I recover from all the sex I've had at the weekend." *I'll make damned sure that sex is with me.*

"OK, so Friday and Saturday?"

"Two nights in a row seems a bit much. Look, once a week is fine. Let's just say Friday or Saturday, depending on other plans we have. Deal?" *I'll take everything you'll give me.*

"Deal. Wanna shake on it? With my penis?" I fill my hands with her backside. She's leaving, I can feel her withdrawing, and I need to touch as much of her as possible while I can.

"No. I need to go home and shower your stink off me before I come to my senses and change my mind." She ducks under my arm, and then she's out of reach and heading for the bedroom door.

"I'll see you next Friday, fuck buddy," I call after her.

"Piss off, Knob."

"Oh, and Hattie," I leaning over the bannister as she skips down the stairs. She turns back, looking up at me. "One more rule. No falling…"

"Don't say it!" She holds her hands up in front of her, palms facing out, eyes squeezed shut.

"What?" I laugh.

"I've read enough romance books to know that saying *'no falling in love'* is as bad as saying Bloody Mary in the mirror three times."

"That's not a real thing."

"Don't care. Don't even risk it. Just shut your idiot mouth." She pulls on her shoes and I take a seat halfway up the stairs.

"We need to work on your pillow talk."

"New rule. No talking full stop. Just make me come, and then go away. That's the deal."

"We're in *my* house."

She swings the door open and doesn't look back. "And now you get to watch me leave."

Chapter 32
Rob

IT GOES ON LIKE this for weeks. She arrives late and we go straight at it until she leaves in the middle of the night, or she appears after work and we fuck, eat, then fuck again.

I don't know why I didn't get a fuck buddy ages ago. Though deep down, I know it would never have been like this with anyone else. I've met my match with Hattie. Obviously I love the sex stuff but I love talking to her too, and even if we spend most of our time arguing, it makes me feel something I've never felt before. It makes me feel alive.

We broke the once a week rule within days, and over time, she stays longer. On warm nights like this one, she lights the firepit in the garden while I make dinner. Yeah, I bought one. Luke and Kara's cosy garden snuggles made me want a bit of that for myself. When I finish plating up risotto, I find her curled up in the garden chair, staring at the flaming end of a stick.

"Didn't have you pegged as a firestarter." She flicks an ember in my direction and pokes her tongue out. "Careful, I don't want tonight to end with a call to the fire brigade. You and I have already wasted both police and A&E time with our fighting, a third emergency service would be mortifying."

"I don't know, if Rennie from *Just a Little Crush* turned up I wouldn't complain," she laughs.

"Who's that?"

"Super hot firefighter book boyfriend with a fit body and dirty mouth." *What the fuck? I've got a fit body and a dirty mouth.* We're not talking about him anymore.

"You haven't mentioned work for a while."

"Not much to report," she shrugs.

"That guy still giving you hassle?"

"Lawrence? Nope. He took my job and I'm seconded to something else for a few months. Apparently there's a promotion opportunity coming up, and they wanted me to *'expand my portfolio'* or some bullshit like that."

"That's good news, right?" She doesn't sound happy.

"Yes, and no. I don't want to talk about it in case I jinx it."

We finish our food in silence, and afterwards Hattie takes our bowls to the kitchen to clean up. I know she's holding back on something, and I hate the thought of her going home alone and dwelling on it. She washes, I dry, and when we're done I lift her onto the kitchen counter and step into the space between her legs.

"Stay," I whisper quietly enough there's a chance she won't even hear it to turn me down.

Hattie bites the edge of her thumb and shakes her head. "No sleepovers, remember."

"I'm serious." I push her hair away from her face, and she looks up at me through her long lashes. "Stay. It's late, but I don't want you to leave. Let me fuck you to sleep and drive you home in the morning."

"How the hell do you fuck someone to sleep?"

I lift her hair away from her neck and pepper gentle kisses across the delicate skin there. "Come upstairs and I'll show you."

There's a moment of hesitation, but when she tips her ear to her shoulder and opens up to me, I know we're about to break another rule.

One Saturday she comes over in the afternoon and there's no point in pretending she's here for anything else. Within minutes, we're naked on top of my bed, warm sun streaming through the window, lighting her up like an angel. I'm in no rush, relishing the fact that since she's here so early, I have hours to enjoy her.

It didn't use to be like this. At first it was all fast and furious, but I think that she trusts me enough to let me slow down now, to enjoy her the way a woman like Hattie should be enjoyed.

When I slide through her wetness and push inside, her knees fall further apart and she moans softly. Eyes closed, basking in the sun, I think I will always picture her like this, blissed out beneath me. I hold her close, kissing her neck, reaching underneath her back to pull her body tighter to me. Nothing could be better than this, until her phone rings on my bedside table.

"Nope, not happening," I growl into her neck, but she wriggles to one side and reaches out for it.

"It's Kara. Ovaries before brovaries, my friend."

"Hey you," she says, switching the call to loudspeaker. She lays her phone on the pillow next to her head. "Don't stop," she mouths and presses her index finger to her lips.

"Hi lovely, Luke and I are out shopping and wondered if you fancy coming over for Sunday roast tomorrow?" Kara says.

"Ooh, that sounds good. Is Rob coming?" Hattie winks at me. It's an over the top, porn star wink. I sit up and spread my knees apart between her legs, one hand keeping her hips pinned to the bed, the other roaming lightly over her chest while I fuck her deep and slow. I pinch one nipple and I feel her tighten around me. I'll never get over how hot it is to feel her body reacting to my touch.

"Probably," Kara says on the other end of the line, "We're inviting the whole gang."

"Ugh, I hate that guy." She rolls her eyes, so I pinch harder, and she has to bite her lip to stay quiet.

"Hattie, play nice. He's a good man. You need to stop being such a bitch to him."

"Yes, Kara," I mouth and give the phone a thumbs up. I like how she sticks up for me.

"Enough about Rob. Can I bring anything? Stuffing?" Hattie looks me dead in the eyes. "I haven't had a good stuffing in ages."

"You little shit," I whisper. "I'm literally inside you." I thrust hard into her and her back bows off the bed, hand flying to her mouth to stifle her moan. Pressing her thighs wide, I lick my thumb and strum across her clit the way I know she likes it.

"Fuck you," she mouths, watching where our bodies are joined. It turns me on so much to watch her see the way her body takes all of me.

"What are you up to?" Kara asks.

"Ohh..." I do it again and Hattie gasps loudly. "Just watching some boring shit on TV."

"I thought I heard moaning? Are you watching porn?"

"Ha. Good idea. I'll see you tomorrow." She scrambles to end the call and throws her phone to the floor. "Keep doing that," she pleads, and who am I to deny her? I withdraw slowly, enjoying the desperate look of need that falls across her face before I plunge right back in. Her moans, unashamedly unrestrained, fill the room.

Seconds later, I hear my phone buzzing from the pocket of my jeans, hastily abandoned by the bedroom door.

"I bet that's Luke. Payback time." I nip at her neck, jump off the bed and pick up the call. "Hey bud, you alright?"

"Hey mate, what you up to?"

I climb back on top of her, but instead of resuming my previous position, as fun as it was, I straddle her chest. My knees pin her arms, and I grip the base of my dick and thrust forward, brazenly pushing it into her mouth. Her eyes go wide but she doesn't fight it. Instead I feel her warm tongue stroking the head before she hollows her cheeks and sucks so hard it makes me want to come instantly. "Uh, just in the middle of a workout. You?"

"Supermarket. If Kara and I do a roast tomorrow, can you join us?"

"Will Hattie be there?" I keep the phone to my ear, but in such close proximity, I know she can hear him, too.

"Yeah, why?" Luke asks.

"Oh, just so I can make sure I'm completely irresistible. You know how much I love to get her all riled up."

"She asked the same about you, you know. When are you going to quit this bollocks and just tell her you like her?" Her mouth and eyes fly wide open in shock.

Fuck. "OK gotta go mate, text me the time!"

I end the call and when she tries to speak I push in further, sliding past her tongue to the back of her throat. I withdraw a little and let her catch her breath.

"You like—"

"Shut up." I push back in.

She's not getting the satisfaction of thinking she has something on me. I reach behind me and bury two fingers inside her. She tightens around them and tries to buck me off, but it's a half-baked effort, and

I glide in and out of her mouth, watching her squirm. She scratches her nails down my thighs, and I yelp, pink welts blooming instantly.

"You'll pay for that," I growl, climbing off and flipping her over.

"Make me," she laughs, pressing up onto her hands and knees.

Sometimes sex with Hattie is a stroll in the park on a summer's day. Sometimes it's war. A fierce battle for control, where it's a miracle we both make it out without having broken the bed. This is one of those battles. She bites me and I bite back. She grips my dick so hard I'd swear she was trying to remove it. The flat of my palm meets the curve of her ass and she cries out, then begs me to do it again.

Afterwards, we lay breathless, sweaty, tangled together. The moment I shift to face her, she does the same.

"You like me," she laughs sleepily, running a fingertip from my forehead down my nose to my chin. It's an unexpectedly intimate gesture from Hattie. I float my eyes closed and commit it to memory, then gather my strength and lift her over me until she straddles my face.

"Let me show you exactly how much I like you."

Lunch is an awkward affair. Hattie makes me drop her off, then circle the block for ten minutes so it doesn't look like we showed up together. I should have expected as much, but it pisses me off, and when I finally *'arrive'* I find everyone around the garden table underneath a blue and white striped parasol. The seat next to Hattie is the only one vacant and I sit and pour a glass of iced water.

Kara and Luke keep disappearing to whisper in the kitchen, and Megan is glued to her phone, which is extremely unlike her.

"Who are you texting?" Hattie asks across the table.

"Nobody," Megan replies, shoving her phone into the pocket of her cardigan.

"I don't believe you. Have you joined a dating app?"

"So I could trawl through your cast-offs? No, thank you." Megan laughs, but I feel Hattie stiffen beside me and she looks away as she sips her wine.

"Hey," I snap. "That was uncalled for."

"I'm sorry," Megan says, her cheeks reddening. "I didn't mean it how it sounded."

"It's fine," Hattie shrugs. "We all know what I'm like."

I haven't had the urge to look at an app since our situation began. Now I'm wondering if the same is true for her, though to be honest I don't know when she'd have the time, given how often she's in my bed these days.

"If you must know," Megan says. "I've gone viral."

"What do you mean, you've gone viral?" Hattie says, sitting up and leaning in.

"One of my Year 10s took a photo of my comments on their homework and now it's on the front page of Reddit."

"Show me." Hattie holds out her hand, and Megan unlocks her phone and passes it over. I lean across to see an image of typed homework with Megan's neat red writing in the margin. *'Please refrain from calling Atticus, 'Daddy Finch' in your exams.'*

Hattie and I give each other a sideways glance and burst out laughing.

"I'm so sorry," she says, "I shouldn't laugh."

"Oh, it's fine. If you believe the comments, half of Reddit now wishes I was their teacher."

Megan heads inside to help Kara carry dishes to the table, and since we have a few minutes alone, I can't resist winding my girl up.

"Hey," I say, nudging her with my shoulder. "Do you think anyone here knows you were screaming on my dick this morning?"

"Stop that right now," she hisses. "I know you're hellbent on breaking all the rules, but this is one I'm not prepared to swerve on. Nobody can know about this."

"Would it really be so bad if they knew?"

"*Yes.* If they know, it will be a whole thing. They'll have questions, they'll get invested, and when this ends, people will feel like they have to take sides. Then there'll be drama, and I hate drama. So keep your stupid mouth shut."

"What do you mean when this ends?" I angle my body towards her and fold my arms across my chest.

"When we've had enough of each other," she says dismissively.

A tight ache forms behind my ribs, forcing me to confront what I've known for longer than I care to admit. I'll never get enough of her, and the last thing I want is for this to end.

Chapter 33
Hattie

CRAWLING INTO BED AFTER a long day at the office, I wish I'd made plans to see Rob tonight. Wish I could have one of those massages where he touches me in the exact way I need. Wish he could make me come so hard I lose all clarity and don't have to think about things like client briefs and project plans. I turn out the light, and my phone dings. If I believed in the power of manifestation, I'd swear I'm the best in the world at it.

    Knob: I need to see you
    Me: Why?

A photo of him, his tight, black boxers, barely restraining his solid erection, pings into our chat. I should have known better than to ask. *Fuck, I want that.*

    Me: I just got into bed.
    Knob: Can I come over?
    Me: You know you can't.
    Knob: Please? Just one time. I'll be quiet. I've been thinking about you all day.
    Me: Isn't there someone else you could text?

What a ridiculous thing to say. I don't know why I'm pushing him away. This past month has been a lot of fun, and I don't want him to be with anyone else.

Knob: I only want you.
Me: Fine. Megan is here so don't ring the buzzer. Text me when you're outside and I'll sneak you in.
Knob: You really know how to make a guy feel loved.
Me: Do you want to get laid or not, pal?
Knob: I'm already in the car. See you soon xx

Rob doesn't even have to speak, one look from the other side of the doorway is all it takes to get me aching for him deep in my core. Actually, scratch that, he just has to be in the same room as me and I feel myself turning crazy. This tight, intense feeling that makes me feel wobbly on my feet, like I need to be held up, and held tight. That the safest way to exist is to be underneath the full weight of him, where I can't think about anything except how good he makes me feel.

I press a finger to my lips, ordering him to be quiet, and he mimics zipping his mouth closed, locking it and throwing away the key.

Leading him to my room, my anxiety disappears, but I can't think about what it means to have invited him of all people here, into my sanctuary from the world. I help him out of his hoodie and t-shirt, push my pyjama shorts to the floor, then lay back on the bed, pulling him down with me.

"Where's Rob?" he whispers into my neck, and a repressed laugh rumbles from inside me.

"Is this a roleplay?"

"No, Rob junior. Pink Rob."

I pull my head back so I can study his expression for some clue. "Are you having an aneurysm? What are you talking about?"

"Your vibrator."

I cover my mouth to stop myself laughing even more. "You don't really think I gave my vibrator your name, do you?"

"Oh," he sits back on his knees and his shoulders slump. "I believed you."

"Such a pretty little narcissist," I tease, reaching out to stroke him through his jeans.

"Shut up." He yanks my t-shirt up roughly and pinches one nipple with just the right amount of pressure to have me writhing under his touch. "I'm serious, where is it?"

"Why?"

"I've been dreaming of using it on you."

I don't know if I'll ever get used to this being the way things are with Rob. The way he always lets me know in these subtle, and not so subtle, ways how much he thinks about me when we're apart.

"Bedside drawer," I say, nodding towards it. He leans across me, his chest looming in close to my face. I breathe him in and get myself high on that deep male scent that never seems to leave my mind.

"Do you need some lube, or are you wet enough already?" he whispers.

"A little extra never hurts."

He drizzles it on the end of the thick head, stashes the bottle and gets himself into position, kneeling at my feet. Need twists its way around my spine.

"Hold your legs apart for me, angel."

I do as I'm told, gripping them from underneath and planting my feet wide.

Rob's eyes flare at the display before him and he dips his head to watch closely as he circles my entrance with the toy. Having him inspect me this way is intense, exposing and filthy all at once.

My gasp is shaky when he slides it into me agonisingly slowly. He teases it in and out for a while and I try to stay silent, which only serves to make this even hotter somehow. When he turns the toy on, the suction part hits me exactly right and I moan loudly, gripping the sheets at my hips.

"Is that position good?"

"So *fucking* good."

"You're supposed to be quiet, remember," he says, heat in his eyes when he leans over me and covers my mouth with his free hand. I know he must be loving pushing me to the edge. "Don't make me gag you."

My eyes widen, and he catches it. "Oh, maybe you'd like that, huh?"

My thighs squirm around him and I nod from behind his palm.

"What else would you like, I wonder?" He leans closer to my ear, his voice a low growl. "Would you let me tie you up and take my time teasing you? Would you let me fuck you outside somewhere, or hitch your skirt up and finger you where anyone could see what a greedy girl you are? Would you let me spank you until your tight ass turns pink?"

I whimper my agreement. *Yes. Yes. All of it.*

"That doesn't even scratch the surface of the things I'd do to you."

This is unbearable. The vibrations coursing through me, the suction hitting just right, his filthy fantasies in my ear. *Him.* I'm so close already.

The sensation builds in waves, my orgasm dragged from the most depraved depths of me. Each one feels like it could be the one to peak and crash, only to retreat at the last second before surging forward again. I could come like this, but I need more.

"I need to see you come too," I plead, tugging Rob's hand away from my mouth. "Come with me."

"Can I come on you?" he chokes out.

"*Fuck*, yes, please."

One hand keeps the vibrator inside me as he unbuckles his belt with the other and pushes his clothes down to set himself free. He is a God knelt before me, the curves and dips of his muscles even more magnificent from this angle.

I prop myself up on my elbows to watch him stroke himself roughly, his thumb spreading the bead of moisture that's gathered at the head. The thick ridges of his cock, hard and swollen in his hand, give me the visual stimulation I crave so badly.

He shifts to hold the vibrator in place with his knee, his hand over his mouth as he jerks harder. I cover mine too, biting into the fleshy base of my thumb. The primal sight of him holding back his moans, combined with the added pressure in my core, is my undoing.

My pleasure peaks, and peaks, and stays for what feels like an eternity on the precipice, then crashes, roaring through my body, a flood of pressure that feels like floating. Everything tightens, my eyes squeeze shut, my stomach clenches, and the band of pressure in my abdomen snaps in a white hot flash that has me trembling around the toy, which is still buzzing and sucking, keeping me high.

My eyes fly open in time to see Rob thrust his hips forward, and the jet of his orgasm sail right over my body in an arc, up and over the headboard where it lands with a splat.

"Oh shit, oh fuck," he moans, toppling forward and landing on one hand. The next release hits between my breasts, the rest painting my stomach as the vibrator wrenches seemingly endless rapture from within me.

He gently pulls it free, turning it off and setting it on my bedside table before collapsing onto his side next to me. My legs are still trembling and he hooks them over his, tucking himself in closer so he can stroke my skin as the wave subsides.

"Did you seriously just come on my wall?" I roll my lips to contain my laugh.

"I'm so sorry," he giggles into my shoulder. "I'm mortified. Give me a second to catch my breath and I'll clean you both up."

The next morning, Rob tries to sneak out of my bedroom, but from my cosy spot underneath the covers I hear Megan's voice.

"Hey Rob, what are you doing here?"

"I just... um, I came to... borrow a charger."

My hand smacks against my forehead. *That's the best you can come up with?*

"Don't lie," I say, appearing from my room. "Just tell her you came over for advice on how to please women because you've realised you're not God's gift after all."

"Huh?" Megan mumbles, rubbing her eyes, still in her pyjamas.

"Yeah, seriously. Turns out he has no idea where the clitoris is and he thought the g-spot was a ride at Disney World. Useless. Anyway, I drew him a diagram, so I think you're all set now, Knob." I open the front door and attempt to shove him through it. "Off you fuck, and God help the poor soul you use for target practice."

Megan stifles a laugh. She clearly doesn't buy it, I wouldn't either, but thankfully she leaves us alone.

"You're in trouble now," he says, looming over me, his voice aggressive in my ear. "Next time I see you, I'm gonna pinch your clit so fucking hard your legs will give out."

My body sways towards him, and I catch myself with open palms against the wall of his chest. I want to drag him back to bed right this second, but a spot of morning sass will have to suffice for now. I look up at him and quirk one eyebrow. "That's if you can find it."

"You know full well I can find it." He grips me roughly between my thighs and, *fuck*, I hate that he's right, my legs are shaking in an instant. Shocked by his boldness, by the jolt of pleasure that strikes straight through me. I'd let him fuck me right here if Megan wasn't home.

I wriggle out of his grasp, shove him through the door and call through the gap as I close it. "See ya later, Knob."

In the kitchen I pour my cereal in silence, then curse when the milk sloshes over the side of the bowl.

"So, you're still sleeping with him?" Megan says, giving me the side-eye from where she's perched on a stool by our breakfast counter.

"No, I'm not." I am *such* an idiot. This is exactly why I didn't want to let him stay over.

"You can tell me, you know, I'm not judging you. Plus, I heard your headboard banging half the night, had to dig out some earplugs around 2am."

Oh my God. I knew we were too loud.

"I can't babe, because if I admit it to you, I'll have to admit it to myself and we both know that me having regular sex with *him* would be the worst thing in the world."

"Didn't sound that bad last night," she smirks.

"What are you doing?" I ask, changing the subject and peering at the phone in her hand. "Are you watching hockey player videos again? It's 7:30 in the morning."

"Listen, a girl's gotta do what a girl's gotta do to stave off a breakdown," she says. There's humour there, but you can't always tell with Megan if that sarcasm is hiding something more difficult.

"What's going on?"

"Just the usual end of year drag. Summer holidays can't come soon enough."

"What do you have planned?" There had been a mention of going to see Max but now that's all off I can't see it happening.

"Nothing," she sighs. "Six weeks of silly little walks for my silly little mental health."

Nah, I'm not having this angel wasting her life away moping over some guy who was never good enough for her in the first place. "Maybe we should take a trip? That could be fun, you and me and a whole load of sun, sea, and sangria?"

I hardly ever take time off work, but with everything up in limbo maybe now would be the best time for it.

"Hmm, maybe. Do you think you could tear yourself away from your boyfriend?" she teases, laughing as she hops up to get ready for the day.

"Fuck you," I tease back, but there's a lump in my throat that tells me leaving him for a week would be far from easy.

Chapter 34

Hattie

I'M LEAVING MY THURSDAY boxing class on an endorphin high when I hear his ringtone.

"What do you want?" I snap, even though I'm smiling.

"Do you want to spend the day together on Saturday?"

"Doing what?"

"I don't know. Whatever we feel like."

Would it be inappropriate to suggest I spend the entire day sitting on his face?

"Why?"

"I don't have plans, and I like hanging out with you."

"Oh, so I'm your last resort?"

"No, Hattie. You're my first. There's nobody I'd rather spend my free time with." I bite my lip and attempt to ignore how fast my stomach flips.

"I have to work."

"It's the weekend."

"There are no weekends in advertising."

"Can I at least take you for breakfast? Maggie's? Promise not to eat into your day too much."

Dammit. He's got me there. I'm a sucker for Maggie's French toast sticks and he knows it. "Fine, you can take me out for breakfast."

"Can't wait. I'll pick you up at 8."

This is so ridiculous. *I* am so ridiculous. I've changed my outfit three times, my lipstick twice, and faffed with my hair more than an overpriced hairdresser. I never make this much of an effort on dates, and I certainly never give a thought to what a guy will think of how I look. That's Rob The Manipulator Morgan doing stupid things to my brain again.

I finally settle on a floaty navy dress covered in little white flowers, chunky boots, and bare legs. I may have to work today, but I'll be damned if I see Rob and don't at least get fingered in his car.

At 7:59am I throw on a cardigan, slip out of the house, and make my way down to the corner where he usually picks me up. Megan might have her suspicions but I won't do anything to fuel them. Thankfully, on weekends she takes the opportunity to sleep as late as her students so there were no witnesses to my pathetic, giddy fawning.

It's cool on this side of the building first thing, only warming up when the sun coasts its way round later in the day.

At 8:06 there's still no sign of him, and I walk up and down the path to keep warm. I swallow my pride and check for a message, even though my phone has been in my hand this entire time.

By 8:10 he still hasn't texted, but it will be a cold day in hell before I text him and ask where he is. I hate myself for checking my phone constantly like a besotted teenager.

I pick at the skin at the edge of my thumb and when I realise I'm doing it I throw my hand away from my body as if it could land beyond my arm's reach.

This is how mum used to get when one of her boyfriends would disappear for a few days. She'd pace around the house as if she was itching all over. She'd start cleaning, pulling things from cupboards, trying to declutter and organise but always making things more chaotic in the process. As if the reason they had left was too many shoes in the hallway and not because they were rotten to the core.

By 8:17, Rob is dead to me.

A couple of minutes late is one thing, but to leave me hanging on the street corner like some secret whore for nearly twenty minutes is unforgivable.

Fuck this guy. I don't care how late he is, if he ever bothers his arse to turn up, he won't find me here. I storm back inside, grab my laptop and my car keys and shout sorry through Megan's door for making so much noise. My stupid heart still hopes to see his car pull up before I slam the door on mine and drive away.

Kara answers the door in her pyjamas, half of her hair falling out of her bun.

"Hey, you OK?"

"Do you have pastries?"

"What happened?"

"I got stood up for a date and I'm raging about it. Can I work here for a bit?"

"Of course. What a dick. Who would stand you up?"

"A gigantic twat, that's who." I follow Kara through to her kitchen and hop up onto a barstool. She rummages in the cupboard and plonks a pain au chocolat down in front of me.

"Maybe he slept in?" she offers.

"It was his idea! If he can't set an alarm then he can go to hell. Honestly Kara, I should be thankful he showed his true colours."

"So hang on, this was a breakfast date?" she laughs, softly. "Wow, your libido never rests."

"I don't want to talk about it," I huff, and thankfully I don't have to because my best friend's husband walks in, looking disgustingly hot in only his boxer shorts. Luke rubs his eye with one hand while the other scratches the soft hair below his belly button. It reminds me of how good Rob looks first thing, all warm and sleepy and dishevelled, and I force myself to look away.

"I thought that was you," he says. "It's early. Everything OK?"

"Shit, I thought you'd be working, sorry."

"Decided to have a proper day off with my wife," he says, nuzzling her neck as he wraps his arms around her from behind. God, people in love disgust me. I swallow my vitriol along with another bite.

"Hattie was just telling me some bastard stood her up for breakfast so she's come here to mope and work."

"I didn't realise you were both off work, though. I'll let you get back to your day of shagging and staring into each other's eyes."

Luke's phone buzzes on the counter and after glancing at the screen he answers quickly.

"Granny, you OK?" Kara looks worried, her hand at her heart as she listens in.

"Rob? What? Why was he calling you?"

My ears prick up at the sound of his name. I try to keep it cool, but my heart sinks when he speaks again.

"Uh-huh... oh no, is she OK?"

I feel a tightness in my chest, my heart racing.

"OK. Yeah I can pass that on. She's right here, actually," he turns to face me, brows knotting together. "I'll tell her."

I feel the blood drain from my face. I don't know what's going on, or why Rob has called Luke's grandma to try to get hold of me, but I know this stupid secret we've been keeping is about to be exposed.

"OK Granny, I'll call you later. Love you."

Luke hangs up and I stare into the layers of flaky pastry, my cheeks burning and head swimming.

"That was my Granny Annie," Luke says, "Rob called her and asked her to call me and get a message to you, Hattie."

Kara looks back and forth between us. "That's weird."

"What was the message?" I ask, attempting nonchalance and failing.

"His mum had a fall. He's at the hospital with her and he doesn't have his phone. That's why he wasn't there this morning."

"What was this morning?" Kara asks.

"I have to go." I grab my bag from the counter and dash for the door, pulling my boots back on.

"Hattie?" Kara asks again, and I can't answer. I just can't have her knowing I was waiting for him, and I especially can't have her knowing I was this bummed out about it. And none of it matters, because his mum is hurt, so *he* will be hurting, and I have to get out of here right now and go to him.

"Rob?" Kara yells from the doorway. "Is that who breakfast was with? What is going on, Hattie?"

I get into my car and don't look back.

I must cover half of the hospital by the time I find the ward his mum is in. Not wanting to intrude, I hang back in the corridor but ask the nurse on shift to let him know I'm here.

He appears from behind a curtain, relief written all over his face as he approaches. When he's finally in reach, I wrap my arms around his waist. His arms come up to pull my shoulders into him, and I settle my head in my favourite spot underneath his chin, my cheek against the skin exposed by the shirt buttons he's loosened off in the night.

"What happened?"

"I got a call at work to say she'd had a fall in the garden. My Auntie Sheila called an ambulance and they brought her here."

"Is she OK?"

"She fractured her arm and hit her head on a step, so they kept her overnight to monitor for concussion. She's sleeping just now."

"I'm so sorry. Are you OK?"

"I'm fine."

"Don't lie to me." I cup his face in both of my hands. "I can see that you're not."

He squeezes his eyes open and shut a few times. "It's just, it's my mum, you know. She's everything to me, I really thought for a minute I'd lost her. I got that call and just panicked and ran."

With the pad of my thumb, I wipe away his tears. "It's OK."

"I'm sorry for standing you up. I left my phone in my office and didn't want to leave Mum's side. The only number I know is Luke's granny, so I got her to ring him so he could reach you."

"Rob, there's no need to apologise. It can't be helped."

"I know, but I was really looking forward to breakfast, and you must have thought I'd stood you up, and I hate that I made you feel that way."

His breath is erratic, he's exhausted and I don't know what to do except hold him tight, maybe the tightest I've ever held him. "It's OK. I'm here, it's OK."

"I slept in a chair and I smell like shit," he sobs into my shoulder and I reach up, stroking my fingers through his hair.

"Do you want to go home and take a shower? Maybe have a nap?"

"No, I can't leave her on her own."

"I'll sit with her."

"You have to work."

"This is more important. Go and get your phone. I'll call you when she wakes up."

In the chair next to the hospital bed I take what feels like my first proper breath of the day. I feel guilty that my first instinct was to assume he'd stood me up. I've never seen him like this, so worried and upset about trying to get hold of me. He's normally so calm and self-assured.

I text Kara to tell her Rob is OK, and that I'll explain everything later and pass the time trying to review documents, but mostly listening in to other patients' conversations. It's impossible not to eavesdrop when the walls are nothing more than a strip of fabric.

"Who are you, then?" Rob's mum croaks, trying to boost herself up to sitting, which is impossible with her arm in a sling.

"Um, hi," I leap to her aid, helping her lean forward while I plump the pillows. "I'm Hattie, Rob's friend. We met at Luke's wedding."

"Oh yes, the woman who slashed my boy across the face," she says, completely deadpan. *Oh shit.* I didn't know he'd told her about that.

"Let me call for a nurse. I'll call Rob, he just nipped home to shower."

"Oh no, no. Don't make a fuss. I'm just winding you up," she says, a warm smile on her face. "He sat in that chair all night, you know. I bet he smells revolting. Leave him be and you stay right here and let me figure out why my son's so obsessed with you."

Chapter 35
Rob

Despite being told to rest for at least a week, yesterday I found Mum in the garden, pulling up weeds. She's never been very good at listening to advice, so I've decided to stay at her house, at least until she can use her arm again. Sheila does her best to help, but Mum tells her off, and she won't get away with that attitude with me.

Being home for more than a few hours on a Sunday night unravels something inside me. I don't know if it's the clutter everywhere you look, Mum and Sheila existing solely on tea and toast, or that the bedroom of my youth remains untouched. If you didn't know better, you'd be forgiven for thinking I'd died and Mum had preserved it as a shrine in my memory.

It's a stark contrast, revisiting the life of a boy who left for university one day, now returning as the man those years turned me into.

Growing up, there was an expectation that Luke, the son of a surgeon, would go to university, and I, the fatherless child of a cleaner and her barmaid sister, would not. And yet the roles were reversed early on. Luke worked in his grandparents' pub before it was even legal, and quickly climbed the ranks in the kitchen. Science was my comfort zone, and once I got the grades to study psychology, there was no looking back. In all that time away, I came back for holidays, but always had a foot half out the door ready to leave again. A permanent position at Branchmore hospital was a stroke of luck. Close enough to

Mum and Sheila to visit, not so close that moving back in made much sense.

I haven't spent a night here in years, which means I'm very much feeling like I don't belong here.

I belong in *my* home. I want to be in my kitchen after picking Hattie up from the station. I want to be cooking her dinner, listening to her vent about her day, before taking her to bed and holding her until the morning. Mum's fall, plus a hectic work schedule, means I haven't seen her all week. There's nothing to do here except poke around the shrine.

Walls plastered in faded posters of semi-naked models and indie bands whose hits are long-forgotten. A shelf of dog-eared novels I barely remember reading. A wardrobe of oversized t-shirts and baggy jeans I can't believe I ever wore. In the bedside drawer, I find a stash of letters and notes written by various girls throughout my school years. Flipping through, I feel terrible realising I can't remember half of them, either.

I'm about to throw them in the bin but one near the bottom of the pile catches my eye, the cursive handwriting summoning a memory of golden hair, one gangly arm around my shoulder, a pure laugh filling my ears.

My Dearest Roberto,

How had I forgotten her nickname for me?

I have a worry and I need to get it off my chest. I'm worried you'll stop being my friend now that Luke and I are officially boyfriend and girlfriend. AND I'm worried you might be worried about it too.

I know it's always been the three of us, and that us two getting together might be a bit of a shock.

Their relationship was about as shocking as the sun setting and coming up again the next morning.

I don't want things to be weird. I know you're his best friend and I won't get in the middle of you two. But I still need you (not just to help me study for Biology!) so please don't friend dump me. I hope we can still all hang out.
Can I tell you a secret? I think Luke is the one. Is that an insane thing to say? I love him so much. I know we're so young, and there's a lot of life ahead of us, but I'm certain he's it for me.

Jesus, that hurts. Heather's life wasn't nearly long enough. She should still be here.

I see it so clearly. He and I will be old and grey and running the pub just like Annie and Derek. You'll visit us as much as you can and bring your wife. She'll be beautiful (obviously) but I hope you'll look hard and find someone who makes you feel the way Luke makes me feel. Alive! You deserve all the good things in the world. I'm so lucky to have you both in my life.

Is she kidding? We were the lucky ones.

Love always,
H xxx
P.S. Choose someone who likes me too. I never want anything to come between us.

A fat tear plops onto the paper, and I dab it quickly before it makes her words bleed into the page. Imagine being that wise at fourteen? Knowing at such a young age that she'd met the love of her life. How did they have so much belief in each other, and what does it say about me that I never had anything close to that?

Would Heather and Hattie be friends? Heather got on with everyone she ever met, young or old. Hattie is much more cautious about who she lets into her life, but I like to think they'd have hit it off.

I have to wonder if I'd have even met Hattie if Heather was still with us. We live in the same town, we're a similar age, even now it seems wild that we hadn't met before Luke and Kara introduced us. How have I never spotted her across the street, or picked her face out in a crowd in a bar?

All this time, I guess I wasn't looking hard enough, but she's the first person I find in any room now. I need to see her, need to make her understand how I feel, even if I only half understand it myself.

Me: I'm sorry about standing you up. Let me take you out for dinner on Saturday and make it up to you?
Hottie: There's no need to apologise.
Hottie: And there's nothing to make up x
Me: Let's go to London. You don't even have to sit with me on the train if you're worried about being seen together.
Hottie: No limo?
Me: Strictly for when you get married, sweetheart.

In the bathroom mirror, I hardly recognise the man I used to be, the man that wanted nothing more than casual sex and no strings fun. Staring back at me is a man who can't get enough of the woman waiting for me out there, the woman who's proved to be more than enough.

Heather's advice from 19 years ago has been circling in my head all week. *'Look hard'*. I don't need to look anymore. Whether Hattie's dishing out fire and ice, or docile in my arms at the end of a long night beneath my sheets, she's the only woman I can see myself with now.

We've had a perfect day together, eating and drinking our way around London, stopping in parks to sit and people watch. She let me buy her a pair of earrings, dainty little studs she's been twisting ever since, and now we're capping off the night in a hip underground cocktail bar she's recommended. The best part, every time I've reached for her hand, she's let me take it. I can't remember the last time I felt this alive, this excited, this hopeful.

When I leave the bathroom, I find another man in my seat, and all that hope comes crashing down. My gaze falls to Hattie's phone in his hand, and I hang back, watching my worst nightmare unfold. She smiles at him, bright eyes roaming his face while he finishes typing. My stomach churns when he passes her phone back and kisses her cheek as he stands to leave.

Even when he's gone, she doesn't stop smiling. She sits back, takes another sip of her cocktail and casts a glance around the room. She seems to look everywhere except right at me until finally our eyes lock through a gap in the crowd that feels like it's doubled since I left her side. Her smile falls, and my feet carry me, reluctantly, back to our table.

"What are you doing?"

"Nothing," she says, shrugging defensively. "Waiting for you."

I point my thumb towards the man she was just talking to, now back in a booth with his friends. "Did you just get some guy's number when you're out on a date with me?"

Hattie scoffs, folding her arms across her chest. "Don't be a dick. It's just a number. It's not like I blew him in the toilets, and anyway, this isn't a date."

"Then what the fuck do you think this is?"

"For your information, he's an old colleague and we haven't caught up in years. I got his number for a job lead. But of course you would jump to conclusions and assume I was trying to fuck him."

Oh shit. "Hattie, no, that's not it. I'm sorry."

"Don't bother Rob, that's literally what just happened. You saw me with a man and you thought *'there she is, Hattie the slutty one'*. I don't know what you're trying to prove here."

"I'm really sorry. I shouldn't have assumed anything." I try to reach for her hand, but she yanks her arm away and downs the rest of her drink.

"Have you paid for these?" she asks and I nod. Grabbing her coat from the back of her chair, she weaves her way through the throng of drinkers. I follow as fast as I can but she's nimble, pushing through the doors and down the street.

"Hattie, wait," I call after her, dodging tourists to catch up. The sun has set while we've been inside and there's a chill in the air. I want to take her hand, as effortlessly as I have all day, but she's tucked both into her armpits as she marches on. "I'm sorry. Please don't go."

"Of course, there's no possible way on earth a man could talk to me without wanting to get in my pants," she shouts, continuing her pace.

"I'm really sorry, I just... I saw him with your phone and thought the worst."

"Darren is gay, Rob. And even if he wasn't, I can sleep with whoever I want. You're not my boyfriend."

"I'm fucking trying to be!"

"*What?*" she stops short, spinning to face me. I drag my hands through my hair and catch my breath. This is not how I wanted to have this conversation. "What are you talking about?"

"Why do you think I really brought you here today? I wanted to show you how things could be with us. Without sneaking around, only seeing each other at night."

"For fuck's sake, Rob," she says, throwing her hands up in the air. "Please don't do this. I already have enough stress in my life. I don't need more."

"Is this stressful to you?" I cup her shoulders and step into the space between us. Dipping my head, I force her to look at me. "The time we've spent together these past few months has been amazing for me. Not stressful at all."

"Then what happens when you decide you don't need this anymore? I'm not waiting around for you to destroy me." She's not the only one who would be destroyed if this ended. Even the suggestion of losing her rattles my heart loose in my chest.

"I don't *need* you, Hattie." She looks hurt, and I wince at my clumsy words. "I *want* you. I'm not here because I'm thinking of my dick, I'm here because I... because I..."

"You don't want this, not really," she interrupts. "This is how it would be. You don't trust me, even though I've never given you a reason not to. You'll always be looking for a reason to get out of this, and that reason will always be something I get the blame for. You'll find someone better."

"You're looking for excuses."

She wraps her arms tight across her chest and shakes her head from side to side, staring at the ground between us. "I'm not capable of having a relationship. You know I don't do that shit."

Can't she see that's what we're already doing? How is it so easy for her to pretend there's nothing going on here? "What if you tried?"

"I can't. I don't know how."

"You need to let me in. Let me help you."

"What I need is to go home," she says, pushing past me, and I let her go. Like a complete idiot, I watch her make her way down to the underground station even though we'll be catching the same train home. I have zero desire to spend another second in London without her. Or anywhere, for that matter.

Chapter 36
Hattie

After a few days apart, and several nights spent replaying our argument, I'm willing to admit that I *might* have overreacted. Or maybe I didn't, I don't know. What I do know is Rob pulled that shit on me out of nowhere, so I'm never getting drunk with him again if he's going to act all territorial and serious about our little arrangement.

I hate feeling like we're in a fight, though, especially when we'd been having such a fun day together. Despite me doing a runner, he did the decent thing and followed me to our train home, but kept enough of a distance that I could cool off. Back home, he walked me to my flat in silence, and didn't argue when I went inside alone.

Obviously, I legged it up the stairs, and peeked behind the curtain to watch him from my bedroom window. The sight of him all slumped in the shoulders as he made his way across the road is not one I want to have as my most recent memory of him, so I'm determined to make amends. And I can't think of a better way than on my knees on his bedroom floor.

August is in full heat, a sticky summer evening where you don't need more than a t-shirt, and the air-con in my car is no match for winding all the windows down instead. Maybe after I've said sorry, I'll make us drinks and we can sit out in the garden and watch the sunset.

Rob takes ages to answer the door and when he finally does, he looks the opposite of happy to see me. "What are you doing here?"

"I came to say sorry." I'll need a little time to warm up before I can give him more of an apology than that. "And I'm horny."

"But it's Tuesday?" he says, pinching the bridge of his nose. "I'm sorry, I'm busy."

"It's OK. I'll wait until you're done."

I step forward, but he doesn't move aside. "Hattie, really, I'd love to see you, but you can't come in. Not tonight."

The realisation hits me as if he's poured a bucket of cold water over me from a great height. "You've got someone here."

"No, it's not that, but I am in the middle of something." He's lying to me. I can feel it in my gut. He glances back into the house. "I really have to get back to it. Can I call you later?"

I'm already halfway to my car when I shout back. "No, don't fucking bother."

Chapter 37
Rob

WHY DID SHE HAVE to pull a move like that? The last thing Hattie needs is me being cross with her, but I can't ignore how angry I am at the fucking mess we're making. Angry that she could be so dismissive of my feelings and not speak to me for days. Angry that she won't try for a second to open up to me. And, most of all, angry that the one time she tried to reach out, I had to make her leave.

I'm not ready to explain it though, and definitely not in under thirty seconds on my doorstep.

Me: You free for a chat?

Luke rings me right away and I get comfy on the sofa. It's been a long time since we've had a heart to heart like this. After Heather died we did this a lot, but it's never been me who's needed the advice.

"What's up, mate?" he says, his face half in the screen as he finds a spot to chat.

"Is Kara with you?" I ask, hoping I'm not about to reveal Hattie's business to her friends, which would only land me in even deeper shit.

"No, she's up in bed with a book boyfriend," he laughs. "What's going on?"

"I slept with Hattie." It feels weird to say it out loud.

"Yeah, I know about that," Luke says, as casually as if I've told him I have two arms. I must look confused as hell because he tells me the answer before I can ask the question. "Kara told me."

"Why didn't you say anything?"

"She said it was a secret. I figured you'd tell me in your own time, and it's not like you tell me every time you sleep with someone."

"It wasn't just one time," I say,

"Ah, I had a feeling that might be the case. You're always making eyes at each other. Is it serious?"

"I want it to be," I say, my breath leaving my body in an exhausted sigh. I've been keeping it in for so long I hadn't realised how heavy it felt.

"Oh my God, mate," he says, sitting upright. "Congratulations!"

"Don't get too excited, that's what I need your help with. You've met her. You know what she's like. How the fuck are you supposed to tell a woman like Hattie Buchanan that you love her?"

Hattie's book club is meeting at Sunshine tonight, so I've walked down to lurk at one of the little tables outside, hoping to catch her as she leaves. As the crowd pour out, she doesn't clock me when she strolls out, arm in arm with Megan. She looks cute as hell, the skirt of her summer dress swishing around her thighs, but her chunky black ankle boots remind me she's anything but cute in attitude.

I see an opportunity here, one I keep forgetting to take. As they make their way across the cobbled courtyard, I pull up her number and hit call. When my ringtone starts playing, she unlinks her arm and digs her phone from her pocket. It takes a second for me to figure out which song she's picked for me.

"It's Rob," she holds it out for Megan to see.

"Answer it."

"No, I'm too scared," I hear her say. *Scared? Why the fuck is she scared to talk to me?* Megan snatches her phone and answers before Hattie can realise what's happening.

"Hey, Rob, this is Megan, Hattie can't come to the phone right now. Would you like me to pass on a message?"

"Hi Megan, would you mind asking Hattie to turn around?"

They both turn, horrified to find me standing behind them.

"*Heads Will Roll*? That's my ringtone?"

"Sorry," Hattie stares at the ground between us. "I did it ages ago."

"It's fine. It's a good song. Can we talk?"

"If you wanted to talk, you should have come to book club," she mumbles.

"It's not a conversation I want to have in front of an audience. No offence, Megan."

"None taken," she says, holding her hands up in front of her. "You should go with him, Hattie. We'll catch up at home."

"Do you want a lift?" I appreciate her nudging Hattie in my direction, but I don't want her walking home alone.

"I'll go back and wait for Kara."

We face each other in silence, each waiting for something, anything to happen. It's unbearable, not pulling her straight into my arms, but I'm nervous about what's about to go down, and still frustrated with her inability to listen to what I'm really saying.

"Can we go back to mine?" I need to be sitting down for this.

"Fine. But this is kidnapping."

"Cut that shit out," I snap, storming off towards where I've parked my car on the main road. I'm about to confess everything, hand her my heart, and she can't be nice for five seconds? I wait for her to get in, and turn the radio up so she doesn't have the chance to piss me off even more.

I can feel the anger pouring off her while we drive. Back at my house she jumps out before I have the chance to open the door for her, and marches up the path like she owns the place. I take my sweet time unlocking the door, and when she tries to budge past me I block her in one direction, and then the other, until she charges against my chest, shoving me out of her way.

"How was your date?" she asks, her voice laced with vitriol as she looks around my living room, presumably for evidence to back up the story she invented about what happened last night. To think she had the nerve to accuse me of not trusting her when she's doesn't trust me either.

"It was great," I lie and she yelps behind her tight smile. If there were weapons nearby I'd be halfway to murdered right now. I don't mind giving her a taste of her own medicine though. She's so happy to act out and make me jealous, if she wants to believe I've been with someone else, let's see how she likes it.

"Good shag?"

"Sure. Cracking blow job."

"How dare you?" she says, her jaw set firm. "Nobody blows you better than me."

"Prove it." I hear the crack before the sting on my cheek registers the slap. Despite it, her nimble fingers unbuckle my belt and whip it free, the buttons on my jeans coming apart the way only an expert knows how.

I'm still rubbing my face when she tugs them down, along with my boxers, and her hand wraps around my shaft the second it springs free. I'm rock solid, I knew I was, but now she knows too, and from the look in her eyes she loves having the upper hand.

"I fucked a guy so hard last night I could barely walk this morning."

What the fuck? I grab the back of her head and yank her away from me.

"Tell me that's not true?" She pouts that pretty little mouth and raises one eyebrow in a way I know will haunt my nightmares. "Is it?"

With a small shake of her head her face softens and she ends her lies. I pull her back further, and loom over her, her body darkening in my shadow. "I never, *ever*, want to hear about you with another man again, do you understand me? As far as I'm concerned, you were a virgin the day I met you and I'm the only man who's ever been inside you."

"You're such a disgusting, possessive, jealous bastard."

I tug harder. "I'm your disgusting possessive jealous bastard, and you love it."

Her eyes flare, then flutter closed. I let go of her hair and she helps me pull her dress up over her head. She's not wearing a bra, and if I'd known those perfect tits and tight nipples were waiting for me, I'd have had my mouth on her before we even left the car. "Get on your hands and knees."

This is no time for niceties. I position myself behind her, drag her underwear down and find her soaking, just like I knew I would. Nothing turns her on more than fighting with me, and right now I've never needed her more. I can only interrogate it for as long as it takes to roll on a condom from my wallet.

Why are we like this? Why do we hurt each other?

"If anyone's going to fuck you until you can't walk it's me. Do you understand me?" I lean over her, my chest against her back, and growl into her ear. She nods, tilting her head to open her neck up to me. I take the fleshy slope of her shoulder between my teeth, tease my dick against her, and inch my way home.

"Say it, Hattie."

"If anyone's going to fuck me until I can't walk it's you," she says, her voice full of need as she pushes back against me.

"That's right, angel." One steady push and I'm all the way in, hot skin meeting hot skin. Hattie groans as I fill her up, her fingers digging into the plush carpet.

"It's you. It's you. It's you," she says, wracked confessions in time with the breath that leaves her with each of my thrusts. She gives as good as she gets, slamming back into me, her back arching as one hand snakes between her legs to bring herself along. I feel the exact moment her fingers find her clit from the way she tightens around me, and I'm tempted to drag her upstairs and fuck like this in front of my mirror. I want to see it all, and I want *her* to see how I'm the one who makes her body feel this good. This alive. This free.

Desperate, and aching on the edge, I need to come, and I need to see her. It's been days since I saw that beautiful face so lost in pleasure. Pulling out, I flip her to her back and lose my mind when I notice the earrings I gave her. The sight of her wearing those and nothing else tugs at something deep inside me. It cools my burning desire, and I still, the weight of me buried between her thighs.

"We're so good together," I drop my forehead to her sternum and breathe into her chest. I can't look her in the eye, but she has to know how much this means to me.

"Don't be ridiculous," she chokes out a laugh. "This is toxic as fuck."

"What are you so afraid of?"

"I'm not afraid of you."

"No, but you're afraid of what this could be. So you push me away, and don't let me get close. Hurt me before I hurt you. That's the strategy, right?"

She tips her head back and lets out a frustrated grunt. "Can you just fuck me already? I was so close."

"I don't think I can." I press up onto my hands, balancing either side of her shoulders, but I still can't bring myself to end this, not fully.

"Why not?"

"Because it's starting to hurt. To be with you and do these things and know that every time I'm getting closer to you, you're getting further away. Fuck, Hattie. I'm sorry. I don't want to keep doing this. Not like this."

"Get off me then, nobody is forcing you to be here."

"That's not what I mean, I obviously want to keep doing this," I flex inside her, forcing a moan from her throat. "I just don't want to do this with anyone else."

"What are you on about?"

"I told you Hattie. I want you. Only you." She stiffens underneath me, her brow knotting together, as her expression races from bliss to confusion to white hot anger.

"I thought you were saying all that shit because you were drunk. I'm not doing this. Get off me."

I pull out and roll to her side, emotions twisting in my chest as she springs to her feet.

"This is just sex for me," she says, scrambling to gather her clothes.

"You're lying to yourself, and you know it." I press the heels of my palms into my eyelids. "Why can't you admit we have something here?"

"You know why, Rob. All my life I've watched men leave my mum. My best friend's relationship was couple goals and then he cheated on her and left after twelve years."

"Kara's happier than ever now." It's a pointless offering. One positive relationship isn't going to undo a life living under the weight of negative ones, just like my best friend's new relationship doesn't change the fact that I had to watch him lose his wife.

All this time I've blamed my father for my shitty attitude to relationships. I hadn't realised until recently how much Heather's death had messed me up too. That nugget of insight shifted everything for me.

I have to tell her. It has to be now.

"I lied to you," I say from my spot on the floor. If she kicks me in the dick now, I wouldn't blame her.

"About what?"

"The blow job. Last night. I didn't have a date."

"Neither did I," she laughs, pulling her dress over her head. A hollow feeling forms in my chest knowing this is probably the last time I'll see her naked. It's all coming out, and there's no going back.

"I've been seeing someone."

"What the fuck? Then why am I here?"

"No, *shit*, not a woman. Well yes, a woman, but not like that. A therapist."

I brace for a scream, some insults about what a useless prick I am, but when I look up Hattie's standing over me, reaching out a hand. I take it and let her pull me up, suddenly aware of how ridiculous I look right now, half-naked on the floor, my trousers still wrapped around my ankles.

"Why?" she asks quietly when I turn away and get myself back in order. I take a seat on the sofa and rake my hands through my hair.

"Because I'm a mess. I've always known it, but I've never looked too closely, didn't want to feel like something inside me was broken. And lately I've been feeling... some things I haven't felt before and I don't know how to deal with them. So I thought I should speak to someone and work through my shit. That's why I can't see you on Tuesdays. I talk to her online in the evening, and then I'm pretty wrung out afterwards."

"That's very mature of you."

"Will you have a drink with me before you go? Let me explain." She just stares at me, that beautiful mouth twitching like she doesn't know what to say. "Please?"

"OK."

In the kitchen I pull two beers from the fridge and flip off their caps. I knew this conversation was coming, knew I'd have to tell her I've been working through decades of shit. Knew I'd have to work up to admitting my feelings, telling her I want more, I just didn't expect it to be tonight.

She takes a seat at the table and I watch her throat roll as she swallows her first sip.

"This is what I imagined we'd do last night. Get naked then have a drink in the garden afterwards," she says with a frustrated laugh. "Why didn't you just tell me you were talking to your therapist? I would have understood."

"I don't know." The booze goes down too easily. "I'm embarrassed, I guess. It's a serious thing. I thought you might laugh. Take your pick."

"Is it helping?" she asks.

"Yeah, loads. I should have done it years ago."

Hattie is quiet, and I can't tell if it's because she doesn't know what to say, or if she's giving me the space to open up. Opening up is something I've talked a lot about in my sessions with Paula, even rehearsing what I might say, but being here in the moment, it's harder than I imagined.

"Remember I told you my dad left before I was born?" I say. Hattie nods, and picks at her thumb. I reach across the table to still her hand but she pulls it away and tucks it underneath her leg. "When she told him she was pregnant he went to the pub and never came back. They'd only been together for a few months but she never heard from him again."

"What a dick."

"Yep. My mum is amazing though. She decided to keep me and raise me with my Auntie Sheila. I didn't think anything of it until secondary school when I started to ask questions. She was honest with me, which I appreciate, but having this therapy has made me realise that finding out at eleven that your dad didn't want to know you kind of fucks you up a bit.

"I love my mum, and so much of me is like her, but I've grown up hating the part of me that comes from him. I hate thinking that her life should have been better somehow, but he robbed her fucking choices out from under her feet. I hate knowing I could turn out like him. My worst nightmare is knowing I could do to someone what he did to her. So I don't let myself get close, I don't let people get attached.

"Unfortunately, I also really like sex, but I'm starting to realise that, despite my best efforts to avoid being like him, I'm actually doing exactly what he did. Avoiding relationships, commitment, avoiding happiness."

"For what it's worth," Hattie says, "I think your mum did an amazing job with you. And she seems really great."

"She doesn't talk about him much, but I don't think she ever got over it. I sometimes wonder if she's half hoping he'll come back. So that's why I don't date. I can't bear the idea of breaking someone's heart. I never met anyone who made me even want to consider changing my mind until you."

Hattie brings her knees to her chest, and her shoulders roll inwards.

"I was seven when my dad left. My sister was four so she doesn't really remember him, but I do. And the thing that hurts the most is that they are good memories. We had a good life, I absolutely loved the guy. He was my hero."

"What happened?" I ask. "Is it OK to ask?"

"He was a long distance lorry driver. On the nights he wasn't with us he was with someone else and he started a new family. He just stopped coming home. My mum told me he was away for a really long driving job but eventually I overheard her crying to a neighbour about it. He didn't even say goodbye to me. Never sent me a birthday card or a present at Christmas. Never tried to contact me again."

"Fuck, that's awful. Come here, sweetheart." I reach out, and she lets me pull her into my lap.

"Mum was a wreck. She had two kids, only a part time job, no family around to support her. She was never the same again after him. I have all these nice memories of her from before, but afterwards she was just exhausted doing everything alone.

"And she thought a man would be the solution, so there were a lot of new boyfriends. They always seemed nice at first, but eventually they'd show their true colours. They'd be resentful of us kids, or they'd shout at us. Mum would usually take their side over ours. Every few years there was a good one, and somehow that would be even worse."

"Why was it worse?"

She makes a pained noise and covers it with a half-hearted laugh. "Because they were nice to us, treated us well, but eventually they'd leave too."

"I'm so sorry, Hattie." She drops her head to my shoulder and I stroke up and down her back.

"I bet your therapist would have a lot to say about that. Probably explains the ice queen act."

"I should never have said that."

"It's fine, I know I'm rotten inside. After watching Mum let those men treat her like crap, I swore I'd never let it happen to me. But..." she laughs softly against my chest. "Unfortunately, I really like sex too. And you're right, I push people away. Men can't leave you if you leave them first."

It breaks my heart to hear her speak about herself that way. Not one person ever took the time to show her how much she's worth. How brilliant, and beautiful, and capable she is. And now she thinks she's rotten? Fuck that. I'd spend every single day showing her just how special she is if she let me have even half a chance.

"I wouldn't—"

"Please don't, Rob," she presses her fingers to my lips and shakes her head. "Don't say it. I'm glad you're getting help. But I'm never going to be any other way, so it's over."

"What are you saying?"

"We have to stop this. The fuck buddies thing. You deserve to get to a good place, meet someone who's also good, and have a happy life. You'll never get that from me, and I really need to focus on getting this promotion. Can we go back to being just friends?"

If I thought my heart was breaking fifteen seconds ago, it's smashed to pieces now.

"I don't know if I can. We've never been just friends. We blew straight past friends and I don't know how to be *just* anything with you."

She climbs out of my lap and shifts further along the sofa. "So what is this, some sort of ultimatum? Keep hooking up or nothing? That's pretty manipulative."

"Hey, look at me," I lean in and cup her chin, forcing her to hear what I have to say. "I don't want to stop any of this. And deep down, I don't think you do either. But I don't want to lose you, so if you really want to end this, then I'll give friends a shot. I just think I'll need some time to adjust because this hurts like hell for me."

It's not the outcome we hoped for, but I know Paula will be pleased with me expressing my needs.

"I'm sorry," she whispers and sniffs, blinking away tears. I can't see Hattie cry right now, not when I feel like bursting into tears myself.

"Hey," I nudge her leg with my knee and raise my glass. "To shitty dads."

"Never. They don't deserve our toast."

"Then to friendship. To us."

"To us."

We clink our glasses together, our eyes locked as we drink, her version of *'us'* feeling so far from mine.

Chapter 38
Hattie

It's been years since I interviewed for a new role, and I'd forgotten how much they feel like an interrogation.

If Andrew was on the panel, I'd feel more at ease, but this role isn't his to manage, so I've got to make do with Bob, Michelle from HR, and an external consultant I've never laid eyes on before.

I've already run through my fifteen minute presentation on what the next six to twelve months would look like under my leadership, and now I'm being grilled with the usual boring questions I've rehearsed night after night for the past two weeks.

"How do you manage conflict in the workplace?" *Fuck you Bob, you spineless prick,* is what I really want to say. I hope he doesn't think I've forgotten his role in the Spirited shitshow.

"I think healthy conflict is essential in the workplace. It's vital that executive decisions take multiple opinions into perspective. If everyone is unanimous in their agreement, then in my experience, it means someone's not saying how they really feel, and those views can bring major stumbling blocks if raised further down the line."

It's a brilliant answer, we've all been tripped up by some dickhead who didn't say what they were really thinking until it was much too late.

"And what about your personal conflict style? You've had a few, shall we say, challenges with members of senior management in the past."

I wish I could say I don't know what he's talking about, but every time I've raised concerns and pushed for better solutions, it's been interpreted as negativity. You'd think they'd want people to strive to be the best in the business, not a bunch of pushovers.

My smile never leaves my face as we go back and forth, and the interview ends with a round of handshakes, and Bob's reassurance I won't be kept waiting too long for an update. That could mean I've definitely got the job, or the opposite, and that they've already made their mind up. If there's one thing Bob is good at, it's his poker face.

"Hattie?" Andrew calls out when I walk past his office back to my desk. I step inside and close the door behind me. "How did it go?"

"Good, I think. I gave it my best, and they said they'll let me know soon." I slump against the wall, my heart rate slowing for the first time all day. "Got any insider info you'd care to share with me?"

"You know I don't," he says, "but I'm really rooting for you."

I let out a heavy sigh. I hate not knowing, and I know I'm going to spend the rest of the day twisting myself in knots. Andrew must sense it, too.

"Why don't you use a couple of flexi-hours and take the afternoon off, Hattie? Go home and rest up for a bit."

"Are you saying I look like shit?" I laugh, weakly. I definitely feel like it.

"I'm saying you deserve a break. You've put a lot of work into this. You're allowed to put yourself first for a bit."

Back home, I change into Rob's t-shirt that I never returned, and crawl under my duvet. The weight of today hits me fast. The interview, all the prep, the months of circling the drain with Spirited and Lawrence Fucking Desmond.

I want to sleep all weekend, but I don't dare close my eyes in case I miss a call. Luckily, I don't have to wait too long, and when I see the number with one of our extensions light up my phone, I sit up, fix my hair, and clear my throat before answering.

"Hello, this is Hattie."

"Hi Harriet, it's Michelle here." I roll my eyes, so bloody formal, nobody ever calls me Harriet, not even my mum. "Bob requested I give you a call before the end of the day, so you aren't waiting all weekend for an update. I'm sorry to inform you that although your interview was of a very high standard, on this occasion…"

I stay on the line, and Michelle keeps talking, but I barely hear another word.

Hours later, a knock at the door drags me out of my bed. It's not like Megan to forget her keys, but when I open it Rob is standing there looking hotter than ever in dark jeans and a tight fitting t-shirt, a massive bouquet in one hand.

"Congratulations!" he says, and I burst into tears.

"I didn't get it."

"Oh fuck," he grimaces. "Then maybe consider these commiseration flowers?"

"What are you doing here?" I say through shaky sobs. "I thought you never wanted to see me again."

"That's not what I said. Can I come in?"

"Sure, whatever, I don't care." *Except I do.* I care very much that he remembered today was my interview, that he had so much confidence in me, and that I've let him down.

"Do you want to talk about it?" he asks, stepping through the doorway and closing it behind him. I shake my head. I'm so tired, so bored with being miserable.

"Can we just go to bed so you can fuck these feelings out of me?"

Jesus, what must he think of me? This pathetic, desperate mess. His t-shirt is damp from hours of crying, but I still use it to wipe away more.

"Oh honey, no, come here." He pulls me into his arms and holds me tight. Everything in me resists until slowly I soften against his chest. "Hattie, you don't have to put on a front all the time, and especially not with me. Whatever you're feeling, it's OK."

"I'm fucking furious," I confess with a howl. "I really wanted that job, I deserved it and now I don't know what's going to happen to me."

In the living room I pick up the bottle of whisky I've already been making my way through, and flop onto the sofa. A deep pull burns my throat.

"They walk all over me. I do 80% of the work for none of the credit. I don't fit a mould, and it doesn't matter if I try to stay in the box or step out of it, it's still not enough. They gave my job to some fucking teenager, bollocked me for calling out the injustice, then let me do this other one for months without reward or recognition, only to give it to some *external candidate*. I don't know why I'm surprised."

"Have you ever considered that maybe the problem is the environment, the company, not you?" he says, prising the bottle from my hand after I've downed another mouthful. "There's nothing wrong with you, Hattie. I mean, I'm sure you're a giant pain in the backside, but you're smart and you're talented. You know your shit and you take no shit. You're brilliant, brave, beautiful, bold. You see what you want and you go after it. They're lucky to have you. Anyone would be lucky to have you."

I'm too messed up to hear his words as anything other than an invitation. Pushing him back against the sofa cushions, I climb into his lap and straddle him, but he grips my hips and lifts me off again.

"Come on, everyone else gets to use me. You can too." I give him a playful poke in the side.

"I'm not using you." His face crumples, and I stand up and take another swig. I don't care if I'm drinking too fast, I want to forget this day ever happened.

"That's literally what friends with benefits is. Using each other for sex. Isn't that why you came here? Threw your toys out of the pram, told me you'd have to stay away, but as soon as your dick got twitchy you've come running back?"

Rob stands too, his big hands gripping my shoulders, holding me steady at arm's length. He bends to meet my glare, but his eyes are full of something far from anger. "Hattie, listen to me carefully and get this in your fucking head. I *don't* use you. I sleep with you because I want you, because I need you. Because I..."

He trails off and presses his eyes shut. A shiver rattles up my spine, time stretching in the space between us. Was he really going to say what I think he was going to say? My throat burns and the tears well up again.

"This isn't friends with benefits for you, is it?"

"That's what I've been telling you," he says, so quiet I barely hear him. But his eyes say it too, until he steps back, dragging his hand over his face. "It hasn't been for a long time. You just don't believe me."

Why can't I believe him? Why can't I be someone who plays nice and gets along with others? Why do I have to make everything so bloody difficult all the time? I'm trying so hard to keep it all together and no matter what I do, it's never good enough. *I'll* never be good enough. Rage, panic, and fear slosh together inside me. I take another long drink, shove the bottle into his hand, and walk away.

"Where are you going?" he asks.

"I need my phone," I say, heading down the hallway towards my bedroom.

"Why?"

"I need to email my boss."

"Oh no, no, Hattie. We don't drink and email. That's like rule number one of having a job." He chases after me, but all I can do is laugh.

"I don't give a fuck." I hit compose and start typing, narrating as I go. "This. is. bullshit. You. are. bullshit. This. whole. company. is. bullshit. Lawrence. can. eat. shit. and. die."

Rob dives across the bed, reaching for my hand. "Hattie, no. Don't do this."

"Too late," I cackle. I throw my phone down on my bedside table and pull my t-shirt up over my head. "Now fuck me or fuck off."

Chapter 39
Hattie

"So I'm not fired?"

Over the weekend, Andrew put an urgent meeting in my diary first thing Monday morning, and even though I was already feeling sick about this mess with Rob, this pushed me over the line.

Of course, he didn't fuck me. He made me dinner, forced me to drink two pints of water, put me to bed, and went home, taking the whisky with him. I don't think I've ever cried over a man, but that night I lost it, and spent most of the weekend under those covers crying and wanking on repeat. A pathetic parody of a woman who has her shit together.

Crawling out of bed this morning, I forced myself to put on an appropriately professional looking outfit; a flowy cream blouse tucked neatly into a black pencil skirt, paired with a matching blazer. I rarely dress like a corporate twat for work, but I made an effort today, even if it was only to walk in and get sacked.

"No, Hattie. The company is restructuring, which has unfortunately rendered your position redundant," he repeats himself, clearly reading from a script HR has sent over.

"So I *am* fired?"

Andrew sighs. "Please don't make me read it again."

"I just don't understand. I said this whole company was bullshit and that Lawrence should eat shit and die. I've barely slept since you scheduled this meeting. How am I not fired?"

"You're being made redundant, Hattie. The company is restructuring, which has unfortunately rendered your position redundant," he repeats. "Listen, you'll get three months' pay, and in addition to that I requested HR give you three months' gardening leave effective immediately. Given your length of service and previously strong record, they agreed."

I'm being fired, but gently, and with a golden fuck off. A decade of hard work, dedication, and loyalty, and I've burned it all down with a fifteen word drunken email. I suspect it was cc'ing Bob that really did it.

Ten years. I've given nearly a third of my life to this place, my entire career, and Andrew has been there every step of the way. He looks so disappointed in me, and that's the thing that hurts the most.

Wait. I get three months' pay? Plus three paid gardening leave? That's not nothing, that's a fucking gift, even if gardening leave is basically code for *'get out of here before you can cause any more trouble'*.

"Did you do this for me?" I ask.

"Yes," he nods, softly. "I couldn't let them just fire you, even though you probably deserved it with that little stunt."

I huff out a relieved sigh and press my eyes together, stemming the flow of tears that are threatening to spill over any second now. "Thank you. Does everyone know I'm leaving?"

"No, we haven't made an announcement yet. You can walk out with your head held high."

I sit there, staring out of the window behind him. This is probably the longest we've ever been silent around each other. "What do I do now?"

"You clear your desk. You go home, and get some proper rest. And then you see where life takes you. I know you've been here a long time, Hattie, but this might be the best thing that's ever happened to you."

See where life takes you. Life has only ever taken me on the path I have pushed myself along, and lately it's been more of a drag.

I stand to leave, smoothing down the fabric of my skirt which has bunched up. I hate these stupid skirts. I'm burning them when I get home. Wherever life takes me, I hope I never have to dress like this again. My hand is on the door handle when he stops me.

"Hattie. I'm sorry for how things have gone down here. And especially for any part I've played in that. You're great at what you do, and I've always enjoyed working with you. If you need a reference in future, come to me personally. Don't go through HR, OK, kid?"

There's a pang in my chest and a lump in my throat. He hasn't called me that in a long time, but for years Andrew has, without me even realising, been something of a father figure to me. He's pushed me out of my comfort zone, encouraged me, and even though he's called me out on a fair amount of shit, he's always had my back. And despite the mess I've made, he still does.

"Thank you, Andrew. That really means a lot to me. I'm sorry I said you were bullshit. You're really not."

Back at my desk, I empty my things from my drawer into my bag and take a last look around the office floor. Other people's desks are adorned with family photos, thriving succulents, and mountains of trinkets. They clutch hot coffees in mugs, matching their personalities as they catch up with each other after the weekend.

The most personal thing I have at my desk is lip-gloss, and an old book club book. The whole thing is clear in under two minutes, so I throw a stapler in there as a last fuck you. God knows what I think I'll be stapling. Maybe I can use it to put my life back together now that I've fully torn it to pieces. *Hahaha, I'm hilarious.* No, that's not actually funny, is it?

I should say goodbye to people, but I can't bear a scene. I'll email people from home when the shock has worn off, arrange some drinks or something. Nobody even bats an eyelid when I walk out of the office, at 9:15am, unemployed for the first time ever.

The train journey home is a blur, and only when I step off at my station do I realise I've no idea when I'll be back in London again.

The house is too quiet when I let myself in. Even on my remote working days, it's not like this. I have breakfast with Megs before she leaves for school, I keep the radio on when I'm not on calls, and meet Kara for lunch.

I don't know what to do with myself, so I strip out of these awful clothes, throw on my favourite jean shorts and a hoodie and walk over to Sunshine.

"Hey," Luke says with a smile when I get to the front of the queue. "I didn't expect to see you today. What can I get you?"

"I need a coffee, a job, and the number for your therapist."

My brilliant, kind-hearted friend has the decency not to laugh. Instead, he rounds the counter and pulls me into a big hug.

"How about we start with the coffee, and you can tell me about the rest?"

Chapter 40
Hattie

I WAITED DAYS TO hear from my old colleagues and, besides a text from Andrew checking in, there was not one single message. It's silly of me really. I've been in that cutthroat industry long enough to know people come and go all the time without explanation. If you're not visible, you simply cease to exist. It makes me laugh to remember how we used to pitch clients with talk of our team being a family. We weren't a family, and I was nothing more than a cog in a machine that could be replaced in a heartbeat.

I still haven't decided what to do, but I don't think I ever want to go back to that life. Rob was right. I spent my days, and a lot of my nights, sending emails to make rich people richer. Even after just a couple of weeks, I'm struggling to see how I was ever so passionate about it.

Luke asked me to help with a few shifts here and there, and it's been surprisingly fun. I had a couple of waitressing jobs in my university days, and though the Sunshine coffee machine is like something out of a sci-fi movie, it didn't take long to get used to it.

I feel freer somehow, with my part time job in a cute little coffee shop. My shifts pass with ease, and it turns out I actually enjoy speaking to people when it's about something other than work. Tonight I'm joining book club from my spot behind the counter, cleaning while I listen to everyone's thoughts.

Apparently, Rob comes to Sunshine Book Club now. I suspect it's to keep an eye on me since I'm not replying to his texts, though I don't dare ask. He'd probably fob me off with some excuse about supporting Kara, and I wouldn't believe him, anyway.

He has a seat up front with Luke and is nodding along as others share their views. I wasn't convinced he's read the book, but I'll give credit where it's due, the man has a lot to say about *Wildfire*. It's the first in the *Buttercup Ranch* series, about a woman struggling to keep control of her family cattle ranch, and the billionaire who wants to buy the land.

It was predictable as hell, and I could tell from five pages in that Winona would win Caleb over the minute she got him on the back of a horse. Throw in a rodeo and a game of pool in a rundown bar and the man was swapping his brogues for Blundstones before you could say *'Giddy up!'* Still, I enjoyed it, as did tonight's group.

"My main question is, when can we have a group trip to cowboy country?" Megan laughs. "I'm desperate to go to a rodeo and see what all the fuss is about."

Maybe that's what I need to do with this unexpected sabbatical, travel a little, see some of the world. I'm certain I'd enjoy hooking up with a Southern man with a belt buckle the size of my face. As usual, I speak before I can shove the words back down.

"I just want someone to put their hat on my head and their dick in my mouth. Honestly, is it so much to ask?"

"Hattie!" Kara scolds me from across the room, but these are my people, and they cannot hide their laughter. Not even the members of Sunshine Book Club, who are in their sixties and seventies.

"I wish I had your energy, Hattie," Janice laughs.

"I wish you had her energy too," her husband, Gerald, teases. I shrug it off, but keep my mouth shut for the rest of the night.

As book club draws to a close I wave everyone off, tell Megan I'll see her at home, and try to ignore Rob who is clearly hanging back for me. There's only so long I can hide in the store cupboard, but when I come out he's still there, waiting by the door.

"Can I drive you home?" he asks, his hands shoved deep into his pockets.

"I don't think that's a good idea." It's a terrible idea. Just looking at him, all big and solid, yet soft and cosy in a charcoal sweatshirt, makes me want to tear my clothes off right here.

"Just to talk."

"What is there to talk about?" We've never been good at talking, and it would be so easy to convince me to take things further.

"I don't want to argue. I just want to hear how you're doing."

"You can head off, Hattie," Luke calls over from where he's putting the furniture back in order. "I'll finish up here and close."

"You traitor," I scowl, wondering if this is something they'd discussed. He mouths a *'sorry'* in my direction.

"What are you going to do now?" Rob asks once I've filled him in on the aftermath of me drunkenly setting off a grenade and ruining my career. Thankfully, he doesn't say *'I told you so'*, though I'm sure he must be thinking it.

"I have no clue, but I'm OK. I feel weirdly free. Luke's going to give me some more shifts at Sunshine to keep me busy, and I'm getting a ridiculous amount of money to not be at DFR, so I have some time to figure things out. I might ask Kara for advice about setting up my own."

"That sounds smart. You'd be great at being your own boss."

I haven't been paying attention to the road as we drive, and it's only when we're pulling into the petrol station I realise we're nowhere near my house. He drives past the fuel pumps and round the back to where the car-wash is.

"Unbuckle your seatbelt," he says, as we roll into position through the first set of sprayers.

"I'm not fucking you, Rob. I told you we have to stop doing that."

"We're not here for that. Get in the back. Like you did with your dad." A gasp slips out of me. I can't believe he remembered. "Quick, before you miss it."

I do as I'm told, scrambling between the seats. When I did this with Dad, I was small enough to climb up onto the parcel shelf and lay out flat on my back. The spray would rain down, thunderous on the window just inches from my body, and though I always jumped when it first started, it soon made me feel so calm.

There's no way I can fit up there now, but I give it my best shot, kneeling on the middle seat and angling my head just right. Even though I know it's coming, I still jump and let out a little squeal, but then I watch the colours blend into one, the foam whipping up until I'm in my little cocoon where the world can't get to me.

Those six minutes are some of the best of my life. I cry my stupid little heart out and let the thunder of the water drown it all out. When I make my way back to the front seat, Rob passes me a tissue then holds my hand the entire way home.

"Are you OK? Do you want me to come up?" he asks outside my building. I really do want that. I'd love nothing more than to crawl into bed with him and be held until morning, but I can't do that. I can't use a man as a sticking plaster over all of the gaping wounds I need to fix myself. Especially not a good man like him.

"I'm really trying to sort my life out, you know? I just need some space."

Chapter 41
Rob

SPACE.

One word.

Five measly letters.

How can it hurt so fucking much?

Chapter 42
Hattie

P*Ar*t*Y* t*His* W*Ay* the sign reads.

It's a unique mix of wonky upper- and lower-case letters that could only have been written by my nephew, Teddy. Today he turns four and, oh to still be the age where everyone makes a fuss of you on your birthday.

I brace myself for chaos and enter, making sure to latch the gate properly behind me. I'm already the black sheep of this whole shindig, the last thing I need is getting the blame for some kid escaping because of my carelessness.

I don't want to be here, but I've been guilt-tripped into it by a barrage of daily texts from my sister.

Georgina has the sort of garden that was made for parties, and here at the tail end of summer it's in full bloom. The borders are filled with big ruffled flowers, the sort someone like me will never know the names of. At the bottom of the garden there's a vegetable patch where she grows peas and tomatoes with Ted and my two-year-old niece, Rosalind (never Rosie).

I only know about it because I've seen it on her perfectly curated Instagram. I don't come here very often, mainly because I'm still being punished for trying to hook up with the vicar at her wedding. In my defense, the second season of Fleabag had just aired and half the country had a thing for hot priests. It wasn't my fault he was young and gorgeous, and I had no way of knowing he was my brother-in-law, Ryan's, best friend since primary school. You'd think someone might have mentioned that. Thankfully he moved to a new parish, or I wouldn't have shown my face today. Honestly, who's best friends with a vicar anyway?

Much like her Instagram, everything about George is perfectly curated. From the hair that looks like she gets daily blow dries, to the tasteful aesthetic she has chosen for her home, right down to the pearly pink nail polish on her pretty little toes. In denim shorts, a vintage t-shirt, and oversized cardigan, I feel like a grubby street urchin in comparison. And this was me making an effort.

It's a garden party for goodness' sake, why is everyone dressed like they're off to Ladies Day at Ascot. Teddy is in a shirt and a waistcoat. No four-year-old should be dressed like that. That's why I've bought him a Nirvana t-shirt in his size so we can match when we hang out, which is basically never. Come to think of it, I'm not sure I've spent more than ten minutes with him since his third birthday party, a similarly over the top affair.

George and I were raised the same way, by the same woman, but somehow she was able to pull herself together and blag the husband-kids-house package, while I scrambled around for what was left and ended up with a heart of stone. Looking around, I think I might have gotten the better deal. Shoot me if I'm ever posing kids for the 'gram or spending time with my friends blathering on about mortgages and school admissions processes.

The garden is full of people, most of whom I don't recognise, but I spy George amongst the masses with Rosie on her hip. I'll need a drink before I see her, so I head for the trestle tables set up along one side, laden with ice buckets full of beers and champagne. Pretty sure the parties of my childhood served cheese sandwiches, Swiss roll, and that was about it. These kids don't know how lucky they are, but of course it's not really about the kids, is it?

Grabbing a bottle opener, I flip the cap off a beer and watch it fly off and land in a hedge. *Oops.* I glance around and make sure nobody noticed, taking a big slug when I'm certain I've gotten away with it.

"Hey, Sis." Ryan appears at my side, the doting suburban dad in a navy polo shirt and khaki trousers. I hate it when he calls me that. I'm not his sister, I'm not his anything. "How you doing?"

"I'm great, thanks Ryan, how are you?" I smile, lying through my teeth. I haven't told any of them I've lost my job, or that I'm working part time in a cafe. George would be mortified, as if it somehow reflects badly on her to have a layabout sister. Ryan would try to get me to invest in some crypto-tech-wank nonsense, though to be fair, he's clearly doing well out of it. And Mum would give me some inane platitude that would make me want to rip my hair out. So I think I'll keep that life update to myself just a little while longer.

I've tuned Ryan out, casting my eyes around the garden so I can find Mum. I don't like to be ambushed by her, but she's nowhere to be seen. I clock Teddy running circles around some old man who scoops him up and, with hands on either side of his waist, zooms him through the air like an aeroplane. With his toes pointed and arms spread wide, I can tell Teddy is a seasoned pro.

"Who is that with Teddy?" I ask Ryan.

"That's Rick," he laughs, like I've asked the most obvious question in the world.

"Who the fuck is Rick?"

"He's Rick. Your mum's partner."

Since when does Mum have a new boyfriend, and what the hell is she doing bringing him here, to a children's party? Has she learned nothing over the years? That little boy is four, completely impressionable. He needs security and stability, not a rotating cast of characters rolling in and out of his life.

Mum appears from through the patio doors and gives me an awkward hug that I don't return.

"So you've got a new boyfriend, have you?"

"Well, not that new, but yes. I'm sorry I've not introduced you before now. I know you're not normally keen to meet them." What she means is that I normally cause a load of drama and they leave soon after.

"You're introducing him to your grandchildren? Are you nuts?"

"Darling, Rick and I have been together for two years. He knows the kids well, we look after Teddy two days a week."

"*Two years?*" I bellow, causing heads to turn. How has she kept this from me for two years?

"He's a good man, Hattie." Her tone is firm, and my throat burns the way it always did when I knew I was about to get told off. "He's not like the others."

"So he's made himself at home has he?" Has it really been that long since I last visited her? I try to remember but memories are a bit of a blur lately. "Have you added him to the will? Let him borrow your bank card?"

It's a low blow and I can tell by the look on her face that it stings. I'm sure she's not forgotten the bastard who emptied her limited savings and disappeared, just like I haven't forgotten eating dinner at Megan's every night for a week because there was no money for food.

"Rick has his own money, and a good job. He's a social worker. He's also got his own house, just round the corner. I'm not really interested in living with anyone at my age. This works for both of us." I take a step back and let her words sink in. That all sounds so... sensible. "He's got his own grown-up daughters too. I think you'd really like them, they're around here somewhere."

She glances around the garden and I take the opportunity to glare at my sister, the picture of serenity, her head tipped back laughing with two glamorous looking women. They're probably laughing about the price of avocados or some smug middle-class shit like that.

"Oh that's them there, with Georgina."

As if I couldn't feel any worse about myself than I already do. George looks like she's found the sisters she's always wanted.

"So everyone's just one big happy family except me, is that it?" I drain my beer and storm inside in search of something stronger.

This is bullshit. I feel ambushed, except it's less of an ambush, more of a stumbling across a happy little life that you've been excluded from. Nothing says *'childhood abandonment trauma'* like everyone having a jolly good time while you want to kick the shit out of everything. Brenda, the therapist Luke recommended, is gonna have a field day with this one.

I've seen her three times now and even in that short space of time she's pushed me to unlock some seriously heavy shit. Most notably, that we have therapy to deal with the crap passed on from the people who probably should have had their own therapy in the first place.

I felt mentally prepared to come here today and hold my own, but I was not prepared to be blindsided by the longest boyfriend my mum has ever had, who apparently my whole family are in love with. Dad didn't want me, and now the rest of my family don't either. I grip the edge of the kitchen counter and force myself to take some deep breaths.

"You must be Harriet," a voice behind me says. I turn slowly, even though I already know who I'm about to see.

"Hattie."

"Oh yes, sorry, your mum told me that's what you prefer."

"Right. And you're Rick?"

"That's me," he says cheerfully, pointing two thumbs at his face. "I've heard a lot about you from your mum, and from your sister, but I would love it if you could come to dinner with us all sometime, and we can get to know each other better." *What the fuck has my sister been saying to this random man?* I'm not agreeing to anything, and George is about to get an earful. I find her in the garden and drag her away from her friends.

"You could have told me about Rick," I say, jabbing her in the shoulder with my finger. "Thanks for the heads up, *Sis*."

"What about Rick?"

"This is the first I've ever heard about bloody Rick," I hiss. Trying to keep my voice down is not easy when I'm this angry and insulted. "I would have appreciated a warning that I was about to meet another one of Mum's dickheads."

"Watch your mouth, Hattie," covering Rosie's ears. "I thought you knew. Have you not met him?"

"No, we haven't met!"

"Well, he's great," she says dismissively, hoiking her nonplussed daughter higher up her hip. "You have nothing to worry about with him."

'Nothing to worry about' is code for he's not going to lock us in the garden in the rain, shout at us, throw our toys away, sell our TV for drugs, be drunk and naked in the living room when we get home from school, hit Mum when he thinks we're not listening, or leave us and start a better family. All the things the rest of the bastards have done over the years.

"He's different, Hattie," she says, resting a hand on my shoulder. "He's not using Mum for anything, he's a great companion for her. He was married until his wife passed away, and he's got his own daughters. Shall I introduce you? They're lovely."

My head is swimming, I can't wrap my head around it all. "No, I'm not in the mood, some other time."

"Are you OK?" George says, ducking her head and forcing me to look her in the eye. "Is something else going on?"

"I'm fine," I say, sulkily. "I think I'm going to go, though. Sorry, this is all a bit much."

"It's OK, I appreciate you coming anyway, and so does Teddy. Do you want to say goodbye to Mum or just go? I can cover for you if you need."

I'm the big sister. I'm the one who is supposed to look out for her, but it's always been this way, her fixing my problems, her covering for me when I've made mess after mess.

"It's fine, I'll play nice and let them know. I'll call you later." I won't. I never call her. She's lucky if she gets a reply to a text.

I find Mum and Rick dishing out burgers at the barbecue and give them a polite goodbye.

"I really would love to see more of you Hattie," Rick says, and somehow I do believe it. "Me and your mum."

"That would be lovely."

I'm not making any promises, but the way Mum's face lights up makes me think it might be worth a shot just to get to see her do it again. I find Teddy for a big squeeze, and then make my escape down the path that runs along the side of the house.

"Hattie, wait…" I turn back to see George chasing after me.

"Yeah?"

"I'm pregnant again," she says, stopping a few metres away from me, one delicate hand pressed to her belly. "It's twins."

"Jesus fucking Christ, you idiot." It's out before I can stop myself. *Why am I like this?* This is wonderful news and I'm being a bitch, as usual. I hold my hands up. "Sorry. I'm sorry."

"No need to apologise, I know that's your own way of telling me how happy you are." I laugh and pull it together for my sister. I can't be mad at her, it's not her fault I'm the way I am. I walk back towards her and wrap my arms around her.

"I am happy for you, really. I think four kids is fucking *unhinged*, but if you're happy then I'm happy."

"You could be happy too, you know." She rubs my back and strokes my hair. My face has fallen against her shoulder and I can tell that she just knows how hard this all is for me. "You could, Hattie. There's enough happiness to go around."

I want to laugh, but I rein it in. If that were true, surely I'd have had a little sprinkle somewhere along the way. Just a splash. A dash even. The only time I think I've ever been happy was...

Oh shit.

Yep. Brenda is definitely earning her hourly rate this week.

I take a deep breath and turn to leave before she sees me crying, but the tears still fall. It's the most heart-breaking realisation. There was a good thing, and as usual, I ruined it.

Chapter 43
Rob

A HANDWRITTEN ENVELOPE LANDS on my desk. The lettering is shaky but I recognise it instantly and tear open the paper, careful not to damage the contents.

Folded inside the letter is a photo, and when I turn it over in my hands my breath catches in my throat.

Marek.

Marek was twenty-six when he was walking home from his shift in a bar two years ago. He was mugged, pushed hard, and never remembered any of the other details. We knew from his injuries and scans that he'd fallen face first and hit the ground at full force. We don't know how long he was unconscious before he was found by a passer-by who called an ambulance.

By the time he made it onto my caseload he was able to stay awake, but he was in a bad way. Everything else was a struggle; memory, speech, attention span. Standing made him dizzy, lying down gave him headaches. He was often confused and angry, and who could blame him? We worked together for months to regain cognitive function, and I know we're not supposed to have favourite patients, but Marek was mine. Eventually he was able to move home under the care of a community team, and the last I heard he'd been well enough to return to work.

And here in my hands is a photo of Marek now, beaming at the camera, with a baby in his arms. I have to blink back tears before I can read his letter.

Dear Dr. Rob,
Our son was born last month. He wouldn't be here without you.
His name is Morgan.
Thank you always,
Marek and Sarah

Baby Morgan. *Jesus Christ, I can't cope with this.* I sit with my head in my hands and take a few deep breaths before standing to pin that photo to the noticeboard above my desk.

Life is so precious, and there's not a person on earth who can predict how things will go for any of us. Sometimes bad things happen to good people, their world can change in an instant, but that doesn't have to be the end of the story.

Sometimes there is good news, and I wish I could share this one with Hattie.

Chapter 44
Hattie

CONSIDERING WE USUALLY READ light-heated smut at Sunshine Book Club, our October book has been extremely heavy. *Happy Ever Sometimes* is about a woman who was abducted as a teenager, and kept captive in an abandoned building for years. Dwayne is a urban explorer who travels around the country visiting abandoned places, disused warehouses, empty asylums, that sort of thing. You can imagine how horrified he is to find Grace, and how quickly he rescues her from her prison.

Forever bonded by her horrific ordeal, Grace and Dwayne keep in touch over the next few years while she processes the aftermath and tries to live a normal life.

It was fucking dark, which matches my recent low mood, but also somehow the most incredible love story I think I've ever read. I'm not feeling especially sociable, but I'm keen to see what others think of it, and I'd hate to disappoint Kara.

"Who wants to kick us off then?" she asks from her favourite spot at the front.

"I will," says Katy, who I've gotten to know pretty well since I started picking up morning shifts here. We've had to force ourselves not to discuss the book too much as we read it, but we both gave each other a huge, much-needed hug the day we finished it. "So firstly, I was not expecting to enjoy this book as much as I did, but I've read nothing like it, and it's safe to say it will stick with me for a very long time."

There are lots of murmurs of agreement from around the room.

"I loved the structure, the pacing, the characters," Katy continues. "I just wanted to hug them both so much."

"I really loved that it wasn't just a case of Dwayne rescuing Grace and then they fell in love," Megan says, keeping the conversation flowing. "She had to put herself back together, so she was strong on her own."

There is a lot of conversation about Grace, and how she changes from the captive victim to the woman she is by the end of the novel. She has so many battles to overcome, both physically and mentally.

"I thought it was a really beautiful reminder that even when people have been through unimaginable trauma, we're still worthy of love," Kara says, looking straight at me. My head is throbbing. I struggle to follow the rest of the conversation, and from my spot behind the counter, I try not to cry.

Trauma. It's a word that's been coming up again and again in my sessions with Brenda. I think I love her, even though she spends fifty minutes twice a week turning me into a blubbering wreck, pushing me to understand myself more deeply.

I've spent my whole life trying to prove I'm not a victim, I'm not weak, and I'm not worthless just because my dickhead dad couldn't be bothered to stick around. Working hard to prove myself, pushing my body to its limit, using sex as a coping mechanism, and attempting to control the uncontrollable.

And, of course, pushing people away before they can get close. I always joked about it as if it was some sort of cliché. Unfortunately, I'm now learning that's a response to childhood abandonment happening at a critical age of my brain development. It's validating, but I'm still figuring out what to do with that knowledge.

Although my situation is nothing like Grace's, this shitty thing that I had no control over, has determined how I've lived my entire life. I've been acting all high and mighty, when in reality I've been carrying around a broken spirit in a strong body all these years. And slowly, I'm piecing myself back together too.

Chapter 45
Rob

The lights are low, the music is loud, and Moonshine is packed out for their first Halloween night. I don't think I knew we even had this many people in town, but with a few live bands followed by a DJ set, I can see why they've drawn a crowd.

Luke told me it was all Hattie's doing. Making coffee all day wasn't keeping her busy enough, so she suggested a move to Moonshine, where she's been spending her time managing their events calendar and social media. She was never any good at resting, but from what Luke tells me, this suits her.

I wasn't even sure I should come tonight, but I wanted to support her. Kara and Luke too. Fancy dress isn't normally my scene, but looking out at a sea of costumes, I'm glad I made the effort. I'll probably just stay for one or two, then head home.

There's a big queue at the bar, but I clock Hattie taking orders and decide I don't mind waiting if it means she'll be the one to serve me. The closer I get, the better I can see her outfit. Dressed in a skimpy white dress, her hair is curled into tight ringlets topped with a tinsel-covered halo. With her full lips painted a glossy red, she looks anything but angelic. My dick throbs at the sight of her, and it's not just because she looks gorgeous. It's because she looks happy.

She smiles at customers, nodding at their orders, her body in flow as she spins her way around behind the bar, fetching their drinks.

When she clocks me, I expect that smile to slide right off her face, just like always, but instead, it pulls wider. Her eyes sparkle and for a moment, the room falls silent and still. Her tongue darts out, wetting her lower lip before she bites down on it. Her eyes drop from my face to my chest and beyond, and when they widen, I know it was a good idea to go shirtless under this waistcoat.

I've sent Hattie the occasional text over the past couple of months, but she never replies, and now that I'm standing here in front of her, she looks guilty as hell. The sad truth is, I was right. We can't be friends after all the shit we went through, and as much as it hurts to admit, we were never truly friends in the first place.

I've stopped going to her gym, I don't drive past her house, and she avoids Friday nights at Luke and Kara's. I never ask, but our friends are sweet enough to give me subtle updates that reassure me that Hattie is doing OK. Luke raves about the latest events she's planned, and Kara tells me she's starting her own marketing consultancy focusing on small, local businesses. Megan says Hattie misses me, and sends her love, but I have a hard time believing those words actually came out of her mouth.

"What can I get you?" she asks in the same tone as all of her other customers. I drove here, so all I want is a non-alcoholic beer, but then she'll have served me in thirty seconds and that won't be nearly enough time in her presence.

"Whatever takes you the longest to make," I wink, and she rolls her eyes but gets to work filling a cocktail shaker with ice, various clear fluids and something bright red.

"How is it working here?" I lean across the bar to ask. She bends over to reach down into the low fridge and I'm treated to a sliver of skin at the top of her thigh and those perfect legs, long and smooth, in bright, white knee-high boots.

This is torture. How the fuck did I ever think I'd be able to get over this woman?

"It's good," she leans back. "Keeps me busy, I like the social aspect. It's always a riot when guys I've fucked come in with their girlfriends. The look on their faces when they figure out how they know me is fun." I imagine it's similar to the look on my face right now, like she's gripped my balls in her fist and won't let go.

"Are those chaps ass-less?" she asks, and I burst out laughing.

"You'll have to take a good look when I walk away and find out," I say and I can tell how much she hates herself for laughing too. "Nah, I considered it, but the last thing I want is anyone thinking they can have a squeeze of the goods."

"Wow," she drawls, her eyes locked on mine as she shakes my drink over her shoulder. "Look at you, all grown up."

She pours the pink, creamy liquid into a tall glass, tops it off with a tower of whipped cream and a bright red cherry. I have no idea what this is, but it looks revolting, like something a kid would order for dessert. A far cry from my usual beer or whisky on ice.

"Open up," she says and I oblige, leaning closer to let her pop an extra cherry into my mouth. I catch her fingertip when I close my lips around it, and her eyes go wide as I suck it in further. I close one hand gently around her wrist, lick the sticky juice from her skin, then release her with a pop.

"Delicious." Of all the things we've ever done to each other, this is right up there as one of the sexiest. Her jaw ticks and her chest heaves and I remember how much I loved getting her breathless. As if I could ever forget.

"Oooh, what are you drinking, Cowboy? It looks *so* good."

Two women have muscled their way to the front of the bar beside me. The one dressed as a nurse flips her hair over her shoulder, and presses her firm tits against my bicep. Old me would have loved this, but now it feels like a violation.

"Can we have a taste of your cream?" her Sexy Cat friend laughs from behind her. I snap my eyes back to Hattie, who looks fucking livid.

Jealous, furious Hattie has always had a soft spot in my heart. She's the first one I got to know, the first one I fell for, but this is not what I wanted at all. I angle my back to the women and shield my drink, making it clear I'm not interested.

"What do I owe you?" I ask.

"It's on the house, dickhead," Hattie shouts, and storms off somewhere up the far end of the bar. I lean over and shove a twenty-pound note underneath one of her bottles, pick up my monstrosity of a drink, and leave before these two make things any worse for me.

I spend most of the night lurking, unable to do anything but watch Hattie from afar. The crowd thins out around two in the morning, and soon the music ends and the lights go up.

Luke and Kara left an hour ago. Megan snapped up their offer of a lift, but I couldn't tear myself away from my favourite girl. Instead, I take a seat in a booth and torture myself a little longer. When Hattie appears, she spots me and pauses, her chin resting on the top of the broom handle as she tries to decide her next move.

"We're closed, you know." She sounds exhausted, and I'm not surprised. Hours on her feet dealing with drunk, demanding customers, loud noise and sticky surfaces. It's the opposite of a rest.

Walking slowly towards her, I take the broom from her hand and get to work on the floor. I'm not in the mood for an argument, and luckily she relents. "I know."

"Where are your friends?" she asks sarcastically, and I frown in confusion. "The nurse and the cat."

Oh, still jealous, are we? "I've no idea. I don't know those women."

"So you didn't come here to get laid?"

I shake my head, and she disappears, returning a few seconds later with another broom. From opposite sides, we sweep our way back to each other in silence. When we're finished, I hold my arms out wide, and she steps into them.

There we stand, in the middle of the empty dance floor, gently swaying side to side. I'm certain she'll make a run for it any second now, but when she breathes out and melts deeper into my arms, I wrap her tight to my chest, happy to do this for as long as she'll let me.

Somehow, in this moment, we don't need words. We don't need to bicker and insult each other, we just need to be held by each other.

"I think you're the best dressed person here tonight," she mumbles, her forehead nuzzling against my shoulder. It might be the first time she's ever complimented me without a hint of sarcasm, and I fold the feeling up and tuck it away with all the other memories I hold dear. She's wrong though.

"I don't think so, sweetheart. You are."

"No, you are," she teases. She always has to have the last word.

I want to coast my hands lower, give her ass the playful squeeze I've been desperate to give it since I saw her bend over earlier, but I keep my hands up high, caressing between her shoulder blades.

"I'm not arguing with you, Hattie."

"That's what we were always best at, wasn't it?" She pulls away a little, tilting her face up to mine. There's a flicker of sadness in her eyes, as if she misses those arguments as much as I do. She was so full of life, and that smart mouth and snarky attitude made me feel alive, too. I used to think we brought out the worst in each other, but I see now it was the best, both in and out of the bedroom. Without her, I'm half the man I was.

Her halo has slipped a little and I reach up to adjust it, my fingers coasting through her hair as I tuck it back behind her ears. Her eyes flutter closed at my touch, but I can't take my hands off her. She's so perfect, I can't believe she's spent so long convincing herself otherwise.

Her teeth sink into her lip and my thumb is there before I know it, tugging it open. She moans softly, body pressing closer into mine all by itself. I'm reminded of a time I had her like this before; soft and gentle, exhausted in the quiet of the night, but still hungry to explore. I won't take advantage of her, of this moment, this ember that's flickering back to life, even though I'm aching to be with her again.

She's so soft, this pillowy lip yielding under my tender touch. I see now that I've loved this lip since the moment I first saw it, pouting away at Luke's dining table all those months ago.

"I think we were pretty good at some other things too," I whisper, and when she opens her eyes, they're full of the same need that's blazing in mine.

I need her.

In my arms, in my bed, in my heart. I can't let tonight end with us going our separate ways.

"Can I take you home, angel?"

"I'm seeing someone," she whispers, and my heart sinks, taking my stomach with it. *How the fuck has that happened? When? Who?* "A therapist."

Hattie has the nerve to smirk, and I wonder how long she's been waiting to get me back for my slip-up.

Fucking hell, this woman.

"Are you really?" I can't take my eyes off her, so beautiful, so bold, so fucking special. It makes me wonder why I haven't been fighting for her this entire time.

"Yup." She nods, pulls off her halo, then lifts my hat and puts it on her own head. "Take me home, Cowboy."

Chapter 46
Hattie

HE'S QUIET ON THE drive home, and I stare out of the window and press my knees together to stop them trembling. Half of me wonders what the fuck I'm playing at. The other half knew I'd find myself here the second I saw him across the bar earlier, smiling at me in full cowboy costume.

Outside his house, he opens my door, helps me out of the car and doesn't let go. I know subtle hand touches are one of the hottest things a romance hero can do, but it still amazes me how so much can pass between such a small area of skin. Heat, tension, and longing, zipping back and forth where his fingers link with mine. Besides a couple of handsy customers at Moonshine, quickly booted out by our excellent security team, nobody has touched me since the last time I was here.

Smiling down at me, Rob helps me out of my coat, and when his hands come to rest on my shoulders, mine sweep along the length of his forearms. This is a different side of Rob, softer, open. He's not pushing for anything, and I know what I want, but I'm in no hurry to get there. If there's anything these past months have taught me, it's that it's OK to take my time, to slow down and see what happens rather than rattle through life at 100 miles per hour.

He'll never make the first move though, and who can blame him after the hurricane of shit I've thrown his way this year. A shiver of nerves rolls through me, but I let it pass rather than push them down.

Of course I'm nervous. I'm giving this man the power to wreck me, but I'm not as afraid as I used to be. The pain of living without him is so much worse than I ever imagined.

I've lost track of time. We could stand here all night, and I'm sure he'd say thank you, but my nerves are rapidly turning to need. My fingertips catch hold of the pulse in his wrist, fluttering away, calling my name. I find the same beat as I smooth my hands across his bare chest, far warmer than I expected it to be. Shirtless in October was a bold choice, but I'm not exactly wrapped up warm in this tiny dress, and the only thing I feel is heat.

I've missed his body so much, the tight expanse of his stomach, those well-defined muscles that demand to be explored. They'll have to wait, my hands are on a mission of their own. Coasting down, I palm his erection through his jeans, though the leather chaps do a pretty good job of framing it like a gift.

"Is this for me?" I whisper, and he lets out a tight hiss.

"My hat's on your head, isn't it?"

"You remember what I said at book club?"

"I remember everything."

I take his hand and lead him upstairs. His room smells like him, and my body sways as memories of our nights here flood my brain. Rob stands behind me, his chin on my shoulder, and there in the darkness, I turn and drop to my knees.

"Hattie," he moans, "you don't have to."

Up close, I can make out the bucking bull engraved on his big brass buckle. I want to laugh and ask where he got it, but that can wait too. I tug his belt free, buttons next. "Please? I want to. I need to."

He steps out of his jeans and his boxers, and I take him in my hand, so thick and solid and manly. My tongue laps at the tip, and from my spot at his feet, I watch his body respond. His is a body that deserves to be worshipped, and I'm determined to show him, properly, without rebelling against it, just how much I want him.

I take my time exploring the length of him, dragging long, wet licks from the base to the crown. My mouth closes around the head, tongue circling the sensitive spot underneath that makes him groan in response.

My hands find his, and our fingers entwine, squeezing each other tight as I push my head down and pull slowly back up. The sound of his moans shoots straight through my core, that low swoop of heat spreading fast. My thighs rub together, my body aching for relief, and I take him deeper, gagging slightly when he reaches the back of my throat.

"Jesus, no, I'm too close," he whimpers, pulling away. "Let me get a condom."

"Wait," I whisper, gripping hold of his thighs and staring up at him. "I haven't been with anyone since you."

A vulnerable silence passes between us. I'm not the same girl he first met a year ago. He needs to know how much I've changed, how much he means to me, but I don't have the language for it yet. I daren't breathe while I wait for his response.

"I haven't either," he says, his thumb stroking my cheek, fingers tucking into that delicate spot behind my ear.

"You're telling me you, Rob Man Whore Morgan, hasn't gotten laid in *three months*?" I laugh, nuzzling into his palm. "How are you not walking around with balls the size of a house?"

"I don't think that's how balls work. But don't worry, I come pretty often."

Heat creeps up my neck and my breath catches in my throat. "Thinking about me?"

"Yup," he nods.

"I don't know whether to be flattered, or disgusted." I can't help myself. I'm working on it, but of course I push his feelings away.

"I'm hoping it's secret option number three," he says, pulling me to my feet and laying me back on his bed. His cowboy hat tips down to cover my face, and he throws it across the room like a frisbee. A real cowboy would be horrified, I'm sure, but the waistcoat goes with it and then his hands are back on me, pushing up underneath my dress to drag my underwear down.

"What's secret option number three?"

"Turned on." He licks a line up the column of my throat, a possessive move he knows drives me wild.

"Oh, I'm definitely turned on." I reach down between us and grip him in my fist, guiding his thick crown to where I want him most.

"Are you sure?"

"So fucking sure."

We move at the same time, him sliding inside me as I push my way down his length. The fullness shocks me, sending a garbled cry from my throat. It's not even that it feels so good, his scorching skin against mine, it's that it feels so special, so right to have nothing between us. I think he must feel the same way too because he cradles my face in between his arms, propping himself up on his elbows, covering my face in gentle kisses while he rocks his hips slowly in and out of me.

"I won't last long like this," he huffs out, his forehead against mine. "I'm sorry. I want to take my time with you, but fuck, Hattie, I've missed you so much."

"We have time. Just stay still for a minute."

And he does. He slows right down, his eyes roaming my face, his hands in my hair. When his gaze settles on my mouth, it's the most natural thing in the world to tip my chin up and press my lips to his.

"Oh fuck, really?" he breathes into my mouth, his voice low and shaky.

I nod and press harder, parting on a moan to let him sweep his tongue over mine. Tears spring in my eyes and I squeeze them shut. *This is good. This is good. This is good.*

"I want you so much," I cry out and he kisses me deeper, the stroke of his tongue full of need. He sucks my lower lip so hard I'm certain he'll bruise me, but I don't care. I take everything he has to give and grip his shoulders while I lose control of my limbs.

I've never had a kiss like it. Never known what it feels like to be so entirely consumed. He cups my face as he begins to move in and out of me again. He fucks me deep and slow, and I don't turn away. I feel it all. Notice everything. Let him in.

I need this so much. Need him closer. Need to feel safe and held and wanted. Need *him*.

His pace builds, and he adjusts his position, making space for his fingers to find where I need him most. Still thrusting, I'm wound so tight it takes seconds for my body to relent, a burst of stars shooting in all directions. Rob pulls my orgasm from deep within me and I flail, actually flail, my body rising from the bed like it's possessed. Only my head stays in contact with the mattress while he pulls me further onto his dick, his fingers still working their magic.

"Give me one more," he pleads. "I love making you come." There's no way I could stop him, one orgasm slamming straight into the back of another, my legs shaking, fists grabbing sheets, core throbbing around him.

He's the only man who's ever managed, the only one who's ever cared to put my needs first. All this time, I thought he was the worst guy ever, and it turns out he's the best.

I feel like crying, and laughing, and screaming all at once. I feel as if I'm on fire, scorched from the inside out. I feel everything, and I let him see it all.

Rob topples forward, bracing on his forearms, his mouth finding mine again. His hips rock, steady and deep and my hands grip his sides, coaxing him closer, needing to feel the weight of him in my arms.

"I missed you too," I confess into his mouth and he groans deeply, surging forward, his orgasm spilling forth until he stills inside me.

We stare at each other, two abandoned souls finding a new home in the dark. Eventually, he rolls to his side, taking me with him. His big, warm hands stroke up and down my back, smoothing my hair, keeping me safe as I come down from my high.

"The way you kiss should be illegal," I laugh, when I've caught my breath. "I'm addicted now. Do it again."

Chapter 47

Hattie

Rob perches on the edge of the bed, fresh coffee in hand. I prop myself up against the pillows and pull the sheets up to cover my chest. Spending the entire night naked in Rob's arms is good, spending the day in A&E after scalding myself with hot liquid is not.

"Are you really seeing a therapist?" he asks, smoothing out the covers beside him. "Or did you just say that to wind me up?"

"I am," I say, taking that first delicious sip and leaning back to observe his reaction. I didn't plan on telling him last night, but I knew we'd need to talk about it at some point. It doesn't feel so scary now it's out there. If anyone understands, it will be him.

"How is it?"

"Terrifying. Enlightening. Makes me want to throw up, but I'm sticking with it. Turns out I *also* should have done it a long time ago."

"I'm proud of you."

"Thank you, I'm proud of me, too," I say, smiling into the cup. "What time is it?"

He checks his phone. "Ten thirty. Do you need to be somewhere?"

"Nope." I set my coffee down on his nightstand, wrap my arms around his neck and guide him back into my arms. "I'm right where I want to be."

"It's not like this with other men," I say afterwards. I'm propped up on his mountain of pillows, and Rob's head rests against my chest, my fingers stroking lazy circles through his hair.

"What do you mean?"

"With them it's just sex and then I go. With you and me it's..." I trail off because I still don't know how to explain it properly, this thing between us. In my head it's crystal clear, but to confess that, open myself up and ask if it's the same for him, that's far too terrifying.

"With you and me, it's all out of order," he says, tightening his arm around my waist and pulling me further down the bed. "We hated each other, then I got to know you, hated you a little less, then we became sort of friends, then the sex happened, and now here we are."

"I never hated you."

"You're such a beautiful little liar." He trails soft kisses along my collarbone. "You couldn't stand me."

"I think I had good reason. You were so rude the first time we met. You took one look at me and assumed I was single and unloveable. It made me feel awful."

He drops his forehead to the pillow next to me then pulls back, pushing my hair away from my face, forcing me to look into his eyes. "All I knew was that one of you was single. I walked into that room and hoped to God it was you. I never once thought you were unloveable, I think I was falling for you even then."

"Ew," I tease, but press my lips to his until I feel him smile against me. "I'm sorry I called you a man-whore. That was very rude and judgemental of me. I felt attacked, and I got defensive."

"I'm sorry I called you a slut. I've always regretted it. You must know that by now?"

I let out a long sigh. I'd shrugged his words off, but they hurt more than I'd ever let on. I've come to realise that from the moment I laid eyes on him, I wanted him to see me differently from the way other men do. Not as a conquest or a bet to be won. As someone worthy of more than a one-night stand. More than I've ever been to anyone else.

"I mean it Hattie, it was the stupidest thing I've ever said. I was completely taken aback when I saw you, and I'd never felt like that with anyone. I was nervous, I wanted to find some common ground, and I blew it. I think you're amazing. I always have."

I press my hand to his cheek, and my lips to the corner of his mouth. "Apology accepted. I forgave you a long time ago."

We lie like that for a while, a tangle of limbs, hands roaming, eyes watching. His teeth worry at his lower lip, and I know he's holding back on something.

"What are you thinking?" I whisper. "You can tell me."

He swallows thickly and curls a strand of my hair around his finger. "I know I'm pushing my luck, but where's your head at on the whole relationship thing?"

I was wondering how long this would take to come up. Even hearing the word, *'relationship'*, makes me feel terrified, but now there's a spark of curiosity too. There's only one person who's ever made me consider the possibility of a relationship, a partnership, and his thumb is circling the inside of my wrist, willing me to give him a chance. I've missed out on a lot in my life because I closed the door too fast, and it hurts to think I nearly missed out on him.

"I would consider that to be a work in progress, but I'm not as opposed to the idea as I used to be."

His relief is palpable. "I'm serious, Hattie. If you want to give it a go, see what this could be, then I'm all in. I don't want to spend another day without you. I've been miserable."

"Aren't you scared?" I ask.

"Of what?"

"Of getting hurt. Of hurting each other?"

"No, sweetheart." He shakes his head and scoots in closer, pressing kisses to my forehead. "I'm not scared. Maybe we won't get things right while we figure out how to be together. Maybe you'll hurt me or I'll hurt you, but I promise I'll always communicate with you, and I'll always do my best to make things better again. Not being with you would hurt much, much more. I'm not your dad, baby. I could never walk out on something this good."

"What about the kids thing?" These are the important, essential, life-changing things people in relationships need to discuss. If we want different things, we don't stand a chance.

"What about it?"

"You want them. '*A whole bunch*', you said."

"Yes, maybe, I don't know. It's not a deal breaker. What about you?"

"I don't think so. It's not that I don't like them, it's that I've got that wild godmother energy. I don't think it's good for kids to be around me too much. What if you change your mind?"

"Then we have another conversation. We'll always keep talking. We don't have to decide everything right now and follow one path. I could live a thousand different lives with you and be happy in every one."

Jesus, how does he come up with this stuff? He's so romantic it makes me squirm and bite back a smile. I can already picture Megan and Kara swooning when I tell them about this.

"What if I never believe you'll stay?" If my biggest fear is him leaving, my second biggest is that I'll drive a wedge between us by worrying all the time. He rolls onto his back, taking me with him, adjusting our bodies until my head rests against his heart. His hand weaves into my hair, keeping me close. His other hand finds mine and gives it a reassuring squeeze.

"I'll prove it to you. For as long as it takes," he says.

And I believe him.

Epilogue

Two months later

Rob

If it's possible, Moonshine is even busier than it was on Halloween, packed with a crowd who've braved the cold December night to celebrate and see in the new year in style.

The space looks incredible, as always. Kara has such a knack for transforming it to suit the occasion. From the ceiling, hundreds of disco balls in various sizes hang at different heights, and the entire room shimmers underneath them.

Hattie booked some achingly cool DJ I've never heard of, but when she launched tickets for tonight on Moonshine's social media, they sold out in two days. Now they're all here, and everyone is living their best lives.

Everyone except me. I'm bored and antsy. I don't want to be here in a sweaty club. If I'd had my way, I'd have whisked Hattie away somewhere, but she refused to let her team down and request a night off on one of the busiest nights of the year. She's always looking out for everyone else, but I'm happy to be the one who gets to look out for her.

Luke and Kara are somewhere in the throng of party-goers after spending Christmas in Scotland. They seem to be constantly off on mini-breaks, but I can't say I blame them. They're both making up for a lot of time life took away from them.

I don't know if Hattie knows, but Luke told me they've planned to spend their first year of marriage taking as many trips as possible before trying for a baby. Hopefully everything will work out in their favour and I'll get to be Fun Uncle Rob sooner rather than later.

There's no sign of Megan tonight. She told Hattie she's staying in to journal and set intentions or something. Apparently this is going to be the best year of her life, and I hope so. She's such a good friend to all of us, and she deserves nothing less than best.

So it's just me, lurking at the end of the bar, keeping an eye on my girl. We've spent most of the Christmas break in bed. You'd think I'd have had enough of her, but now even a few feet is too much distance between us. I need her closer, need my hands on her.

"Can you sneak away?" I lean over to ask when she finishes with a customer and comes back to my end of the bar. "I don't want to end the year or start the new one without you."

She looks around at the rest of her team. There are plenty of them and it's fairly quiet now. With only five minutes to midnight, most people have gotten a fresh drink and found their friends, ready to ring in the new year together.

My pulse quickens when she gives me her most wicked smile, steps out from behind the bar and takes my hand in hers. "Quick, follow me."

She leads me through the door that says Staff Only, down the corridor and into the office where she spends most of her time when she's not on a bar shift or in my bed. Rushing inside, I kick the door closed behind me and pull her into a hurried, greedy kiss.

After denying me her mouth for so long, I still can't get enough of it. I slide my hands through her hair, gripping the back of her head to adjust the angle. She opens to me and I lick inside her mouth, my tongue grappling with hers for control.

I'm rushing. Of course I'm rushing, there's no such thing as going slow with this woman who makes my blood heat and my dick hard simply by existing. She sucks my lip, teeth sinking into my flesh, hands sliding their way up underneath my top. She's my perfect match, who can't seem to get enough of me either.

"Hattie, wait, slow down a second." I cup her shoulders and hold her out at arm's length. *Words first, kiss later.*

"Hmm?" she moans, her eyes glassy and hooded. I love how soft and compliant she gets when I kiss her. I take a deep, shaky breath, and she straightens up and swallows.

"I want to tell you something, but I want to give you fair warning because I'm pretty sure when I say it, your gut instinct will tell you to run."

She wriggles loose and takes a few steps back, resting her bottom on the edge of her desk. *No, too far away.* Her fingers grip the wood and I need to move fast. I didn't mean to scare her. She's probably thinking the worst, but she presses her lips together then lets her mouth pull into a wide smile.

"Come here," she pushes some papers aside and hops up onto the surface.

"I will," I say, locking the door behind me. She's going to run, I'm sure of it, but I have to tell her. "I just need a second."

"I love you too, Rob."

I never used to understand what people meant when they said they had butterflies in their stomach, but I get it now. This fluttering might bring me to my knees. "What?"

"That's what you brought me in here to say, right? So I'm saying it back. I love you too."

"You can't say it back. I haven't said it yet."

"Go on then," she holds her arms out wide and shrugs. "I'm not running."

And she's really not. She's right here in front of me, smiling, open-hearted, and asking me to love her back. The angry, neglected little girl I first met is still in there somewhere, but now her inner child is held, she is loved, and she is reminded every day that I want her in my life. Not just want, *need*.

I'm a better man, because of her. If it wasn't for Hattie, I'd never have peeled back my own layers of bullshit and sorted myself out. I thought I was happy before, free and single, but the man I was back then had no idea what true happiness was.

We still see our separate therapists, but every two weeks we've been seeing one together. It was Hattie's suggestion, but I was very willing to agree. This may be the first serious relationship either of us has been in, but I bet it's the healthiest one on the planet. As a bonus, the sex we have after those sessions is out of this world. Raw, intense, deep, and emotional. Sometimes she cries, fuck, sometimes *I* cry, as we rip ourselves apart and put each other back together again.

In my living room, once considered sparse and boring by Hattie, there is a picture of us on the wall. Next to it, a framed copy of the poem she read at Luke and Kara's wedding. Those beautiful words, about being in each other's clay, that's how she makes me feel every day that we grow together. There may be a few candles scattered around the place too, but who am I to deny the woman of my dreams her obsession.

"I love you, Hattie," I say, closing the space between us. "I love you so fucking much."

Now that I'm standing here in front of her saying it to her face, I'm not sure it's enough. How can three small words possibly convey the depth of what I feel for her.

"You're not scared?" she asks, those beautiful wide eyes looking up at me filled with so much life.

"Of course I am, look, feel." I press her hand to my heart, which was already racing thinking I'd have to throw her over my shoulder to keep her from running away. "But being with you is the best scary thing I've ever done."

She rests her palm there for a second, then coasts it down my stomach, not stopping until she reaches my belt buckle. Her nimble fingers make quick work of it.

"Hey, Rob..."

"Yes, angel?

"I bet you can't make me come before midnight."

Hattie

"Get that fucking skirt up, now," he growls.

I don't need to be told twice. I love everything about this man, but nothing does it for me more than when he bosses me around. Lifting my hips, I move to wiggle my underwear down, but Rob shoves my legs apart and crowds between them.

"No time. Put your feet up." I follow his orders and before I can catch my breath, he's yanked my underwear to one side and slammed his dick straight into me. I didn't even see him unbuckle his trousers.

"Fucking *Christ*," I yell, grateful that the room next door is full of people making enough noise to cover my moans.

I'm sure Rob thinks this was all his idea, but I've got him right where I want him. Hot, hard thighs pressing into mine as I lean back with my palms spread, arms bracing myself upright. This desk is a cheap piece of shit, and every thrust has it scooting across the floor, but it doesn't matter because I've been right on the edge ever since I saw him walk into Moonshine tonight.

I've been thinking about today for a while, wondering if I'd get a moment with him all to myself. Sentimentality has never been my thing, but I didn't want to let one year end without telling Rob how I truly feel about him.

"Fuck, I'm so close," I laugh. Sometimes we try our best to go slow, but it always ramps up into this furious, desperate need.

"Hold on, angel, I want you to come bang on midnight." Apparently, my man has developed a taste for the sentimental too.

From through the wall I can hear the crowd chanting, *'Ten! Nine! Eight!'* and Rob quickens his pace.

I slip down the straps of my dress, grateful I picked something with such easy access, and tug down the cups of my bra, letting my tight nipples free. Rob makes my favourite sound, the guttural, caveman groan he unleashes whenever he sees my tits.

"*Five!*"

I arch my back and he follows my lead, dipping his head to suck hard before rolling my nipple between his teeth, tugging it tight.

"*Four!*"

One hand grips the base of my spine, pulling me onto him in time with each thrust. The other slips between us, finding my aching, swollen clit, slippery at the place where our bodies meet.

"*Three!*"

He strums it with the finesse of a man who's put the work into becoming an expert in everything that drives me wild. Whether it's his fingers, his tongue, or that magical superdick, he never fails to give my body exactly what it needs. My need to come isn't building, it's hurtling through me at a million miles an hour. He's going to win this bet, and I couldn't be more thrilled.

"*Two!*"

"I love you." He lets go of my nipple to moan his words of adoration into my mouth, and I don't think I'll ever get tired of hearing it. I'm right there on the edge of forever with him, breaking apart around his hungry tongue, ready to explode and let him put me back together.

"I love you too," I cry out.

"*One!*"

"Will you marry me?"

"*Yes, yes, yes.*"

I'm not falling, I'm flying, floating, all senses firing. I grip the back of his neck as everything in me tenses and my head rolls back just in time to see the sky light up through the small office window. Fireworks, explosions, orgasms, declarations, it's all right here, coursing between us. I clench down hard, roaring at the sensation as he pounds harder and harder, filling me exactly how I wanted. "Yes! Oh, *fucking hell* yes."

Wait.

Did he say what I think he just said?

And did I just say yes?

No, fuck. Not yes to that. I fall back to my desk and he tumbles with me, his open mouth pressed to my cheek.

"Yes?" Rob pants, one protective hand cupping the back of my head.

"No!" I shout, thumping my fist against his chest. *What the fuck is happening?*

"No?"

"Yes! Yes to no. No, no, no. Absolutely not."

"I'm confused," he laughs nervously. "You just said yes."

"Yes, to coming all over your dick. Not to marriage."

"Oh." His smile falls and I realise he's deadly serious. He pulls away, but I wrap my legs tight around his waist and refuse to let go.

"Hey. Look at me," I say, taking his face in my hands. "We've only been seeing each other for two months, Rob. That's way too fast."

"We're not *'seeing each other'*, we're in love." He cups the back of my neck and pulls me up to him. "This isn't casual for me. You're my girlfriend, and I love you. You know that, right?"

Jesus, so hot. I'm tempted to stay right here until he's ready to go again. "I'm your girlfriend, and you love me."

The first time he called me his girlfriend, I burst into tears. Not because I was happy, because I was upset and angry and confused, still rebelling against the label and the idea that I would be his anything. Rob apologised for springing it on me, and after we talked through our feelings with our therapist, it's a label I've come to wear with pride. Anyone can be a girlfriend, but I'm the only one who can be Rob's girlfriend.

"How about moving in then? You're there most nights anyway, and I hate the mornings where I wake up and you're not in my arms."

"If I knew you were going to be this much of a soppy romantic, I might have reconsidered this whole relationship thing."

"Hattie, stop that." I'm still working on it, not pushing him away or belittling his feelings. Boyfriend Rob is entirely different from the man I first met last year. Caring, attentive, and affectionate as hell. Not just in bed. He loves holding hands or snuggling on the sofa. He does this stupid little act like he can't breathe if I leave the room, and I can't even pretend I don't like it.

He cooks for me when I get home from shifts at Moonshine, or picks me up, stifling yawns so I don't have to close up alone after a night shift.

His affection and adoration are gifts he showers me with daily. I didn't know how amazing it would feel to let someone treat me that way.

The idea that I could have more of it is tempting, and he's right. If I'm not working, I'm at his house. Maybe it's a bit quick, but we've taken our sweet time getting to this point, and it doesn't feel rushed with him.

"Yes."

"Yes? Actual yes?"

"Yes, I'll move in with you." I loop my arms around his neck, basking in his beautiful smile. "Starting tonight?"

"This will be the best year of our lives, angel. I promise you."

I know it will. My marketing consultancy business may only be small, but I have signed my first three clients and have big things planned. Moonshine has a packed events calendar that has people travelling from all over the county. There's a new series of Antiques Roadshow for us to watch with Rob's mum and Auntie Sheila. And my friends are...

"Oh God, Rob. What am I going to do about Megan?"

Megan's story will continue in *The No Rules Roommate*...

Acknowledgments

Ever since Pacey Witter pulled his beat up old car off the side of the road to kiss Joey Potter, I have been obsessed with Enemies to Lovers stories. The tension, the angst, the scowling, the falling. I love it all, and I've had a blast writing this story of two closed-off people who turn out to be just the thing the other needs.

As always, lots of people help make books happen. Thank you to Liz Mosley who I have so much fun working on covers with. Texting is such a key part of Hattie and Rob's love/hate relationship and we were both buzzing to figure out a way to include it on the cover.

Thank you to Sara Madderson, my Fairy Smutmother and biggest supporter in all things indie publishing.

Thank you to my beta readers Katie, Hayley, Alexandra, Eloise, Sabrina, Christina, Nicola, Gina, Beth, and Laura for your kind words and smart suggestions. A special thank you to Eloise who held my hand (over the phone) when I was wobbling, and to Gina who has heard me talk about Hattie and Rob as if they are people we know for over a year.

My ARC readers are the sweetest bunch of cheerleaders, I love and appreciate you so much.

Thank you to every reader who has taken a chance on my books, especially my sisters and my aunt who have no qualms about shoving copies into the hands of their friends.

A number of people were kind enough to answer the most ridiculous questions in the name of research for this book. Thank you to Beth for your hotel security sense-check, Tom for your advertising industry expertise, Gina for your therapy knowledge, Emma for your neuropsychology insights, Mia for the dating app lowdown, and Lydia and The Matelot for your boating wisdom. I'm very lucky to know you all.

And thank you to Alex, for everything, always.

About The Author

Holly June Smith is a writer and romance addict who is constantly falling in love with fictional heroes and dreaming up new ones.

Holly is also a wedding celebrant who helps couples celebrate their beautiful real-life love stories.

Originally from the North East of Scotland, she now lives in Hertfordshire, England, with her partner, their two children, and a TBR that threatens to crush her in her sleep.

You can find her online @hollyjunesmith

Also By Holly June Smith

[Just a Little Crush](https://amzn.to/41mFz4q)

https://amzn.to/41mFz4q

Bec Charlton knows three things for sure.

1. You can't beat a good aged gouda.

2. Her Grandpa's old Ford Cortina is her pride and joy.

3. The women of Thatch Cross are obsessed with Alistair Rendall (who is always just 'Rennie' to her)

Bec can't blame them. When he isn't fighting fires, Rennie runs Rhyme Time at the local library, teaches self-defence classes, and drives his elderly neighbours to their doctor's appointments. The man is a saint in a body made for sin.

They've known each other since they were kids, so the last thing Bec needs is to have him pull her from a car wreck while her latest audiobook blasts out the spiciest sex scenes...

Bec is lucky to escape with minor injuries - and major embarrassment - but the narrow stairs to her flat are impossible on crutches.

When Rennie insists she recuperates at his house, she doesn't exactly have a choice.

All she needs to do is stay put, let him look after her, and keep her outrageous fantasies in check.

After all, it's just a little crush... isn't it?

Just a Little Crush is a standalone childhood friends-to-lovers romance novella packed with heart, humour, and heat.

Printed in Great Britain
by Amazon